Only Slow-Death Man remained, sitting on his coyote dun. Mister Skye stood, stretching after his long immobilization on the gravel. The rain had soaked his heavy graying hair, and now it matted blackly about his skull and neck. He, too, seemed as cold and defeated as the rest, Betsy thought.

"Mister Skye. We talked about whether to kill you all. But we don't need to. The rain will do it. Whites have magic things—and are helpless. We'll go kill buffalo anyway, and go back across the mountains. They will welcome us in our village! We will sing many songs about this day."

Some faint light seemed to flare in the guide's eyes. And then the whites watched Slow-Death Man trot off. They watched the pack animals top the slippery dun bluff and vanish into gray mist. They stared at each other, seeing ashen, cold, gray-fleshed, half-dressed, blue-lipped, barefoot mortals with utterly nothing, and only a few hours from doom.

BY RICHARD S. WHEELER
FROM TOM DOHERTY ASSOCIATES

THE FAR TRIBES

A BARNABY SKYE NOVEL

Richard S. Wheeler

A TOM DOHERTY ASSOCIATES BOOK
NEW YORK

This is a work of fiction. All of the characters, organizations, and events portrayed in this novel are either products of the author's imagination or are used fictitiously.

THE FAR TRIBES

A Forge Book
Published by Tom Doherty Associates
175 Fifth Avenue
New York, NY 10010

www.tor-forge.com

Forge® is a registered trademark of Macmillan Publishing Group, LLC.

ISBN 978-1-250-30529-9

Our books may be purchased in bulk for promotional, educational, or business use. Please contact your local bookseller or the Macmillan Corporate and Premium Sales Department at 1-800-221-7945, extension 5442, or by email at MacmillanSpecialMarkets@macmillan.com.

First Mass Market Edition: March 1990
Third Mass Market Edition: April 2019

Printed in the United States of America

0 9 8 7 6 5 4 3 2 1

For Sara Ann Freed

Prologue

The old Virginian, Colonel Augustus Bullock, USA Ret., eyed his visitor shrewdly.

"You want information about Skye," he said cautiously, surveying the man. "Lots do. You've come to the right place, suh. I know more about Barnaby Skye than any man alive."

The colonel motioned for his guest to have a seat in the wooden chair opposite his desk. "If you're planning on hiring him, I'll send word along. I do that for him. It's part of my business. I'm his agent."

Bullock settled himself into his swivel chair. He liked nothing better than to talk about Skye. "I also do some weeding," he said, and waited for the response. There was none. "Folks clamor for him since he's the best there is. Even back in the States, they know of him. But he's choosy. He's told me a hundred times he wants clients with courage and common sense. Out in those wild lands, the other kinds could get him killed—and themselves."

Bullock smiled at that. It always put them on their guard, he thought. They wandered into his Fort Laramie sutler's store about this time of year, maybe a dozen every May or June, and he sent some of them along to Skye. He stroked his white Vandyke beard, studying the man.

"You ask how he treats folks out there—women, children, cultivated folks. Out there in that wild land, full of hostiles, roaring rivers, hailstorms, starvation, white and red renegades—and heaven knows what. Oh, he'd surprise you, Barnaby Skye. He's read more than you have, I'll wager. He takes people of all sorts—scholars, women, clerks, children—even missionaries. He did that in fifty-five, and no one thought he could. Just as long as they have sand, suh. Courage and common sense."

His visitor perked up at that. Bullock's eyes went soft with memories, with visions of a giant among men.

"Recently he escorted a party composed largely of women—some of them the sort to make a man blush, I say—from here clear to the diggings at Bannack. He pulled them through. Maybe I should say, suh, he showed them how to pull themselves through. Through hell, I'd say. Pure hell on earth. Oh, that was a trip! That was eighteen and sixty-three, I believe. Not long ago.

"But from what you've told me about you and your party, you'd be more interested in one he guided back in fifty-two. Yes, eighteen and fifty-two. He met his party up at Fort Benton, to the north. He hadn't been guiding long. Since the midforties, anyway. He had a new wife then, Mary, and their little boy, Dirk. The lad's back in the States now, getting a schooling. Yes, Mary of the Shoshones, as well as his other wife, Victoria of the Crows . . ."

Bullock saw his visitor startle. "Oh, suh, the mountain men do that a-plenty. Those wives of his are an army—an army. Those and that horse of his, Jawbone. A young animal in fifty-one, but a beast, a *beast*!"

Bullock watched the man, weighing him. "Want to hear that story, do you? Oh, that's a story. It tested Mister Skye clear beyond the limits of his powers—the powers of the best of the mountain men! And he brought them through trouble I lack words to describe, my friend. Believe it or not, life or death hinged on a large cradle his wife Mary used to tote that boy. Life or death! But I won't get into that now, my friend. Just remember this: whenever men of the frontier talk about the best of them all, they all whisper the name Barnaby Skye—*Mister* Skye to you, suh. . . . And it sounds like a prayer.''

Chapter 1

Chapter 1

The setting sun caught Fort Benton like a torch. They rounded the last bend of the Missouri and beheld a gold-flamed building of dried earth, stout and precarious in an empty land. Elkanah Morse watched, fascinated, as engagés in red calico shirts and greasy buckskins boiled out of its single narrow entrance facing the river and hordes of savages poured from brightly painted skin lodges to crowd the levee. These would be the Blackfeet, the most warlike and hostile of all northern tribes. They made an awful racket, fusils exploding in the air, throaty cries, the cacophony of rattles and beads and jingles. But they camped here to trade, not to make war, and that was what brought Elkanah Morse from far off Lowell, Massachusetts, to this desperate place.

Still, the sheer savagery of these tribesmen sent a shudder through him, and he momentarily regretted bringing his dear wife Betsy, and his spinster daughter Arabella. Two months late. Would his guide, Barnaby Skye, still be there with all the horses they would need? Morse scanned the distant levee anxiously, looking for a white man with two squaws and a baby boy. If Skye hadn't waited, the whole trip would be doomed.

He rested on his pole, letting the cordeliers propel the keelboat. These last weeks had changed him. He couldn't bear to watch the brutal labor of the cordeliers while he and his family lounged on the foredeck, so he found a pole and joined them as they made their circling promenade around the cabin, along the narrow passageways on either side of the boat, by turns thrusting their poles into the river bottom to propel the boat ahead. When the current ran swift or it grew windy or they struck rapids, they could not pole the boat at all, and then the long ropes were pulled up from the hatches, and sweating men dragged the keelboats upstream by stumbling along the banks, through brush and swamp and rock, often in water, surrounded by maddening mosquitoes and horseflies. So Elkanah Morse had joined them, and in turn grew hard, sloughing off the soft body of a middle-aged manufacturer and becoming firm-muscled and young. The Frenchmen had laughed at first, then admired the doughty industrialist, and shared the *tabac* with him. All the while they toiled up the swift river, his restless mind sought better ways, ways to meet this need. A small steamboat, he thought. He would offer to build American Fur a small boat just a bit larger than these keelboats, to churn up the shallow western reaches of the great river.

In the second keelboat rode the rest of his party, portly Percy Connaught, a shrewd scholar and Utopian and owner of a successful book bindery in Hartford. With him was Captain Jarvis Cobb, West Point, on detached duty to reconnoiter the unknown lands of the west. And finally, Elkanah's old and dear friend Rudolpho Danzig, Swiss-born geologist and naturalist now teaching at Harvard. Elkanah liked to tease him, call him "the world's greatest expert," which was not a bad description of a man who seemed to be on intimate terms with everything in the universe. Danzig and Cobb had helped the cordeliers pole and haul the laden keelboat, but Percy Connaught, soft and bookish, made excuses and probably, Elkanah surmised, thought the brutal labor was beneath him. He didn't know Connaught well. The man lived down in Connecticut and bought bind-

ery leathers and cloth from him. Cobb he knew even less:
a desk-bound instructor at West Point who had found out
about Elkanah's journey and asked to join it.

This last stretch had been uncomfortable because there
was no room in the keelboats for living space. They had
camped on the banks of the great Missouri each night, beneath incredible bluffs, crenellated white towers of rock cut
into fantastic forms, that had his wife Betsy exclaiming and
painting furiously with her watercolors. Danzig exclaimed,
too, but for other reasons, and could be found in twilight
studying strata and chipping out fossils and making prodi-
gious notes.

Almost two months late. If the river had been higher, the
American Fur steamer *Chouteau* would have continued up
the river, offloading part of its burden at Fort Union and
then pushing on, with higher draft, perhaps even as far as
old Fort McKenzie. Almost August, and Elkanah Morse
had the whole business ahead of him. He would personally
visit the far tribes and see what he might manufacture for
them. He would expand the Indian trade. He would apply
Yankee genius to the labors of neolithic tribesmen, for mu-
tual profit. But 1852 had been a low-water year and the fur
company's steamboat had snagged on every sandbar on the
endless river. They'd skirmished with wild Indians while
cutting firewood, been delayed by vast herds of black buffalo swimming the great river, hung on snags. Once they
anchored for a week in Dakotah to cobble up a patch where
the hull had been pierced by a piece of driftwood that the
captain called a sawyer. For over two thousand miles the
little steamer had fought the mighty river, from St. Louis
clear up to Fort Union at the confluence of the Missouri and
Yellowstone. Beyond that, the water flowed too low, and
the trade goods going on the additional three hundred some
miles to Fort Benton had to be cordelled upstream by fierce
profane sweating French engagés of the fur company.

Two months late. Elkanah scanned the boiling crowd
anxiously, hoping that his guide had waited. Barnaby Skye
was his name. Mister Skye, they called him with obvious
respect. Pierre Chouteau himself, master of the fur empire,
had written Elkanah that no man in all the northwest would

be more capable of taking him out to the far tribes in comfort and safety than Skye. The tribesmen knew him and respected him. He and his two squaws—the idea of two squaws fascinated Elkanah—were a small army. The guide even owned a strange fierce horse, Jawbone, that had become a legend in the far country for its warlike ways. Skye, it seemed, had once been a pressed British sailor but had jumped ship with nothing but a belaying pin and the clothes on his back at Fort Vancouver on the Columbia, and had become a top man in American Fur before turning to guiding.

No man better . . . Elkanah peered anxiously into the savage mob, looking for such a person, hoping the man hadn't given up the long wait.

"Well, Betsy, this is where it starts!" he said, finding the hand of his dear buoyant wife and squeezing.

"I want to paint this place! See the colors, Elkanah! See how the sun brightens the adobes where they're building the blockhouse. These yellow cliffs! All the red calico of these people. Even the river's turned yellow in this light. . . ." She paused. "Do you suppose we'll be safe?" she asked, suddenly cautious.

"As safe as Mister Skye can make us in such a place. And of course Alec Culbertson must think of safety all the time. Look at that fort. Just one small entrance there. I wonder how it feels to live here, one of a handful of whites surrounded by the most savage and warlike tribe of all, and thousands of miles from the frontier."

He glanced at the awesome river, swift and golden in the low sun. Somewhere far to the south and west rose its headwaters, and from those mountain fastnesses known only to a few white men, flowed the snowmelt water past here at Benton, past Fort Union, down through a continental prairie, ever south and east, until it poured muddy and thick into the Mississippi. The sheer distances awed him. Back in Massachusetts he'd scarcely grasped the length of the journey.

What if Skye hadn't waited? Two months the man had been compelled to idle at Fort Benton. Elkanah's letter, sent last winter to the guide, care of the sutler at Fort Laramie, requested that he be at Benton the first of June . . . for a lengthy business trip among the far tribes. The guide apparently was an educated man. In due course a response arrived in Lowell, in a fine hand, saying he'd be at Benton, and the seven-hundred-dollar fee would be acceptable. He would have the necessary riding horses for the Morse party and packhorses and mules for the goods Morse wished to take to the Indian villages. The rest of Skye's brief letter contained advice about what to bring and what to wear. But now it was a day shy of August.

Could the trip still succeed? Could this man Skye get him and his party to the villages he wished to visit so that he could study the Indian life, devise helpful goods that might civilize their life and open new markets for his products? He manufactured a variety of goods for the trade, eagerly bought by the American Fur Company. His Lowell mills spun calico and gingham tradecloth in bright colors. He loomed blankets of various weights, modeled on the Hudson Bay ones, with points, or bars, signifying the thickness. His four-point blankets were prized here in the north. His foundries turned out cooking kettles and skillets, iron arrow points, lance points, ladles, spoons, and knives.

Nor was that the end of it. His busy companies turned out satinets, cambrics, canvas, muslin, laces, silks, carpeting, bed quilts. He produced wallpaper and oilcloth. His tannery produced binder's leathers, saddler's leathers, harness leathers, trunks, and valises. He made steel pen nibs, bar iron, hoop iron, brass and steel wire, coffee mills, church bells, saws and augurs, as well as plows, scythes, spades, shovels, bullet molds, and locks. He had with him a sheet-metal camp stove of his own manufacture, designed to fit into a canvas tent of his own manufacture.

Among the carefully chosen goods he brought here was a complete canvas lodgecover that could replace the buffalo cowhide skins now in use. In his kit were lathed hardwood arrowshafts, more true and perfect than anything manufactured by the tribes. Iron arrow points, large and small, long, barbed, wide, short. He had ready-made arrows, a whole panoply of kitchen goods, knives galore, bolts of fabrics these tribes had never seen, needles and threads, awls, ready-made rubber moccasin soles in various sizes. He would try these out, bring the benefits and blessings of modern civilization to these people, learn how they manufactured their possessions. Hide scraping, for instance. He had several scraper designs in mind that would ease the work. He had the ash and iron fittings for a wheeled travois. He would attach lodgepoles to it and see what these people thought. He would transform their lives! This man, Skye, who came so highly recommended by top people at American Fur, would take him and his party from place to place and deliver them at last to Fort Laramie before cold set in. If it wasn't too late . . .

At last the weathered gray keelboats were poled to the levee and made fast. Elkanah slipped an arm around Betsy and held tight as the boat bumped land and crowds of wild Indians swarmed close, pointing at them, gesticulating wildly.

"I believe they're seeing their first white woman," Elkanah said. The stares of these half-dressed people were upon Betsy and Arabella, and squaws pointed and babbled in a strange tongue. Arabella's face pursed with fear, but Elkanah laughed, and Betsy smiled.

Working through the buckskin-clad throng was a ruddy, stout, bulbous-nosed man Elkanah took to be the bourgeois here, Alexander Culbertson, a legendary veteran of the fur trade.

"Morse?" cried the bourgeois. "That you? We'll get a plank up in a minute." He paused, staring at the women. "I'll be—didn't expect . . . now ain't this a treat," he blustered.

A peculiar burly man stood apart, walled by ten feet of space that none of these tribesmen penetrated. He was a barrel of a man, medium height, whose small blue eyes, almost buried in the crevasses of a weathered face, studied Morse intently. The man had a nose such as Elkanah Morse had never seen, a vast bulging prow, ballooned and battered by brawling, that dwarfed the rest of his clean-shaven features. Beside him stood two squaws and a boy, all of them somehow separated from the rest of the throng.

Elkanah Morse had never seen such a man, though he

was well aware of the peculiarities of mountain men. He had a hunch this one would be Skye, and studied him closely as engagés swirled around him, preparing to unload cargo. The man had dressed Indian, in red-beaded breechclout and fringed leggins. His long tan shirt hung to his hips, and had fringes also. He'd cinched it at the waist with a heavy belt that supported a sheathed knife and a holstered revolver. He wore square-toed whitemen's boots. But it was the grave alert face that drew Elkanah's attention. The man wore his black hair shoulder length, common enough in the mountains, but crowning all this was a black silk stovepipe hat, set rakishly to the man's left.

It was not so much what he wore, but the way he stood, and the way space opened around him, that told Elkanah Morse something about this man. Something about him spoke of calm power, utter competence in the wilds, and faint menace. They locked eyes briefly, and the man smiled, but then his glance turned to the keelboats, appraising them, peering at plank hulls, wide-flared bows, and the low wooden cabin amidships with plank thick enough to stop a rifle ball.

Beside the man the squaws hung close. The older one, rail thin and weathered and seamed, glared angrily at this surging mob. The younger one, full-figured and golden-fleshed, her jet hair in braids, looked more amiable. She clutched the little boy who was plainly a breed, child of the mountain man and herself.

Skye, he thought. Had to be Skye, from all the descriptions. The man had waited! Elkanah was putting his life and safety and the lives of all his party in that man's hands. There surged through him something beyond words, some animal instinct that the man down there would shepherd them safely through a land as dangerous and wild as any left on earth.

"Morse," yelled Culbertson. "The plank's up. Bring your lovely ladies down. Just in time for supper. Here now, the plank wobbles like a drunken Frenchman."

In Culbertson's arm nestled a small, shy, dusky, and altogether beautiful woman, dressed in brown taffeta with an ivory cameo at her throat.

"Mister Morse, I'm Alec Culbertson, and this is my dear wife Natawista," he said. "She's of the Bloods, and the light of my life!"

"I'm so pleased to meet you," said Natawista in flawless English. Her small brown hands caught Betsy's and pressed them, then Arabella's, and finally slipped into Elkanah's.

Everywhere around them now life whirled. Connaught, Cobb, and Danzig waited for a plank that would let them off the second boat. Elkanah caught Skye studying them, even as Skye had studied himself.

Blood and Piegan squaws swarmed around Betsy and Arabella, pinching fabric, touching flesh, muttering and pointing. Arabella looked ashen, but Betsy smiled bravely and touched back, admiring bone necklaces, beadwork, soft-tanned skirts.

"Come on in now," Culbertson yelled. "Your truck is safe. My engagés will haul it all in." He tugged his guests after him, weaving away from the levee, straight toward the burly man in the black silk hat.

"Elkanah, this is Mister Skye. This is your guide. And these are his wives, Victoria of the Crows, and Mary of the Snakes. And this tyke down here is Dirk."

"Delighted, Skye," said Morse, gripping the rough hand of the guide. "Saw you from the boat and thought it was you."

"You'll do, Mister Morse. You'll do indeed. We're set to go in the morning," rumbled this man, with a voice that echoed like thunder. "And call me Mister Skye, if you would, mate."

Engagés had run a plank up to the gunwales of the second keelboat, and soon the rest of Morse's party threaded through the boiling bronze crowd. Elkanah waved them over.

Rudolpho Danzig, a short, compact, dark-haired man, studied the Blackfeet and French-Canadian engagés with amiable curiosity as he came. Young Captain Cobb, with full muttonchops of yellow-brown hair and a receding hair-line, studied things about him as if making notes. But white, soft Percy Connaught looked jumpy, if not terrified.

"Gentlemen," said Elkanah, "come meet our hosts, Alec

and Natawista Culbertson, and our guide, Mister Skye, and his wives Victoria and Mary. And the little lad is Dirk. . . . Now, sirs, let me introduce Professor Rudolpho Danzig, a geologist from Harvard College with a lively interest in natural sciences and everything else on earth. Professor Danzig is Swiss, from Berne, and an old friend who badgers me to make scientific instruments for him.

"Now here is Percy Connaught, of Hartford, who owns a book bindery there and is an old business acquaintance. Mister Connaught has come here to write a book about the west."

"Two books," corrected Connaught. "One for the vulgar—it'll cause a few sensations, I hope—and one serious one, to influence public policy concerning the far west."

"And finally, Captain Cobb, who instructs cadets at West Point about something or other, and is here to gather information for the army, and reconnoiter the west."

"My field's intelligence," explained Cobb. "Knowledge wins wars. It's a pleasure, sir," he said, offering a hand to Culbertson. "And you, sir," he said to Mister Skye. He offered no hand to the Indian wives. Elkanah realized that Connaught hadn't either, but Professor Danzig had cordially clasped hands with each person present.

Mister Skye was visibly sizing up the party, his obscure blue eyes darting from Danzig to Cobb and finally gazing a long moment at Connaught, absorbing the man's pasty corpulence and apparent nervousness.

Then Culbertson steered them toward the fort, which lay thirty or forty yards back from the levee.

"Is our property safe? I should think these savages would snatch it the moment we turn our back," said Percy Connaught in a nasal New England twang. "They're all famous thieves."

"My engagés will have it inside directly," said Culbertson. "They'll be busy all through the night. All these tribesmen—Blackfeet mostly, Piegans and Bloods, and a few Sarsi, Crees, and others—about three hundred lodges, have been camping here waiting for this moment. We'll shelve the trade goods tonight and open the window in the morning.

"The window?" asked Elkanah.

"Right here," said Culbertson as they wove into a long low corridor with a stout gate at each end. "This is the trading window. It opens onto our trading room. They'll bring in the buffalo robes and pelts in the morning and trade for the goods. They'll clean us out of everything—two keelboat loads—in a few days, but the keelboats will bring more from Fort Union. All the trading takes place right here at this window. Only a few at a time, you see, with the inner gate, here, shut."

"Is it that dangerous—that you must deal with these people through a small window?" asked Elkanah.

"Not at all," Culbertson said. "But there are times—when they've sampled the jug, especially—we prefer to be careful." He smiled faintly. "I can't imagine where the spirits come from," he added.

"They're barbaric!" said Connaught, oblivious of Natawista Culbertson, Victoria and Mary Skye. "Animals. I have always opposed white settlement of these western lands. This is like the Sahara, like Australia's Outback, a huge burden the Republic must now maintain for no good purpose."

Mister Skye glanced sharply at the man, and Elkanah wondered whether there'd be trouble on the trail. He thought to say something to Connaught, who seemed utterly unaware that the company he addressed included Blackfeet, Crow, and Snake women. Those he called the vulgar were always invisible to him.

But the moment passed. The inner yard of Fort Benton was redolent with cooking odors and the faint smell of other things—leathers, hides, horses, urine, and human sweat. From a small pen across the yard, an ugly blue roan horse with yellow eyes and narrow head flattened its ears and shrieked, its stare on Mister Skye.

"The engagés live over there," said Culbertson, pointing to a barracks building. "The kitchen's there. Hide storerooms here. My quarters, offices, and spare rooms over there. A few married engagés live nearby in adobe cabins. We've started that northwest blockhouse—my men make about twelve hundred adobe bricks a day—and then we'll build another one on the southeast corner, the river side.''

"Not much wood to build with," observed Rudolpho Danzig.

"Not much," Culbertson agreed. "We cut firewood over in the Highwoods, twenty miles south. Adobe's the only building material here."

"Why here? Why this site?" asked Professor Danzig.

Culbertson shrugged. "These river flats are rare. And up above are the great falls of the Missouri. Also, there's a ford here, and we're close to the tribes we trade with, the heart of the Blackfeet country."

"Ah, so," said Danzig. "Always a reason."

"My friends," said the bourgeois, "Natawista has magically prepared us a great feast of buffalo hump. We'll see you to your quarters now, and expect you in a few minutes."

Elkanah Morse looked forward to it, and the good talk, keenly. He would plumb Mister Skye at table.

Chapter 2

So long had Mister Skye hunkered at campfires that a proper chair felt uncomfortable and strange. He had not sat in one for about twenty years. He tried to remember his manners, dredged up from his forgotten boyhood, and it made him clumsy. Natawista Culbertson had managed a great feast, with succulent buffalo hump, rib, tongue, spiced sausage made of boudins, and potatoes and turnips fresh off the keelboats. Alec uncorked a flagon of good port wine for the occasion, but Mister Skye managed to avoid it. Not now, he thought, not now. In his possibles rested a three-gallon cask of bourbon from the sutler at Fort Laramie. It warmed him to think of it.

The hour was late and he felt sleepy, but across the massive plank table sat one of the most astonishing men Mister Skye had ever encountered. Even now, in the torpid wake of the feast, Elkanah Morse peppered questions at his hosts and guide, his blocky tanned face animated and young in the amber light of the oil lamps. Here lay Yankee genius of a sort entirely new to the guide.

"What are the most successful trade items, Mister Culbertson?" Morse asked.

"Why, blankets, I suppose. Calico. Anything metal, cooking pots . . ."

"I have them all. I have copper kettles that weigh half as much. What about arrows? I have ready-made arrows, with shafts that are truer than anything they can make."

The bourgeois frowned. "I don't think ye'll git far with those, Mister Morse."

"Why not? It's progress! A better arrow. Each shaft milled to a thousandth of an inch. Exactly identical iron tips. Good turkey-feather fletching, scientifically cut and measured."

"Medicine," rumbled Mister Skye. "An arrow must have medicine. So must a bow. Each tribe makes bows and arrows their own way. Each warrior or hunter has his own marks dyed or notched on an arrow."

"Tradition. You're really talking about tradition. That's the barrier to all progress, Mister Skye. I'll show them a better thing, and they'll see it eventually."

"Ah, no, mate. I'm talking about Indian religion. Medicine is how Indians understand power and success and failure and the forces of nature. I'm afraid your ready-made arrows—"

Elkanah Morse laughed easily. "Hope I can prove you wrong," he said. "But that's why I'm here, to get answers. I'll pester you with questions the whole trip!"

Mister Skye enjoyed that. A man who asked questions proved better on the trail than one who had all the answers.

"Now let me try another on you, gents. I've brought a sickle. We make them, too, good hard steel edge. Sickles and scythes, shovels, pickaxes, hatchets, we make them all. Now I thought a sickle might be right handy among these tribesmen. Cut hay. Pile up a winter's supply of prairie hay. Now take a hunting party, out camping somewhere and afraid their ponies will be stolen. They could cut hay, bring in grass, keep their ponies picketed right in camp."

Alec Culbertson laughed. "Woman's work. No self-respecting warrior would cut hay. It's beneath them. That's for beasts of burden, not warriors or hunters, who lounge away their lives like any proper prairie Indian.''

"How you talk!" cried Natawista. "But it is true. Maybe you trade sickles to women."

"Son of a bitch!" cried Victoria, Mister Skye's old woman. "Maybe them damn warriors will learn to use this sickle."

Conversation froze. Betsy and Arabella gaped. Rudolpho Danzig grinned. Jarvis Cobb looked uncomfortable. Percy Connaught pursed his lips, drew himself up in his chair, and peered disdainfully.

Only Elkanah Morse chuckled. "You are a lady after my heart, Mrs. Skye! When I ask hard questions and want straight answers, I know where to come."

"I forget," muttered Victoria. "I learn this talk from the trappers that came to Absaroka. I forget you got some damn good words, and damn bad words. In Absaroka, all words are good words. Son of a bitch!"

"There are occasions, Mrs. Skye, when I envy you your freedom," said Betsy Grover Morse. "A New England woman has a want of words."

Arabella Morse looked bored. "I'm tired, Papa. I think I shall retire."

"By all means," said Elkanah, watching her sweep away and into the shadowed yard. "I dragooned her into coming," he said. "She's bent upon making life as dreary as possible for herself."

Mister Skye watched Elkanah's daughter thoughtfully as she fled the table.

For half an hour more, Elkanah Morse peppered questions at his hosts and his guides, and Mister Skye marveled that a man who had cordelled and poled a keelboat all day, beneath a blazing sun, could be so awake deep into the summer night. The guide studied Morse, studied the others, trying to fathom the character of these people. He had to. His safety, the safety of his family, the safety of these people themselves would be at stake. Arabella seemed pouty and rebellious. A problem.

Covertly Mister Skye eyed the others. Danzig had said little, but seemed as alive and vital and curious as Elkanah

Morse. Captain Cobb seemed an enigma, poker-faced and polite. West Point and competent, he thought. Connaught reeked of trouble, his pasty soft face reflecting disdain and contempt the whole evening. But Betsy, vibrant Betsy the watercolorist, there was a good match for Elkanah, a woman of innate happiness and strength.

Suddenly Elkanah called it off, just as Alec Culbertson showed signs of dozing, and gentle Natawista drooped. "Time for bed. Off in the morning. Try to make up time. One thing, Mister Skye. Before we leave, I'd like to drop in on the opposition, find out what they trade, get the measure of their needs. I see it's just upstream a piece."

Culbertson came suddenly awake. "Wouldn't advise it," he muttered.

"Sounds like there's some animosity," Morse said.

"More to it than that," rumbled Mister Skye. "It's not just competition. There's bad blood. Harvey is, shall we say, hostile to us. To Alec here, and to me. Fort Campbell has not yet been resupplied this year, so he hasn't a thing on his shelves. Mister Morse, I'll put it plain. Alexander Harvey is a killer of the most brutal sort, unforgiving, cruel, vicious. He's murdered Indians and his own engagés without cause. Twice when I was employed by this company, I stopped him from shedding blood. Alec, here, had him thrown out. He will take you for an agent and provocateur of American Fur."

"Sounds formidable indeed, Mister Skye. Nonetheless, I shall visit Fort Campbell in the morning. I'm a businessman and manufacturer, looking for opportunities in the Indian trade. I'll tell him that, and tell him what I have to offer. He may order from my companies on just as competitive terms as American Fur."

There was a bit of steel in the reply, Mister Skye thought. Well then, he'd accompany Elkanah Morse in the morning. Just to keep the unpredictable Harvey from murdering the entrepreneur on the spot.

"I will take you there then," Mister Skye said.

"Why, that's not necessary. I'd prefer that you'd see to the packing. You have the horses, I trust?"

"I do, but I'm going with you to Harvey, Primeau and Company."

"If there's bad blood, why, I'd prefer to go alone, and you may organize our caravan."

"Mary and Victoria will organize it."

"I see you're determined. All right then. I've put myself and my loved ones and friends in your hands because they told me you're the best in this wilderness. I'll defer to your judgment, Mister Skye. If you feel the need to go with me when I visit this man Harvey, why, you must have cause. Come with me, then. Is this man mad?"

It was a question Mister Skye couldn't answer for sure. "No, I don't suppose so. Suspicious. Obsessed. Surrounded by imaginary enemies. And ready to murder."

"Then I am glad you'll be with me, Mister Skye."

In the quietness of a rose and burgundy dawn, Elkanah Morse stared at the ponies. The sun lay so low that a long umber shadow from the engagés' barracks along the east stockade fell across the yard, almost to the horse pens.

"These are Indian ponies, Mister Morse. Small, tough, with hoof horn so hard they don't need shoes. They prosper where grain-fed horses die. High-bred horses from the States can outrun them—for a while. But for sheer endurance, these mustang ponies will outlast them. I have your dozen, and I've picked them for this country."

"They seem small and thin—"

"They're that, mate. Trust them. They'll all take saddle or pack. I dickered half the spring for the best. Now, how do you want this done?"

Beside Morse and Mister Skye lay a mound of gear, all of it so new and clean and well built that it astonished the guide.

"I'll need two to carry my sample goods. Need two ponies to carry the goods up to Fort Campbell. Each of my party will have a riding horse. Those two sidesaddles are for my ladies. The remaining ponies will carry foodstuffs and camp supplies. Of course, sir, you'll be providing us with meat. . . ."

Mister Skye nodded. He caught a tough hammerheaded pony with spots over his rump.

"Let me show you how I want them," said Morse. "I've gone to some lengths so's not to gall the animals." He dropped a fine brown wool saddle blanket over the pony, and then a pack saddle with a fleece lining that astonished Mister Skye. He'd never seen a pack saddle like this, fleece-lined, with cinches of the finest harness leather. After he'd tightened down the saddle, Morse hung the panniers to it. These fine canvas bags astounded Mister Skye as much as the saddles themselves. They were light, durable, riveted along the seams, with fitted buckle-down covers, and probably waterproof.

"Like them? I designed them myself. Had them custom-made in my tannery." Some delight animated Elkanah's square, craggy face.

The river was a live thing, throbbing without pause. It rippled orange and salmon in the dawn light as Mister Skye and Elkanah Morse walked past somnolent Blackfeet lodges toward Fort Campbell, leading two packhorses.

The opposition post was a smaller version of Fort Benton, also on the north bank of the Missouri. Mister Skye banged on the massive plank door with the butt of his Hawken and waited. Fur posts rarely stirred until midmorning, and this one was no exception. He banged again. At last they heard a bar being lifted within, and the heavy cottonwood door creaked open a bit. In the rose light they could see an eye, a hand, and a heavy blue revolver.

"You," said Alexander Harvey.

"We have business, Harvey."

"Not likely. American Fur Company monkey business."

Mister Skye sighed. "I'd like you to meet Elkanah Morse, Lowell, Massachusetts. He manufactures goods for the Indian trade. Harvey, Primeau probably buys them in quantity. He has two pack loads of samples. New goods. Things he thinks the tribes might cotton to. He came all this way to find out."

The door creaked open a bit further, but the heavy revolver never wavered. Harvey had straight coarse black hair, disheveled now, burning brown eyes in a hollowed rough face, and the build of a bear. Now those burning eyes settled on the panniers, noting the fine cut of the canvas, double buckles, and pack saddles that pampered horses.

"Mr. Harvey? I'd like to ask a few questions. Mostly, I'd like to know what the tribesmen want. What to manufacture. It seems to me if I get a sense of—"

"No," said Harvey.

Mister Skye glanced at Elkanah Morse, and at Harvey's unwavering revolver that had somehow lifted slightly until it bored into Morse's breast.

"Well, let me show you the goods I've brought along."

"I don't need to see them. Tell me what they're worth and I'll trade in robes. My resupply isn't in and my shelves are bare."

"Don't you want to see . . . ?"

Harvey shrugged. "They trade for anything I've got. It doesn't matter."

"Well, at least you could tell me what is most—most sought for. I can then make sure your St. Louis people know . . . and I can usually improve the product. Lighter, stronger, more efficient . . ."

Harvey stared at him, then at Mister Skye. "I'm not telling my trade secrets. This is just another damned American Fur snooping party. And you're just another damned American Fur lackey come sniffing around here to find ways to steal my business. Skye, there, is American Fur and always has been."

"It's Mister Skye, Harvey."

The man half-hidden behind the massive door leered.

"I'll show you," said Elkanah Morse firmly. He walked to the nearest packhorse, ignoring the revolver that swung along with him. "I have here six types of iron arrow points; lance points; lathed hardwood arrowshafts. Skillets and kettles, light and heavy, cast iron and copper. Scythes, knives, hatchets, ax heads, double- and single-bitted. Copper rivets, long and short—"

"Rivets?" asked Harvey.

"Why, sir, I thought the Indians might use them in leatherwork. Punch a hole with an awl—I have awls—and run the rivet through leather along a seam, and flatten down the opposite side.''

Harvey said nothing.

''And here I have canvas, oilcloth, calico, cambric, and an entire presewn canvas lodgecover. Do you suppose they'd go for a canvas lodgecover? I had a hide lodge shipped to me a year ago, at great expense, for the pattern.''

''Oilcloth. Waterproof?'' asked Harvey.

''Of course. Red checks, yellow, white. Also a bolt of canvas impregnated with India rubber. Great covering for a canoe. How about wire? I have brass wire, steel wire, fine gauge. Do you think they'd want it?''

''American Fur must be trying to pawn off crazy stuff on me.''

''I'm an independent manufacturer, Mister Harvey. American Fur is a customer. So is Harvey, Primeau. You use my blankets. Now tell me, what colors do the tribesmen prefer? Striped, like the Hudson Bay ones? How many points? Four-pound sell best?''

''I told you I don't share trade information. Tell Culbertson it's a good joke. And you can leave that truck right here. It'll give me a little something to peddle while we wait for the pack train.''

Elkanah Morse drew himself up, eyeing the revolver at last. ''Those are my private samples, Mister Harvey. I'm on my way to the far tribes with them.''

Harvey grinned. ''American Fur samples, you mean. Gonna go out and lure the redskins into AFC. Uncinch those loads and drop them.''

''I think not, Harvey,'' said Mister Skye.

''He obeys or he's a dead man, and so are you.''

Harvey's threat was real, thought Mister Skye. With that revolver the man could put bullets into Elkanah Morse and into himself before he could bring his Hawken to bear. And he was half-hidden behind that door, too. Time ticked by. Morse stood paralyzed. Mister Skye thought the man would be dead before he even started here. Harvey might well murder him after the packs were off the horses.

''I said move,'' snapped Harvey.

"Murder will put you in a federal prison," said Elkanah quietly.

Alexander Harvey laughed cynically.

"Mister Harvey. I'm going to turn my back and lead these packhorses with my goods away from here. If it's murder, you'll do it whether I'm armed or unarmed, whether I face you or have my back turned."

Deliberately, Elkanah Morse turned and walked to the packhorses and took hold of the halter stales. Mister Skye stood rooted, watching Harvey's black revolver follow.

"I will live long enough to kill you," muttered Mister Skye.

Harvey's burning glance caught him then, and the revolver swung toward Mister Skye. A laugh. The heavy door creaked shut, and the bourgeois of Fort Campbell had vanished from sight. Mister Skye stood stock still, his small blue eyes searching out loopholes and finding none. Heart pattering, he trotted up to Elkanah Morse.

"You were frightened?" asked Mister Skye.

"Never so frightened. My legs tremble under me."

"But you did it. Stood him down, mate."

Elkanah Morse shuddered. "I did what I had to. I should have taken your advice, Mister Skye. You and Mister Culbertson warned me. This is a wild land with wild men in it."

"Aye, mate, it is that. There's something a bit wrong, mad I'd say, about Harvey, but you stood him down. Don't think it's over. Harvey never forgets. When he makes an enemy, there's but one thing in his head, and that's the finishing of what's begun."

"Does he really think I'm some sort of American Fur man?"

"No telling. The opposition comes and goes. AFC beat out Bridger, Sublette, Fitzpatrick, Ashley. Beat out Campbell, Fox, and all the rest. They get murderous, thinking about AFC, thinking about the rich Chouteaus back in St. Louis. They get to hating AFC the way a Bible thumper hates the devil. If AFC did half the things they say it does, the government would have lifted its license long ago."

The entrepreneur pondered that as they walked along the

riverbank back to Fort Benton. Life stirred in the Blackfeet lodges now; dusky women bathing at the river silently watched their progress.

"How about these? Piegans and Bloods, are they? We could show my goods to these. Can you talk their tongue?"

"Sign language," said Mister Skye. "I'd say no to this. These Blackfeet are waiting to trade later today, as fast as the keelboat goods are shelved. You won't get an answer out of them. Not the kind of information you want. Mostly they'd be confused, and Culbertson might not be entirely happy. Maybe, if you'd like to stick around a day or two, you could sit at the trading window, see what they want most, watch the whole thing."

"I don't think that'll show me much. What they want shows up in the purchase orders. So many four-point red blankets. So many of such and such an iron pot. No, Mister Skye." He beamed at the guide beside him. "I'm itchy. Let's be off. I've some fancy camping goods of my own design I'm rarin' to try!"

"And you'd like to put a few leagues between yourself and Alexander Harvey, eh?"

Elkanah Morse sighed. "I'm glad to be free of him. We'll leave directly, right after breakfast, and then we'll be free."

"Don't count on it, Mister Morse."

Chapter 3

Percy Connaught kept two journals. One would be turned into a book about far west policy. The other would become a book full of wild west episodes, strange encounters, and amazing sights—for the vulgar, of course. The first book would make him influential among the best minds in the Republic; the second would be a sensation among the masses, and make him rich.

Not that he was poor. He had inherited a bindery in Hartford, and it provided a comfortable return and largely took care of itself, giving him time for more important things, such as advancing civilization. Every Whig instinct in him had fought Manifest Destiny, but in 1846 the avalanche had come, and now the Republic stretched clear to the Pacific, and we owned the Spanish possessions as well as Oregon. But what had we gained? A vast wasteland! A Sahara that could not support civilization and might well bleed the Republic to death. The western armies numbered a few thousand, and should number a few hundred thousand to control and defend this vast waste. Everything on this journey so far had confirmed him in his view, and he intended to write a book so compelling that it would affect the nation's destiny for decades. And here was Captain Cobb, reconnoitering for the army. An opportunity! Percy intended to convert Cobb to his view, and between Cobb's reports and his own, they'd overcome the inflammatory Senator Thomas Hart Benton and his mad son-in-law Fremont and establish a rational western policy.

But now, in the yard of Fort Benton, he labored on his other journal, the one for the vulgar. Each of his journals—five hundred blank pages bound in fine red morocco—was filling rapidly with his penciled fine script. Not ink, of course. Not nib and ink in a wilderness. Here before him labored Skye's two squaws organizing this caravan. The barbarous guide himself had vanished at dawn with Morse—off to the opposition mud pile—but these squaws looked downright industrious. Two squaws, one an old hag and the other comely and voluptuous, wives of a barrel-shaped Briton without a nation, who arrayed himself in scandalous fringed leggins and breechclout like the children of the wilds. Now there was a thing to describe to the vulgar!

Grudgingly, he admired them. In the same way he admired Skye, too. Morse found out Skye was the best to be had in the far west; half-savage himself, fierce, wild, and uncanny. A party could feel as safe as the wilds permitted when Skye was running it. A comfort. He knew there'd be few comforts in the coming months, but having a trained lion along would be one. He chuckled. Trained lion. He'd remember that, use it upon the vulgar. A lion and two catamounts. How they'd laugh, back in the States, to read of a man with black hair to his shoulders and a black silk stovepipe set rakishly on his caveman skull!

"You!"

Percy removed his gold-rimmed spectacles and peered up. Why, it was the old hag herself, the one called Victoria.

"You. Stop making the words, and git your pack on. We're going to go soon. Son of a bitch, we don't go nowhere with a mess of lazy."

"Right with you, old woman!"

"Me old? Maybe tougher. You soft as sheep wool, and you gonna feel it until you get toughed up."

"You have me there, Victoria," he admitted. He paused a moment to scribble it in his journal. He'd record her language as best as he could—using a dash, of course, to form some expressions. Like G——m. It would be inconsiderate to teach the vulgar unfortunate expletives. Then he snapped his red morocco journal books shut and tucked them in his pack.

"That's some hell of a pack. I never seen any so light and strong," said Victoria, fingering the riveted canvas. The packs were, in fact, one of Morse's uncanny marvels. The frames had been cut from thin hickory, tough as steel, and swathed in fleece-lined harness leather pads. The panniers were compartmented with canvas dividers to keep things in place. The canvas itself was lightly impregnated with rubber, making them watertight.

Victoria flipped one of Morse's thick saddle blankets over a scrawny pony and dropped the loaded pack saddle over it, muttering and exclaiming in her strange tongue all the while, as Percy Connaught watched, amused.

Culbertson and half the engagés here hovered around, too, fingering equipment such as they'd never seen, exclaiming, hefting Morse's weapons, bantering with Betsy and Arabella, the first white women they'd ever seen here. Amid the hubbub Mister Skye and Elkanah Morse returned, leading packhorses and looking peculiarly grim on a crisp morning. Connaught wondered at it, but neither of them said anything. They wolfed a breakfast of buffalo steaks and oat gruel that Natawista had ready for them.

Everything seemed ready. The women, in matched gray cotton dresses with pleated skirts, sat their sidesaddles, looking enchanting. Rudolpho Danzig sat a restless spotted pony, eyeing this horde with intense interest. He wore a tweed suitcoat with leather patches, and a flat-crowned gray felt hat that shadowed his pale face and black spade beard. Jarvis Cobb sat easily aboard one of Morse's light cavalry saddles, with a roll tied behind him. They had rehearsed all this over and over in the east, with Elkanah Morse's driving genius organizing everything, inventing and manufacturing devices for every need. They had even gathered in Lowell before embarking and tried it all out, tents and saddles, hatchets, and revolvers supplied them by Connaught's Hartford neighbor Sam Colt. There was nothing more that Yankee genius could do. If the hand of science, progress, and civilization could not conquer the wilderness with such as this, then it couldn't be done.

Mister Skye—how Connaught enjoyed the name!—rolled with a sailor's gait to the pen where that peculiar horse paced. Percy had never seen such a beast. Skye's animal stood tall, ugly, rawboned, with evil yellow eyes and a blue roan hide marred by a hundred scars and cuts. The thing shrieked wickedly as Skye approached, and butted the guide with his head.

"I'll help saddle, Mister Skye," said Elkanah, closing behind the guide. Even as he stepped ahead, Skye's burly arm caught the industrialist and spun him back ruthlessly. Morse gaped, barely holding his temper.

"Sorry, mate." Skye addressed them all. "I don't want any of you getting close to this horse. Never closer than ten or fifteen feet. For your safety."

"He kicks, I suppose," said Elkanah, rubbing his bruised arm.

"No, Mister Morse, he kills."

Even as they stared the strange horse with the narrow-set vicious eyes bared his teeth and snapped at the air, murdering flies and men. He squealed eerily as the guide threw a light pad saddle of Indian manufacture over him and slid his sheathed Hawken over that.

Percy Connaught shuddered. A murderous blue horse would be something for his journal, the one for the vulgar, of course. The guide paused, as if looking for something, studying the high mud-brick walls, testing the cerulean skies with knowing eyes. He rolled over to Alec Culbertson and Natawista and roared like a sore-toothed grizzly, hugging the bourgeois while they slapped each other on the back. And then a gentler hug for Natawista. All much too demonstrative, embarrassing actually, to Percy Connaught's taste. But they'd educated themselves back east about the mountains, and had got that veteran of several rendezvous, Nathaniel Wyeth himself, to tell them what to expect. That taciturn ice dealer had mentioned the mountain hug and a lot of other strange customs, and told them to respect the ways of the mountains and their men because such things were natural and good for the place and the circumstance. They had listened with care.

Outside of the fort, a milling crowd of savages watched silently. Percy studied them a bit fearfully, wondering at their feathers, calicos, half-naked brown bodies, vermilioned cheeks and heads, and calf-high black-dyed moccasins that gave these people their name. *Pieds Noirs*, the French trappers had called them. Stone Age people, without the wheel, without metal, without writing. But no doubt murderous.

Skye's old hag glared at them, and Connaught remembered that the Crows were mortal enemies of these Piegan and Blood savages. Her weathered old body grew rigid, as if she expected an arrow to bury itself in her breast. Even the guide, Skye, peered sharply at the throng. But at the gate of Fort Benton, Culbertson yelled something in their tongue, and the savage mob thronged toward the trading window. Resupplied, Fort Benton was in business.

The ford of the Missouri turned out to be right in front of Fort Benton.

"Follow my path, mates. Water's low. It won't even reach the bellies this time."

He steered his ugly blue horse down the levee and into the swift current, angling upstream. The guide's packmules and ponies followed, each carrying its burden in dyed parfleches. Their skin lodge went over on two horses. One carried the hide cover on its back; the other carried two bundles of lodgepoles that floated behind. The guide's word was good. At no place in the hundred-and-fifty-yard river did water blacken a pony's belly.

Elkanah, Betsy, and Arabella ventured out next, the women laughing and watching the cold water tug at their mounts. And lastly, Connaught, Cobb, and Danzig crossed, each leading two packhorses. They gathered on the south shore beneath a pitched yellow bluff, and the ponies shook off water, violently rattling the packs. But nothing came loose.

It was easier than he had supposed, Percy thought. Maybe all the tales of hardship he'd heard about the wild west suffered a bit from exaggeration.

But over here, away from the dun-colored fort, things

seemed somehow different. Mister Skye sat quietly on Jawbone, letting them all feel it. Feel how it was to be alone
in a vast and menacing wild.

"All right, mates," he rumbled. "From now on, your
safety depends on heeding what I say. If anything happens
to me, trust my good women, Victoria and Mary. They're
better at this than I am. Alec Culbertson told me most of
the Piegans are in the Judith basin, two or three days south.
They were enemies of you Yanks for years; many still are.
Trade and smallpox tamed them—a little. They are great
thieves, and thieving is an honor on these plains. Mister
Morse, they'll want to trade for the sample goods you'll be
showing them, and if not trade, then steal them. I'll be
thinking of ways to deal with it. I don't speak their tongue,
and sign language won't explain it. Be thinking on it."

For several hours they toiled quietly up long yellow draws,
down into an old bed of the Missouri, and finally up again
and out upon a plain so vast it stretched to infinity, with
only a few amethyst buttes and lavender mountains rough-
ing the surface. Percy Connaught found the vast silent emptiness frightening. The old hag rode off obliquely left, or
southeast. Mary and her infant boy trotted off obliquely
right, until each of them turned into black dots, often mysteriously invisible. Scouts, Percy Connaught thought.
Scouts, like cat's whiskers, like the antennae of a bug, out
to search the bunch-grassed silvery prairie for enemies. Sam
Colt's .31-caliber baby dragoon revolver belted to his waist
was a comfort.

Aeons ago, this had been the bed of a great sea. That was
plain enough from the stratified sedimentary rock they'd passed
as they wound upward from the Missouri River valley. The
rock lay angled, broken, and faulted here, no doubt tumbled
by the upheavals of the nearby mountain cordillera. They rode
through a second channel of the Missouri, dry now except for
a small creek, probably in use as recently as the last ice age.
Somehow this land had been lifted up from the sea, and then
the erosion began, thousands of feet of it, leaving those distant
blue flattopped buttes where a cap of more resistant rock had

prevented the erosion. Limestone, probably. Here in an arid climate, limestone would endure.

Before retiring at Fort Benton, Rudolpho Danzig had pulled out his sextant and measured the height of the North Star. The higher in the sky it appeared, the farther north they must be. Fort Benton was, he determined, approximately forty-seven degrees and fifty minutes north. Not far from the forty-ninth parallel, where the British possessions began. Longitude was a tougher matter, and he wasn't particularly worried about it. Someday the world's nations would have to decide where to start, where to run the arbitrary zero meridian. This republic wanted it to run through Washington City, in the District of Columbia. France insisted that the prime meridian run through Paris. Spain was holding out for Madrid. But he guessed that someday the world's nations would settle on London, the Royal Observatory in Greenwich in particular. There were ways to measure just how far west they had come. An accurate clock and a sextant measure of the noonday sun, for one. But he had only a pocket watch. Time was meaningless in these vast and entertaining wastes. He had with him the brand-new book published by the U.S. Naval Observatory, *American Ephemeris and Nautical Almanac*, listing the position of various celestial bodies each day of the year, based on a prime meridian at Washington, D.C. He had also a copy of *Bowditch's Practical Navigator*, for additional help. And, of course, a magnetic compass, which turned out to be several degrees off true here.

None of which concerned him a great deal. He had come for fun, and found every minute, every breath he breathed in this endless land, a joyous experience. He'd grown up in Berne, Switzerland, and won his doctorate in natural sciences from the new University of Berne, and then hastened to the New World and broader horizons than Switzerland could provide, using his doctorate as a handy passport. Harvard had embraced him. He was nominally a geologist, but his mind refused to be straitjacketed and his real study was the whole world and its people, geography. His students got geology enough—plus biology, cartography, topology, botany, paleontology, history, anthropology, and more. Academia couldn't contain a mind like his. Nor his compact body, either, for here he rode, on Morse's expedition, observing everything and setting it down cryptically in his journals. Except for the impressions of a few mountain men, this country remained unmapped and unknown.

From the moment he met Elkanah Morse, he knew they were kindred spirits. The manufacturing genius and the professor had restless tinkering minds, boundless curiosity, and an itch to see what lay beyond the horizon. Rudolpho Danzig had said yes, yes, yes, before Elkanah Morse was half through explaining his westward journey. In Morse's kit lay a mountain of gadgets. Not to be outdone, Rudolpho Danzig had a few of his own, including the whole paraphernalia of Louis Jacques Mandé Daguerre, inventor of the daguerreotype, a photographic image made on a silver-coated copper plate treated with iodine vapor. Elkanah's cousin, Samuel F.B. Morse, had introduced it to the United States, and Rudolpho had hastened to purchase one of the things, seeing at last the tool geologists and naturalists needed to record their finds and help cartographers. He lacked plates—weight was a crucial factor—but he hoped to make a few images of some of the aborigines, perhaps chiefs or headmen.

Ahead of him rode Elkanah and Betsy, side by side, enjoying the wilderness and each other. She perched in her sidesaddle as if she'd been born to it, though in fact she learned to ride only recently. She refused to be left behind. Where Elkanah went, she would go! He'd discouraged her at first, with tales of hardship and danger, but that had only whetted her appetite. She began riding lessons at once and became an equestrienne as swiftly as she'd become a noted watercolorist. Between them, they'd dragooned their daughter Arabella—whose feelings about this expedition were displayed in a fossilized pout—and thus the whole Morse family rode along behind the rude mountain guide.

For a moment Rudolpho felt a pang. His own Sarah declined to come, and he missed her sorely, along with their three boys. But ah, that Betsy! What made these women of the New World so much bolder and more vital than their sisters of the Old World? Scarcely a woman of Europe would

have ventured into a wild like this, but here rode Betsy
Morse, braving it all, enjoying herself, tasting life, risking
everything, drawing air into her lungs as clean and dry and
transparent as any air on earth. How could there be diseases
in a place like this? The sunbaked plains bred health and
life and strength!

That evening they camped in a peculiar gulch on the
northeast edge of a looming flattopped butte, black with
ponderosa on its precipitous slopes. Square Butte, Mister
Skye labeled it. To the west lay the Highwood Mountains,
black-forested and mysterious. Danzig eyed the terrain carefully, noting the white cap of resistant rock that formed the
butte when softer dark rock below it eroded away over aeons of time. This place alone, with its tumbled land, could
occupy a geologist for months, he thought. He had observed
a giant dry riverbed here, and wondered what vast stream
had cut it not too long ago, probably in glacial times. Maybe
the Missouri itself, he thought.

Camping was a familiar drill for all of them now. They'd
camped along the Missouri from Fort Union, on the banks
beside the keelboats, as the burly French beasts of burden
roped and poled them west. But now Mister Skye's choices
of campsites would be based on different considerations:
good water, good grass for the stock, shelter, wood for
fires, and defense. Danzig paused to admire the choice. All
those things seemed abundant here.

Except perhaps defense. They had stopped in a broad
riverbed gulch and could be observed from dun bluffs, not
to mention the vast butte that loomed over them. At least,
Danzig thought, their guide had chosen a place where a
campfire could not be seen far in the night.

Mister Skye addressed them all. "Let the ponies graze
and water freely until dusk, but under guard. Perhaps you
will oblige us by staying out among them, and armed, Mister Connaught. Later, we'll picket them close to camp. My
horse, Jawbone, does excellent sentry duty all night."

"Why—why—I had thought to do my journals, Skye."

"It's Mister Skye."

"Oh, dear, yes, it's Mister Skye!"

"The camp seems to be equipped with fine lanterns, carbide

lanterns, Mister Connaught. Light for your journals later. I will climb Square Butte yonder with an eye to our safety."

He did not wait for a reply from the Hartford man of letters, but trotted off into the russet twilight. A bit later Danzig caught glimpses of the burly guide clambering easily up slopes fit for only a mountain goat. Connaught had ignored Mister Skye, settled before the fine canvas tent with collapsible light ash poles Morse designed, and had taken to whittling his pencil and scribbling in his red book. Rudolpho Danzig sighed, plucked out the carbine Morse had lent him, and strolled out among the loose ponies and mules, keeping a sharp eye upon the nearby tree lines and the rim of bluffs. The ponies rolled in dust, slaked a fine thirst at the cold spring, and ripped the tops off of bunch grass greedily.

Danzig watched the animals, watched Jawbone herd them all, king of this equine tribe. He watched the squaws, Victoria and Mary, erect Mister Skye's skin lodge into its conical form. Back in Massachusetts, Wyeth had told them about these lodges, calling them marvels, perfect adaptations to the nomadic life of these plains people. The squaws adjusted the wind flaps to the direction of the breeze, thus drawing fresh air from the bottom of the lodge to its top and sucking off smoke if there were a lodgefire within. But this amiable summer night they'd cook outdoors after butchering the antelope old Victoria had somehow slain with a silent arrow during the day. Danzig intended to learn about these lodges. Indeed, maybe they'd try out the canvas lodgecover Morse had fashioned.

Mister Skye slid silently into camp a half hour later, just before blackness snuffed the gray northern twilight. He stared hard at Percy Connaught, saying nothing.

"Picket the horses now," he said shortly. "And hobble one or two close to your tents. I'm going for a little ride. We've been followed, and I'm going to find out why."

Chapter 4

Mister Skye rode down the backtrail quietly, through an indigo night, with only a fat amber moon hanging in the east to light the way. Jawbone glided over the undulating prairie, making no noise. Near the hollow, Mister Skye circled west. Not a whisper carried through the silent night. Along the northwest horizon, a faint gray afterlight lingered, the detritus of a spent day.

When he reckoned he was near, he steered Jawbone into a slight crease and left him there. On foot, he stalked the remaining hundred yards up a gentle grade dotted with ghostly sage, and finally to a crest where he could peer down. Nothing. The dished land before him lay empty in the salmon glow of the moon. No fire, but he hadn't expected one. Stalkers rarely lit a fire. He eased silently to earth and studied the inky hollow, seeking the rock or log or thicket of sage that might be something else. His instinct, honed from a life in this wilderness, told him someone lurked there, though he could see or smell or hear nothing.

He set his silk stovepipe hat aside now, and flattened himself, his dragoon Colt in hand.

"If you're Harvey's man," he said conversationally, "forget it. These people are exactly what I told Harvey they were."

Nothing. And yet Mister Skye sensed that his words had reached human ears.

"If you're Pikuni," he said, using the Piegan band's name for itself, "know that I am Mister Skye. I am Mister Skye."

His name was big medicine and well known in every village on the northern plains. All warriors thought twice before tangling with the man named for the heavens and the horse that made war all by itself.

"I am Mister Skye!" he said sharply.

Only profound silence greeted him. He waited, dissatisfied, for a long time, his senses alert. Then he crabbed back from the breast of the earth, and retraced his steps to Jawbone, and rode through a dim night back to camp, the massive black hulk of Square Butte always before and to the right of him.

At his own camp he found them all gathered around a blazing fire, except for Mary and Victoria, who hung back in shadow. His own buffalo-skin lodge loomed off a bit from Elkanah Morse's camp, where the fire flared and spat sparks into the night breeze. From the darkness, he admired Morse's camp, with its lightweight ingenious tents and handy gear. Just beyond the rim of firelight, he spotted the picketed horses, shifting bulks close at hand. But it would not do.

He appeared suddenly in their midst, startling them as he knew he would.

"I'd suggest you douse the fire, mates. It's a comfort on a chill night, but it silhouettes you all."

"You found someone behind us?" asked Morse.

"Someone is behind us," Mister Skye said. "I didn't see him nor do I know his purposes. Probably a man Harvey sent."

"The fire's a pleasure, Skye. I'm finishing my journals by the light. Surely you don't mean some sort of danger lurks out there? Wolves, I suppose, but the rest, why, it's hoodoos and hobgoblins," said Percy Connaught.

"A lobo wolf, in human form, Mister Connaught."

"You make it sound like the nights are full of menace," said Betsy Morse.

"They are that, Mrs. Morse. I have been in the mountains for about a quarter of a century now. About two-thirds of the men I've known here have gone under. Sometimes from sheer accident or disease, and sometimes from carelessness."

"Well, Skye, we'll certainly have to be careful, what with assassins prowling the night," said Connaught.

"It's Mister Skye. Come with me, sir. We'll walk out to the crest of that rise yonder and let you look down into this camp."

Reluctantly, Connaught followed Mister Skye into the blackness.

"I can't see the way," he muttered.

"Of course you can't. Your eyes are fire-blinded. If something lurked out here, you wouldn't know where to shoot."

Connaught laughed.

From the slope a hundred yards out, they stared down into the camp. Each figure around the fire shone brightly against the black canvas of the night. Metal glinted in flickering yellow light. Skye's lodge, off a bit, was a ghostly cone.

Behind Skye, off in the blackness, something scurried through brush. Instinctively, the guide grappled Percy Connaught to earth and flattened both of them on the crest of the hill. Breath exploded from Connaught.

"Now see here, Skye! Are you mad! You demented fool, do you always tussle your employers to the ground?"

Mister Skye said nothing. Some shadowy form in the blur of the moon slid off through dense sagebrush, whisper of cloth or leather scraping brush.

Connaught laughed. "All very dramatic, Skye. And now a hare or a coyote has slithered into the sinister night!"

Mister Skye said nothing. He had dealt with obtuse men before and had come to the conclusion that nothing could change their opinions except bitter experience.

They trudged silently back to camp as Connaught dusted grime off his britches.

"Why, we scared off a rabbit," Connaught announced airily.

But Elkanah Morse read something in Mister Skye's face and hastened to shovel the loose dry soil of the plains over the fire, until they all sat in blackness and only a lingering of smoke remained.

Slowly the night came alive around them. Orion, Big Dipper, North Star. The horses and mules grew visible now, silvery moonlight glistening from their haunches and manes. Sharp night air curled about them. They grew aware of Jawbone hovering protectively in the murk, nipping bunch grass and then examining dark horizons, all senses alert.

From a far hill, coyotes laughed and chattered, but the answer came from wolves, barking sharply into night, or howling like souls caught in perdition.

"Where the buffalo gather, so do the wolves," said Mister Skye as he settled himself cross-legged in the circle of these people. "Tomorrow we'll reach the Judith basin, a bowl of knee-high golden grass, cold creeks full of trout, surrounded by low mountains. Full of buffler, usually. Piegans likely will be on the south side, living fat, making a little jerky and pemmican with these August berries. Until a few winters ago, they killed any white man they saw. Terrorized every tribe south and west and east. My wives hate them. I hated and feared them, too—lost many a friend to them. But times change. . . ."

"It was smallpox, wasn't it?" asked Captain Cobb.

"That and the trade for buffalo robes and white man's goods. Captain Cobb, do you approve of sitting here in the cold dark, without a fire?"

Jarvis Cobb laughed easily. "You want a military opinion, and I'm on detached duty. Well—to answer your question—yes, I suppose. Safety before comfort. Always assuming, of course, that there really is someone out there. I notice you haven't posted night guards."

"My night guard is that ugly evil horse. Captain Cobb, why might someone be following us?"

"You have me there. I'm a textbook soldier with no field experience. I've hoped to organize an intelligence service. The army has none, you know. I'm hoping to prove the value of it with this jaunt. Cartography, topology, detailed information about each tribe, weather . . . all of it. Now— to answer you with a textbook reply—I'd say a stalker is after one of two things—intelligence, what are we up to? Or—damage. Striking us down at a vulnerable moment.''

''If a lone stalker wanted to do maximum damage to us, what might he do, Captain?''

The young officer sat quietly in the darkness. ''Why,'' he said at last, ''kill you, I suppose.''

It was a good answer, Mister Skye thought.

''Who do you suppose he's working for—or is he on his own?''

''I'll answer that,'' interrupted Elkanah Morse. ''Harvey sent him to keep an eye on us. I never met a man so suspicious. He thinks I'm an American Fur man, instead of a manufacturer out to deal with the far tribes.''

''How would you deal with a stalker, Captain?'' asked Mister Skye.

''Snare him and find out what he wants.''

''If he's Indian, Captain, he'd consider torture an honorable death. If he's white or breed, you might get something out of him if you are ruthless enough.''

''I confess, Mister Skye, I hadn't even thought of such means—''

''This is a hard land, Captain. Put that at the top of your notes.''

Mister Skye sat contentedly, feeling fingers of cold air pluck under his elkskin shirt. It always took him a few days on the trail to take the measure of his clients. Now, at the end of their first day, he had some inklings. Connaught had shirked when asked to do something vital. But the thin professor, the spade-bearded Swiss geologist Danzig, had quietly filled in without being asked. Cobb remained an enigma—intelligent, bookish, distant. Elkanah and Betsy Morse delighted him with their natural strength, curiosity, joy, and grace. Pouting Arabella could cause acute problems. He sat amiably in the dark. This would be a better party than some.

* * *

They found Weasel Tail's band of Piegan Blackfeet on the south edge of the Judith basin, where the Judith River emerged from the humped foothills of the Belt Mountains. Through the hot cloudless day they passed innumerable buffalo, most of them shaded up or lying indolent in the August sun. They fascinated Betsy with their dark stupid power, and she resolved to paint them when she could.

Mister Skye's squaws hung closer to the pack train now, Betsy noticed, not wanting to be too far away from their husband in this land of their enemies. Inexorably he led them southward toward the upper Judith, as if he somehow knew where the band would be. Midafternoon, half a dozen horsemen boiled down from the bluffs to the south, dusky men on dark ponies, and Betsy's heart hastened. Fierce almost-naked men surrounded them, pointing and gesticulating. She found herself under their inspection. They stared at her, at Arabella, at their way of sitting sideways upon their horses.

"Easy, mates," said the guide. "They mean us no harm. Curious about the white women, first they've ever seen. These are the police. Every plains village has them. They protect the village and keep order."

Still, their savage power, bows, quivers, and befeathered fusils, alarmed her. They stared flat-eyed at her, revealing not the faintest warmth, and she thought surely she'd be murdered or worse. Beside her, Arabella had gone pale, and she stared back at them with all the arrogance she could muster. Connaught wasn't doing well either. He rode rigid with terror. Cobb seemed self-possessed enough, and that peculiar Swiss, Danzig, positively enjoyed the experience, just as her own Elkanah was delighting in every second of it. She blushed to think how nearly naked the Piegans were, and how attractive their tall, lean, muscled bronze bodies looked to her. She thought to paint them, too. Every one of them an Adonis, she thought wryly, remembering her grand tour through Italy. She smiled. They did not smile back.

Ahead, Mister Skye reined Jawbone and waited. One of the warriors approached, and the flash of hands and arms began. She'd heard of this and now she was witnessing the hand talk of the plains. At last they traveled again, these village police flanking the caravan.

"It's Weasel Tail's village," Mister Skye explained. "These are Brave Dog Society soldiers, doing camp duty. Every one a seasoned warrior. I talked with Blue Heron Running, a headman of the village. Told him we wished to pay our respects to the chief. They're plenty curious about the women. He wanted to know whether you ladies are to be gifts for Weasel Tail."

Betsy blanched. The thought of it suddenly alarmed her—that she might be considered property, traded off to some savage at the whim of some male.

Elkanah laughed and reached across the withers of his horse to clasp Betsy's hand. His eyes danced with mischief. "Maybe they'll trade some dusky beauty to me," he said. She didn't think it was funny.

Mister Skye saw the tension lacing the faces behind him. "Peaceful visit," he rumbled. "Enjoy their hospitality. Have your little gifts ready, Mister Morse. Twists of tobacco will do. They're not painted up, not fighting us—not currently, anyway. Likely just whiling away a sunny August here, making a little meat for winter. You'll be perfectly safe. Even your possessions will be safe."

"About as safe as chickens surrounded by foxes!" Betsy blurted.

"You have medicine, Mrs. Morse," replied the guide. "You ride a trotting horse sideways, and these great cavalrymen of the prairies have never seen such a thing. Wave your wand, and they'll do your bidding."

Betsy laughed nervously, feeling a froth of emotion that was not far from hysteria.

They followed the glinting clear river now—a creek, really, this time of year—and rounding a bend, beheld a forest of conical lodges on a crescent flat.

Bedlam. Her watercolorist's eye picked out yellow and gray curs, all howling. Naked brown babies with jet hair. Girls in leather skirts; boys wearing nothing. Squaws gaudy in red and purple tradecloth, primary colors, yellow calicos, loose billowy skirts, soft dove-gray doeskin shirts. Blue-black hair in glossy braids, hanging loose, tied into a long ponytail. Shrieking ponies. Thick bullhide medicine shields, daubed with white clays, red and black and white—or rather, she thought, carmine, burnt sienna, cream, russet.

All about her rose golden lodges of sewn hide, their tops blackened by smoke, their sides flaunting symbolic suns and eagles and stick figures, and buffalo, and fox, in gaudy color. The lodges seemed to stand in some order, each opening facing east, and she thought some religion must be in it. At the top of each rose a forest of sticks, lodgepoles actually, making the horizon furry with limbs, as if the village were a forest.

They stared at her, pressed, fingered her cotton skirts, boldly peeked at her black high-top shoes, touched her saddle, an excited buzz and murmur, currents of surprise and astonishment running through them. Arabella looked ashen. Betsy followed the lead of the squaws around her. She reached down, touched bone necklaces, claw ornaments, and laughed. In spite of a moil of fear, she enjoyed herself. Everything she and Elkanah had talked about for months suddenly became real.

Before her, Mister Skye rode easily, his silk hat raffishly tilted. These dusky villagers seemed to know all about him, and his blue roan, and they gave the horse wide berth, seeing Jawbone's laid-back ears and wicked glaring eyes, clacking teeth, and lips twisted into a perpetual snarl. Strung out, the visitors made a considerable procession with their packmules and ponies, and the Skye family travois and parfleches bobbing ahead of her. But at last Mister Skye drew up before a larger lodge, this one painted the cerulean of the skies about its lower circumference, with yellow sunbursts above it. Before it stood a tripod, decked with black and white eagle feathers, weasel and ermine tails, and—thirteen black scalps. Betsy watched old Victoria eye the dangling scalps ferociously.

She beheld the chief and he beheld her the same moment. His dark intelligent eyes surveyed her sandy brown hair and oval face, the swell of her bosom within her gray cambric dress. And finally her sidesaddle perch on her pony and slim ankles encased in black shoes. She in turn found herself peering at a young man with none of the seams and weathering of age she'd expected in a chief. This one stood tall, inches over six feet, she imagined, taller even than Elkanah. Lean, the color of waxed cherrywood, scarcely thirty, she supposed, peculiar scars upon his hard-muscled chest, and straight as any captain of industry. He wore a necklace of giant gray claws from some animal she could scarcely imagine, but that was all, save for a skin breech-clout so small she jerked her gaze away. Upon his loose jet hair perched a bonnet, but not the kind she had imagined. This one was a crown of vertical eagle feathers, with no elaborate tail. Only the upthrust feathers and two small ermine tails at either temple. His fierce animal magnetism fascinated her, and only reluctantly did she focus upon his three wives, each a stunning young beauty wreathed in smiles for these white visitors.

She would paint them! Her anxieties eased.

Mister Skye could not speak the tongue of these fierce people, and now his hands and arms flicked this way and that, and the chief's fingers replied. At last the chief commanded something, and a warrior scurried off into the crowd of onlookers. Mister Skye dismounted easily in that circle of quiet space around Jawbone.

"We'll be having a smoke," he said to Elkanah. "When the pipe comes, puff it and pass it along. It's the ritual of peace and welcome. Bring your gifts. Explaining your purposes here is beyond the sign language, but we're in luck. They've a Crow woman, married now to one of their warriors who captured her years ago. They're fetching her now. My Victoria will translate for us into Crow; this woman will translate the Crow into Blackfeet. We'll go slow, but we'll get it across. You're big medicine, Elkanah—the man who makes the white men's magic. They already know that—I was able to sign that much, anyway."

The Crow woman who now lived among these people hustled forward, and Victoria eyed her sharply.

"River Crow—Absaroka of the prairies," she muttered. "Ain't any friend of mine."

Weasel Tail motioned his guests into the lodge—Mister Skye, Elkanah Morse, the Crow woman, and Victoria. The flap fell closed behind them. Betsy gazed at poor Arabella and sighed. The girl hated every moment of this, and didn't need to. It all lay in her head.

"Arabella, dear, enjoy yourself!"

"I hate these savages! I despise them!" her daughter cried.

"They'll sense that. People sense things unspoken, dear. Try to learn about them. Interesting, don't you think?"

"They'll slit our throats while we sleep!" Arabella retorted.

Professor Danzig spoke up kindly. "Not inside a village. Not to guests, Arabella. If I've learned anything about such people, it's that they are most hospitable."

The calm professor calmed her daughter, Betsy thought. And herself.

Chapter 5

Elkanah Morse's fertile imagination ran riot as he stalked through the Piegan village on a shimmering cool August morning. He watched people doing everything the hard way! He paused before lodges, running a hand over his balding brow, smiling at squaws and children, observing the daily work of the village. That's what he had traveled across a continent to see! Already he was concocting new products in his mind, devices expressly for the Indian trade. He paused before a rack of poles burdened with thin slices of buffalo meat being jerked. Every one of those hundreds of thin slabs of meat had been sliced from a carcass with a knife. He'd make it easier! His mind churned with the image of a device that would have multiple blades parallel to each other, all hooked to a powerful lever. One tug of the lever and there'd be a dozen perfect slices of meat ready for jerking in the hot sun. Saving labor! That was the key to progress! He eyed the rack itself and decided to design a lightweight folding portable one these people could take anywhere. Then they could jerk meat far out on any prairie, far away from trees and wood needed for poles. He scribbled furiously in a small notebook, smiled at a busy kneeling woman, who smiled back, and meandered onward.

He spotted a woman making pemmican, battering berries and fat and meat. Why, the woman could use a food grinder! He chastised himself for not bringing his Morse Foundries food grinder, which clamped to any kitchen table and augered any sort of meat or vegetable through a perforated head. A perfect device to help a patient squaw, but one no trader in the fur business stocked. He'd talk to Culbertson about that! Better yet, the Chouteaus themselves, and all the rest of the St. Louis entrepreneurs. That seemed to be the trouble with most businesses. They did things the way they always did, under some rule of inertia, never seeing new opportunities, never experimenting. Well, he'd change that! He'd ease the lives of these far tribes forever. For a few buffalo hides, they'd soon have labor-saving devices that would ease the brutal toil of these women.

If Elkanah Morse seemed curious about the life of the village, the villagers were no less curious about these strange visitors. By the scores, they flocked around the campsite of their guests, touching everything. Trim watertight canvas tents with collapsible hardwood poles intrigued them. Betsy's folding cookstove of hinged sheet metal fascinated them. Who had ever seen such wonders! Betsy laughed, opened the door of the oven to show them the tiny fire of twigs that heated whole pots of food on the oven, and Piegans clapped hands with joy and fascination. Such medicine! Would the wonders of the longknives ever cease?

Elkanah watched amiably, knowing that soon, when Betsy erected her easel and began portraits with her fine English watercolors, she'd be the belle of this ball. And that would be only the beginning. In the afternoon, these Piegans would attend their first trade fair. It had taken some talk, but eventually the Piegan headmen were given to understand that Elkanah Morse hadn't come to trade, but to show his wares, find out what the villagers desired, and discover what they needed. All that, from English to Crow to Blackfeet, had been a difficult exchange, but not impossible. Elkanah inclined to the belief that very little was truly impossible.

All seemed well in camp. Their tents and Mister Skye's

lodge had been erected just upstream from the Piegan village. Old Victoria hovered close to her lodge with a face etched in granite, and Elkanah remembered how bitterly these two peoples regarded each other. Even lush young Mary stayed close, playing with the infant boy.

The old crone glared at him as she fleshed an antelope hide. "Damn! How come you want to sell fancy whiteman stuff to these dogs, eh? These people all killers, murderers, bad. . . ."

She seemed not to understand what he was doing any more than the villagers. "Why, Mrs. Skye, I'm not here to sell. I'm here to find out what they want, what I can manufacture, what I can invent that might be useful to them. I'll be doing the same for your own Crow people."

"They take all these things you make and kill us with them," she muttered.

"Wait until I get to your village," he said.

He wandered back into the village, drawn toward Jarvis Cobb, who had hunkered down near a group of old weathered men and several solemn warriors, who glared at Cobb fiercely. Elkanah wondered if perhaps the army captain wasn't welcome there, even in his civilian clothes. The older men, he discovered, were arrow makers, which meant that the young men with them surely were warriors and hunters. No one forbade Elkanah, so he hunkered down close to Cobb to watch. No Piegan said a word.

There seemed to be no division of labor here. Each of the artisans made an entire arrow. On an ancient fleshed hide lay piles of chokecherry shoots that obviously had dried a long time, some of them bumped and bent, irregular in various ways. Several of the artisans had small heaps of iron arrowheads made from hoop iron. Using an old ax head buried in the ground for an anvil, one old man patiently chiseled a piece of metal from a barrel hoop and began hammering it into a pointed arrowhead. Another old man, with black hair braided far down his naked back, shaped a nock in an arrowshaft with a knife and a thin piece of sandstone. Deftly he sanded the chokecherry shaft until a smooth notch for the bowstring had been cut in it. Other bits of sandstone turned out to be files that he used to shape the hafts of iron arrow points.

Satisfied at last, he placed the chokecherry shaft next to an iron arrow point and chanted quietly for a minute. The nasal chanting mystified Elkanah. What had it to do with making an arrow? The ribby old man had yet another sandstone block, this one with a long groove cut into it. The groove, it turned out, had been perfectly fashioned to sand down the chokecherry shoot into a straight smooth arrow. With practiced but gnarled hands, the old arrow maker ran the shaft back and forth in the sandstone notch, slowly scraping off bark and smoothing nobs until, in a few swift moments, he had a fairly straight shaft of dried wood. Still, it bowed slightly. Where the wood bowed, the old man wetted it with saliva, biting and licking the reluctant wood until the shaft straightened and lay true to the eye.

Swiftly now the arrow maker slitted the thinner end to take the point. With a small tool made from a white man's nail, Elkanah supposed, the arrow maker grooved his shaft, running a wavy little groove—lightning-bolt-shaped it seemed—down each side of the shaft. Why did he do that? Elkanah wondered. Was it to release blood and thus kill an animal—or enemy—faster?

Mister Skye joined them there, observed the surly silence, and began to flash his fingers. For some minutes he finger-talked with one of the arrow makers.

"Not sure you should be here, mates. Making arrows is big medicine and war. It means good hunts. These young braves buy arrows from the old ones, pay for them in ponies or meat or sometimes tobacco. They don't think much of having white men watch something pretty close to religion for them."

"Didn't know I was that obvious," said Cobb.

"I'd like to watch," said Elkanah. "Think I can help them make better arrows, Mister Skye. Could you explain my purpose to them?"

The guide sighed, made signs with flying hands, and waited. An old man nodded at last, but two of the muscular young men stared sourly at the intruders.

"You can watch. Be careful and diplomatic, mates."

"That old gent there is making arrows with obsidian points," Elkanah said. "Where do they find a glassy black rock that chips like that? I've never seen such fine points."

"That rock's famous among all tribes, Elkanah. It used to be traded in every direction, clear back to your States. It comes from a whole cliff of it up in the geyser country where the Yellowstone rises. Whole mountain wall of black glass. They don't use obsidian much anymore. Just a few old men clinging to the old ways. They like iron points and make them from hoop iron they get at the trading posts."

"Probably my own hoop iron. I sell a lot to American Fur."

Cobb scribbled a note on a small pad. The army intelligence man at work, Elkanah thought.

"What about bone? Don't they use bone points?"

"They don't go for bone much. Too light, and not very effective in an animal. If they have to, they can make bone points from buffler ribs, but it's not common."

"What about those wiggling grooves down the shaft? To let blood?"

Mister Skye paused a moment. "That, and medicine— they think of arrows as man-made lightning. But mostly, those grooves keep the arrowshafts from warping. Takes some kind of pressure off the wood."

The old arrow maker dyed the shafts, using mineral and vegetable tints he had concocted, and set them to dry.

"Every warrior or hunter has his own marks, his own colors. And each tribe has its own signature, I suppose you'd call it. That way there's no arguments about who counted coup or who killed the buffler."

Elkanah watched the old man fletch the arrows, anchoring the trimmed and dyed feathers with a glue made from boiled hoof, while another set an arrowhead on its shaft and wrapped it with wet sinew so smoothly that scarcely a bulge rose around the base of the arrowhead. A wizened man examined his finished arrow, peered down its straight shaft, and suddenly smiled at his white visitors. He handed the finished arrow to Elkanah, who admired the craft that had created it.

"Tell him it's a fine thing that will slay the buffalo, Mister

Skye. Would he like to see metal points, and my hardwood shafts, and ready-mades? I suppose this is as good a test as any.''

"Don't see any harm to it," Mister Skye replied thoughtfully. "But I think you'll be surprised by what happens."

"I hope your iron points don't ever pierce the flesh of United States soldiers," said Cobb shortly.

The trial of the arrows drew the whole village. Here would be something to see! Elkanah had brought six of his ready-mades, each as anonymous as the others, differing only in their points. His lathes had milled each shaft true and even; the three turkey feathers on each had been trimmed to the exact same size and glued down. No shaft or feather had been dyed in any way, and beside the Piegan arrows they looked pale and featureless.

Warriors, children, squaws, headmen, Weasel Tail himself examined Elkanah's ready-mades without comment. The arrows passed from one tribesman to another, and Elkanah hadn't the foggiest notion what these people thought of them. Neither did they ask questions about them, although Victoria and the Crow woman were on hand to translate.

Elkanah wondered what they'd use for a target in this grassy flat along the Judith River. A giant headman whose bronze muscles rippled in the high sun snapped some guttural order, and soon a youth led an ancient horse, swayback and mangy, before them. It stank from suppurating wounds that succored armies of flies.

"There's your target, mate," said Mister Skye.

Elkanah was horrified. "But not a live target—" he said. Betsy looked stricken.

"Dog food," said Mister Skye.

A boy led the scruffy brown stallion about forty yards downstream and turned it broadside. No one bothered to tether it.

"I didn't quite expect living targets," said Elkanah tartly.

"This isn't Lowell, Elkanah."

"Why are they so silent? They've passed my ready-mades

around without comment. Without a smile, frown, exclamation. Without pleasure or distaste."

"Medicine, mate. No spirit helper guides your arrows. No dye gives it a home or owner among these people."

"If I make them, will they buy my arrows?"

"We'll see," said Mister Skye. "But I doubt it. Medicine is everything, and nothing is done without it."

The honors went to the headmen. Three powerful men, each a leader of a warrior society, selected two arrows impassively. A squat thick graying man with thick cheekbones, naked but for a breechclout, nocked an arrow.

"He's the leader of the Bulls, the oldest and highest Piegan warrior society," Mister Skye muttered.

Jarvis Cobb scribbled notes.

The headman's richly painted, sinew-wrapped bow seemed short to Elkanah's eye. A sudden silence settled on the crescent of villagers here. Elkanah saw Betsy firmly shut her eyes; Arabella had vanished.

In a single smooth motion, the warrior drew the bowstring while the arrow pointed skyward, arced the bow downward, and loosed the arrow, which flashed white across space, and buried itself in the brown hide just back of the forelegs. The horse shuddered. Its neck lowered. It convulsed. It drew its lips back even as a froth of pink blood slobbered from its mouth. It swayed.

Elkanah scarcely realized the warrior had nocked his second arrow until he saw the white blur. The second one buried itself six inches from the first; a little above. Blood trickled from both wounds. The second arrow penetrated clear to its fletching. The horse shuddered and collapsed, landing with a soft thud. Its lungs still labored.

A gray cur skulked toward the carcass, but a sharp shout from someone stopped it.

The villagers remained silent, raptly watching death creep over the ancient pony. Elkanah had the sensation that death was something these savage people enjoyed and studied. Solemnly, a younger man, tall and lean, with a peculiar reflexively curved bow of wide flat material wrapped in sinew, stepped forward and sent one of Elkanah's readymades into the pony's dun-colored underbelly. The creature

spasmed once again and sighed into quietness. A sudden
whip of air announced the next shot, also into the prone
belly but a few inches back. Both arrows had pierced up to
their fletching.

The third headman, a cruel scar jagging his face, and
peculiar scars on his chest, drew a heavy but short bow back
and loosed an arrow. It pierced into belly just an inch from
the previous warrior's first shot. The final arrow also went
true, entering an inch or so from the previous man's second
shot.

Ah! There was fine shooting! The villagers whispered
and explained and chanted things. They all surged ahead to
the carcass to watch the warriors tug Elkanah's arrows out
of it. The shafts came hard, but finally slid out, slippery
with gore, and the warriors solemnly handed them to Elkanah, who washed them.

To Victoria he said, "I wish to know whether they like
these arrows. Would they buy them?"

She glared at him and caustically repeated the question
to the Crow woman, who raised the question among the
Piegans.

Warriors muttered to each other. A man Elkanah took to
be a shaman cried nasally, picked up dust, and threw it to
the wind. For what seemed hours the Piegans debated, and
when the answer came back, the words had been formed by
Weasel Tail himself.

"Tell the man his arrows are very fine and true. But we
would not trade robes and ponies for them."

That was all. Elkanah wanted more answer.

"Medicine," said Mister Skye. "About what I thought."

Elkanah Morse laughed easily. He'd come to find out
things. He'd offered them a better arrow than their own, but
they'd have no part of it. "Well, perhaps I can manufacture
bows for them. Are bows medicine, too?"

"You bet, mate. And their bows are better than any you'll
ever make."

"Surely you're not serious."

"I am. That third bow is made from osage orange,
brought here clear from the Mississippi Valley, and highly
prized as the best of all bow woods by most of the tribes.

French call it *bois d'arc*. The first headman's bow is local, either willow or chokecherry. Middle man's bow is bone wrapped in sinew and reflexed. Every one is shorter, more powerful, and handier than an English longbow. Try shooting one of your European longbows from horseback and you'll see.''

"The bowstrings are twisted sinew?''

"That they are. A good enough string if handled carefully and kept from water. Indians don't make war or hunt in the rain, Elkanah. Your scalp's safe enough when the clouds are emptying.''

Jarvis Cobb scribbled that, too, and looked almighty pleased.

"Each of my ladies, Mary and Victoria, have light osage orange bows, and each have taken a lot of meat with them. Kept my belly full. But I did insist on one thing: I got some good linen cord from the sutler at Laramie, and made tough linen bowstrings for them. They hunt in rain. In my business we need all the edge we can get.''

"I'll sell linen bowstring!'' cried Elkanah, scribbling his own notes furiously.

Jarvis Cobb frowned. "If you sell them linen bowstring, the savages can strike the army in rain,'' he muttered.

"If the tribes buy it. Lots of medicine wisdom about wet hunts and wet war, mate.''

Yellow and gray curs, half-wolf, mobbed the pony carcass, gashing bloody holes in it, snarling and growling and howling wild songs upon a blue-domed afternoon.

Percy Connaught eyed the carcass disdainfully. He'd disappeared just before the first arrows sailed.

"A fine tale to tell in my journal for the vulgar,'' he said. "Utterly savage and heartless. Oh, it will cause a sensation in the States.''

With all these chattering villagers about, Elkanah thought it would be the ideal moment to display his goods. He corraled Victoria, who stood stonily beside the creek. "I'm going to set out my things near our camp,'' he said to her. "Please invite them all. And explain once again my things are not for trade; I wish to learn what they think of them.''

Dourly, Victoria wheeled off to find the other Crow woman.

At his tents he found Betsy setting up her easel, and before her, perched daintily on a log, sat a silent solemn slip of a girl with loose blue-black hair, small brown eyes, and an unhappy look. But she was adorned in a tiny festival dress of soft doeskin, decorated with dyed bone and rimmed with red tradecloth.

"I'm going to paint her!" Betsy said. "It cost me one trinket mirror."

Even as Elkanah unloaded goods from his panniers and spread them on blue-and-yellow-striped thick blankets he manufactured, Piegan villagers drifted in to finger pots and skillets, sample the textures of cloth, cerise and umber and gray, tug at tan canvas, puzzle over copper rivets, delicately feel the hone of shining hardened steel knives, finger rubber moccasin soles, giggle at a galosh, examine bridles of fine russet harness leather, study awls and drills and axes, red-painted hatchets, black lance points, iron arrowheads, long and short, wide and narrow, barbed and hooked. Solemnly they poked and fingered them all, exclaiming and yet telling him nothing. But all of Elkanah's goods together were no attraction at all compared with the image of a little girl swiftly and surely taking shape beneath Betsy's wondrous brush.

Chapter 6

Arabella Morse wandered through the afternoon up the Judith River, between bald grassy bluffs, feeling petulant. The Piegans were so alarming it had taken all her nerve even to go for a walk along the mountain stream. She scarcely noticed the shimmering beauty around her, the sweet-scented air, silvery-green sage, or the way the cottonwood leaves trembled with each zephyr.

The summer had turned out exactly as she had feared. Unbearable! Her father had dragooned her into this; wouldn't let her stay in Lowell and enjoy lemonades, croquet, picnics, poetry reciting, mental improvements, the pianoforte, calling at teatime, and above all, her serious pursuit of marriage. Unless she married soon, she'd be an old maid, and her life a ruin. Twenty-one was almost old. She had no serious beaux, but many came calling, and she delighted in sorting them out: some wanted to marry money; some were too bold; most were uneducated oafs, like her father, who could think only of business and inventions and sales and new processes, and never of art, or sculpture, or novels, or moral enlightenment, or the world's destitute.

Too many males were like that, unrefined, unaesthetic, insensitive.

But he'd insisted and she was here, and another sweet summer under the green canopies of Lowell had been lost. How could she ever make up the time? Time is lost forever, if it's lost! He'd plunged her into a wilderness unfit for refined people. Thrown her in with savages, brutes who shot arrows into horses for sport, murderous, smelly, cruel, spontaneous human children! Everything had disgusted her, not least the reek of the village when the winds eddied the smell of offal and dung into her nostrils. For what purpose was civilization other than to escape all this, and refine mankind? Maybe they'd even slaughter them all! She felt pity for herself, seeing in her mind's eye a solemn gray granite obelisk over her lonely grave. "Arabella Morse, Born November 28, 1831, Died August 12, 1852. She Lacked Only Life."

So absorbed was she in visions of tombstones that she scarcely realized for a moment that Jarvis Cobb had caught up with her, and walked beside.

"Want company?" he asked.

"I'd love company," she replied. Good company, even if he had left his wife and two children in New York. He was a young man, anyway, and an officer, and that was all she could ask. But of course too old—thirty, he told her.

"Escaping the village?"

"Let's not talk of the village. I don't want to hear a word about it."

"I've filled two pages of my notebook with intelligence about them. Things the army should know. They don't fight in rain, for instance. Sinew bowstrings go soft, their flintlocks get wet. A good time for us to strike. Their buffalo bull-neck shields turn arrows. Even deflect a half-spent ball. But they use no horse armor. I even saw a shield stop an iron-pointed arrow. I know where they get their iron, and how to interdict their supply. If we kill off their buffalo, they won't have much good bone to work into points—or food for that matter. You see . . . some intelligence, some knowledge, and we have the means to win wars. . . ."

She sighed. "Must you?" she asked, putting an aggrieved inflection on it.

He laughed quietly. She liked his laugh. Actually, she knew, Jarvis was bookish, a man of mind rather than action, and she liked that, even if his thoughts ran along military lines.

"This is a valuable trip. I'll revolutionize the army's way of going into battle. 'Know Your Enemy' will become its standard when I publish. And I will rise to the top ranks. But that's not what interests beautiful young ladies."

She felt pleased. Her beauty was borderline, she felt whenever she peered into her looking glass, and she ardently welcomed reassurances. Her nose seemed a bit thick; she preferred the narrow patrician variety. Eyes too wide set, and a mousy hazel color. Oh, to have big azure ones, blue as cornflowers! And a creamy-tinted flesh instead of her fishbelly white! Still, she was molded well, tall and slim, swelling at just the right points. And what she lacked, she made up for with dashing dress that kept dressmakers and milliners gossiping and ecstatic about her tastes.

And now she read frank appreciation of all that in Jarvis Cobb's gaze that so casually floated from her lustrous brown hair to the swells of her bodice and hips. She laughed easily, finding a moment of flirt even here, thousands of miles from home.

"Do you miss your family?" she asked softly.

Cobb remained silent as they strolled through bunch grass, alarming big black and white magpies. "I must confess, privately, Arabella—that I'm glad to be away. My . . . domestic life, my family—has turned sour. Not my children, of course. Delights of my heart. Little Peter's five; the infant—Elise—barely a year. But oh . . . there are difficulties."

She waited, saying nothing. How males revealed themselves to her! She had wormed every secret from every beau, just by listening and clucking and nodding her head!

"We quarrel, my Susannah and I. Her tongue's sharp. Her words cut deep. She tells me she regrets marrying me. It was a great comedown for her, for one of her caste. A captain's pay is unbearable. Officers are all oafs. I'm a slave of the army, at its beck and call. I pay her no regard. I love my books and charts more than I love her. I spend my time by the midnight lamp rather than, ah . . . rather than attending to her needs. I confess, Arabella, I've wearied of it. And am glad to escape.''

''But you're a man of honor, of course, and will endure it rather than pitch her out.''

''Oh, of course. Divorce—that's unthinkable. But how good it is to have a kindred spirit, one whose mind touches upon my concerns. We've shared our deepest feelings for months now. Across a continent. At the bow of the steamer, just you and I, talking. Is there anything about me you don't know? I'll tell you! Tell all my secrets to you! How good you're here a million leagues from anywhere, touching my soul, Arabella.''

She peered solemnly at him and found him returning the gaze, his eyes windows of soft pain. She liked his thick muttonchops and high-domed brow and his wavy yellow-brown hair.

They'd reached a boulder-strewn bend of the river, a mile or so above the Piegan village. The sun had settled into the purple west, and the breezes had died.

''I think I will cool my feet,'' she said. ''If I walk like this, I surely will have bunions.''

''I'll cool mine, too,'' he said. ''I see just the rock.''

He led her to a large rosy boulder that diverted clear water around its base. She settled herself on it, arranging her tan Bedford cord skirts carefully. Then she unhooked her shining patent pumps and wiggled white toes. He settled himself beside her, unlaced heavy grimed boots, and rolled off gray and faintly odorous hose.

''Oh!'' she exclaimed, dipping feet into mountain water. ''I fear I shall wet my skirts.''

She tugged the Bedford cord skirts upward, and the embroidered cotton petticoat up, too, letting a little show, along with shapely ankles and too much calf.

''This is better,'' she said. ''Therapeutic. I do dread misshapen feet. Bunions are terrible.''

''Yes, terrible,'' he agreed. ''We are so far from everything. I'd count it a loss to be so far from sweet feminine companionship but for your tender presence here. Indeed, we share so many things of the soul. To sit here is to enjoy some ethereal union of spirits in a vast wilderness."

Her heart tripped a little at all this—she'd never flirted with a married man before, much less one unhappily married.

"I'm enjoying it, Jarvis. Oh, my!"

Thus they sat, wiggling feet in cool water, neither venturing further, until the sinking sun reminded them that they dallied far from safety and food.

"It's getting chilly," she said, "but my heart is warm."

"Mine is, too! I suppose we should be getting back. The savages set guards at night and would put an arrow through us if we were to surprise them."

"I didn't bring a button hook! I don't know how I'll keep my shoes on."

"I'll carry you if I must, but I imagine you could walk with your shoes loose, Arabella."

"You could carry me easily," she said. "You're so strong."

He sighed. "You flatter me. It's a mile, and I'm a desk soldier."

She smiled and touched his arm. "I'll manage," she said. "I've enjoyed the afternoon. This has been just the nicest day this summer. You're a dear friend, and we have things to seal, two good refined minds uniting, clear out here."

"May I seal our kindred spirits with a kiss?"

"Why, yes, Jarvis. I can't think of a nicer way to seal a friendship than with a chaste kiss of platonic love."

He kissed her lips softly, tentatively, awaiting response. She kissed him back firmly. She felt his strong young arms slip around her and tug her to him, and the hardness of his chest against her breast.

Then he released her.

"Our union of the spirit is sealed," he said, breathing rapidly. "Let's fly back to camp before they come looking."

The small blue pebble in Rudolpho Danzig's hand piqued his curiosity. It looked like blue glass, except that the abrad-

ing of the Judith River had ground and dulled its surface.
But in the warm sun the blue within flared a saucy azure.
He'd found only the one, poking around at a place where
the creek ran shallowly over a rock ledge. Corundum, he
thought. Back at the Piegan village he'd see how it
scratched, and what would scratch it. Corundum was among
the hardest minerals, and if that's what it proved to be, he
had found a sapphire. That amused him. He'd already found
a few flakes of free gold caught in a small crevice in another
creek bottom.

It didn't surprise him, though. Here lay a great mountain
cordillera, with vast hidden treasure waiting for the world
to find it. He squinted up into the Belt Mountains, a dark
featureless range set at right angles to the great north and
south chains of the Rockies. Perhaps untold wealth here for
someone, someday. He laughed. It didn't set his heart
pounding or fire the furnaces of ambition in him. Long ago
he'd wrestled with all that. From boyhood onward he'd been
seized by ambition. He knew he had intelligence; the other
boys in the province had seemed dull-witted to him. He
would conquer the world! He raced through the natural sciences at the new University of Berne, intent upon becoming
the world's greatest geologist and naturalist. He would write
great papers, make breathtaking discoveries, change the way
science viewed the earth, and his name, Rudolpho Danzig,
would be revered through Europe.

All of which, he thought wryly, had made young Danzig
desperately unhappy and discontent. He'd been too busy to
enjoy the days he lived, too consumed with the fevers of
success to enjoy the moment, treasure company. Worse,
when he burrowed into the Alps to win a geologic picture
of them, he'd seen nothing, missed everything. Feverish with
ambition, he'd wrested his doctorate from Berne and skipped
across the Atlantic to begin his teaching career at the great
old American university called Harvard. And there, in quiet
amiable Cambridge, in his thirty-second year, he'd descended into the bowels of hell, living in anxious fear that
greatness would pass him by. Some instinct told him he had
done poorly. Around him, those Americans were doing bet-

ter fieldwork, drawing brighter conclusions. He'd failed, and he'd kill himself.

One January night he sat in darkness holding an Allen and Thurber pistol. He'd neglected to keep his stove fed with channel coal, and now the ice in his digs matched the ice of his soul. But something stayed his hand. An image formed of his native Alps, sidelit just before sundown, one of the few precious images he had permitted himself. His discontents roiled within him. Why had he always been so miserable, so unhappy, so dissatisfied, so alive to the future and numb to the present? He'd rejected everything. He set the old-fashioned pistol down on top of a pile of foolscap and traced the thread of a shadowy idea. If he'd rejected everything in his daily life, then perhaps the thing to do would be to accept everything.

From that night, he'd accepted his life and circumstances. Was he poor? He accepted that. Was he obscure? He accepted that, too. Was he single in a foreign land, and unlikely to find a woman who'd tolerate his accented English? Well, he'd accept that, too. He huddled under cold blankets, and the next morning began to practice his new approach. He'd had no revelations. No blinding light or heavenly voice had felled him on the road to Damascus. No emotion had flooded him. No release, no tears, no joy, no epiphany. But if he could accept what he was, accept his circumstances, he would do it. He began by accepting the grim quarters that his scholar's pittance afforded. Comfortable, really. He accepted the clothes he wore, the breakfast of oat gruel he downed, the dreary winter classes he would teach that day. In fact his callow students found him less snappish that day, and willing to answer their questions instead of merely ridiculing them.

Gradually his life changed. Merely by accepting each day, accepting his circumstances, accepting the people around him, accepting students and faculty, accepting his new republic and its tumultuous politics, and accepting himself, he emerged into a new life. Ambition deteriorated even as he grew more absorbed in his field and began to see pattern and purpose in the workings of the earth. Once geology existed to fuel his vanity. Now he came to his work humbly, fascinated with everything around him, poking and probing, questioning, playing with hypotheses, unaware of self because he was lost, childlike, in a garden of wonders. Rudolpho Danzig gradually disappeared, and in the place of the taut, dark, desperate man with a thick accent came a new creature who enjoyed life around him, and studied it casually, coming to not-so-casual conclusions. That's when he married his Yankee bride Sarah Percival, who adored him and basked in the warmth of his love.

Now in this wild of the American west, he held his dazzling blue pebble in hand and laughed. Wealth meant nothing. Here was a whole world to explore, and that was wealth for his soul beyond imagining. He dropped the pebble into a glassine bag and labeled it. He'd tell them nothing. He understood his contentment, and the discontents of others who didn't practice his daily acceptance of his life. He paused to sketch the terrain in his notebook, and drew a crude map of the whole country, carefully dating it and locating its latitude, which he had determined last night by sextant: forty-six degrees north, fifty-eight minutes.

He wished he had time to probe upstream toward the clay dike that probably held the sapphires, but tomorrow they would leave Weasel Tail's village. August marched ahead, and time grew short even before they got well into the adventure.

Back in the village, Rudolpho found Elkanah displaying his last and greatest innovation. There among the smoke-blackened, paint-daubed lodgecovers made of laced cowhide, stood a virginal white cone of immaculate canvas, triple seams connecting each of the gores to make a perfect cone that rose like a white New England church in the village. Around it stood most of the village, gazing silently at the wonder. A few young squaws ventured inside, past the canvas flap, exclaiming at the amount of light within, fingering the hard cloth, giggling. But old women glared at this thing and wouldn't step inside.

"Danzig! There you are! I borrowed fourteen lodgepoles from Chief Weasel Tail himself and set it up. That drew them in a hurry. Now I'm going to show them something."

Elkanah hastened to the Judith River and filled a canvas

camp bucket brimful and carried the sloshing burden back. He motioned the curious women inside. They saw the bucket and fathomed his purpose and giggled through the hemmed hole. Then Elkanah dumped the bucket, and water rivered down the steep slope.

"Now we'll see!" he cried. From within came chatter and giggles. Elkanah ducked in. "Not a drop!" he cried. "Dry as bone! See here!"

Standing outside, Rudolpho didn't doubt it. Whatever Elkanah Morse manufactured, he made well. This lodgecover had been cut out of his tightest, heaviest canvas and sewn on Elias Howe's new automatic sewing machines, which Elkanah had seized upon for his own manufacturing purposes.

Morse squeezed out of the door hole and into the afternoon sun. "It weighs maybe a quarter of what the buffalo cowhide covers weigh. Why, they have to kill and skin anywhere from eleven to twenty or so hides, and lace them all together with watertight seams, to make a lodge the old way. Imagine, Rudolpho. Imagine what a boon this'll be to them!"

But Rudolpho could sense no great enthusiasm for this wonder. His keen black eye caught these villagers staring impassively, rather than feeling liberated from inferior old ways.

"They'll get used to it. I've learned that wild Indians have to think about new things for a while. I suppose their medicine religion is all tied up with it."

Old Victoria squinted up at him. "Damn right," she said. "This ain't got any medicine. It ain't a lodge. Probably cold as hell in winter. Thin cloth instead of good thick hide with an inner lining to keep out the Cold Maker."

Elkanah laughed. "You always tell me true, Mrs. Skye. Will they buy it? I can make it for about twenty dollars, and I suppose traders here might sell it for seventy or eighty. It wouldn't take many buffalo hides to buy a house."

"Maybe goddamn whitemen kill all the buffalo off, then they buy it."

Danzig thought that was an acutely perceptive reply.

"That's what I'm here to find out," said Elkanah. He

unlaced the lodgecover as one last demonstration of the genius of his device. His whole cover could be dismantled by pulling linen cord out of the eyelets of a single waterproof seam. In only a moment the cover shrugged free and sagged to the ground, leaving naked poles poking heaven. He folded the canvas bundle and dropped the entire cover in one pannier of a packsaddle, while Piegans stared thoughtfully.

"Let them think on it for a year. I won't put any on the market until next year," Elkanah said. "They're steeped in their traditions. All my stuff must seem pretty radical, strange, to people who lacked the wheel and iron. But they'll come to it. They'll see it. And maybe add their own medicine to it."

That was the thing about Morse, thought Danzig. Realism and optimism, and a strange kind of certitude that fueled his genius.

That cool evening, the Morses gave a feast for the chief and headmen, cooking one of the plentiful fat buffalo of the Judith basin. It went well, and even the old Absaroka woman, Victoria, seemed to relax among her tribal enemies, Danzig thought. At its conclusion, while the fire flickered low and the seated headmen smoked contently, Elkanah gave each a twist of tobacco, and then Betsy unrolled her surprise—a fine portrait of Weasel Tail in his full ceremonial regalia. She'd caught him well. He gazed at this image of himself, of the eagle-feather headdress with its ermine trim, at the very face he'd seen mirrored in quiet waters, at his ceremonial shield and lance. And his face kindled into delight.

"It is a good likeness," he said through his translators. "Come again to my village and show us such things."

Beyond the corona of the fire, Rudolpho Danzig thought, the night seemed uncommonly cold.

Chapter 7

Victoria's heart sang. They'd left the Siksika dogs behind and now rode south, toward the lands of her people, the Absarokas. All the while they'd languished in the village of Weasel Tail, she'd made medicine in their lodge and kept her Green River knife close at hand, so she might scalp one first, before they scalped her. That was one thing she didn't like about being Mister Skye's sits-beside-him wife: sometimes she had to visit the enemies of her people. These Piegans were worst of all; more terrible even than the Lakotah people to the east.

She rode ahead and to the west of the caravan, along the Belt Mountains and into Judith Gap, the place where the prairie grasses lay between the mountains. To the east, the black-timbered slopes of the Snowy Mountains vaulted upward. To the west, the black slopes of the Belts. But in the gap lay emerald grasses and buffalo trails, as well as the trails of the People. And that made it dangerous. Great battles had been fought here, mostly between Absarokas and Piegans, but also others, such as Assiniboin and Gros Ventre.

She eyed the somnolent prairie sharply, seeing nothing. She had good eyes, Absaroka eyes, better even than Mister Skye's. She saw the floating eagles and the way the ravens flew. That's what caught her eye now, ravens flapping hard, eastward, in flight. Something had disturbed them upon the western slopes. Some whites thought her people took their name from the crows, but Absaroka really meant the giant bird. Even so, she saw the crows flapping and knew her spirit helpers were signaling. In her mind, the vision of trouble formed. She had the medicine gift, seeing what was not seen.

The verdant prairie that crested between the mountains seemed smooth enough that nothing could hide upon the breast of it, but she knew otherwise. Coulees and creeks, invisible to the eye unless one had almost come upon them, snaked north or south, into the drainage of the Musselshell, or the Missouri. She paused, resting lightly in the pad saddle of her old bay pony. He sensed her alert calm. Far off to the northeast, she saw the pack train trotting southward. Mister Skye directed it into the Musselshell valley, looking for a village of Gros Ventre that Weasel Tail said would be there.

She spat. Gros Ventres killed Absarokas. More enemies. They called themselves Atsina, but the French trappers called them Gros Ventres, Big Bellies. Victoria snorted. The French trappers also called her cousins the Hidatsa, the Absaroka people who lived on the great river to the east, Gros Ventres, too. Couldn't those thickheaded French keep the Peoples sorted out?

Perhaps hunters to the west set the black birds flapping. She scanned the shimmering prairies, seeing nothing. Only the quiet of a warm sunny morning and the snuffle of her pony reached her senses. But something would be there. Not deer or elk or buffalo or antelope, for those four-foots didn't make the ravens croak across the dome of heaven. She glanced behind her. The pack train looked to be a short pony run, maybe five hundred beats of the heart. In the transparent air she made out her husband leading, with that whiteman things-maker beside him. Victoria liked him. He had merry eyes and so did his woman Betsy. She didn't like their daughter, or the one called Connaught, who stared arrogantly—and blindly—upon Creation. The rock collector she liked. Peace shone in his eyes, and acceptance of the Peoples. The other, the young man Cobb, she wasn't sure about, but didn't trust.

She turned west, away from her people, riding crosswise of the grain of the land. Just as she knew, in this direction the land lay corrugated, and at times she slid her pony into long swales where she would be invisible even to someone nearby. She continued westward until she struck a longer coulee, close to where the raven messengers had taken flight. There she slid off her pony and set him to grazing. She found nothing there. No hoofprints of passage, no green horse dung. Nothing to make the blackbirds fly.

Still, she knew something had passed and left its presence behind, where she sensed it, sensed the ephemeral shadow of man passing. Maybe some Piegan warrior dog, going to murder them all, she thought angrily. She stalked up the west slope of this long shallow draw until her black head rose just above the breast of land, so that anyone looking her way would see only a stray dark rock there. Nothing. Softly she padded back to the bottom and slid down upon her knees, sniffing the grass. She slowly drew in the scents of the land, savoring them, and smelled moccasin. So! Now she spotted a bit of bent grass, silver in the sun. Sharp-eyed, she stalked on foot to the south, her senses aware, her Norwester fusil primed and ready. The faint trail revealed itself now, the passage of a single man sneaking south out of sight of her pack train, shadowing it, ahead of it.

She slid up the east slope until she could see Mister Skye and the rest due east. Soon they'd be south of her. Swiftly, she trod along the vague trail, at one point finding the faintest impression of a moccasin in dun dust. A large light man, she guessed, one who stalked with the feet of the mountain cat. Ahead the soft coulee wheeled southeast, and she grew wary. She could not see what lay around the bend. She squatted low, calculating. Whoever stalked them would be gazing east, watching the passage of the pack train. Alertly, she slid around the soft curve, a few inches at a time, and froze. Ahead the distance of a good shot, a white-man peered cautiously through the tall grasses toward Mister Skye's party a mile east.

Son of a bitch! she thought. A whiteman, a killer man. She knew that from the voices within her. Killer, as elusive as a mountain lion. This one had no horse. He padded across this empty land on his moccasins and carried only a small leather bag, which rested beside him. She pulled back a little. If she stared long, he would feel it, the way an animal felt it when stared at. In brief glances she took the measure of him. Black-bearded and thin, so thin the flesh clung to bone and pressed tight to skull. Old, dark-seamed face, black hair almost gone, no good scalp to take! She felt she knew this man. Mister Skye had pointed him out once. Yes, a dangerous man, an enemy. A fur man. She studied his weapon—a fine percussion lock with a black octagonal barrel that did not glint in the sun. A stalker's rifle, she thought, carefully dulled. French. She sensed that. In grease-blackened skins with the fringes half-gone, all so dark that it made him only a shadow even in bright sun.

Tortu. Philipe Tortu. It sent a chill through her to know. Philipe Tortu was a lone lion, killing in the darkness, invisible by day, slaughtering one by one any man his masters bid him to slaughter. Some of her Absaroka people had died at his hand, she knew. He always left his sign, a small cross of Christ, the whitemen's medicine chief, carved upon the back or chest of the dead. Her own heart clutched within her. He had strong medicine. Her own ball would not harm him, but his ball would kill her, his thrown dagger would bury itself in her. Tortu, the wolf of Alex Harvey, come to see what the white toolmakers were doing among the tribes, and stop it.

He seemed restless, peering for something. Looking for her, she realized. He should be seeing her scouting, but he wasn't seeing her. She crabbed back around the bend of coulee, sensing his eyes would soon study his own back-trail. Afraid to turn her back and glide back to her pony, she crouched, her knife out and in hand. Not that it would do much. She possessed no medicine against such a demon as this. Still, Tortu did not come. And she dared not peer around the bend, into his flat brown eyes.

She needed to get back to her pony. For a long way ahead the coulee lay straight. She edged up it, fearful she'd cause birds to explode from her, giving her away. But nothing happened. The somnolent sun arced over a quiet grassland that seemed empty of life in the noonday heat. Everything had shaded up, even birds, until the Heat Maker slid low. She reached her pony and climbed on noiselessly, riding north before cutting east in a wide arc. She cut the pack-train trail and urged her hot sweat-whitened animal into an easy lope. Her man and his party had ridden so far ahead she couldn't see them. But twenty minutes of easy loping brought them in sight. In fact, they were nooning. Mister Skye stood on a knoll, looking for her. Mary, the only one still mounted, sat her pony a little east, the infant slung on her back. Around the sun-pierced camp hip-shot horses stood half-asleep, tails whacking at flies, necks lowered and eyes closed. Only Jawbone stood erect, and at peace, with his ears perked up and his evil yellow eyes calm.

A quiet, pacific place. The whitemen, Cobb, Connaught, and Danzig, each had their pencils out and were making the talk signs in their books of white pages. What did they say in their pages? Did they say this land held no danger, lay sweet and quiet in the August sun? Did the rock-picking man talk of his rocks? They made pictures, too, sketches in their journals. The rock man made drawings of the hills and mountains. As she slid off her pony, she saw him set his journal aside and pick up his curious instrument he called a sextant. What it did she couldn't fathom, except that he made it level with a little ball of liquid metal inside glass— what a wonder, liquid metal—and then peered somehow at the sun without burning his eyes, when the sun was highest, or at the star of the north at night. And then he made more of the talking signs in his book.

But that scarcely concerned her now. Her man stood expectantly on the knoll, watching her, waiting. She loved him. He stood there, thick and powerful, breezes playing with the fringes of the elkskin shirt she'd made for him,

strong with great medicine, his blackened Hawken in hand
and the many-shooter holstered at his side.

He gazed at her expectantly, knowing somehow she had
news. His faded blue eyes were so small and so buried in
the crevasses of his flesh she could never see into him,
scarcely knew when he peered at her. But she felt them on
her now.

"Tortu," she said, and saw his eyes go cold.

By Percy Connaught's standards, the Musselshell wasn't
much of a river. It ran eastward where they struck it, in a
shallow dish of prairie that had turned dun as the grass
cured. The small flow of murky water confirmed him in his
belief that the far west would always be too arid to be of
much value to the Republic. It'd cost more to police and
soldier these wastes than it was worth. To the south rose
remarkably jagged gray mountains Skye called the Crazies,
their north slopes still holding snow in their crevasses.
Anonymous unnamed ranges dotted the west.

The creek—for that was all it was, really—rolled lazily
between thick emerald bands of cottonwoods and brush.
The guide, Skye, had splashed across it to the south shore,
woven through giant shimmering cottonwoods until he
emerged at the low dissected bluffs beyond, and made camp
there well back from the creek. He'd become angry, Connaught thought, and barked at the whole party, telling them
dangers lurked here, there, everywhere. It amused Connaught. Dangers indeed. The Indians seemed peaceable
enough if approached peaceably. What else could there be?
An occasional prairie rattler. Grizzly bears in these cottonwoods, according to Skye. Well, fine, they'd avoid the perils
of nature, especially with Morse's remarkable equipment.
Really, the guide seemed afflicted with ghosts and goblins.

They cooked a meal from provisions on Betsy's portable
stove, because the guide wanted no campfire illumining
them. Really, it all seemed overdone, and Connaught wondered whether this theater was spun out to impress Morse,
and maybe win more money from him, or at least gratuities
later. This campsite, he noticed, had an open field of fire
in all directions, and was a little beyond effective range

from either the south bluffs or the dense riverbank cotton-woods and brush. Well, fine, he thought. Safety, even if it meant dragging firewood some distance. Skye picketed the horses close that evening—how short the days were becoming!—except for that ugly thing he rode, which wasn't picketed at all and hung about Skye's tipi.

No sign of Gros Ventres had shown up in the afternoon, nor of buffalo either. The guide debated it with his squaws, in English, Crow, and what Connaught thought must be Snake. It didn't matter: he had impressions to put down in his journal before the lavender twilight settled into indigo. This would be for his serious journal, the one that would affect public policy.

This arid land, he scribbled, might support light grazing, but everywhere the want of water would prevent serious settlement. True community—homes and mercantiles, schools and churches, industry and husbandmen—could scarcely root in a land without water. Thus would this desolate country be a burden on the public treasury, for no vacuum of power existed long: it would have to be soldiered or lost to rapacious Europeans. Maybe not the British, who seemed complacent with the Oregon settlement, but others: Russians, French, even Chinese. This might well be sold to them and the westward boundary of the Republic drawn at a waterline, east of which enough rain fell to farm the soil.

Satisfied, he slipped his journal and pencil back into its waterproof oilcloth bag Morse designed for him. Cobb and Danzig had finished theirs and sat uncomfortably about the stove, warmed in front but feeling cold-bitten in back, as Connaught felt. He'd beaten the darkness by moments. It seemed an unpleasant camp, with no light save for pricks of orange around the hinged sheet metal of the stove. Skye had not asked again that Connaught do any camp duties, and now that pleased him. They'd paid Skye and the squaws to do all that, and the guide had gotten the message earlier.

Neither Skye nor his squaws joined them that evening. The old squaw vanished into blackness. The young one hovered close to their lodge. They seemed to expect trouble. Then, out of darkness, the guide materialized and squatted beside them.

"We'll be turning east tomorrow, mates. Down the Musselshell valley. My wives don't think the Gros Ventre village is above us—no buffler that way, far as we can judge You can bloody well hear them, you know, Bawling, restless sometimes. Especially at night, when sound carries. Hope to find the village tomorrow."

Elkanah Morse nodded. "Long day," he said to his women, and they silently rose and headed for Morse's taut rectangular tent. Connaught headed for the bedroll himself. A camp without firelight seemed empty and dull, and no one made conversation by the snap of a tiny tin stove. He saw Cobb catching up with Arabella in the darkness, and caught some whispering. The two of them had been visiting with each other constantly for days. The book-bindery executive slid into the darkness to water a dry land, and into his bedroll.

The howl rose eerie in the night and made his flesh crawl under his thick blankets. A wolf? Lion? Bobcat? No. It sounded almost human. In the murk beside him he heard Cobb mutter something and knew Danzig lay wide-awake, too. Cobb scratched a sulfur match on something, and for a blinding moment the three stared at each other until the match blued and the inside of the tent caught wavery shadows.

The howl filtered through night air again, distant and indistinct, and Connaught swore he heard sobs, too, human sobs. He poked his head through the tent flaps. A starflecked dome of indigo sky gave faint light. Enough to see their guide, Skye, wearing only a breechclout, heft his glinting revolver.

The howl rose again, muted and broken. Out in the open air, Connaught realized it rose in the east, down somewhere in the thick brush beside the Musselshell. It became a broken sobbing, ragged and vagrant in the eddying air of night.

Skye disappeared into his lodge and emerged moments later dressed in skins, and much less visible than his white flesh had been.

"Mary," he whispered softly, "stay and guard here."

Jawbone snorted restlessly and tromped sideways, but Mister Skye ignored him.

"You—Connaught. You stay and guard the camp. Guard the women. The rest of you come," he said in a rumble that carried only a few yards.

Danzig and Cobb materialized, dressed and armed. From his tent Elkanah Morse emerged, also ready. A moan rose through the night, ending in a blood-chilling shriek.

"I'm coming, too," said Connaught tartly. He'd make his own choices and not let a hired man direct him so.

"Need someone to guard Mrs. Morse and Arabella, mate," said the guide softly.

"Do it yourself," Percy retorted. If you gave these hired men an inch, they'd be directing your whole life.

In the starlit shadows he saw the young squaw settle herself in shadow, a flintlock in hand, and also her small bow and a quiver. She could deliver death enough, he decided, and followed the other men and Skye eastward.

The guide turned to them. "Spread out, walk softly, keep out of the brush and trees, where you'll snap sticks. Stay in deep shadow. Stay behind me. When we get close, let me go ahead. Don't talk, don't whisper, don't sneeze. Keep your arms ready but don't shoot, don't fire at shadows, don't kill one of us. If you're not sure what to do, do nothing. If we come to Indians, start no wars, kill no one. We're few and any village can mount enough warriors to hunt us down. Do you hear me, Mister Connaught?"

An insult. Plainly, an insult. Percy bristled. "Yes," he said, obviously pained, "I hear you."

"All right then, mates."

They slid silently through bunch grass. The sobbing swelled on the night zephyrs, terrible to hear. Some ghastly thing was happening to some human being. They hurried on, galvanized by the screaming. The sound rose from within the cottonwood belt beside the river, and there, curtained by brush, they glimpsed a fire. A half mile from their own camp, Connaught estimated.

"You stay. Stalking in woods is tricky, mates."

But no one could obey. The sobs impelled them forward, and only the shrieking masked the sound of their passage over snapping sticks and around grasping brush. At last they

pulled up in darkness, fifty tree-dotted yards or so from the
red tableau.

Indians. All males, their bodies copper in firelight, muscular, sinister, laughing softly. All males except for one.
The Indian woman's brown flesh glistened sweat in the amber firelight. She wore nothing. She'd been tied to a slender
tree, her arms bound around the trunk behind her, and her
legs bound as well. She writhed violently, groaning. From
scores of places all over her young body, slivers of pitch-
laden pine projected. They'd been jabbed into her, and hung
from small bleeding wounds across her chest, her breasts,
her arms and shoulders, her cheeks, her nose, her thighs
and calves and feet. Slowly, a few at a time, these pitch-
laden ponderosa slivers had been ignited and burned hotly
toward her flesh until flame consumed her, and the smell of
burnt skin suffused the air. A flaming sliver flared upon a
taut brown breast, and she shrieked.

Never had Percy Connaught witnessed a thing so terrible,
slow torture and inevitable death.

"Ritual torture, mates. She's an enemy of theirs, and
they count it good to kill her as slowly as they can," the
guide whispered. "She looks Flathead. They're probably
Gros Ventres. Stay back and let me handle it!"

Chapter 8

Ritual torture. Killing an enemy of the People. Common enough, thought Mister Skye. Not much time left. The warriors looked to be Gros Ventre, but in the flickering amber light he could scarcely tell. The very people they would soon visit. If he saved the woman, he'd enrage them, break medicine.

A flaring splinter burned into her belly and she screamed, then moaned, writhing against her taut bonds. The warriors gazed approvingly. This enemy dog screamed and wept, and that was good.

He turned to the taut transfixed faces dimly white behind him. "I'm going in. Let me handle this. Don't shoot. If I call out, Elkanah, put a shot in the fire, scatter some sparks to let them know I'm not alone. I'll save her if I can. But remember, I'll break their medicine. We'll be visiting these very people."

He peered at the appalled men shadowed in the cotton-woods.

"Mister Connaught, please hand your weapon to Elkanah."

"But—they might kill me!" Connaught refused, clinging desperately to his revolver.

Mister Skye didn't have time to argue. The woman shrieked again in mortal pain and fell into a wild sobbing, slumped against her rawhide bonds.

"Spread into a half circle. Two of you on that flank," he whispered, and glided softly toward the glow. The seven ponies had sensed him, and stared into the night straight at him. But torture has its own fascination, and the warriors didn't notice—for the moment.

A stick cracked under him, masked by a shriek.

When their backs were to him, he slid into the open, his Hawken cocked, his big Colt revolver ready.

"I am Mister Skye," he roared.

They wheeled violently, recognizing a name and man who had become a legend among all the northern tribes. Some carried glinting knives, awaiting the next step when they would slice living flesh from the woman bit by bit, keeping her alive as long as possible to prolong her agony.

Some circled, so they could rush him from all sides.

"Stop!" he roared. He didn't know their tongue, but his command had its momentary effect, backed by the swinging bore of the Hawken.

A burning splinter flared against the woman's nose and she shrieked, too lost in pain to notice her salvation.

One of the Gros Ventre, a tall, muscled warrior the color of mahogany in the wild waving flamelight, snarled something to the others.

The leader, then. But they were about to rush him.

"Elkanah, let them know," he commanded.

From the darkness a heavy shot boomed, and the fire blew apart, careening glowing brands in various directions.

"That's enough," yelled Mister Skye.

"Sit," he commanded, pointing a finger at the grass before each of them. These were fine experienced warriors, not young ones. As dangerous and murderous a band of Gros Ventre fighting men as the village possessed. A scar laced across the cheek of one, cocking an eye. Amber light shadowed the scar furrows across another's chest, a place where battle-ax or lance had gouged a vicious trough. Not one of them, he realized, studying each one by one, had the unmarked body he started life with. Medicine bundles hung from their necks, but beyond that they wore little. Some had painted, great greasy slashes of white clay mixed with fat, black ash, yellow and ocher.

War it was, and war they celebrated, he thought.

As fast as they settled sullenly, peering sharply into the blackness beyond the aura of the tiny fire, Mister Skye raced to the woman, who slumped nearly senseless and out of her head. He yanked the remaining slivers of pine from her tormented body, each tug another burst of pain. Blood oozed from the small wounds. Where the burning brands had reached flesh, there were ugly festering cauterized holes.

With his free hand he cut her rawhide bonds. She fell sobbing, curled up at the foot of the tree, still lost in her torment.

"Mister Cobb," he said quietly. "Please attend to this woman. Find her clothes, and carry her, if you must, back to Victoria and Mary."

Cobb materialized out of darkness, his revolver glowing orangely in the light.

"Holster it, mate. The next part of this is peaceable, and they know me anyway. I've already broken their medicine."

Reluctantly Jarvis Cobb sheathed his weapon, staring sharply at the sitting warriors. He found the woman's torn red calico blouse and skirts, but when he attempted to slide them over her, she wailed. She couldn't bear the touch of anything upon her brutalized flesh.

"Let her stay, mate. Let her weep. I'm going to have a little talk with the headman here, and I'd take it kindly if you'd keep an eye upon the others, watching for the throw of a knife."

The captain stood beside the huddled woman, ready for trouble. Mister Skye settled himself on the grass before the headman. He would do the rest of this with sign talk.

The warrior watched him impassively, with eyes as flat and feral as a rattler's.

"I am Skye," he said, making the arched sign for the heavens. "I come at peace. We come to your village with gifts. We wish to buy the woman to be our slave. What will you sell her for?''

For a long time the headman said and did nothing, until Mister Skye thought he didn't understand.

"Who is with Skye?" he finally signaled.

"Whitemen who make pots and iron arrowheads and blankets. Friends of the Atsina, come to see what Atsina people like."

"They will give us many things for the slave. She is a Flathead and a dog and deserves to die. She has no bravery in her."

"One bolt of blue cloth for the woman. A fair price," signaled Mister Skye.

"Cloth, ten twists of tobacco, and one pony."

"No horse. The tobacco, yes. She is a Flathead dog and that is all we will give."

"One iron arrow point for each of us." The headman's hand included the six others.

Mister Skye lifted his voice to the darkness. "Elkanah, can you spare seven iron arrowheads?"

From the blackness the entrepreneur called back, "Anything at all, Mister Skye. Anything to spare that wretched woman."

The guide nodded, and his fingers flew again. "Ten twists, seven iron arrow points, and a bolt of blue cloth."

The headman pondered. "One thing more," his hands said. "You have broken our medicine. Our hearts are on the ground. The night is bad. We will take those things for the dog, and we will all count coup on Mister Skye. That will make our hearts good."

"No. No warrior counts coup on Mister Skye. It is death." The guide's hands jabbed angrily. "The great blue medicine horse would kill each of you."

"We are Atsina warriors. We must have our medicine back. You have taken it. You cannot enter our village until we count coup."

From the thickening dark, the other Gros Ventres watched intently, following the fingers.

"You have counted coup upon the Flathead woman."

The headman retreated into stony quiet.

Mister Skye pondered. To let them count coup on him would end his medicine. The news would race like wildfire from tribe to tribe, wiping away the respect and wariness he'd fostered. No. He'd have to offer them some other atonement, some other christ.

"Mister Danzig," he said into the black shadows. "These Gros Ventres wish to count coup. It restores their medicine. Would you volunteer?"

"They wish to touch me, right?"

"Right, mate. They will each touch you. Maybe hard."

"I will be the Gadarene swine, and maybe even rush into the Musselshell afterward," said the geologist amiably.

He sauntered easily into the light, his dark eyes filled with concern for the weeping woman curled near Jarvis Cobb.

They watched him, seeing a compact graying man with wise eyes, walking fearlessly to them.

"You are a brave man, Mister Danzig," said the guide. "Walk to each warrior and let him strike you. Some may wish to hurt you."

The geologist ambled easily to the first and waited. The warrior gravely tapped him. The second warrior shoved hard, staggering him. The third touched him lightly. The others tapped firmly, and then he stood quietly before the headman.

"What is your name?" signaled Mister Skye.

"I am called Snow Hunter."

"Snow Hunter. This is Rudolpho Danzig." The guide spoke the name aloud. "He is a wise man, a medicine man of the whites. A teacher. He studies the earth. He knows about the rocks upon the breast of Mother Earth."

That was as much as Mister Skye could convey with his sign talk.

"Now you have counted coup upon a great man of the whites," he signed gently.

The Atsina leader stared hard at the quiet professor, sensing some fine thing about Rudolpho Danzig. Then he offered a handclasp. Surprised, the geologist found himself shaking hands.

Mister Skye felt pleased. "Now we will smoke," he said.

"Mister Morse, We'll need a bolt of blue cloth, ten twists of tobacco, a pipe, and seven arrowheads. And please bring Victoria to tend to this woman. We have acquired a slave."

"I'm here," came a familiar hard high voice from the dark. Victoria padded into the glow of the coals, her bow strung and an arrow nocked in it. "I'll fix her good. Flatheads, they friends of the Absaroka people."

Her presence astonished Mister Skye's clients. They peered distrustfully into the dark, wondering what other surprises it might harbor.

The episode shook Percy Connaught to the depths of his Whig soul. Civilized people, he wrote in his public policy journal, can scarcely imagine the savagery of these inhabitants of the plains. They must either be civilized and enlightened, or meet the fate that nature reserves for inferior species.

Then he turned to his journal for the vulgar and described the same episode in lurid terms, alluding delicately to the burning brands that blistered the woman's limbs and face but avoiding the brands that burned pits in other flesh. It would make a sensation in the east, he knew.

The whole business set his mind churning. No longer did he feel comfortable in these distant wilds. Not even Mister Skye offered much protection against barbaric tribesmen such as these. He saw himself tied naked to a tree, convulsing as each pitch-laden brand blistered into his flesh, slowly dying in an agony beyond the comprehension of civilized men.

In such desperate pain had the short broad Flathead woman been that they could not clothe her. The softest touch of calico set her to gasping in the night. Victoria muttered and cursed and finally asked Skye to carry her back to their camp, after he had smoked with the barbarous Gros Ventres.

That took an hour. Percy had crouched suspiciously in the outer darkness the whole time, unwilling to let those murderous Indians know of his presence. But at last the warriors left for their village to the east, and Mister Skye solemnly carried the groaning Flathead woman to his lodge.

There the woman's moans lifted through the night, and

he saw Victoria scurry in and out, digging in parfleches, stirring balms and salves of root and powder of her own barbarous manufacture, muttering and cursing while the others sat silently, unwilling to return to sleep.

When finally he slipped into his tent and bedroll, he slept not at all. He lay rigid, and not one muscle relaxed.

The morning found him crabbed, tired, and full of nameless terrors. He sipped coffee dourly and turned silent. He tended to be honest about himself, and discovered a truth in the middle of the night he didn't much like: he had no particular sympathy for the Flathead woman. Indeed, where he ought to feel pity, he felt wild fear that a similar thing might happen to him in this terrible desert. That was not the only distasteful discovery he'd made about himself this trip. He knew he was a slacker, sloughing off camp duties on the pretense that he had more important things to do. He did: the journals were priceless records. But he knew that he alone wasn't carrying his weight, and he felt half-annoyed with himself, and slightly ashamed, and he couldn't rationalize away his conduct.

When Mister Skye emerged at last from his lodge, yawning, Elkanah Morse cornered him, bursting, as usual, with questions.

"How is the poor woman, Mister Skye?"

"She'll be all right, mate. Nothing internal got hurt—just her skin. She'll be scarred the rest of her life. She's in such pain we can't dress her, and not the lightest cover either."

"Who is she—do you know?"

"Just found it out this morning, Elkanah. She's Flathead, all right. Kills Dog Woman. She and a few other women, and a party of Flathead hunters came over here to make meat. Flatheads think the Musselshell country is their buffler ground. The Gros Ventres jumped them, got her."

"Barbarous!" exclaimed Percy.

Mister Skye fixed him with a stern gaze. "Don't know that some slaves in your south get treated much better."

"That's barbarous, too, and I'm ashamed of the white south!" he replied.

The guide nodded. "Those Atsina aren't exactly appreciated by the people around here."

"I suppose Mrs. Skye has a few simple unguents for those wounds," said Elkanah.

"Lot more than that. She has medicines made from roots and leaves. Powders she blows or dabs into terrible wounds and they don't ever mortify. She put Kills Dog Woman to sleep with a leaf tea last night in spite of the woman's pain."

"You're saying they have effective medicines, better than our scientific ones?" Elkanah asked.

"I don't know what your medicine back in the States is about, mate. But yes, Victoria and most any tribal practitioner here can do amazing things."

"Would she share her secrets? Get me leaves and roots and tell me what they do and how to use them?"

"Ask her, mate."

"I may have a new business," Elkanah said. "One that'd bring healing to the world. That's what business is all about—bringing good things to everyone. I'm not a chemist and know little about pharmacopoeia, but Danzig knows chemistry and I'll set him on this."

"What of the woman? You said you'd bought a slave last night. Is that what you intend?" asked Connaught indignantly.

Mister Skye laughed heartily. "No, that's what I bloody well told the Atsina. We'd buy the slave. Why else would a whiteman buy a Flathead woman? That was for their understanding, Mister Connaught. She's welcome to stay with us; welcome to return to her husband. But for a while she'll be with us."

Elkanah asked, "Won't she be terrified when we visit the Gros Ventre village?"

"More like hate. She'll know she's safe with us. Gros Ventre won't harm a hair on the head of my slave."

"Will we be welcome?"

"I imagine." He paused, hesitant. "But the Atsina—Gros Ventre—are known for treachery. One of the reasons they're hated. They're even quarreling with their old allies the Blackfeet just now." He sighed. "We smoked. We gave them their medicine back. We bought rather than captured the woman. I think we'll be out of harm's way. But let's put it this way, Elkanah. That tribe, above all tribes, needs watching. Stay alert, pick no fights, never use your arms or you'll be tortured to death before every man, woman, and child in the village."

"Let's just go elsewhere!" Percy Connaught exclaimed.

The guide's flinty gaze rested on the man of letters. "Can't. I told them we're coming. They said we'd be welcome. If we turn tail now, they'd say our medicine left us. Do you know what that means?"

Percy Connaught felt annoyed. This barbarous man lectured him, presumed him to be utterly ignorant, even though Percy had taken pains to read every journal of wilderness travel he could lay hands on. He supposed, secretly, that he actually knew more of Indian medicine than the guide.

"Why, we must save face," he replied.

The guide's gaze rested on the distant yellow bluffs, dotted with cedar and jackpine, missing nothing. "I suppose you could put it that way," he muttered.

The rest of the camp stirred. Betsy had a fire kindled in her portable stove and the aromatic smoke of juniper sticks perfumed the camp. Arabella vanished into brush. Mary and Victoria busied themselves around Skye's lodge.

"We'll go to the village as soon as our guide wishes," said Elkanah briskly.

"Tomorrow," said Mister Skye. "Today we'll let our guest heal."

"I have a theory," said Elkanah. "And this is the place to prove it out. I hold that trade brings peace. Traders are the emissaries of one civilization to another. They bring goods and goodwill and buy what the others have to offer, making valuable exchanges that bless both parties. Let's go to the Gros Ventre. I'll wager my products will excite them, kindle the desire for trade—"

"Or theft and murder," broke in Percy.

"Yes, that's possible, Percy. But I'll wager on trade. Wait until they see what civilized men can offer them. Every modern convenience. Freedom from famines, as soon as they learn to till the earth and plan ahead. I have for sale every implement that will help them transform themselves into modern men with all the blessings of true civilization. Trade, gentlemen, is the unifying and civilizing force of modern times!''

Jawbone screeched, and plunged away wildly.

Mister Skye responded by diving to the grasses.

A distant shot racketed and a ball plowed earth where the guide had stood, barely missing his flattened body.

A faint bloom of blue powder smoke spread along the top of the bluff a hundred fifty yards distant.

''Son of a bitch!'' snarled Victoria. She dove into the old lodge and sprang out with her flintlock, hard fierce gaze upon the rim of distant dun rock. She fired, and the bark of a gnarled pine flew into the sky.

''Tortu!'' she muttered, a word that baffled Percy Connaught.

Mister Skye scrambled to his feet, running to fetch his Hawken. His evil horse kept on screeching and whirling.

''Mister Morse, your theories aren't worth a bloody damn,'' the guide muttered.

Chapter 9

Hunting down Tortu would be as futile as snatching smoke. Harvey's assassin had a way of vanishing into wilderness. Even so, Mister Skye trotted up the south slope to search for the faint tread of moccasin he expected to find, and follow it. Probably that human phantom had crossed the river by now and had holed up far to the north. But it had to be done: if Mister Skye hoped to live to ripe old age, he had to stalk the stalker.

It all puzzled him. Why now? Years ago, Mister Skye had booted Alex Harvey out of American Fur for brutally murdering two Blackfeet who had come to Fort McKenzie to trade. That, actually, was the culminating incident in a long string of brutalities Harvey had inflicted upon his engagés, tribesmen, and those above him in the fur company's chain of command. Plainly Harvey wanted him dead and had set the most vicious and elusive killer in the northwest after him. Tortu meant twisted, and that described him perfectly. No man possessed more cunning and cruelty, less warmth and human kindness than Tortu.

All of it had something to do with Elkanah Morse, too.

Mister Skye puzzled that one, because Harvey, Primeau could as easily stock Morse's products as American Fur, though perhaps at higher prices. The opposition couldn't afford to buy in the quantities that were routine for American Fur. Surely Harvey didn't believe that the Morse party engaged in actual trade. Morse had only two packhorses laden with goods. A trading venture out among the tribes would have required scores of packhorses or mules. No, it had to be that Harvey, Primeau couldn't afford to risk loading its shelves with Morse's new trade items. Harvey'd always hated anything new. And Morse brought the new and untried to the far tribes, threatening to weaken the opposition even more.

He stared hard as he approached the bluff, his eyes alert for the glint of a rifle in the dawn sun. But he found nothing, not even the faintest moccasin track. Any good assassin avoided horses that might betray him with noise, droppings, and a trail easily followed. About him lay a vast and silent wilderness where a man without a horse could hole up silently in any crag of rock and wait. Mister Skye sat quietly, watching for the explosion of birds or the flight of antelope on a distant slope. Nothing.

He had little time. Tortu meant death. Not only to himself, but also Mary and Victoria and the child; to Elkanah and Betsy and Arabella Morse; to the rest. The only safety lay in a village. Almost any village. Tortu would be unlikely to assassinate guests in a village and face a hundred or so howling vengeful warriors, as skilled at rooting out elusive quarry and as knowing of the wild as Tortu himself.

Mister Skye would get them to the Gros Ventre village, then. Not that the treacherous Atsina would offer much more shelter than the wilderness. Below him, he spotted Victoria stalking angrily, checking out every scrub pine and juniper bush within rifle shot of the camp. Nothing.

He eased down the slope, his flesh flinching, awaiting the explosion that would be the last thing he ever heard. Nothing happened.

"Victoria," he muttered. "We'll head for the village. Rig a travois for Kills Dog Woman. We can't stay here."

"We go among dogs to hide from rabid wolf," she snapped.

Nonetheless, she began at once to break camp and ready a travois to carry the tormented woman, who'd face screaming pain with every jolt of the poles over a rock or into a gulch.

"Captain Cobb, I could use your counsel," said Mister Skye.

"What was that all about?"

"Killer named Tortu. Sent by the opposition. Harvey's nursed grudges for years, and probably thinks Elkanah's venture here works against him in every way he can imagine. That's how his mind works. I know it well enough . . . Tortu. Shadowy French-Canadian fur man who's turned lobo. Always on foot and shadowy as a panther at night. We get him, or he gets me—and you. I'm heading for the Gros Ventre village at once. How would you suggest we defend ourselves en route?"

Captain Cobb scanned the mounded hills and their copses of pine and juniper nervously. "In pairs," he said at last. "If you set single flankers and scouts, he'd murder them. Pairs are harder to deal with."

"I was thinking the same bloody thing." Mister Skye lifted his black stovepipe hat, tugged at his long hair, and screwed the hat down again.

"You and my Mary on one flank—and don't underestimate her, Mister Cobb."

"I certainly don't."

"Victoria and I on the other. The Morses and Mister Danzig can handle the packhorses, travois, and the rest."

"What about Connaught?"

"He can do what he wants."

Jarvis Cobb stared, smiled faintly, and turned to break camp.

They splashed across a ford and up the north slope, onto level open bench land that offered few possibilities of ambush. Kills Dog Woman lay on the travois stoic and silent now, in acute pain but drained of the terror of death. Mister Skye watched her pass, repelled by her swollen gashed face, angry and scorched, the nose so bloated she could barely breathe. Their eyes caught a moment and then hers closed. No one had told the burned woman where they would go today.

The morning remained cold, a haze robbing the sun. Not long, he thought. He had to hurry these people to Fort Laramie and army transport down the Platte. He and Victoria rode the south flank, keeping an eye on the breaks tumbling down to the river, where Tortu would likely lurk. Far off to the north, Captain Cobb, erect and military in his saddle, guarded alertly, along with Mary, who rode twenty or thirty yards back of him. In the pack train itself, Elkanah Morse rode with his revolver in hand, as did the doughty professor, and Connaught.

Beneath him, Jawbone sensed the wariness and minced with ears pricked up and his nose testing the chill air. At the faintest scent or sound of trouble, the ferocious horse would alert him in various ways. But the morning slid by quietly, broken only by a burst of antelope bounding white-rumped to the northeast.

They ventured at last into buffalo grounds. They lay, for the most part, in the lush dun cured grasses, having filled themselves early in the morning. A few black hulks stood on distant swells of prairie, sentinels. One group caught the scent of the intruders and indolently trotted over the horizon. Others didn't bother to stand and seemed oblivious to their passage through the haze-chilled morning.

They nooned on a dry swell that offered no chance of surprise in any direction. Even so, Victoria hovered angrily, her old flintlock in hand, while Betsy and Arabella doled out slices of cold antelope that had kept well in the cold night.

The wiry dark professor took the opportunity to shoot the noon sun with his sextant.

"Where are we, Mister Danzig?" asked the guide.

"Why, sir, I believe—given my lack of adequate equipment—we're at forty-six degrees and thirty minutes north. I get that by deducting the sun's altitude from zenith, or ninety degrees, and then adding the zenithal latitude of the sun on this date from a table I have. In fall and winter one deducts the zenithal latitude."

Mister Skye laughed. "I'd say we're on the north bank of the Musselshell, with the Snowy Mountains off to the north, the Crazy Mountains over there in the southwest, and some of the best grazing land in the world beneath our feet."

Connaught bridled at that. "More a desert waste," he muttered, scribbling something in his endless journal. "Can't imagine human beings surviving here in any but the most barbarous circumstances."

Elkanah approached him. "I've been pondering this whole business of Harvey's assassin," he began. "It appalls me. Have I misunderstood something? Is my trade expedition at fault here? Is my family endangered? Should we turn back to Fort Benton to put a stop to it?"

The more Mister Skye saw of the entrepreneur, the better he liked the man. Elkanah asked questions, got to the heart of things, and had a mind open to possibility. Mister Skye tackled the history first, describing Alex Harvey's troubled, brutal, unstable years working as an officer of the American Fur Company until Skye booted him out. Now he had a powerful opposition company, backed by the amiable Robert Campbell himself in St. Louis, as wily a master of the fur trade as the Chouteaus.

"Yes, to answer your question. Harvey sees a threat. They don't have the cash to risk on new shelf goods—all these items like ready-made arrows you've toted along."

"But surely that's not an excuse for bloodshed—for murder—for taking the lives of, of you and yours, and me and mine!"

"This isn't the east, and what you're seeing is not competition among trading companies, Elkanah. Out here beyond law and civilization, the struggles of the fur companies are something else, more primitive, brutal, vicious. The walls and that bastion being built at Fort Benton protect not just against Indians, Elkanah. They bloody well protect against pirates. Consider this an ocean, and consider it full of privateers and freebooters."

Elkanah Morse grinned wryly. "I can see that free trade and certain civilized rules and order complement each other. Mister Skye, are my wife and daughter in grave danger?"

"Yes."

"What do you propose?"

"Get to the safety of the Gros Ventre village. And then I'll have to deal with Tortu somehow—stalk the stalker."

"Let's go then," said Elkanah sharply.

These Gros Ventre looked terribly poor, Elkanah thought, with few of the ornaments of the proud Blackfeet. They fashioned their lodges from ragged mended hides, rarely daubed with the medicine decor that leaped to the eye when one viewed a Blackfeet village. Few of the haggard tribesmen they passed wore decorated clothing. Most of it was simply crudely tanned hides or rough-sewn tradecloth in various subdued earthy colors, carelessly cut and laced, all of it ill-fitting.

"These are the homeless wanderers of the prairies, Elkanah," Mister Skye said. "They rarely stop long enough to manufacture what they need, and spend a lot of time mooching on other villages until they wear out their welcome."

"Maybe I can help them. For a few buffalo robes, they can have my ready-made lodges, arrows, and all the rest."

The guide sighed. "Not that simple. They steal and war and sponge for a living, and that's the way of it with them."

These people seemed less eager to have visitors than the Blackfeet. Perhaps hospitality wasn't a part of their way, thought Elkanah. The camp crier had announced them, and the village police escorted them as they rode into the concentric circles of lodges on a cottonwood-dotted flat along the Musselshell River. Few dogs met them, no doubt because the rest had vanished into the stew pots. No one seemed surprised. News of their coming had preceded them. But many a brown eye gazed boldly at the delirious Flathead enemy bound tightly to Victoria's travois, now a slave of Mister Skye.

"The Blackfeet camp was like a rainbow," observed Betsy, "but this is all brown and dreary. I didn't know villages and tribes could be so different! It'll be a challenge for my paints."

The whole trip Betsy had fussed and worried about Kills Dog Woman, begging to help any way she could. But Victoria had shooed her off, and the woman herself remained barely conscious. The torture had unsettled Betsy and turned Arabella silent and distant. But his dear bright wife hadn't thought of herself; her heart had gone out to the suffering woman, and Betsy's innate love for the creatures around her had worked into a rage against torture, against these Gros Ventres, and a determination to preach Christian love to them all. That was his Betsy! Elkanah thought. Never content just to observe, and always eager to make herself a part of things, and change things for the better.

"They're an evil people!" she had said. "I shall rebuke them and teach them!"

"I'm afraid most of the tribes engage in ritual torture, Mrs. Morse," the guide had replied. "It's medicine, part of the way they dominate their worlds."

Elkanah realized as they threaded through the quiet village that few people watched them. The young men had vanished, and only the ancient ones, with furrowed brown faces, observed their passage, along with scampering children. It puzzled him.

"Out fetching buffler. There's a pishkun near here, about a mile east."

"A what?" asked Elkanah.

"Buffler jump. Natural place where they can stampede a herd over these cliffs and make meat."

"How can they possibly make use of hundreds of carcasses at once?"

"They can't. They take what they want, and feed the wolves and coyotes with the rest."

"Can't they do it some more efficient way?"

"They're horse-poor. Don't know much about training a buffler runner, either. They bloody well steal what few buffler runners they've got, so why learn to train them?"

"Are there no other ways?"

"In snow, they can sometimes drive buffler into a drift so deep they can't escape the arrow. Or they can kill an old bull or cow before the wolves do."

"Can they do anything well?"

"Steal, war, and kill. They're as fierce as any around here, and their women are fiercer than the men. Some years

ago, some trappers tangled with them near a rendezvous
and took a licking no fur trapper's ever forgotten.''

''Mister Skye,'' said Betsy, ''will we be safe here?''

''Your persons, probably. But not a single item you own.
We'll have to set guard over the supplies and ponies, even
though we're guests.''

''Mercy!'' exclaimed Betsy. ''I shall give them a piece
of my mind!''

They drew up before the lodge of the chief, who stood
with his befeathered staff of office in hand, awaiting them.
This dreary lodge stood no taller or wider than the others,
and its only decor was a collection of black scalps laced
around the entrance flap.

He'd lost his front teeth and muttered amiably to Mister
Skye, ancient hands lazily making sign as he mumbled. But
his cataract-fogged old black eyes shown merrily, and his
ancient body, withered down now about his bent frame,
jerked and bobbed spastically as he talked. A merry old
rogue, Elkanah thought. An ancient crone, as withered and
toothless as the chief, sidled out of the lodge and grinned
her gummy pleasure.

''He's called Horse Medicine, mates,'' explained the
guide. ''He says the whole village is up on the prairie north
of here driving buffler. There's some squaws east of here,
waiting to slice up the bloody herd. The village is mostly
run by the war chief, White Beaver. Younger man. We'll
smoke now. Have some tobacco and a few things ready,
Elkanah.''

An hour later, after a lot of finger talk, smoke, an old
man's babbling, and a long hard effort by Mister Skye to
explain their purposes here in the village, the guide and
Elkanah emerged into a cold sun. The village dog soldiers
had led a sullen Victoria and the wary visitors to a campsite
just east of the village, hard by the banks of the Musselshell. There'd be wood and water, but no graze for their
ponies for a mile or so.

''We're invited to watch the jump, mates. But you'd better have the stomach for it. A whole herd of terrified buffalo
going over a cliff and dying in a heap, bones and blood,
isn't a pretty sight.''

"It's not a sight for women, Betsy!" said Elkanah. "You and Arabella had better—"

"Oh, pooh! If squaws can manage it, so can I! I'm going to paint it later anyway."

"I think I'll stay here," said Arabella dryly.

Elkanah himself wondered whether he could stomach a sight like that. But he'd go. He'd find ways to make the labor easier. He'd study what they did, how they dealt with a pile of black limp carcasses, and what they salvaged and abandoned.

Victoria came with them, muttering, intending to make meat herself, and maybe snatching a hide or two after the Gros Ventre squaws had abandoned the pile.

"I suppose they'll leave this village site soon. The smell of decaying flesh will be awful here," said Jarvis Cobb.

"Few days. It doesn't rot all that fast in this colder weather, Mister Cobb."

"Interesting erosion," said Danzig. "Lot of it from wind over countless years. Wind-whipped sand hollowed that yellow sandstone. Frost cracked those slabs loose, and there they perch until something tumbles them."

Percy Connaught came along, pinch-faced and white, looking so grim that Elkanah wondered how long he'd last when the horror of it slammed into them. They'd all come except for Mary, Arabella, and Skye's little boy. Elkanah hoped Mary would guard the camp from these thieves, and relaxed only when he realized that Mister Skye didn't seem concerned about it.

The jump itself loomed above them, its lip about a hundred feet up, and the fragmented face nearly vertical. At its foot lay a pile of yellow detritus that had weathered off the rim. The cliff rose only forty yards or so from the lazy river and was naked at its crest here at the jump, but to either side thick stands of jackpine and juniper sprang almost miraculously from native rock, their roots jammed between loosened sandstone strata. In the detritus lay ghastly heaps of white bones, hollow-eyed skulls, grown dry and porous in the relentless prairie sun. In fact bone was spread over a wide area, an acre or so, Elkanah supposed.

A dozen or so squaws waited solemnly, some of them

kneeling and making medicine of some sort with guttural chanting. They eyed the whites curiously. Several wore only filthy old skin skirts, nothing covering their sagging brown breasts. Elkanah glanced tautly at Betsy, who seemed to be perfectly at ease with the nakedness.

"They won't be wearing their Sunday best while slaughtering the sacred buffler," Mister Skye explained softly. "If the hunt is good, you'll see them all fixed up tonight in finery for a happy dance and a lot of medicine making. They'll thank the One Above. Most of these tribes know what gratitude is, and reverence of nature is born in them. And likely they'll apologize to the buffler spirits they've taken."

It seemed a strange, mysterious place, Elkanah thought. On a tripod hung some sort of medicine, a weasel tail and feathers and other things. But there was something else: some palpable power he felt here as they all stood quietly, anticipating thunder and death, some brutal climax that would sunder the sun and earth.

Then a strange excitement shivered through the squaws, and their keening crescendoed into whispers and new alertness. Elkanah heard nothing and wondered. Some of the women lifted naked arms toward the bluff, in some kind of supplication. A strange fear settled on them all. Percy sweated, drops of wetness blooming suddenly on his forehead as he licked his lips. Death lurked and prowled here, setting teeth on edge. Victoria glared contemptuously at the whites about her, daring them with her sharp black eyes to weaken and flee this place of carnage. From above now the wind carried faint hoarse cries, and Elkanah spotted a boy on the edge of the tawny cliff, far to the west, waving a red trade blanket frantically.

The earth trembled. They heard nothing, but felt a strange vibration in the soles of their feet, a tremor that rustled grass and turned the cottonwood leaves silver-sided. Then came a faint mutter, a throaty boom of distant thunder, fearsome. Elkanah involuntarily stepped back, stepped away from this tawny lip of death looming above. The others did, too.

"Oh, God!" cried Betsy. "I shouldn't have come!"

The squaws wailed now, mouths open, dancing small circles, even as thunder rolled toward them and the sound battered ears with the howl of death.

The first buffalo, a great bull, sailed over, legs flailing, grunting and whistling, defecating as it somersaulted down, and smacked the earth shoulder-first with a sickening thud, twitching. Even as he fell a dozen more sailed into space, grunting, thundering, spinning and tumbling, smacking earth on their backs, splintering legs, breaking necks, spewing blood, geysering guts and urine, dying fast and slowly, shuddering and spasming, landing on the ones underneath, ten, a hundred, two hundred, thunder, and awful silence.

From above, the chanting of the hunters.

Next to Elkanah, Percy Connaught vomited and huddled into a ball, sick. Betsy stood pale, her lips drawn down. Elkanah settled his own stomach and turned to watch the squaws attack.

Chapter 10

From the top of the heap a calf bawled piteously, its forelegs shattered. The terrible black pile did not lie quiet, but pulsed with fading life. Limbs rose and settled and shuddered. Bright blood gouted from compound fractures. Yellow bone pierced through woolly brown hide. Mouths yawned open and black lips drew back into eerie grins. Dun dust twisted upward in a column and drifted east. Above, on the lip of doom, bold gray wolves surveyed the feast below.

Elkanah had never seen death wholesale, and it sickened him. Betsy couldn't bear it, turned her back upon it, and clutched him.

"Oh, God," she wept. "I didn't expect—I hadn't thought—"

On all fours, Percy Connaught heaved up everything in his stomach. Even Rudolpho Danzig, who took life as it came, looked unusually solemn, if not shaken. Mister Skye didn't like it either, Elkanah realized. His face had a drawn look in the presence of so much death.

He estimated a hundred seventy or eighty, old and young bulls, cows, calves, yearlings. Dead or dying in two or three minutes of cataclysm. Even as he watched, Gros Ventre squaws in ancient tattered skirts swarmed into the heap, often carving upon the still living. A hundred, maybe a hundred and fifty women materialized, each with glinting silvery knives, and began sawing. Tongues first. Easy to butcher, and a delicacy. The women crawled over the pulsing pile, slicing out tongues and tossing them into a bloody heap on the grass.

"I ought to make a daguerreotype," said Rudolpho, "but they're so black I'd have only a black mound on my plate. Too bad. No one has made an image of a buffalo jump."

"I had thought to paint it, but I can't. I never will," muttered Betsy, still in Elkanah's arms. "I think I'd better go back to our camp," she said softly. "It will be a long time before all this fades from my mind."

Elkanah watched her go. Even his buoyant Betsy, who rode storms and troubles like a cork, had suffered some sort of shock. He wished he had discouraged her, but then he smiled. No one ever discouraged Betsy when she set her will upon something.

Mister Skye's gaze had shifted to the rimrock and the cottonwoods along the riverbank and studied the far shore, and Elkanah realized that even here, surrounded by Gros Ventre, he watched for the slightest sign of that madman who dogged him—and maybe the others. It filled Elkanah with rare anger: he'd had enough of slaughter.

"Where are the men? Where are the hunters?" he asked the guide. "There's work to do here, more work than I can imagine!"

"They've ridden back to the village. They'll celebrate and smoke now, and laugh. Their work's done."

"But if they helped—these creatures must weigh a thousand pounds or more—if they helped turn the carcasses, pull them out of the heap—"

"Woman's work."

"But that's madness. They could butcher so many more—start meat to drying—collect hides—"

"Woman's work. No self-respecting warrior would think of it. If you tried it yourself, these squaws would chase you away, or just laugh at you."

Instead of slicing down the stomach cavity and pulling off the hides, these women sawed down the neck and back, cutting a good hide in two.

"Why do they do that? What a waste of a hide!"

"They can get a split hide out of it, mate. Sew the two pieces back together with sinew. The buffler are too heavy to turn over—too heavy for women to drag at all. So they're slaughtered about the way they fall. See, they're going after the hump meat, best of all meat, and that thick white backfat there—great delicacy. From the stomach they'll take some boudins—intestines—and liver. Raw buffler liver, now there's something to taste. Kept many a fur man alive and happy."

"I'll make block and tackle! I'll show them how to set up a simple tripod and pull these carcasses up with good rope and some hardwood pulleys. Then they can slaughter the whole animal, take the whole hide off—"

Mister Skye laughed. "Don't think you'd get far, mate. Look at those hides. Few of them worth anything. They've been torn to shreds by horn and hoof landing on them."

"You mean most of this is waste?"

"That's the way of it."

"What'll they get out of this?"

"Why, more meat and trim than they know what to do with: hump roasts, boudins, liver. Plenty to jerk before it gets too cold, and plenty for pemmican. Backfat, that adds flavor to stews. Sinew. Hides. Dorsal bone, off the hump, for kitchen things. Brain for tanning. Maybe twenty, thirty hides to trade. Mostly splits—worth less, but still something they can give for whitemen's truck."

"What percentage of all this carnage'll get used?"

"Oh . . . ten, twenty. Rest feeds the carrion eaters for a week or two. See the wolves, mate? They're waiting. You'll hear them all night. Coyotes, wolves, badgers, crows, hawks, magpies—you'll hear them at dusk, soon as the squaws clear out."

Rudolpho said, "It seems a waste, at least to a European, to whom meat is always precious."

"Millions of buffler," said Mister Skye. "Sometimes the land is black with them, far as the eye can see. But if the robe trade builds, they'll thin down."

Jarvis Cobb said, "It's their whole economy, isn't it? Kill off the buffalo, and the warriors of the plains are tamed. I'll discuss that in my reports."

"Hate to see them go, Mister Cobb," said the guide.

"These buffalo prevent forward progress of civilization," Cobb replied. "These tribesmen won't stop roaming and warring until we destroy the buffalo. Then it'll be easy to start them farming and ranching."

"I suppose you're right," said Mister Skye crisply. Elkanah was not surprised at the bitterness in the guide's voice. Abruptly Mister Skye left them, stalking toward the Gros Ventre village and his own lodge.

"He hates to see his own way of life fade," said Rudolpho gently. "I can understand it. They get to love this life, out beyond the known world. The freedom. Even these tribesmen who are traditional enemies of his wives seem to command his respect."

"We've witnessed something few whites have ever seen, or will see," Elkanah said softly. "Write it up, Percy—" He peered around, discovering that Connaught had vanished, too. "Something for Percy's journals."

Before them, blood-soaked squaws sliced and tore red flesh from black carcasses. Greasy gray guts covered the grass. Flies swarmed in great green masses. The Gros Ventre women chattered among themselves in a hoarse sharp tongue, and sometimes slipped morsels into their mouths to chew as they worked—chocolatey liver especially. The silent heap of buffalo turned redder and browner, and yet scarcely diminished. On a far side of it, Elkanah spotted Victoria, fiercely hacking back hide with a honed hatchet to get at hump roast. Elkanah scarcely felt like eating, and wondered if he'd manage even the succulent rib roast coming that evening, a roast more tender and tasty than anything beef cattle could offer.

Most of that chill afternoon Elkanah watched, while squaws chipped away at the dead, not even touching a hundred or so animals trapped at the bottom. If they wouldn't hang the animals for slaughter, there seemed little he could offer to save labor or make this gargantuan task easier. It boiled down to humble whetstones. These squaws butchered with dull knives, making hard work brutal work. The other possibility that came to him was smocks of some sort, some sort of cotton shifts they might use for this filthy work and then wash easily. The whole thing might go easier with some division of labor. Teams of strong men to hang the beasts from a stout rafter. A group of hide specialists who did nothing but peel back the valuable brown skins. Gut specialists, who gathered the boudins and liver. Head specialists, who scooped out brain for their tanning process. Backstrap specialists, who cut out the fine hump meat, took sinew and backfat, and the succulent tenderloin. Then it'd all work.

But even as Elkanah thought it, he knew it'd never happen. This monstrous mound would feed wolves rather than people, for the most part. While he watched, shamans snatched bits of buffalo—eyes and noses, ears and tails, magic and power for them. This entire labor seemed infused with tribal medicine and religion, as warriors raised arms to the One Above, as squaws followed ancient rituals and would do things no other way. How, Elkanah wondered, could you offer a people a better way if it invaded something sacred in their life? He had no answer for it.

In the village he found old women, crippled women, and girls engaged in the same relentless labor. Patiently they sliced each thin strip of red meat to be jerked, while children hung loads of the slices over cottonwood racks for the blessing of the sun. Warriors and hunters loafed, smoked, gambled, joked, snatched bits of meat to chew, and enjoyed the late afternoon. Whetstones, thought Elkanah. He'd make whetstones and ease this labor.

Tomorrow and maybe the next two or three days, these people would be much too busy to examine his wares, study his ready-made lodgecover, finger his remaining arrow points, axes, kettles, saws, hatchets, bolts of cloth, thick blankets, and the rest. Percy would scribble. Cobb could study the warriors and their fierce ways of war. Betsy could paint. Danzig had whole cliffs of weathering sandstone to probe for fossils. Working with his pocket watch, which he'd set to the riverboat's chronometer at Fort Union, he found that noon at this location came two hours and twelve minutes later than noon at Washington, D.C. In each hour, the earth turns fifteen degrees of longitude, and in each four minutes of time the earth spins an additional degree. Thus they were thirty-three degrees west of Washington City; one hundred-ten degrees west of a prime meridian running through the Royal Observatory at Greenwich, England. Elkanah grinned. He measured it as twelve or thirteen hundred miles from the farthest edge of civilization.

Barnaby Skye came all awake at once in the blackness of the lodge. The preternatural quietness had jolted him awake. His mind cleared swiftly, and he listened for Jawbone's warning mutter or shriek, but heard nothing. Through the smoke hole above, a few stars winked in a clear moonless night. He sat up in his robes, senses tingling. Victoria sat up with him, listening, but Mary and the child slept peacefully. Kills Dog Woman didn't stir. He could see none of them.

The silence itself had awakened him. The whole night had been alive with the eerie howl of carnivores feasting on the heap of buffalo a little to the east. They'd heard the throaty howl of wolves inviting their brothers to feast; yapping of coyotes, the scream of foxes—now all gone silent. One thing—no, two—might do that. A grizzly at the carrion, lord of the wilds, whose very presence chilled every living creature around. Several times, Mister Skye had experienced a sudden silence, when bird songs caught in their throats and the shimmer and rustle of forests ceased, and even wind seemed stilled. That meant Old Ephriam lumbered near with small weak eyes, vicious temper, and claws that could shred any creature in moments. Maybe a grizzly had found carrion. Or maybe Tortu. Fresh, still-warm liver for the stalker, boudins, hump meat to take somewhere else and roast over a tiny smokeless fire.

In the blackness Mister Skye found moccasins and pulled them on, and buckled his heavy belt with its holstered and sheathed burdens.

"Son of a bitch, Tortu," muttered Victoria. "You go kill him now. He is rabid, like a bad wolf." She paused. "You kill him first. I want you to come back. You be careful, Mister Skye.''

Her fear reached him. Rarely did she admonish or caution, but now her terror spilled from every taut word. ''I don't know why that Harvey sent him. If he hurt you, if he send you to spirit land, I'm gonna kill him back. He don't see an old squaw with a knife.''

Her crabby love reached him, and he drew the taut old woman into his arms and hugged her. She hugged back ferociously. ''You be careful, Mister Skye. He got bad medicine, lots of it. Baddest man there ever was. You come back to hug your old Victoria. I'll fix you good hump ribs and make a new elkskin shirt. . . .''

''I don't know what's in Harvey's craw either,'' he muttered. ''It's been nine years since I booted him out of the fur company. And if I hadn't done it, Alec Culbertson would have.''

''Maybe these people. Maybe this maker of things, Morse.''

''Maybe,'' Mister Skye agreed, thinking of Alex Harvey's suspicious mind, seeing threats where there were none.

''I'll come with you now.''

''Stalking has to be done alone, Victoria. You'd best watch over our lodge and the two tents.''

''I got a bad feeling. Tortu's bad medicine. Has the medicine power of hydrophobia and wolf. Never so bad.''

The old woman's nervous outpouring troubled him. He'd never heard her worry so much. He pulled open the door flap and peered cautiously into an inky night with not even a sliver of moon. And yet, some sort of light shimmered, an eerie green that undulated and wobbled and made shadows writhe on the black ground. The eerie light triggered alarm in him. He'd never known such a thing, as if heaven had released every soul trapped between heaven and hell, and now they all danced. He spotted Jawbone, ears laid back in the weird light, head up but not sounding alarms. Good. Victoria knew Jawbone's language.

His senses screamed. He peered hard at shadows, at the quiet prim tents of Morse's party. He padded softly past wavering cottonwoods, alive with the greenish light, padded lightly through quivering bunch grass toward the great black pile of carrion. Things passed him, soft as a feather. Creatures with sharp teeth slinked his way, giving him wide berth. Quietness clamped down on the night like plague. Had he been wrong to leave Victoria and Mary and the child? Would a cruel killer strike swiftly, killing all that he loved in a few silent slashes? Would the killer murder a great entrepreneur, a genius, in his bed, and exterminate a brilliant scholar, a captain, and Connaught as well? Plunge a cold knife into bright, bold Betsy's breast?

He felt the silence thicken as he approached the black mound. He smelled no bear. Abruptly, fear crawling in him, he retreated and padded almost back to the Gros Ventre village. There he cut north to the dark bluff and scaled a steep watercourse until, puffing hard, he stood on the rim of sandstone and beheld a night alive above the prairies. Across the whole northern quarter of the heavens, curtains of wavering green light plunged and erupted, fountains of weird light, mostly green, but sometimes phosphorescently yellow or pink, the color of long-bruised flesh. Northern lights. He'd never seen such a frightful display of them, a heaven gone mad and devouring stars, devil's light turning the earth to dancing jelly.

Swiftly he padded east across open prairie, up a small cuesta that angled northwest, down its rock-strewn far side— it formed a natural wall to funnel buffalo toward the rim— and then, warily, toward the lip of the buffalo jump. He crept on to its other side, where scrub pine grew and their shadows quivered in the phosphorescent light. There, in the rock and pine, he peered down over the edge, into the shadowed mass of dead buffalo below, where the northern lights didn't reach. Slowly he studied every night form. Nothing. But something stalked there.

"Tortu!" he said in a silky, carrying voice. "Go back to Harvey. Tell Harvey to forget it. A long time has passed. The people I'm guiding mean him no harm. Go now, or meet your fate."

He slid sideways to new shadow, not wanting to be where his voice had risen. Nothing. He peered sharply about him.

The wavering light made it tricky. Every shadow undulated, multiplying Tortu by a thousand.

Some violent thing hissed by and shattered on sandstone a few feet ahead. Arrow! From up here! He rolled violently, finding cover behind jagged sandstone rimrock. Another thing slapped rock, this time inches from his face. Now he sweated. Tortu stalked, but the wavering green light hid the stalker. Mister Skye felt his heart trip, the pulse so loud in his ears that it surely reached Tortu's. Arrows in the green night. Bad medicine, bad as Victoria had feared. He lay still. To crawl would be to die. His elkskins blended with the sandstone, and his head pressed deep into the grasses. But he inched his arm down to his dragoon revolver until he gripped it. In that position he waited, his nerves screaming. Time ticked, and the weird light faded back into blackness until he could scarcely see a few feet ahead of him.

The voice lifted from somewhere in the blackness of the jackpine. "Ah, Monsieur Skye! So it is a standoff tonight, eh? Too black now. The lights of the north died before you did!"

"Tortu! What does Harvey want?"

A weird chuckle drifted back, from a different locale. "Why should I say, eh? You want to know why you die, *oui*?"

Mister Skye remained silent. Tortu seemed inclined to talk.

"Harvey, he don' care about old times. He's making much more as the opposition. American Fur pay him a little. But now, he's—how you say?—a principal. Naw . . . he wants dead the man Morse—*mort*! Morse *mort*!"

Mister Skye waited in the blackness, alert for the slightest shadow against the stars. The metal of his revolver wouldn't shine now, with the liverish light gone. He slid it out and pointed where last Tortu's voice had floated over the cold air to him.

Nothing. Tortu said nothing. Mister Skye wondered what Harvey, Primeau and Company had against Elkanah Morse. Why they'd sent an assassin to kill the businessman. He had no answer, and he wasn't about to speak up again. An endless time slid by, and Mister Skye felt bone-cold in the freezing night. But still he lay rooted to the spot, relatively safe in the sandstone cleft, every sense alert. Vision came with gray dawnlight, and still Mister Skye lay quietly, feeling his life at stake. Gray gave way to color, gray sky and grass and trees turning pastel blue and dun and jade. He lifted an arm and waved it. Nothing. At last, with a blinding sun creeping over the east horizon, he sat up. Still nothing. He stood, stretched, pumped life into locked muscle, and padded back to camp.

Victoria stared at him sharply, more angry than relieved.

"You scare me bad," she muttered, turning her head aside. "How come you stay away all night?"

He saw wetness rimming her crabbed old eyes. Mary, who was feeding his boy, Dirk, looked up at him solemnly, anguish in her eyes, too. They'd been sharing their fears, he knew.

"He had me pinned. Better eyes than mine," Mister Skye said quietly. "I never got a shot. Never even saw him. But he talked a little. He's after Morse, and I haven't the faintest inkling why."

Chapter 11

The terrible death of so many buffalo darkened Betsy Morse's spirit. She had witnessed something too brutal to fathom, and the memory seared her mind. Of course animals were slaughtered for meat. But in the east she'd been insulated from it, and in any case the throat-cutting of a single cow or ox seemed different in its very nature from this violence she'd observed.

This wild land frightened her now, though she hadn't started the trip with Elkanah harboring fear. In the space of hours she'd seen a woman rescued from ritual torture and death; seen a mad assassin shoot at their guide, Mister Skye. The importance of order and a policing hand and punishment of crime dawned on her. She had taken them all for granted in civilized Lowell. If someone stole or murdered, why, punish him! But here . . .

She hastened back to their tents, glad that Arabella hadn't witnessed the buffalo hurtling to their doom. She wanted only to rest quietly until the searing images left her. Perhaps then she'd set up her easel and paint. How the tribesmen—especially the children—loved to watch! But there at their camp at the edge of the Gros Ventre village, the tortured Flathead squaw, Kills Dog Woman, sat quietly before Mister Skye's lodge, beside Mary and the child, Dirk. The woman's face remained a ghastly ruin, her nose blistered and swollen, arms pitted with vicious suppurating pockets of burnt flesh, feet swollen and blistered so badly the woman couldn't stand on them.

And yet, she noticed, the Gros Ventre paid the woman no attention. Hours before, their warriors had started to torture her to death. Now the woman belonged to Mister Skye, and she had ceased to exist, even as a curiosity, to the Gros Ventre. Betsy's heart tugged, and she sat down beside the Flathead woman and smiled, unwilling to touch her tormented flesh.

Mary sat quietly, sewing a new sole on a worn moccasin, using an awl and sinew.

"Perhaps you could tell me, Mrs. Skye—is the Flathead woman comfortable?"

"You bet. Soon she'll be fine."

"But isn't she—afraid? These are the very people who tortured her!"

Mary shrugged. "No. They be enemies of Flatheads—Crow and Shoshone, too. She gets caught, she expects it. If the Flatheads catch the Atsina, the Gros Ventre, maybe they torture the Atsina squaw. This one, she wasn't very brave. She wept and cried and screamed, so they did it slow. After burning, they'd slice off little bits of skin, make as much hurt as they could but not kill her. If she didn't say nothing, just stood quiet, they'd kill her quick, honor her medicine."

Betsy tried to digest all that, but the very ideas repelled her. She gazed gently at the impassive woman, who was dressed in a loose orange calico shift that lay lightly on tortured flesh, and felt pity.

"Mrs. Skye, would you ask her if I can help—I could whip up a new dress in no time, very light cloth. . . ."

"Hard to make Flathead words." But Mary muttered at the woman, her fingers gesticulating.

The woman replied through lips too swollen to speak.

"Maybe later. You make a dress and maybe she becomes

your slave. She thinks that's a good idea. Take her with you back to your home in the east. Maybe good medicine.''

Betsy sighed. Some instinct warned her not to say no to this or express her dismay. ''She'd be a fine helper, I'm sure,'' Betsy said. Mary seemed satisfied with that and translated it. Kills Dog Woman managed a smile through puffed lips.

On a nearby gray cottonwood log, Percy Connaught scribbled furiously in his two journals. He had the red-bound one open now—the one he would publish for ordinary people. No doubt he was describing the killing of the buffalo in language as florid as he could muster, Betsy thought. And no doubt he would not mention that through it all, he was on hands and knees vomiting! She laughed suddenly, some of the horror of the day sliding away.

Rudolpho Danzig rummaged through one of the panniers near his tent and pulled out his daguerreotyping apparatus. A strange device, Betsy thought. He set up a wooden tripod with telescoping legs that he anchored in place. On this he attached a curious box with black bellows and a spyglass lens in front. Well, she thought, what on earth would he make an image of?

He approached the women diffidently, his warm eyes resting gently on Kills Dog Woman. To Mary he said, ''I'd like to make an image of the Flathead woman.''

''But why on earth now!'' Betsy exclaimed. ''Wait until she's healed. I imagine she'll be rather pretty.''

''Ah, Betsy, that's the point. I wish to record the life of the tribesmen as it is, for my colleagues who are ethnologists. The picture of the tortured flesh would be most impressive. . . . But of course, if this is an affront—''

Mary eyed the apparatus suspiciously. Rudolpho turned to her. ''This makes an image, like a painting. Like Betsy's watercolors, but faster. In just an instant. I'd like to make an image of Kills Dog Woman. No harm will come of it.''

Mary tried to convey all that to the injured woman, who finally shrugged and muttered something.

''She says she is a slave and awaits her fate.''

Betsy's spirits sagged. What strange people! But Danzig

nodded and pointed his contraption at Kills Dog Woman, and then vanished under a black velvet hood.

"Ah!" exclaimed the Flathead at the peculiar sight. A white man wiggling around under a black hood in bright sunlight. "Ah!"

Something clicked. The eye blinked. Danzig emerged, beaming, with a rectangular thing in hand, and vanished into his tent. Betsy waited, wondering what these squaws would say. Her whole family had been daguerreotyped, and now the lovely images in oval frames rested on Elkanah's polished walnut desk at home. Betsy had been astonished that hers had come out so well. But not so well as a good color portrait, she thought. Those black and silver images lacked life compared to her clear, transparent watercolors splashed gaily on good absorbent paper.

Danzig's image making had caught Percy's attention too, and he scribbled that into his red-bound journal while Danzig fussed inside his tent. Betsy thought to have Danzig make images of Arabella and Elkanah, too, mementos of this astonishing adventure, but Arabella had vanished. Oh, yes, she was strolling with Captain Cobb. A good thing, Betsy thought. At last Arabella had found someone to talk to. Ever since she'd befriended Cobb, Arabella had become almost amiable. Or at least less sulky.

At last the slim professor emerged from his tent, carrying a thin copper plate. He knelt before Kills Dog Woman and showed her the silver and black image on it, an image of herself, blistered and wounded.

"Aiee!" wailed the woman, startled. She peered at the image and lifted a swollen, blistered hand to touch her puffed cheeks. Her tormented eyes darted to the daguerreotype and then to the dress she wore, and she wailed.

"Bad medicine," said Mary solemnly. "You have stolen her spirit and made it evil."

Betsy peered at the image. The likeness was perfect, but shocking. The wounds had become black blotches, and the grotesque swelling of her face had become monstrous on the plate. "Oh, dear, Rudolpho. I think this was a mistake!"

"I fear so," he said contritely. "I was most callous, and

now I've done some black magic. So much for science and knowledge! How can I make it up?"

Betsy turned to Mary, but Mister Skye's squaw wasn't following the drift of it.

"Mary," he said gently. "I have injured her, and wish to express my apologies but don't know how. May I give her something according to the traditions of her people?"

Betsy watched Mister Skye's beautiful dusky wife frown silently. What a golden beauty! she thought, a bit enviously.

Mary tried again to convey something of Danzig's feelings to the Flathead woman, but ended up shaking her head.

"She says the bad medicine is because she is now a slave."

"Ah—Mrs. Skye. Tell her I will make her a good-medicine image of her. When she is healed, I'll make an image that will show her beauty, her virtue, her—strength!"

When that was conveyed, Kills Dog Woman smiled.

"Professor, would you make an image of Mrs. Danzig in such condition?" asked Betsy.

"Why—I don't believe so."

"Well," Betsy said triumphantly, "Kills Dog Woman feels just the same way!"

"I am duly chastened," said Professor Danzig. "Do you suppose old Chief Horse Medicine might sit for a portrait?"

"Let's find out!" said Betsy. "You'll either be a sensation or they'll torture you to death!"

Jarvis Cobb helped Arabella up the last steep grade to the top of the amber stone cliff, northwest of the Gros Ventre village. Twice as they puffed their way up, rattlers slithered off, while the city-bred young woman yelped her fear. Below, dog soldiers—the village police—watched them impassively. At the top, on a rough plain dotted with somber green jackpine, they got their wind. But what struck them at once was the view. To the north lay a blue belt of featureless mountains their guide had called the Snowies. Far off to the south, maybe even fifty miles in that crystal air, rose jagged gray peaks with snow still trapped in the north crevasses, a range called the Crazies. Still others lay blurred on distant dun horizons.

"It's beautiful, Jarvis . . . but I cherish smaller vistas, green canopies, tea and tarts in our side yard in Lowell."

"It's a lovely place," he replied. "Bereft of people we know and cherish. We must make our own companionship here."

"Yes! The wilderness is so stern. I've been writing poetry. Everyone is keeping notes and journals, so I thought I would write, too. My poems keep me from going mad here!"

"I hope you'll share them sometime."

"Oh, would you read them? But I must see whether they'll embarrass me first."

The slim maiden before him looked, if not beautiful, uncommonly pleasant, and everything about her had been enhanced by costly clothing that fit her lovely form to perfection, tantalizing the male eye. With her cheeks flushed from the hard climb and a faint glisten of moisture on her temples, she seemed vibrant to him. Stray locks of glossy brown hair—all the Morses had rich brown hair—fell over her forehead in enchanting disarray.

He sighed. Honor raised its firm barrier. To violate it would stain his career, offend his host, lead to endless difficulties. She flirted and more; she teased and toyed and aroused. They waded one day at a creek, and she had lifted her skirts high, flashing visions of trim ankles and calves, knees and thighs. She'd had every advantage of education, grooming, training in the women's virtues, and all these dazzled him, and no doubt a long procession of beaux. Each day they'd wandered off to some private bower and hugged, and the hugs had ceased to be merely affectionate. Each day they'd come closer to a brink, but hadn't fallen over it. So far. But just being here away from prying eyes would tempt fate again.

"You're ravishing, Arabella," he said, almost involuntarily.

She smiled gently. "It's so grand to have a dear friend. I would die here in this awful place without someone to cling to," she replied.

He wanted to cling and dreaded it. Something about this wilderness over two thousand miles from his home and family had loosened bonds, commitments, ties. He could scarcely conjure up a vision of his Susannah, or his boy Peter. Some savage force severed the threads, one by one, crumbling promises. He cringed at it and yet welcomed it, heart pounding, drawn ever closer, each day, to the time of no turning back. Even now she stood before him smiling brightly, soft lips parted, eyes shining instead of pouty.

"I'm rested; let's walk," she said, waltzing toward the somber copse of gnarled ponderosa and juniper piercing out of the crannies of broken dun sandstone. He trotted after her, scarcely keeping up with her rushing strides toward a new bower deep within the pines.

They plunged into dappled shade, surrounded by yellow-barked pines with long needles. They treaded down a long gentle slope covered with brown needles, into a bowl that emptied over the bluffs they'd scaled. She pushed ahead, aiming toward a ledge of lichen-covered stone that formed a natural seat in a sunny place. She'd done it again, he thought restlessly—found a very private bower for them to dally in, surrounded by curtains of needles as opaque as bedroom doors.

"What a place to rest!" she exclaimed. "See how secret it is! This is where friends can share the things in their hearts and souls. Tell me what's in your soul right now."

She sat down, leaning back on her arms until the polished tan cotton of her dress strained over her bosom. She waited quietly, her large shining eyes intent on him, wanting confessions and intimacies.

"Why"—he said hoarsely—"I am missing my Susannah. It's been so many months now. My family. My little cottage. My fine staff position . . ."

"You must miss her embrace."

"Oh, I do. A great sweetness. A great tenderness."

Arabella sighed. "I sometimes can't bear being a maiden and unembraced. But of course I must be patient."

"Yes, be patient. Be patient, Arabella. You'll find just the right gentleman for you."

"I don't know that I want a gentleman. This wild land does strange things to me. Naked Indians. Blood. Life and death in the raw. I fear it's making me half-savage myself."

''There's honor, Arabella. One of the things a good officer tries always to live up to—at the Point we encourage duty, honor, country.''

She laughed wildly. ''Honor,'' she said, and giggled.

It seemed time to turn conversation away from these dangerous things. Why was it, every time they strolled, they ended up at the very brink? How weak he was! He let her lead him toward forbidden things each time, as fascinated and hungry as she, as probing and eager as she. He glanced into her face, and found her wide eyes intent upon him.

''Arabella, let's talk of other things,'' he said quietly. ''We may be alone and unchaperoned and free and two thousand miles from our friends, but what could happen here might lead to our ruin, your shame, and my disgrace, divorce, the end of my happy posting as a teacher and scholar at the academy, ostracism for us both. . . .''

''I know.'' She sighed softly. ''I don't mean to violate honor and I'm sure you don't. I only am curious about things I—haven't experienced, and the wilderness drives me.''

''Then let us be friends, comrades of the soul and mind,'' he said, relieved.

''Yes, let's.''

They sat quietly side by side, sunning.

''It's so private here,'' she said. ''There's not a view anywhere, only the trees. Tell me what it's like to be a soldier. To be someone called upon to shoot human beings if necessary.''

''I'm not really that kind—the army has all sorts of people, and my work is scholarly, really.''

''You research better ways to shoot people,'' she said saucily.

He winced. ''If the army didn't exist, would you feel safe?''

''No, of course not. Lots of people want Daddy's money and factories. I suppose lots of countries would like to possess ours.''

''But that's only one view of it,'' he rejoined. ''What if the army exists to help take land and possessions away from other people—these Gros Ventres, for example.''

''You sound like you're speaking against your own army.''

He shrugged. "I'm a realist. Manifest Destiny is making this whole continent—its central area at least—the property of the Republic. My army will soon be corralling these tribes, one by one. My task in the field of intelligence is to learn how to do it efficiently and without bloodshed."

"I suppose it's going to happen. But I hope not for a long time. This land is just right for these savages, and I can scarcely imagine whites living here. They'd turn savage because the land would make them savage."

"The key is buffalo," he said quietly. "The army doesn't need to wage war at all."

She seemed bored, and they lapsed into silence again. Mountain bluebirds flitted boldly from branch to branch around them, splashes of color.

"Would you hold me again?" she asked shyly.

"I'm afraid to, Arabella."

"I know. I'm afraid, too. But we can still be friends of the soul and mind if you hold me. I just—this wild land stirs up some need, is all."

"Honor," he said quietly.

"I know. But hold me gently anyway."

He knew he would. His heart tripped with the mounting hunger that galvanized him. "All right. Just for a moment, Arabella. Then we must let go."

She stood and faced him, her gaze intense, her wavy fine hair tumbling loose about her face. She smiled and still he hesitated, feeling out of control, not wanting to stand, not wanting her to experience his desire. But slowly he stood, drawn up by some relentless force larger than his will. She glanced briefly at him, with quick intake of breath, and they slid arms about each other softly, not pressing, a last crumbling barrier still between them.

Then they pulled each other desperately close and he felt her melting into him, felt her loins molding to his own thickening desire, felt her breast upon his.

"Oh! Jarvis!" she whispered, and kissed his lips with her own parted ones. He returned the kiss furiously, finding her lips sweet, touching her tongue with his. He kissed her lips and eyes, kissed her nose and throat, drew the fine hair away from her ears and kissed them, kissed the cotton fabric over her breasts, felt her hands slide down to his buttocks and draw him tighter to her, felt her arching her own inviting loins against his throbbing.

"Stop! We must stop, Arabella!" he cried.

"*Non!* Eet is ver' entertaining. Don' stop."

Jarvis felt the shock of terror pierce his lust. He whirled. Arabella gasped, withdrew, pulled down high-hiked skirts.

"What a pity. Ver' pleasant to watch," said a cadaverous man with coarse black hair and sallow skin stretched over a skeletal face. One hand held a bow with a nocked arrow; the other rested lightly on the haft of a sheathed bowie knife.

"Tortu," said Jarvis tightly, his own mind a turmoil of fading lust and sudden terror.

"I'm going to take this lady, daughter of Morse. You go back and tell Monsíeur Skye, tell Skye and Morse, and then they come out of the village after me to save the mademoiselle."

"I won't go," snapped Arabella.

Tortu laughed wickedly.

She sat down. "Drag me," she said, fear and defiance blazing in her.

"You have no horse, Tortu. I think it's a standoff," said Jarvis. Something of his long training, his own life work and passion, intelligence, began to assert itself even in the midst of his terror. "Tell me, Tortu. Why do you want her?"

"It make my task easy." He glared at Arabella. "Up. Up or taste the blade."

She shook her head, weeping now.

"Who, Tortu? Who do you want? Morse? Skye? And why?"

Tortu gazed at him with hooded black eyes as flat and opaque as a rattler's. "You are full of queries. But it make no good. I am paid to send Monsieur Morse to paradise." He laughed softly. "Ah, paradise, where the spirits float. Who has employed me? Ah, *mon ami*, that is amusing."

"Where'll you take her? What will you do with her?"

Tortu smiled. "Not far. Far enough to choose my . . . ah . . . terrain. Maybe I keel her, *oui*?"

"You've stolen a guest from the village. All the Gros Ventre will swarm after you."

"And the belle Arabella die, *oui*? *Non*."

"And what if Skye doesn't come?"

"The mademoiselle, she is good sport."

"She can't go far on foot."

"Ah, the prick of the knife—what miracles it can perform!"

"What if only Skye comes?"

"Then I kill but one, and the way is open to Morse."

"Morse is wealthy. He could make you rich the rest of your days if you forget this."

"Ah, bribe! Ver' entertaining. But I like to keel. Tortu—the name, a legend of the north. But enough talk. Now you go back to the village. I will leave clear tracks to follow, *oui*?"

"No!" screamed Arabella. She began howling at the top of her voice, a piercing scream that would carry beyond this grove, maybe to the ears of a village dog soldier.

Catlike, he jabbed the glinting blade lightly into her side, his gaze never leaving Jarvis. She gasped. Red blotted her cotton dress. *"Allons, mademoiselle."*

The pain subdued her. She rose shakily and followed Tortu, her last desperate glance on Jarvis.

He watched until they disappeared into the northwest.

Chapter 12

Jarvis Cobb stopped before them, wild-eyed, running his hand over his high forehead and receding hair.

"Tortu! He took Arabella!"

Mister Skye felt cold dread run through his blood. Elkanah Morse heard it and dashed to the guide's lodge. From her cookstove, Betsy gaped.

"We—were—strolling up the rimrock. He—just—materialized out of nowhere, where the pines are thick."

"Oh, God," breathed Elkanah. Betsy sagged, holding tight to the entrepreneur.

Mister Skye waited, already knowing.

The captain got his breath and gradually composed himself into a military officer. "He had a bow and arrow, and a knife at hand. He made Arabella go with him. He told me to go back and tell you. . . ."

"Wants us to follow."

"Yes. Said he'd leave tracks. He wants to suck you out of the village and kill you."

"What else, Mister Cobb? Why did you stray so far from the village when you knew—"

"The view!" he cried. "We climbed up to see—to see the Crazy Mountains and the Snowies. . . ."

Cobb seemed peculiarly flustered. "I was able to ask—to gather some intelligence. He's—threatening to kill her if you don't come. He's—really after Elkanah, not you, but sees you as a barrier. He . . . wouldn't say who employs him or why. He's on foot, can't go far; can't haul Arabella far. When she—she refused to follow, he pricked her—pricked her with a big knife."

"Oh!" cried Betsy. Elkanah looked ashen. "Oh, dear Arabella," she wept.

"I offered a reward—a bribe—for him to lay off, but he just laughed."

"What did he say to the offer?" Mister Skye asked thoughtfully.

"He said he likes to kill. Likes to be a legend, a terror, in the northwest."

"You're not telling us everything, Cobb," said Mister Skye.

"I swear that's it. I wasn't expecting—wasn't even armed with a revolver."

"Your mind was upon other things, perhaps," said Mister Skye. "As an army officer, surely you know better. Unarmed. Taking a young woman beyond—"

"I know, I know!" he cried. "I am in torment!"

"We have no choice but to go after her and try to trick or overwhelm him, Mister Skye," said Elkanah quietly.

Mister Skye shook his head. "No, mate. This isn't something for you. I'd be pulling an arrow out of your chest in minutes. I want you and Betsy to stay here." He stared at the others, who had gathered around. "Mister Danzig, Mister Connaught. Please guard the camp. Captain Cobb will stay here as well, guarding the Morses. For the moment, say nothing to our hosts. In fact, Elkanah, if you can summon the courage, I'd be pleased to see you begin your presentation to them—your trade show. Their buffler cutting and hide fleshing's slowing down now."

"I couldn't possibly do that, sir."

"Very well, mate."

He nodded to Victoria and Mary and began to saddle

Jawbone. Behind him Betsy wept, and the others gaped silently. Danzig finally galvanized himself into action and found rifles for them all.

Mister Skye slid his sheathed Hawken over the saddle, checked the loads on his dragoon Colt—the caps were all seated—and clambered on Jawbone, waiting. It took Victoria longer to fetch her pony, which had been grazing in the Musselshell River brush. She anchored a small pad saddle over her bay pony and the sheath containing her old fusil. Over her shoulder hung her quiver and unstrung bow. She glanced at him solemnly, a small taut aging Crow woman perched lightly. Mister Skye loved her in that moment.

"What are the chances we'll—see Arabella alive?" asked Elkanah hoarsely.

"Pray," said Mister Skye.

"I'd like to go. I think I could offer money—enough—"

"Tortu doesn't care about money." He turned to Cobb. "Where do we pick up the trail, Mister Cobb?"

"Climb the bluff west of the village—there's only one way. Walk west. Continue into a ponderosa pine grove—a thick one sloping down into a hollow. . . ."

"Some view, Mister Cobb. All right then."

They walked leisurely through the village. The squaws paused in their labor to stare, and to summon children away from the terrible medicine horse, Jawbone. They walked through quiet space, the village opening silently and closing behind them. They passed the lodge of the war chief, White Beaver, who sat smoking before his tipi, watching them intently.

"Hunting," Mister Skye said with his fingers.

An odd thing to do with a village groaning under buffler meat, he knew. But all Indians honored whim. The chief nodded amiably.

"How you do this?" asked Victoria irritably. "Maybe we both die for those people. Tortu stalks and they go for a walk."

In truth, he didn't know how. He was going by invitation, with ambush in Tortu's mind. Going because he had to. Cobb had gathered some useful information, at least. No horse. On foot—well, maybe. It'd be easy enough for Tortu to snatch a couple of Gros Ventre ponies. He could do it even under the watchful eye of the youths herding the ponies. No one could stalk so invisibly as Tortu. . . .

Why? How? Where? He might never catch Tortu. He might find Arabella with a slit throat, a simple pawn to draw him away from the village. Or he might find her—violated, demented . . . Cobb should have had more sense. He'd acted as if he didn't understand about these wilds, as if the quiet sunbaked plains were as safe as the streets around West Point. . . .

Put him out of mind. What Cobb did or failed to do didn't matter. Tortu mattered. . . . And a plan to outwit the craftiest and most dangerous killer he knew of.

He found a steep watercourse breaking the dun cliff and rode cautiously up, feeling Jawbone gather muscle under him to spring up the crumbling rock and over clinging juniper. Behind him Victoria followed. Three of them—Skye, Victoria, Jawbone—against one. That'd help. But Tortu had a hostage, a living shield to prevent shooting, to prevent even aiming. Mister Skye sighed. He probably would disappoint Elkanah and Betsy. This trip among the far tribes would probably come to a bitter end today.

The view above was stunning. Cobb had that right at least. To the west lay the wooded hollow, densely covered, a place with no view at all, neither in nor out. A place to hide, Mister Skye thought, and with the thought came some inkling of how it might be between Cobb and Arabella.

He reined Jawbone lightly. The forested slope loomed darkly ahead, and a rifle poking from any shadowed pine within it would be invisible to him. Jawbone minced, feeling the guide's tension. Jawbone knew; he always knew, and his ears pricked forward and his nose sniffed high, bobbed, sniffed, and pointed. He'd picked up man scent in the woods island on this vast prairie.

The woods covered a dished depression that emptied over the bluff and into the Musselshell. Open prairie lay around it. He turned Jawbone north, steering around the woods. He'd try to pick up a trail on the far side. Northwest, Cobb had said. Intelligence. Observant officer. Give him credit for that. Victoria followed quietly. She rarely spoke in tight moments, but always knew what to do, often better than he knew. They circled the dark woods, always out of rifle shot, and studied the open prairie as well. Tortu was famous for rising up out of nothing, a place of no cover, a place that might seem as safe as the slope of a field outside of London.

Mister Skye grew desperate for want of a plan, but he couldn't think of a thing. He'd simply been invited to his own death, and he had to go or lose Miss Arabella. North of the copse he'd realized the sun had sunk low, and the late August chill had already pierced into his buckskins. Arabella would be spending a bitterly cold night—if she lived. Tortu might just slit her throat and wait, free of any encumbrance.

Twilight was always the most dangerous—a time when stalkers stalked invisibly, hidden by tricky light. This twilight would be no different. It might also obscure the trail, but Tortu didn't want that. He wanted to lead his prey to the slaughtering place. Off to the west, the plunging sun sank behind a purple cloud bank turning the heavens amethyst, jade, and pink. A band of ocean green lay along the horizon, reminding Mister Skye of the high seas he knew so well. The western flanks of the mountains flamed yellow, while the eastern slopes turned indigo. Beneath his feet, the grass glowed burgundy and rose. He'd rarely seen such a sunset.

They found the light tracks of two unshod horses in a dusty patch on the far west side of the grove, two or three miles west of the Gros Ventre village. Tortu had deliberately steered the horses into the dry dusty area. And for good measure, Tortu had dropped a strip of tan cotton cloth—a mocking signal. The tracks headed straight into the sunset, west by northwest, across an utterly empty land, with scarcely a slope or ridge to distinguish it. So it would be like that, he thought. The thing Tortu did best.

He reined Jawbone, feeling a prickle of fear, even though Jawbone sent him no signals. Victoria reined beside him.

"Son of a bitch!" she said crossly.

In minutes the path ahead would thicken into a purple murk. He studied it, seeing nothing but sensing murder.

Beneath him Jawbone stood rigid, not even swishing his tail, turning the horse and man into sunset-splashed statues.

No, he thought. Why do what Tortu wanted? He dreaded what they'd say in camp when he returned without Miss Arabella.

"We'll go back," he said. "If he kills her, he's lost his chance to draw Morse—and me—out of the village."

They rode quietly back, around the forested area, and finally down the cliff to the Musselshell valley. The fragrance of buffalo ribs broiling struck them. In the village an idea struck him.

"Victoria," he said quietly, "let the Morses know I've returned temporarily, and that we followed a clear trail of two unshod ponies."

She glared at him. "Dogs fight dogs," she snapped.

He grinned. She rode toward the Skye camp in the east edge of the village. He turned Jawbone toward White Beaver's lodge, dismounted, and scratched softly on the door flap. Light shone translucently through the amber lodge-cover. A massive square-faced squaw invited him in.

He settled in the guest's place proffered him. The war chief, who wore only breechclout and leggins, seated himself in his proper place, his powerful torso and shoulders glinting in the tiny fire. He offered no pipe. Mister Skye and his entourage were scarcely friends of the Gros Ventre.

Mister Skye regretted that he had only his hands and arms to convey meaning. The sign language of the plains was crude and failed to convey detail. Still, he would try. It took a long time, hands whirling, an occasional word, Tortu. Arabella. White Beaver knew Tortu. What northern Indian didn't? Knew Harvey, too. At the news of the abduction, White Beaver frowned. Stealing a guest from the protection of his people? Ah, there was war. And where were this Tortu and the woman?

Hovering close, northwest, mocking. The guide said nothing, letting the whole story run through White Beaver's mind.

Why does Tortu do this to your people? he asked, fingers flashing.

We don't know. Could be many reasons. Morse makes

the trade goods stocked by the trading posts, both American Fur and the opposition.

White Beaver reached above him and lifted a sheathed medicine pipe from a hook on a lodgepole. They smoked quietly. The evening raced by. Darkness settled on the village. The war chief seemed lost in thought. At last he signaled. This is a great wrong done to the village of Horse Medicine. I, the war chief, will lead our warriors this very night. Tortu might hide from white eyes, but not from the eyes of the People. We will kill him and bring the girl. You will not come—my medicine says we must do it, avenge the wrong done this village. I will gather every warrior, young and old, ten times the fingers of my hands, and we will kill Tortu. Go to your camp and wait.

I'd like to question Tortu—find out reasons, the guide replied with his fingers.

White Beaver frowned. We will try to bring Tortu here alive, he replied. And shrugged. The gesture dismissed Mister Skye. He stood, nodded, and slipped into the icy night. Even as Mister Skye rode back to camp, he heard the town criers quietly summoning warriors from their lodges. Within a few minutes, something like a hundred of them would be mounted and begin a vast infiltration of the prairie where Tortu lurked. This one would be beyond his ability to solve himself, he thought, glad he'd recognized it. He'd bloody well learned to be humble in this wilderness—be humble or die. What would he prove, riding out to rescue a maiden in man-to-man combat, like some Arthurian knight? He was no knight, and here no rules, no fairness, governed the way men warred. Why did he always take battle so personally? Was it some male pride in him? They'd think ill of him in camp, turning the task over to the village. Coward, they'd think—Connaught especially. Well, they bloody well could think what they would. He smelled frost in the eddying air, and would be glad of the fire in his small lodge.

They heard him coming and waited quietly in the night. He dismounted, slid the saddle and bridle off Jawbone, and turned the ugly blue loose to graze.

"It's a tribal matter, Elkanah. Every warrior in the village is mounting up right now. Abducting a guest of the village is a mortal insult to them. Think what you will—it's the one way to fetch Miss Arabella back. She's safe enough, I think. Wouldn't be if Tortu killed me. We'll have to sit and wait.''

"You're not even going?'' asked Connaught disdainfully.

Mister Skye fixed his gaze on the man. ''Say it, Mister Connaught. Say what you think—that I'm too cowardly to go at this alone.''

''Why, I—well, yes. You're the vaunted guide, a white man, too. This conduct is, well—''

''I think Mister Skye is doing the right thing,'' broke in Elkanah firmly. ''We must wait. This wilderness and its tribes do things in ways we would be wise to understand. Don't you agree, Jarvis? Rudolpho?''

''Of course,'' said Jarvis. ''What better safety for Miss Arabella than a hundred dusky warriors swarming through the dark?''

''Keep your guard up, mates. With every warrior out of the village, nothing keeps Tortu from coming here. I'd suggest lights out in your tents and patience. We may not know anything until morning.''

''Oh, Mister Skye, thank you for doing what you could,'' said Betsy. ''We trust your judgment. You've lived here and we haven't. If our dear child can be made safe and this strange threat to us, to you, ended this way, why . . .''

''We'll give this village gifts,'' cried Elkanah.

Mister Skye nodded. ''Tell me again, Elkanah. Has the opposition company any reason to hold a grudge? Have you treated them differently from American Fur?''

''No . . . Well, maybe. We offer volume discounts. American Fur's orders of trade goods are larger, and qualify for larger discounts. But that's scarcely reason to send an assassin . . . or kidnap my innocent daughter.''

''Doesn't make sense,'' Mister Skye agreed. ''But someone wants you dead for some reason. And this wild land is a perfect place for it to happen.''

With that they adjourned sadly into their tents and lodges to wait while the desolate night slowly passed. The village lay quiet in the frosty night, with only the dog soldiers present to protect it from wolves of all descriptions. Mister Skye sat in his dark, warm lodge, playing with his little tyke, Dirk. An odd name to these Yankees, but a British one he'd always liked. Scarcely a Dirk in this American republic. His women sat quietly through the somber night. None of them could sleep. He feared for the lively, bright, spoiled young woman. His reputation as a guide who could get his clients past any peril of the west hung in the balance here, and it lay in the hands of tribesmen who had been enemies of the fur trappers, enemies of his wives' tribes. He didn't like it. But his every instinct told him that Tortu would be more than a match for him.

He peered out of his lodgeflap into the blackness and eventually made out Cobb, who sat with his back to a cottonwood, holding a fowling piece. A soldier faithfully at guard. Good enough. Cobb and Jawbone made a formidable force against an intruder.

Midnight passed according to Mister Skye's reckoning, and a bit later the heavy thud of hooves reached him, the sound of returning warriors. Muffled cries. Harsh commands. By the time the horses and warriors had arrayed themselves before Mister Skye's camp, every person there had bounded out of a tent or lodge and stood waiting, dreading.

Mister Skye made out White Beaver on a white medicine stallion, and sitting behind him, skirts hiked high, rode Arabella.

"Oh, dear!" exclaimed Betsy. "Oh, thank God! Oh, Arabella!"

The warrior lifted the young woman easily and set her on earth before her parents, who hugged her.

"It was awful, Daddy. What a pig! He stabbed me a bit to make me docile. And then he put me on a horse and we rode to a place where he waited—he called it a buffalo wallow. Just mud and smell."

"Where is he? Is he dead?" cried Elkanah.

But Arabella was sobbing, pent-up terror flooding out of her. "Pig, pig, pig, pig," she sobbed.

At last, Elkanah turned to Mister Skye. "Please tell them

we are grateful. Please tell them I have gifts—much of what I brought—for them in the morning.''

"Hard to make finger sign in the night, mate. You get her story. I'll walk back to White Beaver's lodge and get his story by the firelight, where we can see each other.''

Mister Skye trudged wearily toward the war chief's lodge, more tired than he thought he'd ever been. There before the lodge lay a dark hulk, a human being on his side. In the soft light radiating from the skin covering, he saw Tortu—and an arrow protruding clear through his belly. It had entered from the rear, and its metal trade point projected through his buckskin britches in front, dark with blood.

The assassin breathed raggedly, wheezing. "Ah . . . Skye . . .'' he said, coughing. "You are coward. Afraid of Tortu . . .''

Mister Skye knelt down to hear the whispered words. "Yes,'' he said simply. "Afraid is right, mate.''

Tortu grinned, wheezing. "So I am more man. Tortu, you send the whole village against Tortu.''

"Tortu!'' said Mister Skye sharply. "Why did Harvey send you? What started this?''

The dying Frenchman laughed, a rattle in his throat. "Not Harvey! He don' know about it. I get employed by St. Louis men, and they say they get money from . . .'' The last words mumbled and blurred into a spasm of choking. Tortu's mouth leaked blood. And Tortu died.

Mister Skye stood up slowly. White Beaver and other warriors stood, seeing death slip into their midst. Then the war chief barked something, and warriors hauled the dead man away. He beckoned to Mister Skye to enter the lodge where they could finger-talk in wavering firelight.

Chapter 13

Elkanah stood before the opened panniers, puzzled. "What would be appropriate?" he asked.

"Tobacco. Powder, galena. One of those bolts of cloth if you can spare it. But they don't value material things the way we do. Have Betsy paint his portrait—he'd be truly honored. That or one of Mister Danzig's daguerreotypes."

"Gold?"

Mister Skye hesitated. "Yes, if White Beaver understands it."

Moments later they stood in chill pale sun before White Beaver's lodge and waited. Perhaps they'd come too early, Elkanah thought. He'd noticed that male Indians arose at a late hour and lounged through most days having fun and accomplishing little.

The flap parted, an eye peered out and they waited some more. At last White Beaver's squaw, Hide Scraping Woman, ushered them into the warm, softly lit lodge. A boy slid outside. White Beaver yawned. They had awakened him. He seated them, and slipped outside to the bushes a moment, and returned wider awake.

The guide's fingers flew once again, and Elkanah wondered whether he might invent some way—maybe pictographs—by which these plains tribes could communicate faster. Little cards, the size of playing cards, with lots of pictures—ah, there'd be something to sell them. . . .

Questions and gift giving. They wanted to find out from White Beaver what had happened. Arabella's account of the night was semicoherent. The assassin had prodded her along, leering and laughing, making obscene jokes and threatening to violate her. That much Elkanah had found out. And now he wished to give generous gifts to the war chief. Mister Skye had assured Elkanah that the chief would share them with the others who rescued Arabella.

He watched White Beaver reply, doubting that much real information could be transmitted in such fashion. At last Mister Skye turned to him with the story.

"White Beaver says their best scouts sniffed out Tortu—he stank, it seems—and worked around him. He'd left the buffler wallow and had dragged Arabella back into a gulch. It was White Beaver's arrow that got him. Some of them diverted Tortu in front, and the war chief slid in from the rear. Turned out to be easy."

"You've thanked him?"

"Not exactly a concept like that. But honored him, yes. Gave him your praise. And debt. Told him you're owing him, and had gifts. You can fetch 'em now."

Elkanah ducked out into sunlight and dug into the pannier. He found the bolt of royal blue velveteen, shimmery in the sun. On it he piled the other things, a pound of powder, bar of lead, a spare skillet, ten twists of tobacco. These he carted in and laid before the chief, who grunted, fingered the cloth, and then smiled, saying something unintelligible.

"He's well pleased," said Mister Skye. "Now I'll tell him about Betsy if I can."

In a moment it was arranged. White Beaver would put on his ceremonial dress, bonnet, bearclaw necklace, and sit for Betsy. She'd paint others if she had time. Elkanah would at last show his trade goods and the guide would try to get some reaction to them.

White Beaver dismissed them—he was obviously hungry

for breakfast—and Elkanah and the guide led the pack pony back to their camp.

"Mister Morse, before Tortu died he told me Alex Harvey had nothing to do with all this. Tortu was working for someone else."

Elkanah felt puzzled. "This whole thing makes no sense at all," he muttered. "But I'm so glad it's over. I've been sick with worry—for me, for you, for dear Betsy and Arabella—"

Mister Skye waited. Then, "Tortu said he'd been hired out of St. Louis. I don't have more than that."

"St. Louis? Why—you mean, someone back in the States?"

"You have enemies back in the States?"

Elkanah puzzled that. "No . . . business rivals . . ." A thought came to him. "One firm grew very bitter, or at least a principal in it did. I'd undersold them on many things— kettles, arrow points, cloth . . . American Fur finally quit buying from them because I simply had better and cheaper goods."

"Mister Morse, for as long as I can remember, this wilderness, out here beyond the frontier, has been a place of revenge, murder, plots spun out back in the civilized east but executed here. Back in the trapper days, the rendezvous days, there were often some hunters showed up at the frolics—only they hunted heads, not pelts. That's what a frontier does, mate. The things they can't do back there, they hired done out here. If you think life's savage here, maybe you might see just how savage business competition is back there, on your manicured lawns, in your safe cities."

"You really think a business rival . . ."

"You have any other ideas, mate?"

In fact, Elkanah didn't. Always, like the dark drone of bees, men had resented his successes, his inventions, his bright new marketing ideas, his sheer interest in improving the way people lived, and the fact that he'd earned a fortune doing it. Why did the world hate progress?

"You think it's over, Mister Skye?" he asked, shaken.

"We'll keep our guard up and look for a confederate. But

Tortu was a loner if there ever was one. He'd have gone into a rage at the idea he couldn't handle it alone.''

"It never occurred to me that others might resent my successes so much," Elkanah muttered.

The kidnapping shocked him. Arabella's terror had turned into smoldering hatred of everything in these wild lands, and especially of its people. "I want to go back to civilization!" she'd told him at dawn. "Take us back! Wildmen and savages! I didn't want to come and be exposed to madmen! It's all your fault, making me come. This is the most awful place!" Elkanah couldn't think of a thing to say. He wished devoutly he'd left her back in Lowell, well chaperoned and safe.

Within an hour, Betsy had her easel and watercolors set up at White Beaver's lodge. The war chief refused to sit, and stood patiently while Betsy brushed fine transparent color on the white sheet until a stern proud war chief began to emerge. Around her stood a horde of children and squaws, watching in astonished silence. Some of the young warriors feigned not to notice, but ended up staring at this amazing spectacle anyway. At last even old Chief Horse Medicine watched enviously.

Betsy saw him. "I'll do you next!" she said.

A while later she rose and carried her swiftly done portrait to the war chief.

"Ahiee!" he said, and Elkanah wondered what that meant. But White Beaver held it up solemnly so that all the onlookers might see. Then he paraded it back and forth, holding it in a way that suggested pride and magic. Then he motioned abruptly to his squaw, who ducked into the lodge and emerged with a handsome bone necklace. The hollow white bones had been strung like two small washboards, forming a V at the center. Solemnly Hide Scraping Woman tied the necklace thongs around Betsy's neck.

Betsy smiled. "I'm so pleased," she said. "Thank you. It's beautiful!"

They understood the tone but not the words.

That day Betsy painted old Chief Horse Medicine, his wife, Makes the Moccasin, and an old cross-eyed medicine woman, revered because she could see in two directions and into herself. She sketched three of the warriors in their finest regalia, holding their bows and quivers and trade fusils studded with brass tacks, and feathered lances. All of these she gave away, though Elkanah wished she'd keep them to take east.

"Don't worry, dear. I've made pencil sketches, too, and I'll fill them in with the colors later. I remember just the colors," she said happily. "I'll have a fine portfolio to display in Lowell."

Elkanah's own trade show turned out to be disappointing. The enigmatic Gros Ventre stared at his goods, exclaimed in guttural tones at his canvas lodgecover, fingered his fabrics, studied his russet leather bridles—and kept him in the dark. No one in the village could communicate with him. He held up his milled-perfect arrowshafts and ready-mades, and warriors stared politely at them. No medicine in them. No medicine. He'd never sell goods that lacked medicine. Disappointed, he packed things back into the fine panniers and gave up.

Rudolpho Danzig was having a better time, he noticed. The professor had his daguerreotyping apparatus out and was making portraits. He had too few plates to make images of one at a time, so he was lining up Gros Ventre into rows, like some chorus back east, and then squirming around under his black hood, adjusting focus. Whole crowds of villagers waited patiently while he finished the process by treating the silver-coated copper plates with iodine vapor in a box inside his tent. Each time he emerged with a new plate in hand, villagers mobbed him, exclaiming, pointing. They passed the plate from hand to hand, chattering and laughing and fingering themselves.

This visit to the Gros Ventres had been a failure, Elkanah thought. He'd learned nothing helpful to his business. No one could even talk to him. At least he was coming to understand the daily life and labor of the villages, although their religion continued to mystify him. And the whole alarming business of Tortu had ended—in death—and he and his loved ones could hope for safe passage through this wilderness now. If anything, he felt even more confident about Mister Skye.

Back in camp he found Arabella sitting sullenly, saying nothing to Captain Cobb, who had attended her faithfully during and after the ordeal. Good man, Cobb. But a bit careless to wander so far from the safety of the village. Percy Connaught attacked two journals at once, whittling his pencil furiously and scratching in one and the other leather-bound journal in a fine hand to save space.

Connaught looked up at Elkanah. "These are becoming priceless!" he exclaimed. "So valuable. I'm pouring out all my impressions. Forming policy about these people. Recording every nuance. Describing every chief. Examining every event. Can you imagine how the tale of that Flathead squaw's torture and rescue will be received back in the States? So valuable!"

"Wrap them in oilcloth," cautioned Elkanah.

"Oh, I do that! And in your bag, too. The safety bag you designed for me!"

Elkanah smiled, glad to see one of his little things in good use. He glanced over at Mister Skye's lodge and saw the injured Flathead, Kills Dog Woman, sitting solemnly beside Mary, talking in some fashion with uttered phrases and finger signs. She had healed somewhat, and had the affection of Mary and Victoria to help her along. That pleased him.

From the Musselshell valley their guide took them south over rugged humped prairie and down the east flank of the Crazy Mountains. Outside of the Alps, Professor Danzig had never seen mountains so glacier-sculpted. They were crested by knife-edged ridges of extruded igneous rock, volcanic in origin, with flanks as steep as sixty or seventy degrees. A little like the Alps, he thought. Cirques lay between the ridges, with traces of snow still in some of them. The range seemed to extend forty or so miles north and south and looked to be narrow across, maybe fifteen or twenty miles. Sometime in recent geologic history, molten rock had pushed up through a crack in the crust of the earth to form these stunning razor-edged purple peaks.

The caravan rode easily now, with the danger from that madman gone. Betsy and Arabella perched comfortably in their familiar sidesaddles. Danzig thought that Arabella had weathered her abduction well enough. The girl was too ill tempered to brood about it, and all they'd heard from her for days had been sulfurous comments about natives, red and white. A good spoiled-rotten rich girl would be too busy living to let a mere abduction get her down. Still, he thought, for all her nastiness, Arabella could be witty and warm when she chose to be. He liked her, somehow, against all odds. She'd be slow maturing, but would finally blossom into a lovely woman.

Back a way, Cobb handled the packhorses easily. Far ahead and to either flank rode Mister Skye's squaws, like the antennae of a caterpillar, looking for trouble and finding none in this somnolent country. How the old woman's eyes shone! he thought. They were riding into her country, the home of her people, the Absarokas. She seemed to know this land, steering them to water and safety and sheltered campsites each evening. Her people were Kicked-in-the-Bellies—what a name! He had written it in his journal, and no doubt so had Connaught and Cobb. She would find them without difficulty, Mister Skye had said. She always knew mysteriously where they would be, any time of the year, including this bright beginning of September.

They crossed Sweet Grass Creek, which angled southeast, but Mister Skye hewed to the eastern flanks of the mountains. When they reached Big Timber Creek, the vast valley of the Yellowstone lay ahead. Mister Skye followed the creek, along cottonwood-dappled banks and still-green meadows that drew moisture from the high water tables. Frost had yellowed some of the foliage, Danzig observed, and it faintly worried him.

He touched his heels to his pony and trotted up to Percy Connaught.

"I've never seen such a land, Percy. What noble mountains—a little like my Alps. And how rich these lands. We ride in perfect comfort day after day, dry sweet air, lush cured grasses for our horses. . . ."

"It soothes the eye," agreed Connaught. "It lends a nobility to these savage people. These mountains and vast prairies have shaped them, I suppose. A harsh people fitted to a harsh land. In the space of hours we've seen torture and death as well as cheer and festivity and feasting.''

"I suppose you're recording all that in your journals.''

"I am. Few whites have been here, and those who came didn't record it properly. Not even Frémont in his explorations south of here. But I am. I am not only catching every detail—especially about these savages, who fascinate me—but recording my observations about them. Oh, Danzig—when this is published, I'll—I'll—''

"You'll make your name,'' said Danzig, who knew Connaught's churning ambitions very well.

"I'm forming a theory,'' said Percy, almost ecstatically. "Maybe someday it'll bear my name. The land forms the people. We whites live in moderate climates without extremes, you see. Flatter land, fertile, well watered, temperate. It affects our character, you see. With natural industry we make our soils yield, our mines produce. Our own nature is temperate, measured, thoughtful. Now you take these savages out here—everything is extremes because the land is extreme. Little water, so they must hunt instead of farm. Vast prairies, scarcely a tree on them. How radically they must affect the soul. Vast barbaric mountains like these on our right. Barbaric! Violent walls of rock, not at all like the gentle slopes of New England or Appalachia. It must provoke these savages to war, to violence, you see. There's not a stitch of temperance in them. Give them spiritous drink and they'll instantly stupefy themselves. Give them weapons and it's an excuse for bloody battle. Give them buffalo and they slaughter whole herds! Why, the more we wander here, the more my journals fill up with the true picture of savages!''

"I come from a country whose landscape is even more violent than this,'' said Danzig quietly.

"Well, yes,'' admitted Connaught. "But Switzerland is an exception. A mountain island in a settled temperate continent. It doesn't really challenge the truth of my theory. Look at Skye's squaws. Wild and savage, even after living for years with a white man. Of course this savage land has turned Skye savage. He's a deserter from the Royal Navy, I hear. No wonder he lingers out here, afraid to go home. He wouldn't even dare to step into the Canadian possessions.''

"He was impressed," corrected Danzig. "A man who's dragooned onto a ship against his will has a right to free himself, don't you suppose?"

Connaught didn't reply. Then: "It's a mystery why he stayed here. He could have gone east to the States safely enough, made a good life for himself. He obviously has nothing put by. A ragged tipi and two squaws and a half-breed brat. Oh, I tell you, Danzig. This land is dangerous! It tears away every virtue and civilized restraint in a man! I fear for the Republic if it's ever settled! And I am going to publish on it—these journals, this trip, why, what I have packed away in oilcloth here will be the most important book of the decade!"

Rudolpho Danzig grew silent. He could scarcely imagine a more enchanting place to settle, a place that would invite warm Swiss villages, healthy living with mountains and meadows stretching from one's very yard, game, crystal water and air. . . .

The water-worn cobbles in Big Timber Creek were igneous and metamorphic, he noted, granite, diorite, down from the mountains, but the country they rode through was sedimentary, an ocean bottom once. Rising to the south were the snow-tipped Absarokas, as formidable as any range he'd seen. They rode, he mused, along the farthest western edge of the Great Plains, a corner of the plains that he increasingly described within himself as paradise.

At the shimmering Yellowstone they paused, admiring the wide clear river with its gravelly islands and easy banks. The river ran slow this late in the year, and it didn't seem formidable to cross. Across the river a large stream debouched, and Danzig knew at once where they were: Lewis and Clark had called it Rivers Across and had camped here. Danzig had their journal in his bags and had studied it closely.

"That's the Boulder flowing in across there, mates," said Mister Skye. "We'll cross here, a little above, and camp on the Boulder. Victoria says her people will be up the

Boulder valley a way. We'll find them and have a good visit.
Some speak English. They've been friends—give or take a
little horse stealing—of the whites from the fur days. Many
trappers stayed with them. That's how I met my Victoria.
Their customs are, ah, a little unusual. . . . ''

Mister Skye looked pained, at a loss for words. But Danzig laughed. He knew what the guide was trying to say. The
Crows were notoriously bawdy. The journals of the mountain men brimmed with it. He glanced covertly at those
prim New Englanders, Elkanah and Betsy and Arabella, but
their faces didn't register understanding, and the guide
couldn't bring himself to say more.

"Son of a bitch!" muttered Victoria. "Let's cross!" She
slipped off her pony and began unloading a travois. In minutes she and Mary had strapped Mister Skye's lodge and
parfleches on the backs of their ponies and mules and were
ready. Confidently she led them west a bit and struck into
the water at a southwest angle. Danzig watched her progress as the swift current tugged her pony's legs. But the
ripples scarcely reached its belly and it bounded up the far
side, shaking and spraying violently, while Victoria laughed
and chattered like the darting black and white magpies along
the great river.

Rudolpho Danzig was pierced with understanding. Victoria had come home. For a moment he felt a pang for his
own Switzerland, for his Berne, for the sweet people who
lived there. Homesick, suddenly. Homesick out upon a
North American wilderness half a globe away from Berne.
But Victoria danced and laughed on the far shore, trans-
formed, the heartland of the Crow people beneath her feet.
These people Connaught called savages—these people loved
their homes and families and villages as much as any on
earth. Was Connaught, beside him, seeing love? Seeing
Victoria's joy and anticipation? Tomorrow, the Kicked-in-
the-Bellies! Parents, brothers, sisters, cousins, nieces,
nephews, chiefs, headmen, clans, news, births and deaths,
the old squaw's people! He doubted it. Theories could im-
prison the mind, he thought. And Connaught's mind lay
trapped deep in a prison of his own making.

They crossed the gentle Yellowstone easily and made

camp on the south shore, with breathtaking views in most directions as the setting sun painted the mountains.

"Tomorrow, mates, we'll head into one of the most beautiful intimate valleys in the west and find Victoria's people," said Mister Skye. "Enjoy yourselves. With Tortu behind us, this looks to be the happiest journey we've had."

Chapter 14

Victoria dashed ahead of the caravan, looking for her people. The Kicked-in-the-Bellies usually camped here in the
valley at the beginning of the coolness. She touched moccasins to her pony and it spurted ahead, galvanized by her
excitement. She ran beside the boulder-strewn river, following it upstream, through mounded plains at first, and then
foothills, and finally into the great mountains, where forested slopes shot upward from the intimate verdant bottoms.

And then before her sat two Kit Fox Society warriors,
camp police, on restless ponies. Her people! She knew them
by their society shields. She knew all the warrior societies:
Lumpwoods, Big Dogs, Hammers . . . They sat easily, almost naked even in the icy morning air, watching her.
Close, then! These were the guardians of her village, ever
alert for surprises from the Piegan or Lakotah—she spat the
names of the enemies of the People from her mouth.

"Ah!" she cried, reining before them. She couldn't think
of their names; they'd been boys when Mister Skye had
taken her away from the People. But they knew her. Every

person in that village of almost two hundred lodges knew her.

"Many Quill Woman!" cried one, a powerful bronzed youth with massive cheekbones and a single braid of jet hair. Victoria loved to hear her Absaroka name spill over his tongue.

"Ah, Kit Fox Society man! I'm so happy to come to my people! The others come, my man, Mister Skye, and white-men we are taking from place to place."

"It is a good day to visit," said the other, a thin hawkish young man. "Tonight we have a dance. The Kit Fox Society is done with the village policing, and we will dance. Then the Lumpwoods will dance, and they will become the village police. But we do better. We guarded well and kept the village safe."

"A dance! We will be happy to see you dance!" exclaimed Victoria. "And how is our chief Many Coups?"

"He has blessed the village. We are rich with buffalo meat and new hides, and the women are busy making pemmican and gathering roots for the time of the cold," replied the heavier youth.

"I will not wait. I'll go ahead to the People!" she cried. She kicked the pony forward, and one of the Kit Fox warriors rode beside her. The other would escort Mister Skye.

Ahead a mile lay a thin layer of blue smoke from the village fires, trapped in the narrow mountain valley. Close now! Here and there along the river, Absaroka women plucked berries, pulled up good roots. Others busied themselves on the steep slopes, gathering pine nuts. Her people! How she ached for news, ached to hug them all, gather her own Otter Clan loved ones about her and chatter with them into this night! She loved Mister Skye and knew it was a great honor to be the woman of the great white warrior, but this visit would be pure joy. Always, unless her village was grieving, these visits marked the high points of her life. And the Kit Fox warriors had no bad news to give her!

The camp crier, old Coyote Tongue of her own clan, met her and wheeled about to announce her, crying among the lodges, galvanizing women and children. Many of the young men had gone off to hunt, but would ride in soon for the great dance.

She rode her pony into a great forest of bright-daubed lodges, whose doors opened to the east to greet and revere Sun when he came to make the new day. She collected a crowd, scampering, shouting children, boys who drew mock bows and sent mock arrows at her, and laughed. Women who rose up from their hide fleshing and moccasin making to welcome her. The Kit Fox escort pushed through them all importantly, guiding her to the great lodge of Many Coups.

The chief was not there to greet her when she and the crowd halted before his fine lodge with its black-painted suns and new moons. Beside the lodge a brush arbor had been erected, and in its soft dappled shade his sits-beside-him woman, Black Deer Nose, scraped a new hide. Many Coups was off counseling with the medicine men this afternoon, she explained. Soon he would come.

By the time Many Coups appeared, Mister Skye and the whole entourage had also, wending through the shouting villagers who kept a respectful distance from the terrible blue roan, Jawbone.

"Big feast and Kit Fox dance tonight," she said to Mister Skye. "Son of a bitch, we gonna have fun."

The powerful chief threaded his way, unhurried, among his people, stared at the visitors, his eyes long upon Elkanah and Betsy and Arabella—he'd never seen white women except once at Fort Laramie—and vanished into his lodge. Welcoming required ceremony. A welcome formed a sacred bond between the village and its guests. In a moment he emerged, wearing his ceremonial regalia. His chief's bonnet of black and white eagle feathers above a blue-beaded headband was without a tail. He held a staff of office, befeathered at the top, with totems hanging from it.

Victoria barely heard the welcoming as Many Coups droned on. She had spotted her father and his new woman, one she'd never met. And her brother and two sisters. And others of her Otter Clan, the clan of her dead mother, to which she belonged by birth. Mister Skye, Elkanah, and the other whitemen vanished into the lodge for the ritual smoke and gift giving. Then at last they emerged from the chief's lodge, and Mister Skye led his party to a place on the outskirts of the village and made camp there.

Crossly—she wanted to be free—she erected Mister Skye's lodge with Mary and Kills Dog Woman and looked to the comforts of the Morse party.

"Big doings tonight, mates. Kit Fox Society dance. And a feast of buffler. Boudins and tongue, hump meat and ribs. They'll honor the spirits. Honor their guests. Thank the One Above. There'll be a solemn ceremony transferring the police duty to the Lumpwoods—that's another warrior society. This is the season of dances and feasts and medicine. Last fling before it gets too cold and winter closes in. Tomorrow night, a Lumpwood Society dance and another feast. We're among friends—Victoria's people—and you'll enjoy meeting them all," Mister Skye explained. He turned to Victoria, who stood muttering. "I figure there's some folks you want to see, old woman." He grinned and pulled her to him with his massive paws, and she felt happy in the tight circle of his arms.

"No one here I care about. All dogs," she retorted. He laughed, more at ease than she'd seen him in many moons. In a way, this village was his home, too, the place he'd always returned to in the winters of his trapping days, so that he was almost Absaroka himself, and had counted coup and fought beside many of the graying men of the village. Crow enemies were Mister Skye's enemies.

"If you find a beautiful Absaroka girl and pay fat gifts for her, I could use another slave. Got too goddamn much work. Got Mary, and maybe this Flathead, Kills Dog Woman, unless she goes back. But they're goddamn lazy and I got to do everything! Damn. You find a pretty Absaroka girl and go into the bushes with her!" She laughed raucously. Mary grinned impishly. The healing Flathead women, who didn't know English, smiled politely. Victoria glanced covertly at the whites and saw the strange one, Percy Connaught, gaping. She cackled and winked at him.

With that, Victoria fled into the large village to find her old father and meet her stepmother, who came from a band of river Crows. Her heart felt as light as her feet as she dodged shouting children and barking yellow dogs and passed smiling women who had returned to their endless labors. Many of them, she noted, were making winter moccasins from the smoke-blackened tops of lodges. The smoke-and-grease-cured leather turned water and made a fine outer moccasin against the Cold Maker's fiercest weather. And that would come all too soon, she thought, feeling the late-afternoon chill as the sun slid toward the towering western slope, plunging the valley into a lavender cool.

Her people! How rich they all were. Fat times, plenty of buffalo. Parfleches full! Fresh red quarters hanging from alder branches and heavy tripods! And here in this green valley, she knew, roamed more deer and elk than could be counted, and sometimes the great brown bear, too. Bear spirit claimed this valley and would hunt fall berries and eat pine nuts and catch trout and maybe roar at them here before going off to his den for the long winter's sleep. But now as she threaded through the lodges looking for her father's, everything delighted her approving eyes. How fat they looked! She saw few women with hair cut off—not many warriors had died this year. Fat women beaded and quilled together, or strung thin white bones into handsome heavy necklaces. They knew Victoria and smiled, but did not detain her, for she would first visit with her clan, and then the People.

She passed young bronzed men sitting with graying elders and scraping and sanding bows of six-month seasoned chokecherry and willow, good medicine bows to kill the Piegan dogs. The Blackfeet were as numberless as the stars on a moonless night, and the Absaroka were few, and her people survived only by sheer force of will, and much good medicine, and a determination to hold on to this Elk River land, what whites called Yellowstone, that gave them food and skins and health and cool summers and protected winters. Where else could life be better?

She passed the lodges of great warriors, lodges daubed with red or yellow figures showing them counting coup, killing the sacred buffalo. Before them on tripods hung the medicine of the lodge and the trophies of war—Piegan and

Lakotah scalps, dry and black. She knew instinctively where to go, what quarter of this giant village her father's lodge would be in. And at last she found it, and found him, ancient, rheumy-eyed, toothless, and grinning as she swept him up in her arms, an old woman greeting an ancient man.

"Come tell us the news, Many Quill Woman. And meet my new woman, Digs the Roots, who was two times widowed by the Piegan and Assiniboin dogs."

She slipped inside and found brother and sisters, nieces and nephews she barely knew, her father's medicine bundle hanging from a lodgepole, and her father's new woman, much younger, with two fingers cut off in mourning, smiling at her joyously.

"It's good to be home!" she exclaimed. "I will stay here for a few days and let Mary and Kills Dog Woman, the Flathead, take care of my man."

Oh, he had a thirst. It felt worse than the rendezvous the day before Broken Hand Fitzpatrick's pack train arrived. He thought lovingly of the juices corked into the soldered tin cask in his panniers, juices he had saved just for this.

Absaroka was home, and the Kicked-in-the-Bellies his people. Tonight at the feast and the dance he'd gather old gray Buffalo Tail and others of his friends around, and roar like the grizzly. He could jabber passably in Crow, and they could hump along in English some, and what more did they need, except plenty of the amber juice to light the way? Ah, what a thirst! Oh, what a night! He would disappear, go over to the Other Side, as Victoria angrily called it. She'd be too busy with her kin to notice, he thought smugly.

But he had business to attend to first. He hoped to conclude it before evening, before the great feast and dance, before he corralled his warrior friends and slapped backs and hoorawed and bellowed. What a surprise he had for Buffalo Tail, the widower! But it would take some doing, he thought.

It took only an hour or so. First he corralled the headman, Buffalo Tail, and had a smoke. Then they invited in the shaman, Bull's Eye, and smoked again. Then they trotted among the conical lodges until they found the squaw of

Raven Wings, who was one of several Flathead women in the village. Mister Skye still needed to round up Elkanah Morse, but the businessman had disappeared someplace. Probably somewhere where something was being manufactured, he thought. He steered them all toward a gathering of middle-aged men patiently sandstoning wood into trim bows, and there sat Elkanah, studying it all.

"Come along, Mister Morse. You have business to attend," rumbled the guide.

Puzzled, Elkanah followed Mister Skye's party back to the guide's own shabby lodge, where Mary and Kills Dog Woman sat happily, minding Dirk and resoling Mister Skye's moccasins.

At once the Flathead squaw cried out and ran to Kills Dog Woman, babbling in the tongue none of the rest understood. They hugged, and the squaw tenderly examined the healing wounds, turning Kills Dog Woman's face from side to side, running a finger over the new pink flesh on her arms, all the while muttering and wailing. The Flathead woman had nearly healed now, and as the swelling receded her beauty had blossomed. Her eyes shone to discover her friend here among the Crows.

More translating now, thought Mister Skye, but the Flathead squaw of Raven Wings would do.

"Would Kills Dog Woman like to go back to her Flathead village now? She's free to do so."

The answer came in a flood as Kills Dog Woman poured out her story, which finally was repeated in Crow, which Mister Skye could understand.

"What's this all about?" asked Elkanah impatiently.

"Why, mate, she's saying that the Gros Ventre killed her husband when they jumped the Flathead buffler hunters. That was before they caught her and started to torture her to death. She's saying that it'd be fine to go back to her people, but the Absaroka have always been good allies of the Flatheads, and she likes it here, she's happy here. But she says the decision is not hers—she's been bought and is a slave of the whitemen."

"Well, what has that to do with me?" asked Elkanah impatiently.

"You bought her, mate. She's your slave."

"What!"

"You own Kills Dog Woman. That was your bolt of stuff that bought her. Your goods and arrow points. She's all yours, Mister Morse."

Elkanah gaped helplessly. "But that's ridiculous! I was merely trying to keep the poor woman from being brutally tortured to death!"

"Well, you got yourself a slave." Mister Skye could not quite keep the grin off his face.

"But I'm an abolitionist! I give her her freedom right now!"

"Not that simple, Mister Morse."

"What would Betsy say? How did I get into this?"

Mister Skye enjoyed this hugely. All the more because an audience had collected. Professor Danzig watched with a cocked eyebrow. Captain Cobb stood quietly, enjoying himself. Even Percy Connaught observed the affair with stuffy interest. And then, to make it all perfect, he spied Betsy coming, her paper and colors in hand, and waited a moment until she joined them.

The headman, Buffalo Tail, eyed Kills Dog Woman closely. A comely woman, Mister Skye thought. Slim, with liquid brown eyes and heavy cheekbones and a full chunky figure. Tall and strong. Buffalo Tail stared and nodded. Kills Dog Woman, sensing what lay ahead, smiled shyly.

"Ah, Elkanah, and Betsy. Meet my old friend and war companion Buffalo Tail. He's a headman here, leader of the Kit Fox Society, maybe the next chief of the village. Buffalo Tail is a widower. The pox took off his woman a year or so ago. He thinks maybe this Flathead lady of yours would make a fine fat bride for him, warm his nights, make his moccasins."

"Woman of ours?" asked Betsy, puzzled.

"Good God," muttered Elkanah. "Is it that simple?"

"No, quite complex. We've consulted the shaman, had a smoke. And we've come to see the woman. They admire her, of course. Anyone who's been tortured by those dogs the Gros Ventre is a friend of these people. Especially a Flathead."

"Well, fine," said Elkanah, relieved. "I'm pleased. I'll just give her to Buffalo Tail here." He sounded hopeful.

"Well, that'd be an insult, Elkanah. You're putting no value on her. Break her heart. You're saying she's worthless."

"Oh."

"Tell you what, mate. Buffalo Tail here is offering two fine ponies and a rare cream-colored buffer robe for her. Those cream robes are mighty precious, and this one is tanned so soft it's like velvet. A whole robe, too, not a split."

"But what would I do with two more— Mister Skye, I am in your hands. Let me be putty in your hands."

"Now don't be hasty, Elkanah. You must think over the proposition. Shortly, two good ponies and the robe will be placed before your tent. You think on it. If the ponies are a suitable bride price for Kills Dog Woman, then put them out in our bunch and take the good robe into your tent. Buffalo Tail will observe that you have accepted his gifts and come fetch his bride."

"What is this about?" cried Betsy.

"Sounds like a right good proposition, Elkanah," said Rudolpho Danzig. "If two ponies aren't enough, maybe I'll trade my sextant for her."

Elkanah Morse sighed. "I came to find out how to trade," he muttered. "Will I be invited to the wedding?"

"Not exactly, mate. Buffalo Tail will just come and claim her, move her into his lodge."

"That's it? No blessings, no ceremony?"

"Oh, you might hold a feast to celebrate it if you and Betsy are inclined. But that would be more correct if Kills Dog Woman was your daughter rather than your slave."

"She's no slave of mine! You bought her!"

Mister Skye howled gleefully and slapped Morse on the back. "Well, mate, you don't have to trade her off to Buffalo Tail. Maybe you'd like another wife, eh? Why, Betsy just might be delighted to have all her burdens shared."

"Another wife!" Betsy gasped. "Elkanah, how could you?"

"Mister Skye, you are a rascal."

"I think two wives would be a good proposition, El-kanah," said Rudolpho. "It might take a little explaining in Lowell, though."

"I think Betsy would be pleased to share," said Cobb.

"Like those Mormons," added Danzig.

"Why! What? How dare you!" Betsy howled.

The guide's laughter boomed across the happy village. He addressed the Flathead squaw. "Tell your friend Kills Dog Woman that the headman here, Buffalo Tail, is mighty pleased to take her for a wife."

Kills Dog Woman listened, smiled broadly, ran a finger tenderly over her pink wounds, and then suddenly wept softly. She clung to the other Flathead woman, weeping. Then at last she pulled herself free and walked to her new man and solemnly took his hands in her own and pressed them gently to her lips, saying something in her own tongue.

"She says she's proud and pleased to be chosen by the headman, and grateful that the whiteman has given her, and she'll do her best to bring good medicine and good work and love to the lodge of Buffalo Tail."

Love suddenly hung on the air. Elkanah muttered to himself. Connaught raced off to find his journals and pulled out the one intended for the vulgar.

"I must explain all this to Betsy," muttered Elkanah.

"You don't have to explain anything. I don't want to know!" she snapped. "Don't you ever tell me! Sometimes I don't understand men!"

Buffalo Tail wandered off to fetch two fat ponies and a robe. And Mister Skye dug into his panniers for a tin cask. A happy journey, he thought. Almost idyllic, in spite of the bad moments with Tortu. Fine people he was guiding. Yes, a good trip, nothing wrong with any of them, even Connaught. A fine little adventure among the tribes. He found his soldered cask and tipped some gurgling amber juice into a crockery jug.

"Ah!" he exclaimed. "A happy trip."

Chapter 15

To Jarvis Cobb, the Kit Fox Society dance seemed less a dance than a military parade passing in review. It had begun about twilight after a vast feast on a grassy area rather like a village square or plaza near Chief Many Coups' great lodge. The society apparently numbered about fifty warriors, plus those who still stood guard vigilantly out on the periphery.

Captain Cobb's business was intelligence, and he'd spent the afternoon counting lodges. One hundred and sixty, he numbered them, times an average of eight persons to a lodge. The Kicked-in-the-Bellies numbered twelve or thirteen hundred people. A huge village, he thought. Feeding a community so large must be a pressing, constant problem. This feast, this single meal, had consumed ten buffalo, six elk, and uncounted deer, plus a vast array of roots and berries patiently gathered from the abundant Boulder valley. One meal! Cobb grew suddenly aware of the burden on Chief Many Coups, the importance of buffalo to the Crows and all the plains people, the power of the shamans and village site selectors to name each place where the village would stay and to set the times of travel. How long could it last? he wondered. Only as long as the buffalo lasted. Food was everything: cut off food, and the plains tribes would be brought to heel without war.

Carefully he recorded his intelligence in his journal for future military use. On its pages he numbered the lodges and people, named the warrior societies, and wrote in the names of every headman and war chief and shaman he'd learned of so far. Knowledge wins wars, he thought.

Before him, to the quiet throb of drums, the Kit Fox warriors paraded in endless naked array. No intricate dance step here, but every lance, shield, scalp, bow and quiver, and rifle, paraded over and over before the people, as if to tell them something of the power and prowess of this society, of these protecting warriors. Chief Many Coups stood solemnly the whole while, rather like a president or general reviewing troops. Each of these seasoned senior warriors paraded his personal medicine, his shaman-blessed war shields made from the thick hide of a buffalo-bull neck and so strong they could sometimes stop a rifle ball as well as an arrow. They carried befeathered coup sticks proudly, many strung with withered black scalps. Enemy dead, big medicine.

The village watched respectfully: the Kit Fox Society's fame and honor were known to every adult and child. Cobb wondered when it would all end. The warriors had circled fifteen or twenty times now, in continuous parade, and showed no sign of stopping. It seemed a little boring actually. Then at last a change came: one at a time, the warriors began to address the chief, probably telling him of their personal feats at war, Blackfeet and Sioux killed, coups counted, praising their personal medicine, the personal help of badgers and buffalo horns, mountain sheep and pack rats. . . . So religion took a part in it, if medicine could be called that, he thought. The things that whites separated from one another seemed blended together here, war, power, personal prowess, spirit help, God, magic. Captain Cobb wondered how he could describe all that in his journals; how it might help future officers in future Indian wars deal with savage peoples.

Indigo night settled, and still the drums throbbed in the darkness, at the rate of heartbeat, mesmerizing in their intensity. Several small bright fires lit the parade route, casting amber light upon brown faces. Squaws and children sat quietly in their ceremonial best clothing. Affairs of state seemed to be dress occasions, he noted. The women wore softly tanned and fringed doeskin dresses, almost white in the night, with bone and bead necklaces and exquisite calf-high moccasins on firm comely legs.

Close by, the Morses sat quietly enjoying the pageantry, Betsy making small pencil sketches in the dim gold light. Arabella looked pained, and kept glancing at Jarvis. But across the way, near Many Coups, Mister Skye sat cross-legged, methodically lifting a brown jug to his lips, smiling stupidly. That savage oaf of a guide was imbibing spiritous drink, Cobb thought distastefully. Connaught had noticed Skye, too, and was whispering to Danzig about it.

"He's drunk!" whispered Percy Connaught. "Skye's drunk as a lord! What an insult to our hosts. I've never seen anything so disgusting! It'll go into my journals along with a description of this barbaric parade."

"I hope he stays quiet and doesn't insult these people," replied Captain Cobb. "These are his wife's people and there he is, making a spectacle of himself."

"He looks quiet enough to me," rejoined Rudolpho Danzig. "Just a quiet little drunk, eh?"

"Why, he's passing the jug to his Mary, the young one!" exclaimed Percy. "A swine of a man. I knew it all along!"

"These drums are giving me a headache, Captain Cobb," whispered Arabella. "Would you walk with me? I don't think I can stand another minute of them."

"The beat's so steady it's like the human pulse. Have you noticed that when these savages pound those drums faster, our pulses speed up? Fascinating!" said Cobb. That, too, would go into his valuable journal.

He rose and escorted Arabella beyond the vibrant arena and into a vast blackness in which countless lodges loomed conically in the night, each with a forest of sticks thrust into the starlit sky. Something like a thousand villagers had gathered there at the dance, Cobb thought. And now these silent tipis seemed deserted, though many others, infants, the very old, slumbered in them. Slowly the drumming faded as they wound among lodges, and the other sounds, crickets, the ripple of water in the river, the soft flurry of breeze on the ear, restored peace in him.

"Thank you, Jarvis," she said, taking his arm. "I was going mad there. I never want to hear another drum."

He paused, not quite sure where they walked. In a village so vast, on a black night, getting lost seemed all too easy. Still, there was the river, and he knew they followed it generally south, away from Mister Skye's camp at the north end of the village.

He felt Arabella's presence beside him, and found himself struggling again. Not since the moment they'd been surprised by Tortu had they been together like this. Arabella had been so shaken that she had avoided him. He, in turn, cursed himself for his carelessness, for letting temptation overcome his own scruples. But here they were, and he found himself keenly aware of her lush form in the black night, the lithe young figure tightly wrapped in beige gingham, the softness of her lips. . . .

At the south edge of the village they could scarcely hear the drums.

"Oh, Jarvis," she whispered, taking his hand and pressing it in hers. "I had to get away. I'm so lonely. So alone here. You've been such a comfort. Would you hold me gently? I draw such peace from your quiet embrace. . . ."

"I'm married, Arabella," he replied hoarsely. "I can't let what almost happened—"

"Of course not," she said. "But we're friends, and we share something in our souls. We both hate this barbarous life and yearn for the comforts of civilization. Oh, Jarvis, hold me gently or my heart will break!"

She faced him eagerly. He hesitated, feeling the stir of his loins and the race of his pulse. Perhaps for a minute, he thought. They still walked among the lodges, though open meadow lay just ahead. Not a private place at all. A village street, though a midnight-black one. It'd be safe . . . and wouldn't lead to anything. He'd return to his dear family at West Point in honor. . . .

He drew her to him, slid his arms around her crisp dress and under her shawl, drew her tight until her breasts crushed against him and their thighs pressed tightly through layers of cloth and restraint. Her lips lingered on his. His lips found her eyes and cheeks and then pressed hard. He felt her arms and hands tugging him tighter, racing greedily up and down his back. . . .

"Oh!" she cried, and pulled back a moment, uncertain.

A woman's nasal voice erupted softly close by, and they leaped apart, discovered, hearts racing. Their eyes, long free of the mesmerizing fires at the dance, could see clearly now in the starlight. An old crone, bent, wizened, toothless, grinning. One of the ancient ones, probably very poor by the looks of her. She grinned, gummed strange words, hissed in sibilants, and beckoned.

"She wants us to follow," Arabella said tightly, her voice quivering. The toothless grinning woman clawed at Jarvis's sleeve, tugging. They followed her reluctantly between black cones. The old one tittered and giggled, like a girl, and pointed at the door flap of a small sagging lodge.

"She's inviting us to come in," said Arabella. "I guess she wants to entertain us."

They clambered through the low door hole. Within, a tiny twig fire flickered, supplying more light than heat. Black buffalo robes lay thickly, making a bed along the far side. Three dyed parfleches contained the woman's whole possessions, except for a bow and a quilled quiver with a few arrows in it, hanging from a lodgepole. The lodge smelled pleasantly of leather and smoke and sagebrush. A poor lodge, a poor woman, Captain Cobb thought.

"It's so quiet, so . . . private!" exclaimed Arabella. "Why, I can't even hear the drums. I didn't know a skin lodge could keep out the world so well."

"Yes," said Cobb.

The old woman grinned, tittered, pointed cheerily at the mounded robes, and waited. Cobb understood. The Crows loved lovers, loved dalliances, loved assignations. That drunk, Skye, had told him that. Told him that Crow squaws had become famous among the mountain men, famous for their boldness, for their incredibly bawdy jokes . . . and here stood an old toothless crone grinning and waiting.

"What does she want?" asked Arabella.

"I think she wants to leave us here, so we can . . . talk. . . ." said Cobb. "I think she's given us a little bower. I suppose she's expecting a gift."

Gifts he had, a pocketful—a hank of crimson ribbon, a polished tin looking glass or two, some twists of tobacco. He dug in his pockets, found a ribbon and a twist of tobacco, and presented them to the old woman.

"Ah!" she exclaimed, sniffing the tobacco happily. Then, suddenly, she darted out.

Utter silence embraced them. Cobb stared across to Arabella, his pulse hastening. Her lips opened, her eyes shone brightly. She pulled a ribbon out of her glossy brown hair, and it cascaded loose about her shoulders. Artlessly she undid the top button of her gingham, and then the next. He struggled one last time with duty and honor. "I think we should just talk, Arabella. Just share the things of the soul as friends must. We have the future to think of. My . . . family. My career. Your reputation . . . I mean, your future marriage . . . . If we just sit down now, it'd be best."

"I don't care about the future!" she cried. "We'll probably be killed or scalped anyway. I don't want to—to die without knowing about—about . . ."

She rushed to him, pressed her hungry body against his, knowing his thick desire. He pulled her to the mounded robes and began undoing buttons while she kissed and tugged him furiously.

Elkanah Morse spent a ragged night. The throbbing of the drums had a residual effect on him, like some savage narcotic. It had heightened all his senses, made his hearing, vision, smell sharper. But most of all, the lingering throb of them prevented sleep, like black coffee.

Arabella had come in late, just when he had become alarmed about her and was considering going out into the darkened village for help. But he'd been daunted by that prospect. With Mister Skye apparently stupefied by strong spirits, he didn't know where to turn. But she'd arrived at last and slipped into her bedroll.

"Where were you, Arabella?" he asked softly.

"Talking," she replied crossly. "We had lots to talk about."

"We were growing worried."

She didn't reply.

Had the night been still, he might have drifted off then among the chirping crickets. But it wasn't. Periodically, from the vicinity of Mister Skye's lodge, roaring and bellowing shattered the peace. It sounded like a sore-toothed grizzly, but he knew the voice rose from a human throat. Between the roars, he heard cackles and giggles, not to mention the splash of someone making water very close, and other grunting he hoped Betsy didn't recognize.

But she did. "Dear me," she said. It struck her funny. "Dear me!" she said, lacking words. "Oh, my!"

Elkanah Morse laughed, feeling irked at the same time. Back in Boston, that former mountain man Nathaniel Wyeth had warned him that nature held sway in the wilds of the west, that one could only be tolerant of voluptuary excess. That was how he'd gently phrased it: voluptuary excess. One New Englander to another.

Jawbone shrieked and snarled, an unearthly snapping scream Elkanah could scarcely believe erupted from a horse. The creature obviously hated Mister Skye's excesses.

Mister Skye had roared back, shivering the night.

Once, when Mister Skye had bellowed louder than usual, a night-shattering honk that vibrated the earth and stilled the coyotes in the hills, Elkanah sat up with a jerk. He'd step out and still the monster. He clawed open his tent flap and peered out into the starlit tableau. There indeed sat Skye, cross-legged, before his lodge, jug in hand, muttering softly, baying at the North Star. Leaning on him and in worse condition, slumped his younger wife, Mary, who snatched the jug and guzzled and barked like a coyote while he pawed her with his big hands. Nor were they alone. Sitting to the other side of Skye, an Indian Elkanah made out to be Buffalo Tail, teetered like a slowing top. And flat on the ground lay Kills Dog Woman, her skirts scandalously high.

"Oh dear," muttered Betsy beside him. She peered out, too.

"I must do something," whispered Elkanah. "You mustn't look."

But Betsy had fallen into a fit of giggles.

"Be quiet!" snapped Arabella from her black corner.

"Look!" cried Betsy as she peered out the flap. She pointed at two ponies picketed beside their tent. And a mounded something in the grass.

"It's the bride price," muttered Elkanah. "But I think Buffalo Tail has jumped the gun."

Buffalo Tail wobbled to his feet and began to make water.

"Oh dear," muttered Betsy, and ducked back in.

Elkanah peered around sharply, thought he saw Connaught's distraught face peering from the other tent, and then closed the flap. It'd be a night to endure.

But Betsy had other ideas. Silently, in the total blackness, she snuggled tight against him and hugged.

In the haggard dawn he crawled crabbily into the gray light, finding frost on the grass. Mister Skye had vanished along with Mary. In their lodge, he supposed. Buffalo Tail had vanished, too, with or without Kills Dog Woman. The ponies stood patiently. One looked to be a dun, the other a chestnut, both fattened by fall grasses and clean of limb. Before him lay the dew-soaked buffalo robe, amber, almost yellow in color, lighter than any of the buffalo he'd seen. He spread it out, admiring its rare beauty.

He'd had no sleep at all, and felt it. He'd speak to Mister Skye, of course. Tolerance indeed; he could understand the ways of these mountain people. But they might at least have reveled somewhere else, away from camp, away from the eyes of his women. Yes, he'd say that to the guide when he sobered up. It would have scandalized most white women, and maybe did scandalize Betsy, though she'd made light of it. And of course he would prefer that Arabella not see or hear such things. The girl had lived a protected proper life, and while this trip and the sight of naked Indians had surely informed her about certain things, he hoped it wouldn't affect her grace and innocence and the lovely purity he enjoyed in his daughter.

Wearily he tugged on his boots and laced them, and wandered into the misty river bottoms for his ablutions. The others slept, or pretended to. He slapped cold river water on his stubbled face and enjoyed the icy shock of it.

"Wakes a man up, eh?" said Rudolpho Danzig.

The professor had kneeled nearby to wash.

"Can't say as I needed awakening this morning. Up all night," replied Elkanah sourly.

Professor Danzig laughed. "At least we're in a friendly village," he said. "Do you suppose our guide might remain in this condition for some while?"

"Maybe until he runs out of spirits," Elkanah replied. "He can't possibly have a bottomless reservoir of them."

"We could spill them," Danzig replied.

Elkanah sighed, "Let's wait and see. Today I'm going to show my wares, pitch the canvas lodge. These people know English! I can talk with them, Rudolpho. I'm not going to worry about Mister Skye today. But tomorrow, if he's not with us, we'll have to find our way down to Fort Laramie without him. Or find some other guides to escort us. I have no idea just where we are."

"Why, to be exact, we are at forty-five degrees and forty minutes north, provided that I was holding the sextant exactly level when I shot the North Star. At sea, there's always true horizons, but here on land, surrounded by mountains, we have none, so land sextants have a spirit level or some similar device. If I didn't get the bubble right last night in the dark, I could be off a few degrees."

"You're a big help, Professor!"

Danzig grinned. "I always know where we are," he said. "All we need is a sober guide to get us to the next place."

They laughed, and the day seemed better.

The valley lay deep in cold blue haze, but far above, the rising sun blazoned the eastern slopes of the mountains, fired the ridges yellow and white and orange.

"The warmth'll be welcome, Professor," said Elkanah softly. "Frost last night."

"So I've noticed. Elkanah, we should hasten on, I think.

In these latitudes, the weather can turn on us—turn into brutal icy rain, mud, snow. . . . This summer's over. Indeed, my fall term has started; I'm missing classes. Hoped to be back about now . . ."

"You're right. I'll talk to Victoria if I can find her. These lodges all look alike. I'll show my wares today, and tomorrow we'll be off for Fort Laramie and the military caravan home. I'd hoped to visit half a dozen tribes this summer, but we've gotten to three at least, and I'm getting some idea of what can be done and what won't sell. It's less easy than I thought to change the lives of traditional people, Rudolpho. But that's what I came out here to find out about."

Percy Connaught joined them at the misty riverbank.

"Discharge that lout," he said. "Worthless."

"You'll guide us safely home, Percy?"

"Hire these Crows. Or find some other white renegade who's at least sober."

"No . . ." said Elkanah. "Mister Skye pulled me aside at the beginning to offer some words of advice. As I look back on it, it almost seems as if he knew he'd stumble along the way. Trust old Victoria, and young Mary, he said to me. Those women would be better guides than he could ever be. That's what I'm going to do, Percy."

"Put our lives, our safety, into the hands of two savage squaws?"

"That's it, Percy. Two squaws."

Chapter 16

Mister Skye lay stupefied in the shadowed lodge. The bad-medicine smell repelled Victoria as she peered in. Gone to the Other Side again, she thought crossly. He often did that in the village of the Kicked-in-the-Bellies. The People didn't mind. Mister Skye had married into the village, had fought beside its warriors, and had helped them all many times. And when Mister Skye guzzled the spirit waters, they smiled and helped him to his lodge. Actually the spirit juices gentled him. He always roared like a wounded grizzly, but it was only roaring. Still, Victoria hated it when he uncorked his jug. Hated it when Mary joined him. That left her to take care of little Dirk, because Mary slept as stupidly as Mister Skye.

She had to feed Jawbone. The horse hated it, too, and laid his ears back and snarled whenever Mister Skye went to the Other Side. Jawbone turned even more menacing in these periods, and eyed the world murderously from narrow-set yellow eyes. Still, she had to feed him.

"Damn, you gotta eat grass, Jawbone," she muttered, approaching him cautiously, wondering if this would be the time he chose to slaughter her with his vicious hooves or teeth. But he stood evilly while she tied a halter on him and led him to fresh pasture. It would be a long walk because the pasture close to the large village had all been chewed down to dirt. The evil blue roan followed her reluctantly, unhappy about giving up his sentry duties. When Mister Skye drank, Jawbone stood like a soldier over him, letting no one close except Victoria and Mary.

She thought she'd try the hills rather than the Boulder River bottoms and steered Jawbone up a long western slope and into a pine-park area where grass flourished thickly. She'd leave him there unguarded. No one could capture that fierce animal. A rope landing over him was signal enough to him to attempt to butcher any human in sight. Big medicine, she thought fearfully. Bigger medicine in Jawbone than in any horse of any tribe. She left him there, chewing and glaring yellow-eyed down upon the long village below. He'd return soon and resume his duties.

Winded from the long steep climb, she paused. Below, her people's village spread along the river flats, and she could see the women working on robes, sewing, making clothing to ward off the cold. Far to the south and north she made out the horse herds, two of them for a village so large, each guarded by youths as well as the Lumpwood Society warriors now policing. In the northern band, picketed close together, grazed Mister Skye's and Elkanah Morse's horses and mules, including the two fine ponies given to the whiteman by Buffalo Tail, for Kills Dog Woman. A fitting price for the Flathead squaw, she thought. Two fat ponies for the fat woman.

Down below, she spotted Elkanah Morse setting up his displays. He'd borrowed some lodgepoles, and even as she watched, he erected his ready-made canvas lodge. When he got it up and laced, it gleamed whitely, and drew hundreds of villagers to it.

She hurried on down the slope because she'd promised the things-maker she would translate for him, tell him what her people thought of all his big-medicine wares. She liked him. Elkanah Morse seemed to be a good man, not contemptuous of brown-skinned people. He spoke truly, asked questions, respected the sacred ways of her people, and had a good laughing heart, just like his squaw Betsy, who enjoyed people and accepted the differences among them.

"There you are, Victoria! Now we'll begin," he said. She wove through the silent villagers, who stared impassively at pots and skillets, bolts of cloth, blankets, ready-made blanket capotes, assorted awls, saws, knives, axes and hatchets, arrow points, ready-made arrows, and above all, at the canvas lodge. Not a soul among her people said anything or gave the slightest indication of how they felt. That would be impolite. But she sensed something more than politeness here. She sensed fear and worry about all these new ways. She'd have to press them for answers, she knew, because they'd say not the slightest thing critical about the things of these guests.

"I'd like to get some sense of how they feel about these goods—whether they'd trade robes for them at the posts. And so on. Your people are so polite!"

Victoria smiled at him and began questioning her people one by one. Ah, Many Quill Woman, how can we tell? We do not know the medicine of these things! The more she queried, the more evasive they became. Maybe these things are not the Absaroka way. Maybe the medicine men, like Buffalo Bull's Eye, would find evil in them. Maybe they'd be good to have. Maybe they shouldn't tell the whiteman anything, so that he has no power over them. Maybe this man Morse is a bad-medicine man, a witch, and these things are witch things? Who can say? Maybe we'd trade robes for these. Maybe we won't. Witch things are bad medicine. Do his arrows know our bows? Have our bows met his arrows? Who can say, Many Quill Woman! How can one talk about such a lodgecover as that? We see not a medicine picture on it, just cloth. Who would live in cloth, unprotected from witches? Who is this man that Mister Skye brings here? Have you brought us a witch or a demon, Many Quill Woman?

At last, she returned to Elkanah. "Son of a bitch!" she muttered. "I don't get the answers you want. They say maybe yes, maybe no. Maybe good, maybe bad. Maybe they'd trade robes, maybe not. Maybe it's the Way of the People, maybe it ain't.''

"Could you tell me more? Am I violating your religion, Victoria? Do these ready-made arrows violate—is something spiritually wrong?''

She shrugged. "Goddamn. They say their bows don't know these arrows. Ain't never met these arrows. These here arrows ain't met the bows. Bows and arrows got to meet. Feathers and arrowshafts got to meet. Arrow points got to get to know their brothers.''

Elkanah looked baffled. "But these arrows will shoot true—go truer.''

"Naw. Each warrior knows his arrows and arrows know him. He can make his arrows go where he wants. But not yours.''

"Well, what about the canvas lodgecover? Isn't it a convenience, something new and better—especially in the summer? Won't it save them labor? Isn't it lighter, easier to carry, easier to set up?''

"Damn,'' she muttered. "I can't say it right in English. It's no place to live, they say. No spirit helper, not the One Above, to protect it. They think maybe you're a witch.''

"A what?''

"Bad-medicine person, making bad things. They'll go visit the medicine men, find out about you.''

"Good God! I mean them no harm! I wish them no evil!''

"I'll go visit the shaman, tell him whitemen son of a bitches ain't bad medicine. Unless he says so. If he says so, we got to get out of here. No one will want us to stay in the village.''

"I'd like to go with you—would you translate for me? Let me make my case? He'd listen, wouldn't he?''

She squinted at him angrily, unable to make up her mind. Maybe this man she liked was a goddamn witch. That's what the People thought. "Go get a good pony. Get lots of twists of tobacco. I'll take you to Buffalo Bull's Eye. Maybe he accepts your gifts, maybe not. Maybe he tells you to stay, and you're not a witch. Maybe he says you're a witch and you gotta go. It ain't just you. The professor man, he gets inside his black cloth and steals the images of people, bad magic, takes the image of a good Absaroka person. And last night they see him out with a thing, stealing the North Star. He looks in, and aims at the star to take it from us. And your squaw, she makes the images, and the people see she's captured their medicine. Maybe she's a witch, too. Goddamn, if you're witches, I'm staying with my people and you and Mister Skye can get out!''

Elkanah stared at her, speechless. ''Are we in danger?'' he asked quietly.

''Naw. They maybe make you go, and burn all the witch things you got.''

''I'd like to talk with Buffalo Bull's Eye. And also the village headmen. Would you translate?''

''Goddamn,'' she muttered.

He hurried off, pausing long enough to warn Rudolpho Danzig and Betsy of possible trouble. The silent crowd of villagers drifted off, leaving Elkanah's displays naked and forlorn. In a few minutes Elkanah returned, leading one of the ponies he'd received and carrying a handful of tobacco twists. He followed her silently as she threaded through the village, heading not for the small lodge of Buffalo Bull's Eye, but toward the emergency council of village elders and shamans gathering in the grass before Chief Many Coups' great lodge.

She squinted at Elkanah, who looked drawn. Mister Skye gone to the Other Side, too. Maybe Mister Skye could explain to his Absaroka friends about this white witch. Maybe he could make things right. But he got drunk, and he was no damn good now.

Seated in a semicircle in the grass, the elders and sub-chiefs waited, along with two shamans. Victoria stopped at the edge, awaiting an invitation.

''You have business with us, Many Quill Woman?'' asked Many Coups.

''Yes. Elkanah Morse here has brought a gift to Buffalo Bull's Eye, and a twist of tobacco for each of you. He wishes to talk with you and tell us what he is here for, and that he is not a bad-medicine man. Not a witch. That is what he will say.''

The elders sat quietly, not responding, waiting. Then old

Bull's Eye rose slowly, lifted his medicine staff with a rattlesnake head at its crest, shook it in each cardinal direction, and slowly walked to the pony, circled it, and led it to a nearby shaded place. They would listen, let Elkanah Morse address them.

One by one the other whites arrived, looking solemn, and settled themselves in the grass opposite the headmen. Danzig's arrival seemed to evoke some sort of tension among the Crows.

Elkanah stood, eyeing the assemblage amiably. "We are pleased and honored to be guests in your village, gentlemen," he began graciously. He praised the headmen, Victoria, and the Crow people, and admired their way of life and their arts.

Victoria translated easily, except when ideas didn't translate well. Oh, if only Mister Skye hadn't gone to the Other Side! Elkanah began to explain his reasons for making the arduous journey among the far tribes.

"I employ many workers to make things that people find useful," he continued. "We make new things to make life easier, too. Things to make less work. Just as a steel knife makes cutting meat easier than one chipped of stone or shaped from bone, so does a canvas lodge make life easier for your women."

The shaman interrupted, and Victoria translated now for Elkanah. "Why should we want to make life easier for the women? Then they would have nothing to do and feel worthless."

"They would have more time for fun, more time to enjoy their children," replied Elkanah.

"But you steal their worth from them, things-maker. If they have much to do, they are proud and happy and know they are good wives. That is our way. If they have nothing to do, they will get into trouble. It is for women to labor, and men to hunt and war. A woman is valuable and revered among us if she works. Would you have our women become like men?"

Betsy smiled amiably. Arabella looked cross.

Buffalo Bull's Eye stood, raising his arms. "The First Maker, Ah-Badt-dadt-deah, has made our ways!" he cried.

"Where is the First Maker's hand in these cloth lodgecovers? The lodges must be made of the sacred buffalo, our protector and our food. Why do we worship buffalo and dance around the skull of a bull? So that we may have his blessing upon our lodges. Who blesses the cloth lodges of this whiteman—except ghosts from under the earth and demons from the dark waters? Evil spirits profane the cloth lodge!"

The shaman sat down suddenly amid silence. The enunciation of the sacred name of the First Maker required silence and reverence. The lesser spirits, even Sun and Earth Mother and Moon, the Absaroka might joke about, for they were like magic people. But not the One Who Made All Things. Victoria translated quietly, using the whitemen's word, *God*, for the more fearsome one she barely dared pronounce.

Elkanah paused, finding words. "I do not wish to violate the beliefs of the Absaroka people," he began. "No evil spirits from under the earth live in my canvas lodgecover. I made it so that the life of the Absaroka people might be easier, and I might be paid something for the making of it."

A powerful headman, No Scalp, stood in his ceremonial robe of wolfskin. Over his brow rested a desiccated wolf head, the medicine of his spirit helper. "I despise the arrows of the white things-maker," he began in a nasal harangue. "They are not made in the proper way, and the bad spirits in them would turn them around in war so they come back at us. What Absaroka made incantation to the spirits? Who prayed that the arrows would fly true, into our enemies, or into the buffalo, or into other meat? Who set the arrow points next to the shafts so they might get to know each other in harmony? Who told these whiteman arrows what bow would shoot them, what Absaroka warrior or hunter would possess them? These are arrows made by the underwater spirits to weaken and deceive us and make us think we will be safe."

Elkanah nodded. "I suppose these things are not for your people, then. That is what I came to find out. I will pack the things and put them away."

Many Coups himself rose, holding his hooked staff of office. His word, Victoria knew, would decide their fate. He addressed the whites in English. "The man Danzig, with the black hair flowing from his face. Some among us say he is a bad-medicine man, a white witch. At night he goes about with a strange weapon and steals the star of the north from the Absaroka. And when Sun comes to visit, he makes images of the People with another strange thing, secretly under a black robe where we cannot know what medicine he practices. He steals images from us and takes them to the demons under the earth. So it is said among us. No man can make images as perfect as these, so they must be made by demons. The evil ones then can possess my people and bring evil upon them, and upon the village."

Rudolpho arose thoughtfully. "Chief Many Coups, no harm is intended, and if you could see inside me where my spirit is, you would know I am a friend. The thing you refer to is called by whites a sextant, and it is a little like a spyglass. With it I can tell how far south or north we are. The farther north we are, the higher in the night sky is the North Star."

"We know where we are! Why should it be a mystery to whites?" asked Many Coups impatiently. "We are at the center of the world. To the south it is very hot. To the north it is very cold. But First Maker brought the People here because here it is perfect."

"Ah but—my good chief—you see, we whites believe the world is round like a globe, like a perfect ball, and right here we live very far to the north—"

"A ball? We would all fall off of a ball, and the sides would be too steep!" cried the chief.

Professor Danzig retreated. "The other device that makes images was invented across the sea by a Frenchman, the kin of the French trappers who often visit your people. It does not steal images, and no demon or bad medicine is in it. It works with metals and chemicals—elements of nature, not evil spirits."

"We believe no man, white or of the People, could make images so perfect," Many Coups retorted. "You are hiding from us the demon people under the black robe who do these things.''

"No demon people are . . ." Professor Danzig paused, helplessly. "I tell you what. I will give the images to you, so each of your people will get his image back and no evil spirit can take it away. Would you and your people like that?"

Many Coups consulted with his elders and headmen for a while. "We will take the images the bad-medicine people have made," he said.

Danzig had the plates with him and handed them to the chief, who gave them to the shaman.

"Now my council will talk about these things among ourselves. You will go to your camp and wait, and do not leave it or wander in our village." He turned to Victoria. "Many Quill Woman, we will let you know, too. You have translated well."

She followed the whites back to the camp, her heart heavy; her own people shunned her because she might be in the company of a witch. She ached inside, and felt ripped apart. At camp, the whites vanished silently into their tents. She peered into her own lodge, where Mister Skye lay muttering, and the sour smell of his spirit juices smacked her. She elected to sit outside with Mary and Dirk and to tell Mary about all the terrible things that were happening.

Her people deliberated slowly, and she knew it would be a long time before a message came. But at dusk one did come, and it was delivered by Many Coups himself, flanked by two shamans. She knew by the set of his face that things were bad.

"We find that this man with the black beard, Danzig, is a bad-medicine person. We are divided about this man Morse, the things-maker. Some say he is not a bad-medicine person. Others say he is. I cannot make up my mind."

Witches, Victoria thought. Mister Skye is guiding bad-medicine men of the whites.

"The council says that the whites must leave the village at once. We cannot permit witches to stay in our village and harm the People. Evil would come to us in the night. The spirits would rise out of the earth and sicken us with pox or make us starve. We must honor our way and cleanse ourselves. After you leave we will burn everything of the whites, and purify ourselves in the way, and make offerings to the First Maker and the others who protect us.''

''At once?'' asked Victoria.

''At once. Before the darkness. If you do not go, the Lumpwood soldiers will kill them. We have spoken now. Be careful, Many Quill Woman; you are among witches. Come back with Mister Skye when you are not among witches.''

The chief wheeled off into the quiet village. Not a soul stirred in it; each villager knew that bad-medicine whites would send demons upon them unless they stayed within the safe circles of their lodges.

''We must go,'' Victoria said sharply. ''If we stay, you will be killed. When the dark comes, we must be away or you die!''

Elkanah stared at her. ''We are not bad-medicine people, Victoria,'' he said firmly.

''The medicine men say one here is,'' she spat. ''They have all-knowing. They know!''

Elkanah chose not to argue. ''Let's get packed and off,'' he said quietly. The whites had already loaded their panniers, and the Lumpwood Society police had already brought their horses and mules. In a few moments they could leave. Jawbone snarled, ears back, as she lowered her lodgecover and loaded the travois.

I will have to lift Mister Skye upon him, Victoria thought, despairing. She wanted to weep.

''Son of a bitch!'' she cried. ''Hurry up! We go now!''

Chapter 17

Mister Skye defied the laws of gravity. Rudolpho Danzig had never seen the laws of gravity suspended before, and observed the matter with scientific curiosity. From his vantage point on the back of a pony a few yards behind Mister Skye, the professor maintained a constant vigil, awaiting the moment when gravity, king of all natural forces, would reassert its dominion. Danzig had heard of only one previous case, in which the Subject had walked on water. But there the similarity ended. Mister Skye belonged at the opposite end of the spectrum from the Other One, and seemed inclined to sink like a stone to nether regions rather than float or defy nature's law.

But the professor's own eyes recorded the fact that Mister Skye tilted considerably further than the Leaning Tower of Pisa, first to port, and then with a shudder and desperate convulsion, to starboard. His degree of declination fell clearly into the impossible.

"I will bet you two bits, payable in Lowell, that the silk hat falls to earth in the next five minutes," said Elkanah, riding beside Rudolpho.

Indeed, it seemed likely. Mister Skye rode heavily starboard, and the black stovepipe jammed rakishly over his cranium leaned even further starboard, virtually horizontal, and seemed to cling to the guide's skull only by force of habit.

"Done!" said Professor Danzig. He was witnessing one miracle; why not two?

"I believe Jawbone is unhappy," observed Elkanah Morse. It had to be the understatement of the day. Jawbone loathed every moment of the journey, and minced with his ears flattened back and a snarl frozen on his lips, staring viciously at the topsy-turvy world through yellow eyes.

Mister Skye reached the apogee of his starboard journey and convulsed himself back to equilibrium, muttering and clutching his brown jug. A moment later he began sliding to port side, and Jawbone clacked his teeth.

"I think you lost, Elkanah," said Professor Danzig.

"Five minutes aren't up yet," the entrepreneur replied, consulting his silver-cased turnip watch, a gift from Betsy.

They rode quietly through an icy morning. Victoria had led them out of her village the previous twilight and pushed on into the dark, seeming to know where they would go. North of the village, she suddenly cut east, riding out of the Boulder River valley and into rough foothills for several miles until her mysterious trail led down into another drainage, a cottonwood-lined creek. There they camped, eating a late supper from their few stores in the panniers.

Victoria had turned sullen and wouldn't even speak to Professor Danzig, whom she firmly believed was a bad-medicine man, a witch. When they awoke this frosty morning, she continued to ignore him and wouldn't even come close to him. Apparently she thought he was the author of all their troubles. Her village medicine man had told her so.

She rode a hundred yards ahead, as if to dissociate herself from these evil whites, a lithe angry ancient woman resting lightly on her rawboned bay pony. She steered them due east, too, by Danzig's magnetic compass, taking them across drainages, up and down vast swales and ridges, rather than following the easier route of the level Yellowstone valley. It puzzled Danzig a little. To the south loomed vaulting mountains that looked to be the roof of the world. From the ridges he could see the Yellowstone valley way to the north and angling northeast. And between them, the country had convulsed into giant shoulders of the mountains, half-forested, half-prairie, rocky and cut by rushing clear creeks. Not a good place to take a caravan, he thought, but she seemed to follow a fairly easy Indian and game—probably buffalo—trail. Ahead, Mister Skye's travois-laden ponies and mules negotiated the rugged country with no difficulty beyond an occasional jarring bounce of the travois. But Mary rode ahead, keeping an eye on all that, and on little Dirk, sitting on a travois as well. Unlike Victoria, Mary revealed not the slightest hostility.

"How does it feel to be a witch?" asked Elkanah, whose mind must have run in the same direction as Rudolpho's.

"About the same as feeling Swiss," he replied. "About the same as feeling married."

"It's not a good thing. Is there any way you can reach her? Change her mind? Stop this superstition? I dread to see our little party divided."

"I will ask to speak with her at this evening's camp. I'd like her to look through the sextant and see what I'm doing."

Mister Skye slid almost horizontal and then righted himself heavily, like a half-flooded ship wallowing in heavy seas.

"You owe me two bits," said Rudolpho triumphantly. "Once a man defies natural law, there's no stopping him."

The horses straggled up a long grade. Sandstone, Danzig thought. So convulsed by the upthrust mountains that the strata stood on end. Wind-eroded, too, hollowed and curved into fantastic shapes by the abrasion of sand upon sand. Indeed, a violent cold gust whipped at his back, lifting dust and debris from the slope.

"Cold, isn't it?" said Elkanah. "I asked Mrs. Skye to take us to Fort Laramie directly. I fear time's run out. I'd hoped to get to two or three more villages—Sioux, Arapaho, Northern Cheyenne—but that's out. We'll be lucky to scrape by in pleasant fall weather."

"Those army ambulances from Fort Laramie to Leavenworth may not exactly be comfortable either in October and November," Danzig observed.

He felt the pony bunch its muscles under him and plunge over a sandstone step in the trail. He'd come to an understanding with this line-backed coyote dun—that's what Mister Skye had called the beast—long before, soon after they'd left Fort Benton. His diplomatic protocol with the beast required that he sit quietly and let the horse make all the decisions in true monarchial fashion. It had been hard for the republican Mister Danzig to swallow, but in time the dun showed the wisdom of it. The little malformed lowrumped mustang picked gentle grades, carried him uncomplainingly, and seemed to survive on snatched mouthfuls of bunch grass and weeds. Its unshod hooves were remarkably hard, and never wore out, even in such rock as they now traversed.

Professor Danzig's head had found the protocol with his mustang agreeable, but his tailbone didn't. The Harvard geologist had rarely been on a saddle horse for more than an hour or two in all his life. But here he lived atop this animated conveyance, and he'd discovered new ways to experience pain. He believed his hammered behind would no longer rest comfortably upon cushioned Harvard chairs or even outhouse seats and he would have to install saddlelike chairs in his home for future comfort. Still, he rode easier now than when he started the voyage. The mustang had become affectionate, too.

Behind him rode Betsy and Arabella in their sidesaddles, their pleated long riding skirts tucked neatly about their legs. Professor Danzig had always marveled at Betsy, but never more so than here in a vast empty wilderness. Her natural buoyancy turned all hardship and discomfort into adventure, and her ready laugh and affection turned each camp into a happy picnic. Even dour Arabella had relaxed her tart hostility, and seemed softer and more a woman, he thought.

Behind the lovely ladies rode Percy Connaught, always complaining of discomforts or exclaiming about the entries in his priceless journals, and last, Captain Cobb, who tended the pack animals and seemed competent in his phlegmatic and deliberate way. Elkanah had asked the pair of them to handle the pack animals and supplies, but only Cobb did, patiently saddling and unsaddling each animal each day, making sure the loads in the panniers were even, taking the horses to water and pasture, and all the while being useful. Connaught had not helped. He alone was the slacker among them, forever finding his morocco-bound journals more important than the camp chores. So they'd all waited on him because there was no help for it. Saddling his horse mornings, unsaddling and picketing it at night. Danzig had done much of that. Good training for a geologist in North America, he thought privately.

That evening Victoria sullenly halted them beside a twisting creek, barely running in this dry season, that had cut a deep narrow canyon in its rush to the Yellowstone.

"Has this creek a name?" Danzig asked politely. Victoria glared, and turned away silently. Through the whole journey he'd sketched maps, inserted creeks, given peaks and rivers whatever white trapper and Indian names he could commandeer from Mister Skye or his wives. But now his principal source had become unavailable. Indeed, incoherent. Danzig watched Victoria and Mary ease the inert muttering guide off a twitching and biting Jawbone. They couldn't quite support him, and he landed in a heap, trembling the earth, gazing stupidly from his obscure blue eyes at his new universe before vanishing into his own world again.

"Goddamn," Victoria muttered fiercely.

She avoided Danzig through all the camp chores, but at last he cornered her before their shabby lodge.

"Victoria," he said softly. "May I say something?"

She wheeled, glaring, frozen, waiting.

"For me to be a bad-medicine man, a witch, I'd have the wish in my heart to do evil to you and your people and others. I have no such wish. You call God the First Maker. I hope the First Maker blesses you and brings you goodness."

She glared, muttering, and returned to her butchering. Sometime during the day she'd put an arrow through a doe, though no white in camp knew just when, and now she and Mary peeled the hide off of it.

He tried again. "Tonight come look at the North Star with me through my sextant. I will show you that I only look. I am not stealing your star or making bad medicine. I can use it to look at the sun, too, when it is highest at noon, and tell you how far north or south we are."

She glared, muttering. "Maybe I'll think about it," she snarled. "Maybe you a witch and make Mister Skye stay on the Other Side. He never stay over there this long before."

"We could take away his whiskey," he said.

"No. I don't take away nothing. He got to make up his own mind. You take away his whiskey and I get mad."

He left it at that, detecting some softening in her that might turn into something better soon. He wanted to poke around the stratified sandstone here before dusk anyway.

Two things happened at the equinox. It rained, and Mister Skye sobered. Jarvis Cobb surmised that the former caused the latter. They awoke to leaden gray overcast the first day of fall, and a temperature barely above freezing. Indeed, the water in the camp buckets had iced over, a clear solid skim reminding them to hurry to safety.

For days, old Victoria had steered them east by southeast, following the humped prairie foothills of the Absaroka mountains. Grand country, Jarvis thought, but hard to travel compared with the flat belly of the Yellowstone angling to the north. They'd pierced through a vast silence, made all the more profound by Victoria's dour hostility to them all. They'd seen not a soul, not even another Crow band. It seemed almost as if the whole Crow nation knew a bad-medicine party pierced through its lands and had steered far away.

They'd splashed across a laughing clear river horse-belly deep, beneath towering blue peaks, that Danzig identified as the Stillwater. Then another, less formidable one he called Clark's Fork of the Yellowstone, boulder-strewn and murkier than the first. Lewis and Clark's careful journals had become Danzig's basic source because Mister Skye remained lost in his own world. Elkanah bet Danzig that Mister Skye would fall off Jawbone and into Clark's Fork. It looked as if it might happen. The angry blue roan splashed viciously across the slippery rock-strewn bottom, as if weary of the leaning stupefied load he carried. At one point Mister Skye defied gravity again, righting himself at the last moment, but not before Jawbone splashed him thoroughly by pawing icy river water. Danzig won another two bits. Percy recorded the bet in his fattening journal for the vulgar.

The Crow woman swung through a wide dry gap in the mountains. Pryor's Gap, Danzig called it, after consulting Lewis and Clark again. At once Captain Cobb could see its strategic importance. They'd come to the eastern end of a vast range of mountains that blocked southward passage. But off to the east rose the featureless Pryors, and beyond, the Big Horns. A strategic gap, he thought; a gap that funneled villages, armies, and horse-stealing expeditions. The country grew sandy and arid, with thick bursts of silvery sagebrush and sharply eroded dry watercourses. All the beauty and grandeur of the Yellowstone country vanished, and a new dark mood lay upon this lunar land: loneliness. This huge empty basin seemed somehow inexpressibly lonely. The Big Horn basin, Danzig called it. A natural home of wild horses. The explorers' journals recorded that the Pryor Mountains—which they named after a sergeant on that expedition—were full of them.

They'd dined the last evening of summer on an antelope Victoria had shot. The white-rumped pronghorns seemed abundant here, and were gathering now into vast winter bands. Prairie-goat meat seemed tough and gamy, and didn't please him. But it filled his belly. In these frosty days it kept well, so they tied unused haunches on their packs against the time when Victoria might not be able to down an animal. Rudolpho pulled out his sextant as night thickened, and shot the North Star again in a sky growing cloudy.

"Just south of forty-five degrees north," he said. "Let's call it forty-four degrees, fifty minutes."

Jarvis Cobb recorded that in his tersely written journal, along with other military considerations. White haze ringed the full moon, and Captain Cobb recorded that, too. Also that their lout of a guide, Mister Skye, had now completed his eleventh day of inebriation. Victoria no longer eased him off Jawbone; she yanked him hard and let him crash to earth. Always his first act upon smacking into dirt was to stumble to his feet and make water, which invariably caused Betsy and Arabella to hasten elsewhere.

"Have you no decency!" Connaught bellowed.

Bitter wind flapped at their tents that night and eddied into them. This expedition had not outfitted itself for winter, and their shelters and bedrolls seemed barely adequate as the days shortened and the night frosts clung to the bunch grass far into the days.

Icy horizontal rain whipped them just as Betsy got her portable tin stove fired with sagebrush stalks for breakfast. Each drop hissed as it hit the hot stove. Eventually the rain drummed so violently that it cooled the metal surfaces in clouds of steam, and she could cook nothing. In any case, she got soaked in icy water while the rest huddled in their tents. Cold breakfast, then. Or no breakfast. They crawled inside their chattering tents to wait.

Captain Cobb, the army man, knew it would only be a matter of time before water oozed into their dank, gloomy, crowded quarters. Neither of Elkanah's tents had been set up on high ground or ditched to carry off water. The prairie clays under them would turn to grease and soak bedding. And everywhere a hand or finger touched canvas above them, it perspired, coating the inner walls and ceiling with collected water.

From out in that icy drizzle, Victoria bellowed at them. "Pack up now! We got to git!"

Captain Cobb stuck his head out the flap, into the stinging wind-borne spray. She stood before him, small, soaked, and glaring. Astonishingly, Mister Skye's lodge had been neatly folded and anchored to its travois, and its poles hung in two bunches from the second horse. Mister Skye sat upon Jawbone, rain dripping from the brim of his silk hat, the shoulders of his buckskins black with water. He looked almost sober. Mary sat her pony impassively, cuddling little Dirk before her, bundled tightly in some sort of capote.

"Surely you're not traveling on a day like this!"

"It gets cold soon. And you ain't got anything for cold. We got to get you to Fort Laramie fast."

"Well, we're not going," replied Cobb. "We'd take pneumonia in this."

"You got those slickers. You each got the slickers."

True enough, he thought. Elkanah had provided each of them with a bad-weather coat of canvas impregnated with India rubber. That was another of his strokes of genius. Ever since his friend over in New Haven, Charles Goodyear, had learned to vulcanize rubber by adding sulfur and heating it, Elkanah had experimented with rubberized fabrics. When Howe invented the sewing machine, Elkanah had plunged into ready-made storm gear.

From the other tent, Elkanah peered around, observing Mister Skye sitting silently and possibly soberly on Jawbone. The guide said nothing—not yet ready to speak—but stared back with knowing in his eyes at last.

"I think we'd better be off, gentlemen," Elkanah said quietly.

"But that's madness!" cried Percy. "We'll all be soaked and take the fever. My journals will be ruined!"

Mister Skye said, "Have you looked around the walls of your tent, Mister Connaught? Do you wish to sleep in muck tonight? Perhaps we'll find a better place down the trail a bit. Do you see any firewood here to dry out with? Only sagebrush, sir."

They stared, astonished, at the guide.

In fifteen minutes they packed and broke camp, settling themselves gingerly on cold wet saddles. The whites, in fact, had more protection from the driving rain than Mister Skye's family, who sat stolidly absorbing the drizzle in their water-black skin clothing.

They struck southeast under a leaden sky, through a day without light, across a landscape without feature. Arabella turned sullen and vicious, snapping at her mother. Percy muttered complaints and imprecations. But off they went into a gray gloom, as hungry as when they rose.

By noon the clay beneath them turned to gumbo, treacherous and slick. Horses skidded, and not even the utility of four legs kept them from sliding and careening. Water trickled down Captain Cobb's neck, slicing vicious streaks of cold down his back and chest. Travois poles skidded silkily behind the guide's horses, cutting clean furrows in the liquid clay. And still they rode across a land that seemed almost desert. The only happy creature in the whole caravan was Jawbone, whose ears perked forward and whose step had become bold again, now that he carried a man on his back rather than a drunk.

Connaught's complaints turned into hate.

"If you hadn't gotten drunk, we wouldn't be in this mess your squaw got us into, Skye!" he cried.

"Mister Skye, mate."

"Drunks don't deserve to be called mister. Why don't you and your stupid women find us shelter and warmth? Where are caves? Overhangs? You'll kill us with the ague, the chills. Have you no thought for the Morse women?"

"Hard to find those things in this basin."

"Well, find them! And we'll wait for sunshine there."

"Might not be sunshine for days. And we're a long way from Fort Laramie." Mister Skye spoke with a peculiar gentleness that seemed to rise from some remorse and sorrow. Cobb noted it, and found himself oddly sympathetic even to a man who had been falling-down drunk for eleven days.

"Percy," said Elkanah, "let's endure. Let's get along. Let's see what the day brings. We're not suffering terribly in these slickers. Not as much as Mister Skye and his brave women."

But the rain kept driving, mixed with sleet, and they found no place to hide. They crossed a swollen muddy river Mister Skye called the Greybull, and made a miserable wet cold camp in a grove on its south bank. That night they were all sullen and quiet.

Chapter 18

All the next grim day he led them southeast under a sullen sky that blotted all landmarks and emptied icy water in gusts and bursts the whole hard trip. He knew where he was going by instinct. Four times horses skidded to their knees, usually when clawing up the slick gumbo of a grassless draw. In places hock-deep muck mired the horses, clotting on hooves and pasterns and exhausting them. They splashed so much muck on their legs and bellies, and on their riders and packs, that not even drenching rain washed it off. It caked heavy on the beasts, adding to their burdens.

Late in the day, when the dull light imperceptibly melded with twilight, he struck the valley of the Big Horn. Just then orange sunlight pried at the world from under the belly of the storm, turning it purple and gold, and blazoning a vivid emerald smear of valley set between ocher bluffs. The light lasted all of thirty seconds, and then vanished like a vision, or a visitation of angels, spurring strange yearnings in him for the sight of England.

A bruised dark cloud spat ice at them as they skidded

downward, horses mincing and going rigid under them, into the bottoms.

"We'll camp down here tonight," he said to the sullen people beside him.

"I hope there's dry firewood," snapped Percy.

"We'll show you how to find it," Mister Skye replied. He had started to hunt for the right sort of place, preferably sandy and a bit up from the bottoms; protected from the gusty winds, and with a thick cottonwood forest nearby, plenty of brush. He would have preferred a good overhang, but little rock lay exposed in these gentle water-cut bluffs.

He swung south, up the Big Horn, riding under the west bluff through a bottom partitioned into parks and dense thickets. They scared up mule deer. Partridge exploded from brush, spraying rain. They crashed through thickets of fall-yellowed foliage that drenched them as they passed.

He chose a place on a gravelly delta beneath the bluff, a place that had shed the water. Thickset majestic cottonwoods loomed darkly in every direction save for the bluff on the west, and masses of brush burgeoned up in the gloom. He preferred camps with sweeping vistas, but this cloistered one would do on a drizzling and bitter night.

He'd gone numb long ago. The ice water had purged the last of the alcohol from his body and forced his mind out of its long haze. He felt subdued, stung by nature and guilt, quiet and humbled, in need of forgiveness.

They all dismounted, mud-caked and hard-eyed, surveying this brush-walled place in obscure light. Victoria and Mary erected the lodge. The two wall tents rose. He'd chosen well. They'd sleep dry and warm tonight and wouldn't even need to trench around the tents because the rain vanished into the gravel. Wordlessly, Victoria slipped into the gloom of the forest with her hatchet and reappeared later with semidry wood. A lot of the small sticks looked entirely dry, ripped from some obscure corners. Other wood seemed moist-black on top, but gray-bottomed. Elkanah and Rudolpho examined her load with interest and plunged into the gloom to duplicate it.

Percy dove into the erected wall tent and refused to budge, leaving the camp and horse chores to Captain Cobb once again. Elkanah rigged a fly sheet he'd rarely used this trip in front of his tent, giving protection from the drizzle. It chattered in the wet gusts. Betsy could cook comfortably under it, using her little folding camp stove. But this night none of them would be as comfortable as the Skye family in its skin lodge with the smoke vent and wind flaps above, to draw off the smoke from a small hot fire in the very center of the lodge, a fire to cook on and radiate heat into a cone of comfort.

Well, thought Mister Skye, they had slickers all day; my Victoria and my Mary and my Dirk have a warm dry night ahead. The smoke-cured lodgeskins turned even a driving rain and captured warmth within. The smoke of Victoria's fire lifted lazily into the rain and then sank to earth, oddly perfuming the little park. Betsy's stove pumped smoke up its tiny chimney, too, and Elkanah's party crowded close to it, heat-starved, under the canvas fly.

The guide sighed. They'd not collected wood enough for a night like this, and gloom lowered into gray now. He braved the stinging rain some more, and checked the horses, too. He found them in a neighboring park, greedily chewing grass at the end of their pickets. All except Jawbone, who ranged freely and would return to the lodge shortly. They seemed safe enough here, though invisible from the camp. It wouldn't be a night for horse thievery. He snapped squaw wood from trees and carted it to the Morse camp. Three armloads. Then another for his lodge.

"Is that enough?" asked Rudolpho. "I'll help you. And watch how you select dry wood."

"Glad for your help, mate," the guide rumbled, and together they examined wood, finding it dry on sheltered sides, finding sticks caught in brush that seemed barely moist.

"This is the Big Horn. And upstream a way it becomes the Wind River on my charts. How do you explain that?"

"Cuts through a red and purple granite mountain, Mister Danzig."

"But it's still the same river!"

"No . . . not really. On the other side of the mountain it's another river, headwaters in the Wind Rivers, pulsing out onto the Great Plains, or anyway an arm of the plains. When it hits the canyon, it starts running uphill.''

Danzig laughed. "You mountain men,'' he said.

"Tremendous hot springs this side of the canyon. We'll go there for a little holiday. You might even feel warm again. We could make it in less than two days.''

"Connaught claims his writing fingers are frozen stiff.''

Mister Skye didn't laugh.

In his lodge he pulled off his clammy soaked fringed shirt of elkskin and let the tiny hot blaze warm his naked flesh. His wives had anchored down the lodgeskirts with rock to keep chill gusts from sliding into this haven. Soon, when it became colder, they'd tie up the inner lining and anchor it with rock, giving them double-walled comfort that made lodges livable even in bitter cold. Victoria looked up at him from her cooking pot and the sliced antelope and bread root she was dropping into it, and suddenly crawled over and hugged him.

"Goddamn!'' she exclaimed angrily, squeezing him. It was her signal that she'd forgiven him, and more. Her way of telling him she loved him. Mary smiled, too, loving without words.

He sat peacefully in his small home, cleaning caked wet powder out of the cylinder of his dragoon Colt and setting the soaked powder to drying safely back from the spitting fire. On occasion a gust of cold wind rattled the lodge and sent a few drops whirling down the smoke vent, but it didn't matter. This rain seemed relentless but not vicious. He half expected to see a sheen of snow in the morning, though. He poured fresh Du Pont into six bores of his cylinder and rammed balls home, and pressed fresh caps over the cleaned-out nipples. The old caps had vanished during its long neglect. That done, he set to work on the soaked Hawken, gouging gummy wet powder out of it, cleaning the chamber and nipple, and replacing powder, wad, ball, and cap.

He'd order some of Elkanah's slickers for his women, he thought. Maybe even buy Elkanah's if he'd sell them to him at Fort Laramie. Mostly, Indian ways worked better here—he glanced at his comfortable lodge and thought about the cold wall tents of Elkanah's—but those slickers had value and might save his family from a death of a cold or ague or lung congestion.

Almost over, he thought. Maybe two weeks of autumnal travel to Laramie if they could make thirty or so miles a day. He'd give these half-frozen mud-caked pilgrims a little comfort where the hot mineral waters boiled over white-limed rock and into the Big Horn. That'd lift their spirits. All in all, it had been an easy trip, without calamity, and Morse had found out what he came for. Morse's party still faced seven hundred miles of prairie travel with an army supply and mail train east, but they'd have excellent covered wagons to ride in.

Even stripped to his breechclout, he felt perfectly comfortable in the warm lodge. His leggins and shirt steamed in the radiant heat. Little Dirk was in a jolly mood, freed of the cradlebasket that trapped him on Mary's pony, and Mister Skye horsed with the tyke in the glow of the lodge. Everything inside seemed golden and tan and brown tonight: the dark inviting buffalo robes, the tawny lodgeskins, the rosy brown faces of his women, the amber smoke of the fire coiling out upon a lowering blackness. He felt happy to have the rot out of his blood and to be here, now, at peace. His soaked silk hat lay to one side, and he'd tied a red bandanna around his head to keep his long graying hair out of his face.

The Skyes entertained visitors that night after supper. All except Percy Connaught, who scribbled in his tent by the light of Elkanah's lantern.

"Back in Boston, Nat Wyeth told me these skin lodges are marvels," said Elkanah. "I was slow to believe him . . . but I'm learning."

The entrepreneur's grin, along with his endless capacity to adjust his thinking to new insights, delighted Mister Skye. Betsy and Arabella sat to either side of Elkanah, at first a bit put off by Mister Skye's furry near-nakedness, but warming to him and to the fire and the radiant cheer of this little home.

"Well, mate, what have you learned this trip? What'll ye be manufacturing for us?" asked the guide amiably.

"I've learned to trust the trading companies—for the most part," Elkanah said. "They seem to know what the tribes will buy and what cuts against the grain of their lives. Like those ready-made arrows of mine.''

"I think you'd find a market for your slickers," Mister Skye said. "Handy things. I don't fathom any medicine problems with them."

"I'll remember that," Elkanah said.

Beside Betsy sat Rudolpho Danzig, quietly avoiding talk and glancing from time to time at Victoria.

"You, Danzig. Dammit. How does your star shooter work?" she asked suddenly, in a stutter of the conversation.

"Why, I'll show it—"

"Nah, I seen it. Don't go out. You couldn't look at the star tonight. We know where we are, but you don't know where you are!" she said triumphantly. "Inside my head is better than them charts you draw."

He laughed easily. Victoria had forgiven him, too. Or declared him a nonwitch just by talking with him.

They didn't stay long. The visit had been a reconciliation more than anything. Shared comforts, shared anecdotes about a brutal day, and a renewal. Drowsily Mister Skye saw them off, his gaze following them to their dark chill canvas tents. For all of white men's genius and innovation, they didn't know how to live out here, he thought. Didn't know how to live Injun.

That blustery night two wives snuggled up tight beside him, and he enjoyed them both, slipping at last into an amiable dreamless sleep.

Jawbone's screeching awakened him. He knew that wild screech, and his heart labored from rest to violent banging, not catching up with his need for blood. He yanked his robes aside and clutched his Hawken, easing out the door flap. A dull streak of light shone through black cottonwoods to the east. That was the last he saw. Something cracked his head from above, and he sagged into the wetness.

Mary bolted up in the robes. Victoria slid up in the blackness. Outside, a shot, a thud, a male yell, a woman's scream. Another shot. Naked, Mary crept toward the lodge door, stumbling over her man's prone form, half in, half out, blocking the way.

"Son of a bitch," muttered Victoria, her old fusil in hand. She peered out, into murk. Mary did, too, seeing the shadowy forms of warriors. One leaned over Mister Skye, just a few feet away, a scalping knife catching the gray of dawn. Victoria fired, flint on frizzen. Spark and sizzle. She'd failed to clean out the soaked powder.

Mary grabbed Mister Skye's legs and tugged violently, yanking her man's entire body back into the lodge just as the warrior grabbed a handful of Mister Skye's long graying hair. She yanked so violently the warrior tumbled in with Skye, muttering Shoshone words Mary understood.

Victoria clubbed the warrior with her fusil.

Dirk squalled in his robes. Mary lifted the big chunky boy, slid him into the lined cradlebasket she used now.

Then the entire lodge ripped away from earth, yanked by some giant force, leaving them naked in dawnlight. The old lodge crumpled in a heap. Around them crouched more warriors—nearly naked even in this bitter air—than Mary could count, ready to kill, lances and war clubs poised, trade iron tomahawks in hand. No bows. Rain had softened the sinew bowstrings.

Wildly she peered out. Both the wall tents had vanished, ripped from their pegs and thrown aside. One dark form— Cobb's, she thought—lay inert. Danzig sat quietly. Percy Connaught in white linens whimpered, choked, pleading for mercy in a strange whine. Where the other tent had been, Arabella cowered in her bedroll. Betsy sat up in her petticoats, a blanket drawn tight about her. And Elkanah in a nightshirt struggled to his feet, his face wild, his receding hair prickling in all directions.

All this Mary absorbed in a glance. Jawbone screeched, wheeled through camp, tumbling these raiders, kicking murderously at one and another, biting viciously. They turned to lance him, missing because of his demonic speed and violence. A flaying hoof caught a warrior, crushing his thigh into bloody pulp. He fell, writhing, screaming words Mary understood: "demon horse . . . medicine horse . . . I am gone. . . ."

She crabbed around her possessions, found her own fusil, probably wet, too, and brought it up, but a cold hand clamped her, ripping away the rifle. "I'll take that, squaw," said a voice in a tongue she understood. Shoshone? Would her people, ancient friends of the longknives, friends of Mister Skye, do this?

"Stop!" she cried in her Snake tongue. "This is Mister Skye! I am Mister Skye's woman! This is the medicine horse Jawbone. Do this and you die!"

Jawbone screeched and plunged, berserk and murderous. A lance caught his flank, drawing a thin sheet of blood, and he bulled into its thrower, toppling him. Mary screamed. Victoria crawled to Mister Skye, who stirred woozily.

Elkanah Morse managed to stand, but a warrior smashed him to earth with one brutal blow. Betsy screamed.

"Don't hurt me, I'm a friend," Connaught whined. "I'm a friend, a friend. I'll give you anything, anything."

The light had intensified a little. Cobb, flat on his belly, stirred. Mary could make out a bleeding gory lump on his head where he'd been knocked unconscious.

Mary stood up, naked, and yelled. "If you hurt Mister Skye or us, you will die! The spirits will kill you. The spirits will torture you and take away your children." Some of the milling warriors glanced at her, understanding her words. Her Shoshone. She felt shamed beyond description. The warrior who had ripped the rifle from her tossed her to the ground again, and she sprawled over Victoria and Mister Skye.

"Goddamn," Victoria muttered, drawing her dagger. "They kill us all, but I will kill one."

Jawbone went insane, screaming an eerie sound that could not possibly rise from a horse throat, plowing viciously into one after another of these night raiders, scattering them. From the little park where they'd picketed their horses, she heard screaming and hooves and finally a thunder of fleeing animals.

Mary wheeled upon the warrior beside her whose hand gripped her hair. "You! You've disgraced my people!" she snarled. "You've attacked friends!"

"Not Snakes," muttered the powerful stocky warrior. "Bannock. No friends of these longknives."

Bannocks! Not her people. Not exactly her tongue, either, but one she'd understood. They lived in the mountains to the west, like her own people.

"We come for the sacred buffalo," he said with a strange accent. "We see no buffalo for our winter meat and hides, but this is almost as good." He laughed, and deliberately slapped his lance across Mister Skye's naked back, raking flesh and drawing blood with its iron point, counting coup again. "We will all count coup on the big-medicine whiteman who lies at my feet."

Mary stared at the hard-muscled warrior. He hadn't painted for war. This had been sport, at least until Jawbone went berserk. Now two of them lay injured or dying, one with a crushed hip, the other with a caved-in skull. So many! A few had taken off after the captured herd. Jawbone bolted after the herd, too, intending to turn it back, as he always did. So many! Bannocks slid out from behind cottonwoods where they'd fled from the terrible medicine horse. Mary counted swiftly. Maybe twenty more.

"This is Mister Skye. We have captured the greatest of all longknives," cried the warrior. "Come count coup before we torture him to death!"

"You will die! His ghost will haunt you forever and soil your villages forever," cried Mary fiercely. Her words were different but somehow the same as theirs.

They laughed easily. One by one they filed past, each slapping a lance or a war club across Mister Skye's back. One snapped a hatchet down, and Victoria deflected it ferociously. The warrior snarled, shoved old Victoria aside, and swung the ax viciously. Mary sprang into him, sent him sprawling. "You will die!" she hissed. He grabbed her hair, lifting her bodily, intending to bash her skull with his hatchet. That's when Mister Skye bit him. The guide gripped a calf and sank in his teeth and spat out a mouthful of flesh and blood. He'd ripped a mouthful of calf from leg. The Bannock screamed. Betsy screamed. Victoria snarled and snatched the hatchet from the staggering warrior and clobbered him with the flat back of it.

Victoria stood wildly, a vicious old naked squaw daring any of them to come closer, to count more coup on Mister Skye. The Bannocks laughed. Over twenty of them had counted coup on the greatest of all whites. That made the Bannock people the greatest of all tribes!

Mister Skye sat up dizzily, staring about him in the dawn-light. He felt the lump on his skull where he'd been clubbed. His back bled from a score of wounds where the coup counters had jabbed lances and knives into him.

Elkanah stood again, and they let him. "Who are they, Mary?" he asked weakly.

"Bannock!" she hissed. "I know their words. They live far to the west. They came for buffalo."

Elkanah peered around him. "We are all alive," he said.

"Not for long. They will torture us! They will kill us slow, just like Kills Dog Woman."

She stood ferociously, utterly unconscious of her young voluptuousness until she grew aware of staring. She knew the One Above had given her a perfect body. Imperiously, she picked up her dried doeskin dress and slid it on. Then she picked up Dirk's cradlebasket and anchored him into it, pulling its well-greased elkhide cover over Dirk's head to keep the rain off of him.

Mister Skye stood nakedly, a hairy barrel of white flesh, and as he did, a dozen warriors lifted their deadly lances and pointed them at him.

He made signs with his hands. Signs for medicine, for killing, for bad medicine. What he was saying to the one who seemed to be the Bannock headman was, leave at once or die of bad medicine.

The stocky scarred gap-toothed headman, who wore waist-long hair in a single braid plaited around German silver medallions, grinned back. "I don't hold with medi-cine," he said, letting Mary translate. "It is foolishness. White trappers taught me it is foolishness. I know of only three things: The power of warriors. The power of hunters. The power of squaws. Right now we have the power of warriors over you, and we will do what we please. Slow-Death Man has said it."

Chapter 19

A Bannock freethinker, Mister Skye thought to himself. His head ached. Cold penetrated his naked body. He turned his back to the whites and tied his elkskin belt—a gift from Victoria—around his middle and picked up his breechclout. This he slipped between his legs and stuffed the red-beaded ends under his belt fore and aft and let them drop.

"Get dressed," he said to the rest sharply. If they didn't get dressed, and fast, they'd likely not have any clothes.

Victoria slid her fringed doeskin dress over her and tied on her high moccasins. Mister Skye slid his elkskin shirt on and immediately felt warmer. He pulled up his heavy leggins and tied them with thong to his wide soft belt. He started for his square-toed whiteman's boots.

The pocked headman growled something at Mary.

"He says no shoes. Whitemen have tender feet and can't go anywhere without shoes," she said.

The guide stared toward his clients. Elkanah was tugging trousers up under his nightshirt. Arabella cowered in her blankets. Betsy pulled a woolen emerald dress over her night shift. Cobb had been dressed when he plunged from his tent and got clobbered. He sat up now, rubbing his head. Danzig dressed quietly, his back turned to the women, buttoning the fly of his black britches. But Connaught seemed paralyzed, cowering in white linen smallclothes that stretched down to his knees.

Mister Skye's mind whirled with possibilities. Their herd had bolted, and several Bannocks had ridden off to corral it. Jawbone's occasional shrieks drifted through the morning fog. He would be gathering the horses, too, or maybe conducting his one-horse war on the mounted Bannocks. They might put arrows into the horse—if they had dry bowstrings.

He turned to the smirking headman. "If your friends were trappers, you know English," he said flatly.

The headman said nothing, his eyes mocking.

Deliberately, he reached for his big boots and slid his feet into them. The lance stabbed earth viciously, half an inch from his fingers. Mister Skye stood again.

"So you don't believe in medicine," he said calmly. "But you counted coup twice—big medicine—and invited all your warriors to count coup. You believe in medicine, my friend."

"Medicine is nonsense," replied Slow-Death Man in slurred English. "Counting coup is like the ribbons your soldiers wear. Bravery ribbons."

He spoke something sharply to the warrior nearest Rudolpho, who threw the geologist into the gravel and yanked his shoes off.

"Oh dear," cried Betsy faintly.

Danzig rubbed a sore arm and sat quietly.

"They have been told," said the headman.

"Slow-Death Man. How did you get that fine brave name?" asked Mister Skye, meeting mock with mock.

"In the New Grass Moon, after the trappers had wintered with us, I killed them slowly. Three days it took because I am expert. They told me medicine is not real—just cloudy thinking. There is only power. Power to kill, that warriors and hunters have. Power to grow life, that squaws have. Spirits. Ghosts. Witches. Vision quests. All nothing. Animal helpers, spirit helpers, whitemen's God, all the same. I asked them about the blackrobe, DeSmet, who came to us with the cross, and black book. They laughed. Medicine, they said. No good. Only rifles and axes and bows and arrows make power. So I killed them slowly to see if they were lying. They lied. They screamed and prayed to their medicine, the one called God. So I took my new name."

Mister Skye nodded. A headman without the constraints of medicine. Bad business. He'd known whites like that, trappers in particular, turned murderous and brutal by the very mountains.

"These people with me have come peacefully—even their women are along—to show new things, good things, to the people like yourselves. That gentleman there makes these good things, arrow points, metal pots—and he came to find out what you like, and make them for you. We wish to smoke the pipe with you, and then be on our way."

The headman laughed sarcastically. "One of my men lies dead, kicked in the skull by your horse. Another lies badly injured, his hip smashed by your horse. And another, there, you have bitten in the leg, and he hurts."

"That's the price of war and horsestealing," replied Mister Skye. "Your power was not enough."

"Bad medicine," snapped Victoria. "You got bad medicine."

The headman turned serious for a moment. "Some of my warriors think it. They keep to the Ways of the People. I am different. I think of luck and power. I think we will do what we please. You are helpless. We have power. We will torture Mister Skye to death, and kill your horse. I don't know about the others. I will think about it."

The remaining Bannocks returned, driving the stolen herd before them. Five more, Mister Skye thought. Jawbone hovered beside the herd, bunching it, doing Bannock work, squealing and dancing like a spirit animal, making the Bannocks restless.

"See how your great medicine horse does our work for us, Mister Skye. It has killed one of us, and we will kill it soon."

"Unless it kills you first," Mister Skye retorted. The blue roan looked confused, he thought. Never had it seen him captured. It didn't know friend from enemy just now. It paced restlessly, ignoring the Bannocks. One warrior tried to touch it with a coup stick, but Jawbone whirled, arcing murderous sharp hooves inches from the warrior's chest. After that they let it alone.

The headman barked some nasal command, and the newcomers slid off their ponies one by one, paraded before Mister Skye, slapping him with lances and coup sticks, counting coup. Jawbone paced nearby, half-frantic.

Mr. Skye felt the club and scrape of their lances bruising him. They had not counted coup gently. Twenty-five Bannock hunters, sporting. He wished Jawbone hadn't killed one. But it was what he'd trained the ugly blue roan to do. Crazy horse. Jawbone walked along an edge. Mister Skye stood obdurately, never flinching as the coups rained over him, staring each bloody warrior in the eye.

"Now we have all counted coup on the great—and helpless—Mister Skye," said the headman, mocking. "Now we will see what these whitemen have in their bags for us."

The breath of their ponies fogged the cold air. The whites looked miserably cold, standing half-dressed beside their torn-down tents. Warriors trotted gleefully toward the plunder. One reared back on his heels and burst into coyote song, barking and yapping in coyote joy—the sound of a fresh kill.

"Be patient, mates," said Mister Skye softly. "We have our lives so far. Remember that."

"So far. So far!" The headman snickered. "Maybe I will drain it away slowly to pay for our losses."

"Sir, I will help your injured men!" Betsy said. She walked resolutely toward the two who lay groaning, one with a lacerated and smashed hip, the other with a gouged calf.

The headman beamed. "See, it is as I say. Squaws have power to heal and grow. That is woman's power. Man's power is to kill and be a lord over the world. That is all there is—power."

Betsy ignored him. The warrior whose calf had been bitten sat on the gravel, clutching his calf, trying to slow the sheeting bright blood. He'd lost a great deal and sat sternly, gray-faced, ignoring pain but weakening.

"Oh, dear," she said. "I can't stop this."

"Let the dog die," snarled Victoria.

The headman snapped a command, and two warriors shoved Betsy aside and wrapped soft leather that had been a saddle seat around the bright-blooded wound and tied it tightly with thong. The other warrior's problem was different: his hip was broken. The lacerations on his thigh had crusted over and barely bled at all. Bouncing brutal travois all the way back to bitterroot country, Mister Skye thought.

He considered turning Jawbone loose. A sharp command would do it. But not against twenty-five able-bodied Bannocks. They'd kill Jawbone with their lances, and then slaughter the whole party. Maybe drive arrows into the roan if they had any dry bowstrings.

"Easy, mate," he rumbled at the horse. Jawbone shrieked.

"You're wise, Mister Skye. We'll count coup on the famous horse, too, the terror of the plains." He laughed again.

"Not before he kills half of you," muttered Mister Skye. "And you first. If power's all you know, then taste Jawbone's when you're ready. Your widow will wail and cut off her finger. And because you don't believe in anything, your spirit will wander without a home forever."

Slow-Death Man nodded solemnly. He understood the language of power, even if he laughed at the language of medicine. He stared triumphantly at the huddled fear-stained whites, the captured herd steaming in the cold fog, and then at the bags and parfleches, the debris of Mister Skye's lodge, the canvas and ropes and metal pots of Elkanah's, the thick blankets that still covered Arabella, and all the rest, wet in the mist.

"We will see what the whiteman makes!" he said, muttering something to his warriors. At once they prodded the whites toward Mister Skye, yanking Arabella out of her blankets. She wore a loose white nightdress that hid little of her. Terrified, she tenderfooted her way across gravel, too frightened to object. All the whites minced on bare feet over coarse rock until they gathered close to Mister Skye. Connaught, dressed only in his white smallclothes, had gone blue with cold, and sat down shivering beside the others.

"Easy, mates," said Mister Skye. "We're going to be all right if we stay patient."

Slow-Death Man heard it and laughed nasally. Betsy and

Arabella huddled close to Elkanah, drawing and giving warmth. Mary, clutching Dirk in her cradlebasket, and Victoria settled down, glaring hot and defiant, beside Mister Skye. The others—Danzig, Connaught, Cobb—sat huddled and cold in the bitter wet fog of dawn. The sun had vanished behind a new cloud bank, and Mister Skye thought it might rain hard again, or sleet. If a wind came up, these people could die of exposure, even partly dressed as they were.

"Mister Headman, my name's Elkanah Morse. I'd be delighted to show you my goods and demonstrate their uses to you. I've brought fine things to show your people. . . ."

"Quiet!" snapped the headman. He pricked his lance into Elkanah's back, making the industrialist wince.

Squat muscular warriors spread gleefully through the camp, wrestling goods from panniers and parfleches. Bolts of cloth, blue and red, flower-patterned and gold, velveteens, canvas, rubber moccasin soles, ginghams, cottons, wools . . . shiny tin pots, gleaming copper kettles, iron arrowheads, steel awls with wooden handles, red hatchets, blue axes, the black slickers, silvery knives, ready-made arrows, black iron lance points, Betsy's folding tin cook stove, thick four-point blankets with Hudson Bay–type stripes at either end, rubber ground sheets, the tan lodge-cover, ghostly in the fog, copper rivets, rolls of wire, cord and string, scraping tools, files, augers . . . collapsible tent poles with brass fittings . . .

"No!" cried Percy Connaught. "No!" He bolted up and ran, stumbling barefoot, toward the one who lifted his journals. "No!" he shrieked as the warrior solemnly unwrapped the oilcloth bag and slid the blue leather and red leather volumes out into naked day and leafed through them. "No!" screamed Percy, ripping them from the warrior. The Bannock whirled, smashed Percy into the gravel, and kicked the sobbing man. The thump of it jolted them.

"Oh dear," said Betsy. "Oh dear!"

"Those are everything. Those are my life! My work of months! My reputation and fortune! Every insight my mind possesses!" Percy babbled. The warrior stared, flicked through the pages of fine writing. He ripped a page and set it floating to earth.

Behind him, Mister Skye heard the headman chortling. "What is in the sign books, Mister Skye? Big whiteman medicine!" he mocked, drawling out medicine. "White power!"

"His journals of the trip, Slow-Death Man. You might leave him that. Means a lot to him."

"So does our dead warrior—Falling Buck—mean a lot to me! What is writing compared to a Bannock life? All one winter trappers showed me the letters and words. They said those were power, too, power like guns and arrows. I can read. I will take the books with me and cipher the words. See what this weeping man thinks is so important."

"Oh God, no," wailed Connaught. "I'll read them to you. I'll pay anything. I'll send it, send gold, give you whatever—"

"Quiet, weeping man. Your words are all foolishness. See how you wail like a dozen mourning squaws."

The headman muttered something, and a warrior handed him the two journals, along with Cobb's and Professor Danzig's.

"I will see what's in them!" cried the headman.

Both looked stricken. Cobb sat tight-lipped, saying nothing, but his dreams and hopes rested on his journal, Mister Skye knew. Cobb's might be damaging. If the headman really could read, he'd find coldly gathered military information, cold assessments made for armies bent upon defeating Indians. Professor Danzig's would be a compendium of geological notes, sketches, maps, weather notes, anthropological observations about the tribesmen, flora and fauna notes . . . But Cobb's journal—it could get them all killed, Mister Skye thought. He'd never thought of that, that a military intelligence journal could pose such menace.

He peered up at the headman behind him, who stood thumbing through pages, frowning. Mister Skye felt sudden relief, discerning that Slow-Death Man could pick out very few words. "Want me to read it for you, Slow-Death Man?"

The headman glared at him and slid the heavy journals into a soft leather sack dangling from his pad saddle. He strutted out among the goods strewn about by warriors. Everywhere, gleeful muscular young men—were there no old ones in this party?—dug through goods, shouting. These

Bannocks were a squat broad wide-cheeked people, with lidded Oriental eyes. They seemed impervious to cold, stripped down for the buffalo hunt to breechclouts and calf-high moccasins. Most wore their coarse hair shoulder length and loose. A few guarded the herd, their own poor ponies—the Bannocks had never been a horse tribe—and the stolen animals. The rest dug industriously through the loot, howling at women's chemises and pantalets, yapping at Elkanah's folding razor, brush, and strop, wiggling Arabella's black lisle stockings in the fog and then making a neckerchief of one.

One found Betsy's portfolio, jerked out her watercolors, forty-three of them now, and bugled like a rutting elk. "Ah!" he cried, waving them. Warriors gathered around, exclaiming, admiring. He waved a watercolor, bugling and howling, making his elk medicine.

"Atsina!" cried one, staring at a portrait of a Gros Ventre warrior. "Ah!" he bellowed, and tore it to shreds. An enemy. Then they found portraits of the Blackfeet, squaws, little girls, warriors. . . .

"Ah!" they cried, spreading Betsy's deftly done works on the gravel and grinding their moccasins into the soft absorbent paper. "Piegans!" they howled.

"Oh, Lord, no, oh dear . . ." breathed Betsy, and sobbed into Elkanah's arms. Elkanah Morse held her tightly, his face resolute and wary.

"I'm so sorry, Betsy. Who would suppose that these tribesmen would—hate portraits of others? How little about them I understood . . ." His voice trailed off.

"Mrs. Morse," rumbled Mister Skye softly. "We have life."

That set her to sobbing more, and Arabella, too, and Mister Skye supposed it was the wrong thing to say. And yet it made a point among them. Some of them. Percy Connaught had sunk into some desperate blubbering despair.

"Mister Connaught. Go get dressed," Mister Skye snapped. "Miss Morse. You too! Now or never. Before they take—do you understand?"

Arabella clung tighter to Elkanah and wouldn't budge. Percy huddled in a heap on the gravel, his white knees lacerated.

Mister Skye watched the warriors shake and flip clothing item by item and toss it into the growing pile. They'd take it all, this loot for Bannock squaws, whitemen's clothing. Connaught and Arabella would go almost naked in the wilderness in late September.

Mister Skye stood. He'd try it himself. With his rising a half-dozen warriors surrounded him with lances. He walked anyway, ignoring them until the iron points pressed viciously into his guts and thighs.

The headman leered. "Power, Mister Skye. That's all there is. See what we have got! Two hundred fine robes could not get us this at the posts. Warrior power got this!"

"I am going to get a dress for the young woman and some britches and a shirt for that man whose books you've stolen."

"Whitemen need clothes. See us, with only our breechclouts. We don't feel cold. Whites are clever but weak. They die without all their clever things, food, weapons, clothing, tents. Let them see if they can live—like us."

A pocked warrior handed the headman two of Danzig's devices.

"What is this?" asked the headman, holding up the sextant.

Professor Danzig himself answered quietly. "It tells me how far south or north we are," he said. "I will show you how to use it." The lithe dark Swiss seemed calmer than the rest.

Slow-Death Man laughed and set it on the ground. The other device before him was the daguerreotyping machine, varnished box, glass eye, black velvet. Plus a handful of exposed tintypes.

The headman examined each, passing them along to exclaiming warriors. Miraculous images. Like Betsy's only all in brown and white and exact, just as the eye sees. One warrior burst into wild talk, gesticulating, pointing. The headman grabbed the tintype.

"He knows this Atsina. He counted coup on this Atsina. He wants this image so he can make medicine and kill the Atsina in the future!"

"Medicine," muttered Mister Skye, feeling the lances pressed into him.

Slow-Death Man said, "Yes, medicine. I do not follow the way of my people. But all the rest follow the way. I think White Weasel is foolish, wanting this image to make medicine. If he wants to kill this Atsina, he should go kill him. No medicine!"

"I will give him the image," said Professor Danzig.

The headman looked amused. "You talk like making gifts!" he exclaimed.

Danzig said, "I am making him a gift."

"Make me a gift. Make an image of me."

"I can do that. I will need this, and these"—he pointed to a box of unexposed plates—"and other things. I have nine plates left."

"Make nine images of me. Ah! Make nine images of me counting coup against Mister Skye."

He would show the world, thought Mister Skye. Very well. It might win them something.

Professor Danzig set up his wooden tripod, screwed the daguerreotyping machine to it.

"You will have to be very still. There's little light, and this needs lots of sunlight. But if you stand still, perhaps I can make an image."

He vanished under his black cloth. The warriors halted their plundering to gape. The headman grabbed his coup stick, rammed it roughly into Mister Skye's ribs, and held it there, proudly. Danzig fussed. They heard a whirring click and the eye blinked.

"Now I must pull my tent over me and do some things," Danzig said calmly.

"Son of a bitch!" exclaimed Victoria in a rage. Counting coup meant a lot to her. Sacred business to a Crow, Mister Skye thought. And Slow-Death Man would count it eight more times before the whirring lens. He didn't much like it himself, but he'd gotten the message of the lance points. The message wasn't medicine; it was power.

Chapter 20

Betsy wept as these whooping naked savages destroyed the work of months, work she could never replace. Every rip of matted paper ripped her heart. She remembered each of her subjects, sitting before her in high summer sunlight. Little girls, proud warriors in all their regalia of fur and bone and feather, work-worn women, some dressed in softly tanned finery, others in shabby bags of skin worn for messy and grueling tasks, such as fleshing a buffalo hide. All gone, each delicate stroke that had caught shadow under cheekbone, sheen on a bearclaw necklace, pride in a chief, mystery in a squinting sour shaman.

"I have lost everything," she whispered to Elkanah, sitting beside her. He squeezed her hand.

"Not everything. Not life. They'll take my display goods and we'll be on our way," he said. "Memory will help you redo them."

She shook her head. Memory wouldn't help at all. Memory wouldn't sort out quillwork, beads, the slant of a feather, the scars on a warrior's arm, the sag of lodges. No, it was gone.

"I'd hoped to have an exhibit. I'm the only woman. . . . Hardly anyone's been here. Catlin. Bodmer. Miller . . . I thought—I could almost read the Boston papers . . . 'Splendid Exhibit of Wild Indian Scenes at the Athaeneum . . . Fine Transparent Colors Boldly Put to Paper by the Lowell Artist . . .' "

She sighed shakily.

"We'll pick up the pieces! We'll gather every scrap, and when we get back, we'll puzzle them together. Then you can copy, Betsy."

But even as he whispered, gusts of chill air scattered fragments of color into wet grass and off into thickets of brush.

Beside them sat Jarvis Cobb, pale and drawn. She glanced covertly at him, wondering if he'd suffered a concussion. And poor Percy in his muddied smallclothes, huddled on gravel into a ball of anguish. Everything he'd scribbled gone, too, unless they could get it back from that strutting smirking chief. She didn't particularly like Percy, but she pitied him now and felt a kindred loss. He was a fusty bachelor, too, and lacked the ties she had, so he probably had wrapped his whole life, his future, his dreams, in those vanished journals.

They were dividing the weapons now. That dreadful smirking headman had buckled on Mister Skye's belt and holster with his old revolver and had claimed Mister Skye's heavy dark Hawken. Except for that, they hadn't plundered Mister Skye's belongings. Too many things of Elkanah's and Rudolpho's fascinated them. They'd gotten Elkanah's weapons, too—everything. The custom fowling piece, and English rifle, and Sam Colt's revolver. Some subchiefs of some sort fondled them, along with every other weapon they could find, plus powder horns, paper cartridges, and all the rest of it. She felt a chill. The more these Bannocks plundered, the more helpless they all became.

"I don't think they're going to take just your trade goods, Elkanah," she whispered. "I think they'll take everything. Everything!"

"We're alive," he replied, echoing Mister Skye. "Surely they'll leave us a few things to get along with."

"But . . . !" she exclaimed, and then couldn't say what

dread thoughts crowded her mind. Would they . . . kill? Would they torture? The image of poor Kills Dog Woman of the Flatheads filled her mind, and she shuddered. What if they killed Elkanah? Tortured him before her eyes? What if—what if— She tried to chase a terrible thought away, but it wouldn't go away. What if they used her, crawled on her and used her, and used Arabella, right before Elkanah's eyes? She'd die; she couldn't bear the thought; she couldn't imagine this profane thing happening to mock what had been sacred and sweet and private between them alone. Elkanah might go crazy and they'd kill him. Arabella—she might go mad, poor thing, those things unknown to her. . . .

Betsy shuddered and stared around. What-if's could drive a person mad, she thought. Just thinking about what-if's. It hadn't happened. They all sat here unharmed. She clutched her arms tight around her in the vicious cold and stared helplessly at the whirl of her small wet world.

Professor Danzig emerged from under a huddle of canvas, toting a tintype. Slow-Death Man had grown impatient and had gone back to plundering, but at the sight of Danzig he leaped to the professor and snatched the daguerreotype.

"Ah! I am here, counting coup on Mister Skye!" he cried. "I will show this to everyone, to the world! I will have another now!"

Mister Skye hadn't moved, indeed couldn't move with three lances jabbed into his belly and back. Danzig quietly ducked under his black hood, the headman brought his coup stick down viciously on Mister Skye's skull, staggering the guide, and the next click trapped an image of humiliation.

"That is all," the headman said to Danzig. "This image making takes too long." He barked something in the Bannock tongue at some of his cavorting band, and they began at once to load Elkanah's fine panniers with their loot. And exactly as Betsy feared, they weren't stopping with Elkanah's trade goods, either. She watched in horror as every scrap of equipment—things that could mean life itself—vanished into the bulging panniers of the pack saddles. Their whole kitchen. Her shoes and dresses. Everything of Arabella's. Their sleeping blankets. The rubberized ground cloths that Elkanah had invented for cold damp earth. Everything of his—razor, strop, shoes. The lanterns and lastly the tent itself with its shining fittings. Everything. Everything! A sudden sense of utter nakedness and helplessness swept through her, and a vision of death from exposure.

Instinctively she clutched Elkanah. "We must be brave!" she whispered. "We will be brave!" She reached across Elkanah's lap and patted Arabella tenderly. The girl looked stricken. "If worse comes to worse," Betsy said softly, "I wish to be worthy before our Maker. I want to find the courage to bless them, whatever they do to me—to us."

Elkanah stared at her, some anguish boiling bleakly in his eyes, some guilt.

She read it. "Do you think for an instant I'd have let you come here alone—without me? Keep your wild west adventure from me?" She smiled. "If you had, you'd have found me curled up in the bottom of a pannier!"

She felt his hands responding, his fingers intimately tugging her closer, pressing her rib cage. Maybe, she thought with renewed dread, they were saying good-bye to each other. She stared at his familiar face, seeing it in profile now, his high forehead and receding brown hair and the clean strong line of his determined jaw. She would remember it while there was breath in her.

Danzig crawled out from under his sprawled canvas, stood quietly, and handed the second tin-backed image to the headman.

"I suppose I could show you how all this is done," Danzig said. But Slow-Death Man didn't hear. He studied the new image gleefully. "See! See how I have power over Mister Skye, greatest of all the whitemen! See this! I am the greatest."

"Don't know about that," rumbled the guide. "Let's you and me find out."

"You are my captive," the headman retorted.

"You take a knife. I'll fetch me a wooden club I've got in my things. I've busted a lot of sailor skulls with it; might as well bust yours. Belaying pin."

"Goddamn," muttered Victoria.

The headman glared. "I have heard of how you fight with this club. I will think about it. Maybe this is not the day."

"Any day's the day to smash the skull of a Bannock coward."

"I will think about medicine."

"Ahhh!" mocked Mister Skye. "Maybe those images showing you counting coup are lies. Three of your warriors have lances against me, and you count coup. Great warrior you are, my friend."

Mary heard all this and instantly translated it into the Shoshonean tongue Bannocks understood. The headman's boasts; Mister Skye's challenge.

"What is Mary doing?" Betsy whispered.

"I think she's telling the Bannock warriors that Slow-Death Man is refusing to fight Mister Skye—even when Mister Skye would have only a belaying pin against his knife."

"Mercy!"

"They're about the same height—medium. I think the Bannock has longer arms, but Mister Skye is heavier. But a belaying pin . . . I've never heard of such a thing. . . ."

The young warriors had stopped their plundering and stared at their headman. Slow-Death Man rose and paraded before them, showing them the images—counting coup against the big-medicine whiteman. Swiftly his nasal voice rose and raged.

Mary translated. "He is saying they should torture us all to death. That Mister Skye's challenge is nothing, a bluff."

Betsy felt a sickening fear flood through her. Torture . . .

Mister Skye tried to stand, but the lancers thrust at him and kept him sitting.

"Slow-Death Man," muttered Mister Skye. "If I kill you, we will take all our things and leave. You will not kill me. I always have medicine."

The warriors waited for the headman to translate. Just to make sure his message reached them all, Mister Skye repeated himself with the hand language of the plains. His three guards permitted it warily.

"No such thing as medicine. Only power," the headman retorted. But his warriors stared. At last one of them began his own oration, snapping strange-sounding words to the others. Betsy listened, mystified by the man's powerful oratory and fierce gestures. He pointed at the piles of booty, at Mister Skye.

"He says they should take everything and go," translated Mary. "He says Mister Skye got big medicine, and the Bannock chief don't got medicine because he says he don't follow the Way of the People. So Bannock chief get killed and Mister Skye takes everything back. He says they'll take everything, and he's chief now, and Slow-Death Man ain't anything anymore."

"I don't understand," whispered Betsy.

Victoria heard her. "They want all this stuff and think maybe that son of a bitch gonna lose it because he ain't got any medicine or spirit helper. So they say he ain't the headman anymore and maybe they all go away."

"I'll fight the new headman," rumbled Mister Skye. "Tell him that, Mary. Give him a knife. I'll have my belaying pin. He's got Bannock medicine. Let him try it."

Mary translated that back to the new headman, a young stout one with protruding eyeballs. At that moment Jawbone screeched eerily, feeling the tension in camp.

Theft or glory? Loot or prowess? They argued briefly among themselves and settled for loot.

"They're afraid," snarled old Victoria. "Goddamn!"

"Of Jawbone," whispered Elkanah. The warriors eyed the terrible blue horse warily, afraid of a murderous shrieking assault that not even lances would stop, at least before the horse would slaughter several of them.

The new headman-by-consent snapped commands, and warriors loaded Mister Skye's possessions, the parfleches of pemmican and jerky, the fine robes, the women's old fusils, and their osage orange bows. One of them discovered the linen bowstrings and exclaimed. They nocked the strings of both bows and drew them, howling. One of them dipped the bowstring into a puddle until it was soaked and drew it. The string didn't fly apart. The bows passed from warrior to warrior, and each pulled the string to its limits but it didn't break. Magic! It dawned on them what those bowstrings meant. Horse raids in rain! Hunting in rain! Defeat of enemies in rain when sinew bowstrings went soft and flew apart!

"Ah! More whitemen's medicine," said Slow-Death Man, ignoring his recent humiliation. "Bows that shoot in rain."

They folded Mister Skye's lodge and bound the cover to a travois. They abandoned the lodgepoles, which would only hinder them on the long trail west. When they were done, everything from Elkanah's party, and every possession from the lodge of Mister Skye, had been stuffed into panniers or bundles and tied down on horses and mules. Victoria muttered angrily. Betsy watched with fascination and terror, knowing her fate in these autumnal wilds. Even as she clung to Elkanah, the numbing cold—just above freezing—relentlessly chilled her. She couldn't get warm. Poor Arabella—even worse off in her gauzy white nightdress!

"Slow-Death Man! Tell them I want my belaying pin back. If I don't get it, I'll come after you," growled Mister Skye.

The deposed headman had recovered something of his mockery. "Maybe not," he said. "We maybe still torture you to death. That is to be decided. You and the others."

The bleak news chilled Betsy. She felt an overpowering urge to go to the bushes. None of them had done it. They'd been dragged from their tents an eternity ago, though now she realized it had scarcely reached midmorning. In the back of her mind lay another purpose: she hoped to find a piece of sharp-edged stone, sharp enough to sever the artery at her wrist, sharp enough to spare her and Arabella days of utter torment, hours of debasement too evil to imagine. Fast death would be a mercy.

"I must do chores," she whispered, freeing herself from Elkanah's comforting grip. "Come along, Arabella."

No one stopped them. In fact, Victoria and Mary joined them. They wobbled tender-footed over stone, cringed over grass and sticks, and finally turned around a drenched thicket that sprayed ice water over them, intensifying the cold. She found no sharp stones there; only river-rounded cobbles. But along the bluffs lay fragmented sandstone. . . .

Victoria stared at her. "What are you looking for?" she asked sharply.

"Nothing."

Victoria, all-knowing, discerned Betsy's mood. "You got to die proud," she said. "Kill them if you can. If they torture, you say nothing. Don't cry. Don't scream, no matter what. Laugh and make them see you got a big spirit. You show them a big spirit and maybe they kill you quick, honor your spirit."

Arabella wept. Betsy tried to comfort her, drew an arm around the girl's soaked cold nightdress and gasped at the coldness under her hand. Her daughter could not be far from danger from cold.

"Run, Arabella! Dance! Wave your arms! You're much too cold!" she cried. "We all will. I will, too!"

Betsy began running in place, swinging arms. Arabella stared.

"It's no use," mumbled Arabella. "We'll all be dead."

"What are you talking about? They go away, we get fixed up quick," growled Victoria.

"We have nothing," mumbled Arabella.

"I don't understand goddamn white people," muttered Victoria. "We got a whole world here. We can walk two days and sit in hot springs, so warm you can hardly stand it. We got a whole river valley here full of stuff."

"Two days without shoes! Two weeks to walk there barefoot!" cried Arabella, actually saying what Betsy was thinking privately. "Without clothes! Without food! Without fire! Without shelter! And if it rains again—it looks like it—the cold will kill us. I don't want to die!"

"Who's gonna die? I ain't," muttered Victoria crossly. "You do like your mother now, make your heart pound. Only don't make sweat or do too much. Just enough to make your blood go fast."

It began to mist, fine cold drops that wet Betsy's face and hinted of death. It occurred to her that this day had scarcely begun. It would stretch into the longest of her life, or mercifully the shortest. She'd come to an age when she'd thought about her own death. One does that upon turning forty. And yet it had always seemed so distant, and she felt so young and full of life that she'd put off coping with it. But here it was, sitting right here like a wolf on its haunches, waiting.

For her. For Elkanah. For Arabella. And the others . . .
Now that she peered about, she saw death lurking everywhere, but no more than in the lowering dreary clouds that
blanketed heaven with bulging black bellies and hid horizons as surely as they hid the future.

They limped back in the thickening icy mist and found
the Bannocks loading the last of the stolen pack animals.
Not a scrap of the comfortable camp remained, except for
the shreds of Betsy's paintings, scattered forlornly. The mist
settled on the scraps, blurring the watercolors, streaking the
remains of hundreds of hours of loving labor.

The Bannocks seemed excited, and she realized they
clustered around those bows that had been Victoria and
Mary's, endlessly pulling back the linen strings. Others of
them fondled the percussion lock rifles they'd commandeered.

Mary listened to their excited talk. "They're thinking they
can hunt the buffalo now, even in the rain. They can shoot
them bows. They can shoot them rifles with the caps. They
got one or two flintlocks that ain't no good in the rain. But
now they got these new ones they can shoot. They're saying
they can shoot buffalo now."

"Maybe the rain will rescue us, mates," muttered Mister
Skye.

But Betsy couldn't see how. It'd kill them in this desolate
cold place in hours.

Their minds made up, the Bannocks herded the pack animals west, and up the bluffs. Betsy felt so cold in the thickening mist that she scarcely cared what the Bannocks did.
Everything she possessed went in that caravan. At the last
moment, the three grinning Bannocks who had guarded
Mister Skye with lowered lances released him and swung
up on their waiting ponies.

Only the deposed headman, Slow-Death Man, remained,
sitting on his coyote dun. Mister Skye stood, stretching after
his long immobilization on the gravel. The rain had soaked
his heavy graying hair, and now it matted blackly about his
skull and neck. He, too, seemed as cold and defeated as
the rest, Betsy thought.

"Mister Skye. We talked about whether to kill you all.

But we don't need to. The rain will do it. Whites have magic things—and are helpless. We'll go kill buffalo now. Maybe it'll rain for many days, but we'll kill buffalo anyway, and go back across the mountains. They will welcome us in our village! We will sing many songs about this day."

From under the black slicker he'd commandeered, he pulled out Mister Skye's old hickory belaying pin, flared thickly at one end, but lathed narrower at the other. He tossed it to earth.

"Here! Take your wooden club, the club that Mister Skye always has. Maybe you can kill buffalo with it!"

Some faint light seemed to flare in the guide's eyes.

They watched the Bannock trot off and catch up to the others. They watched the pack animals top the slippery bluff and vanish into gray mist. They stared at each other, seeing ashen, cold, gray-fleshed, half-dressed, blue-lipped barefoot mortals with utterly nothing, and only a few hours from doom.

Chapter 21

Mister Skye faced them. "You are alive," he said. Numbing rain stung him. "I want you to listen. But before you listen, I want you to huddle together."

No one moved. Jarvis Cobb stared up at him. "No use," he muttered. "Don't rally us with nonsense. I'm an officer. I know about this."

"Huddle anyway. Press together. Mister Connaught, get up."

The man lay curled in a ball on the gravel, his white underclothes mud-smeared and soaked. He peered up and said nothing.

Mister Skye walked to him, feeling harsh gravel under his soles. He lifted Connaught to his feet, but the man didn't help and would have sunk to earth but for Mister Skye's support.

"All gone. Let me die. I know perfectly well what our true condition is."

Mister Skye dragged him to the others. Listlessly, Betsy helped Connaught down and drew him close, her face a mask. Professor Danzig stood, flapped arms to make blood move, and walked over, squeezing close to Arabella and slipping an avuncular arm about her shoulders.

"Cobb?" The officer sat apart, head sunk into his chest.

"Goddamn," snarled Victoria. She and Mary slid over to Cobb and embraced him from two sides, making a tight ball of human flesh.

The icy rain fell heavily now; not a deluge but a cruel drizzle.

"We don't have much time. I won't take time to explain everything now. We have important things to do. First, forget about your hunger. We can live for days without food. Second, fire and shelter will keep us going. Fire is the first priority. If not fire, then shelter."

"Have you flint and striker? Sulfur matches? Dry wood?" asked Elkanah wearily.

"No. But with luck, we'll have a fire. And if we can't start one in this, we'll have a shelter. But tonight and the next days will be the worst."

"I suppose you have a convenient cave, with dry wood stashed in the back and a pouch of lucifers hanging on the wall," muttered Cobb.

Mister Skye gazed at this country. The Big Horn cut through gently sculpted hills here, occasionally baring outcrops of gray sandstone. No caves or even overhangs in this country. But maybe, just maybe, an upright cliff of rock that'd form a warm wall they could prop brush against for a shelter . . . He'd set them looking.

"No, we're not so fortunate. But I intend to get us through. Get you safely and comfortably to Fort Laramie."

Connaught laughed crazily.

"It's midmorning sometime. We have enough daylight. If all this had happened late in the day, we'd be in trouble."

"We're not in trouble?" asked Cobb, mocking.

"Captain Cobb, I'll argue later. Just now there's no time. I'm going to set each of you to a task. Do it. Your lives depend on it."

Arabella started laughing crazily too. Her body convulsed and shivered, a bad sign.

"Elkanah and Betsy, press yourselves over her. Pin her down and warm her with your own bodies."

Betsy stood. "I'll give her my dress—"

"No, your body heat's more important."

Reluctantly—this intimacy ran against their grain—the Morses clambered over chattering and shivering Arabella and pressed her. Professor Danzig helped, too.

"Damn," muttered Victoria. She stood, slid off her soaked doeskin dress, and handed it to the Morses. Her old withered naked body seemed to defy the elements, and Mister Skye knew that she could go awhile with nothing. Indians seemed to have a gift of endurance. Elkanah and Betsy wrestled the trembling young woman into the dress, and then pressed over her again.

"Thank you, Victoria," said Betsy.

"Cattails," Mister Skye said gently to Victoria and Mary. Instantly they trotted off on hardened feet toward the river, hoping to find a slough.

The tall flat leaves of the cattail could swiftly be woven into good mats. Weak ones but usable tonight. The bulbs of the cattail were edible, and could be dried and pounded into a good flour.

"Mister Danzig. Your training as a geologist might save the day for us. We need flint or obsidian—both actually. And any rock with a sharp edge."

"These hills—there'd be little flint in them. Obsidian—not likely here. That's volcanic glass. Flint's a type of quartz. . . . But the river. It's low and there's gravel beds exposed, and I'll probably find it. . . ."

"Flint for weapons, knife edges. But mainly flint for fire, if we can find something to strike against," said Mister Skye. "Let me see your belt buckles, gentlemen."

Cobb's was brass. Elkanah had no belt on. Neither did Professor Danzig. No steel.

Disappointed, he turned to other things. "Mister Cobb, work your way north, downstream, as far as your feet can stand it. Look for a cave, an overhang, a vertical rock wall or cliff. Look also for deadfall limbs or thick grasses. If you see any chunk of rock—from these bluffs—that has a sharp edge, get it. If you find an antler, bring it. If you find vines, wild grape or anything like it, mark the place. If you spot animal burrows or dens, remember them. Look for dry-

bottomed thickets. Carry a stick to club any small animal—
sometimes in bad weather they sit stupidly. But food is
secondary. Our first business is shelter and warmth.''

Captain Cobb sighed, ran a hand tenderly over the blood-
ied lump on his head. ''This is utter futility, you know. I'm
not feeling well,'' he muttered.

''Give up and die then,'' Mister Skye retorted sharply.
He didn't have time to argue. With a cliff, some deadfall
limbs for rafters and beams, and grass for thatching, he
could make a serviceable and almost waterproof shelter.

The rain bit at them all. He felt icy water sting down his
back and belly. So little time. He saw Danzig walking off,
each step tentative, bare feet testing. Slow going.

''Mister Connaught. Stand up. Run in place. Make your
heart pound at once, until you're warm.''

The miserable man curled tighter into a ball and didn't
reply. ''Break off brush as thick as you can manage, Mister
Connaught. I want to find you under a large pile of it when
I get back.''

The man laughed weirdly. Mister Skye didn't have time
to argue.

''Elkanah, we're going south, upstream, together, looking for shelter and gathering some things. We have things
to talk about.''

Even buoyant Elkanah seemed rudderless, shocked, and
shivering cold.

''Up! Up, man! I need your manufacturing wisdom!''

Actually, he needed his squaws' Indian ways more, but
Elkanah's inventive and flexible mind would help. The entrepreneur stood, hollow-eyed, and wobbled over harsh
gravel, grimacing whenever a sharp pebble bit his white wet
feet.

Good. He'd come.

''Mrs. Morse. When my wives return with cattails, they'll
show you and Arabella how to weave simple mats from the
leaves. If you weave the leaves tightly, they'll turn into a
mat that will hold heat and turn the wind, and even shed
some water.''

Betsy, who lay over her daughter, peered up, wet hair
falling over her white face, and nodded.

"Come along, Elkanah," he said. They walked slowly and silently south, the misery of the icy drizzle subduing them.

"Lots of ways to make shelter and fire, Mister Morse. Lots of ways Indians survive in these circumstances. We're going to turn Indian for a while. Don't give up! Don't let any of the others give up! I'm regretting I spoke sharply to Mister Cobb, though he and Connaught are the ones most likely to collapse and die. You and the professor and Betsy— I have to rely on you. Captain Cobb seems—I think he's got a concussion."

Elkanah sighed. "Tell me honestly, Mister Skye. Our chances are about zero, aren't they?"

"Fifty-fifty, Elkanah. And better than that if we can get through tonight alive and well. Our enemy's despair—that more than nature or weather."

They struggled painfully southward at the base of the gentle western bluff of the river, past cottonwood parks and thickets closer to the stream.

"I don't see it," Elkanah said.

"The Indians managed very well before they had a single trade item from whites, Elkanah."

"But the things they had took time to manufacture. It took time to shape a bow with bone or flint knives, sand it with a block of sandstone, sand arrows, chip arrowheads. . . ."

"You're going to find ways of doing it, Elkanah."

The industrialist winced along silently. "I'm already starved. I'm sure the others will soon be dizzy with want of food. I don't know where we'll get the strength—"

"My women are gathering cattails right now. There's other edible roots and nuts and berries. Fall's a good time, in a way. We can rob squirrels, snare ducks—lot of things. Tools. You'll be in charge of tools, Elkanah. Knives. Flint's only one way. If we find a new buffler skeleton, we'll have good knives. Those dorsal bones that make the hump, they're flat and wide and can be sanded down with a chunk of sandstone into useful knives. We'll need knives and clubs, stone hammers and flint-edged hatchets. Lances whittled to a point, the point hardened in fire. Arrows, bows . . . Put your mind to it, Elkanah. The Indians call you things-maker.''

Elkanah laughed shortly. "Maybe we can scrape and sand green wood into some kind of bow, but how would you string it? Surely not with these whangs on your buckskin shirt.''

"No, they won't work. Jawbone, Elkanah, will supply us with a temporary bowstring. Plaited from his long tail hair. Poor doings, but maybe we can make a weak bow.''

"Horsehair!''

"I'm looking for a sharp-edged stone right now to cut tail hair. Need it for a fire bow.''

"Fire bow?''

"With a wrap of bowstring around some bone-dry hardwood, a bow can get that wood spinning into a hollow of another piece of hardwood until it smokes from friction. We've got to get a bit of dry tinder in there to ignite.''

"But this rain! This water!''

"Squirrel's nest in a knot, in a tree hollow, should have plenty of tinder. Dry wood'll be harder. And we'll see what Danzig comes up with by way of flints.''

"But we have no steel.''

"I've seen spark from smacking rocks, Elkanah.''

"Ow!'' cried Elkanah. He'd stepped on a vicious stick. He lifted his cold white foot and found blood.

"My feet aren't much better,'' said the guide. "I never cottoned much to moccasins except around camp—always wore big square-toed boots.''

His own feet had been lacerated by this walk, he knew.

Elkanah stopped. "Mister Skye, I've never been this cold. I'm cold down in my center. I'm wet and numb, and—I'm losing heart. We don't have much time. Poor Arabella! Poor—''

"Look here,'' muttered the guide. He stood before a small corner of stratified stone with roughly vertical walls about five feet high, with sloping prairie above it. It needed only deadfall limbs propped against it and thatching. Not much, but something.

"This might do,'' he muttered. "But I want to check thickets first. Animals hunker down in hollows under thick brush and stay warm and relatively dry. But getting to them in the river brush is going to be bad, Elkanah.''

Step-by-step they threaded into the dense brush closer to the river, placing tender feet with care and even then wincing. Slow, wet, miserable going. Nothing. Just water-laden willow and serviceberry and chokecherry brush, open at their bases and cold as January.

They heard a crashing behind them and discovered Jawbone, following and curious. The horse! He'd barely thought of the horse. He'd grown as cold as Elkanah but wouldn't admit it. He'd never been as cold as this in all his years in the mountains.

''Elkanah, I'm going to help you up on Jawbone and take you back. I want you to huddle together with the others—make each other warm.''

''But Jawbone—he'd kill me.''

''No, not now.''

He hoisted the exhausted man up, while Jawbone twisted his head back, wary and ready for trouble. Wearily Mister Skye stumbled back, step by painful step, the horse following unbidden. The three hundred yards seemed more like three miles to him because his muscles weren't working right and his feet bled from scores of small lacerations. But he trudged ahead.

''The horse feels warm under me,'' muttered Elkanah. His feet dripped blood.

Back at camp, or what remained of it, things had gotten worse. Betsy still lay upon Arabella, but both of them convulsed with shaking. Victoria, still naked, pressed close beside them.

''I am sorry, Mister Skye,'' she muttered. ''I got goddamn cold.''

The guide's heart sank at the sight. But Mary sat stoically, weaving cattail fronds into a mat as fast as numb fingers could manage it. She'd found a sharp piece of sandstone to cut off the bulbs, and these she piled beside her. Her dress had blackened with cold water, and the icy rain ran down her goosefleshed arms, off her braids and face. And yet she endured. His heart went out to her, too. A cattail mat would be a pathetic barrier in such a cold as this—but a start.

Time. He needed much more time. An hour more and these people would be beyond help. He helped Elkanah down and bade him lie close to the others. A vicious gust of wind sliced through, chilling their numb bodies further.

"Mister Cobb!" he roared. "Get over here! Get tight against the others."

Jarvis Cobb had curled into a small ball, shaking spastically inside of his drenched tan shirt and britches. He peered grayly up at Mister Skye and laughed through clenched lips.

Mister Skye grabbed him by his shirt, lifted him bodily, and slapped him. The wet smack echoed weirdly.

"Oh!" muttered Betsy.

Cobb laughed harder, maniacally. Mister Skye slapped him again.

"Very good of you, Skye. Hit me again," muttered Cobb, teeth chattering beyond control.

Mister Skye didn't know whether he had the strength left to drag the man to the others, but he tried. He hauled Jarvis Cobb across abrading wet gravel and dumped him next to Victoria. Then he hauled a whimpering Percy Connaught to the same pile and jammed him hard against Cobb. His heart thudded painfully. A small task, but the coldness had sapped him.

Mary finished a cattail mat, and Mister Skye laid it over the pile of them, a pathetic green thing. She didn't have enough cattails for another.

"Let me borrow that stone," he muttered. The sandstone had a rough jagged edge, not bad as a cutting tool. He found Jawbone's tail and grabbed it.

"Easy, boy," he muttered. The horse peered evilly at him, through yellow murderous eyes. "Easy . . ."

He sawed at the tail hair. It didn't cut readily. The horse shifted restlessly, barely tolerating it. He sawed more and cut some of the long hair loose until he had a fistful.

No time, he thought. No time. They'd be dead of exposure before he got enough done. . . .

He took the hair to Mary, who stared at him soberly.

"Mary, you're beautiful. Did I ever tell you how beautiful you look in the rain?"

A flash of smile rewarded him, and he hugged her, feeling the sopping cold of her doeskin dress, and the warmth of her faintly. "We have to hurry," he whispered.

She nodded, pressing tight to him. It felt good.

"Lots of cane grass in these bottoms. This knife of yours—cut it fast. We'll gather it into bunches and I'll tie a horsehair around one end . . . thatch."

"What is thatch?" she asked.

"Grass'll shed water," he muttered. "Hurry!"

He had to find Danzig. Probably half-dead somewhere. He tried to crawl over Jawbone and couldn't. The strength had gone out of him and the horse's back was slippery wet. He led the horse toward a cottonwood log and managed to clamber on. He could steer Jawbone with his knees. He trotted north, weaving through majestic cottonwoods with yellowing brown-specked leaves, glistening with water. A long silvery log caught his eye, and he steered Jawbone toward it. Hollow end, rotten reddish wood reduced by weather and insects to pulp along the bottom. Maybe, he thought. He slid off the horse and peered in, on his hands and knees. Hollow and dry, the gloomy light showing distantly from the other end. Big enough for women, two women. His naked Victoria, and Arabella, the farthest gone.

He climbed up on Jawbone, knowing he himself had reached his limits, and trotted back to the inert shivering people. Mary had cut and tied three grass bundles and laid them on the others.

"I've found a safe warm place for two women," he said. "Victoria, come with me. Arabella, I'll carry you."

Nothing. They peered at him dumbly. He slid down from Jawbone once again and gently pried them apart, lifting the mute Betsy off her daughter. Arabella shook violently. He lifted her, dragged her, to Jawbone, who sidled warily from him.

"Steady, boy," he muttered. He lacked the strength to seat her properly, and slid her over the horse on her stomach, hanging on the animal like dead game. He turned around and found Victoria standing grimly behind him, her eyes desperate and ice water trickling down her naked flesh.

They followed him, Jawbone with his half-dead cargo, and Victoria, silently. The log lay two hundred yards distant, close to the Big Horn. It took a long time, and then they stood before it.

"Help me," he muttered. Together they slid Arabella off Jawbone and twisted her wet skirts tight and wrestled her feetfirst into the hollow log. It got harder and harder to do as the friction increased, but with a last vicious push against her shoulders, he got her head under cover. They stood panting.

He stared at her, then wrapped his tired arms around his old naked woman. "Forgot to tell you how I love you, Victoria. Forgot to say thanks. Maybe we won't get out of this. It's getting worse by the minute. If we don't, I want you to know—to know—you've given me a good life. Most lucky man in the world to have you. I love you now . . . love you in the spirit land to come. . . ."

She hugged him mutely, too tired to talk. Then she slid herself into the other end of the log.

"Goddamn, it's warm in here," she said.

Chapter 22

Life-and-death crisis galvanized something in Professor Danzig's mind. As he limped through cottonwood forest and brush toward the sprawling Big Horn River, his keen, analytical mind surveyed possibilities. He'd never felt such cold as this, with icy rain slicing into him and sluicing heat out of his compact body. But he ignored it. Rather, his fertile mind furiously examined one material after another in these bottoms.

Not much time. Perhaps an hour for the weakest; two or three hours for the strongest. He reached the river at last, after wincing his way through a barrier of thick rushes and sedges, dense stalks as high as three feet. They could be cut and thatched, he thought. They had insulating qualities. But cutting them would be a problem. He tried tugging some, breaking some, and found they resisted, as he expected. Oh, for a knife! In an hour they could have a shelter of bulrushes.

He stumbled at last out upon a gravelly streambed area. In spite of these first autumnal rains, the Big Horn ran very low, exposing long beaches of mud and gravel and cobbled stones, rounded by aeons of river passage. The variety of them surprised him. Red granites and gray gneisses, pale rhyolite, gabbro and basalt, most of these igneous rocks probably from the great Yellowstone batholith to the west. But also sandstone from the surrounding area, gray limestone, mudstone, shale, chunks of quartz, good news because it might mean flint. Other rocks he couldn't identify. Some of them looked burnt.

But finding flint on a dark gray day in a sheeting rain presented problems. Flint had a luster and could range from translucent to opaque. But in this relentless rain, all the rocks had luster. He stumbled slowly over gravel, hunting the telltale gray or brown, seeing nothing. Then, before him, an arrowhead, finely chipped of tan flint, with two knife edges and the haft intact so it could be anchored to a handle. He fondled it, rejoicing, and slipped it in his pocket. He debated. Head back with this or search further. He decided to search. This would give them a knife, but they needed flint for a fire striker and many more tools. He wobbled on, feet numb on wet icy rock. In ten minutes he had one additional piece of flint he felt sure of, and two rocks he classified as doubtful. Only then did he notice that his limbs were refusing to function and he was shuddering spasmodically, as his body fought against the murderous cold. Time to get back, hug someone for dear life.

In the thick bankside rushes he paused and began cutting. Slower than he thought, a few stalks at a time. Too long. He began slashing savagely, forcing work from his numb body, feeling his heart begin to pump. When he had an armful of the wet rushes and sedges, he unbuttoned his shirt and stuffed them in, working them around to the back until he could jam no more into available space. The rushes dripped cold water but then, slowly, caught a bit of body heat and began to feel warmer than his drenched cotton shirt. He rejoiced and slashed at the rushes around him until he had another armful, and began carrying them back. They might be the salvation of someone back at camp.

He worked his way through dense cottonwood bottoms, noting that the huge rough-barked trees seemed relatively dry on their eastern sides. People could lean against their trunks on that side, somewhat protected from the northwest winds and the driving rain. As he walked, his restless mind hunted for burial scaffolds—he'd like nothing better than to rob the dead of robes and blankets and weapons, so the living might live. But he saw nothing. Only wild things in an empty land.

That's when he came upon Mister Skye, riding Jawbone.

"Worried about you, mate," the guide said, his gaze taking in the bulky deformed shirt and Rudolpho's armload of rushes.

"I'm a stuffed shirt," said Rudolpho gleefully. "It helps. It keeps bunching up but if it's spread evenly in my shirt, it insulates."

"How'd you cut it?"

Danzig grinned, dug in his wet pocket, and pulled out the flint arrowhead.

Mister Skye took it, admired its sharp edges, and handed it back. "A treasure. It could bloody well save our lives." He slid down. "Hop up here now. Your feet are leaking blood."

"That horse'll kill me. No reins either."

"No. Not now. First week or so he might have. He'll allow it now." Mister Skye relieved the professor of his armload and helped him up.

"Warmth between my legs," said Danzig. "Feels almost royal."

Oh, for horses, Danzig thought. They could all ride, barefoot or not, to any sheltering point. Or even down to those hot springs Mister Skye had talked of, a day or two south. And just wait out the storm immersed in hot water. His convulsing stopped, thanks to Jawbone's warmth and the rushes in his shirt.

"Professor, I think we have less than an hour, at least for some. I found a hollow log for Victoria and Arabella."

"Any chance of a fire?"

"A chance," Mister Skye muttered. "If only things would be a bit easier. I need to make a bow. Need to find a bone-dry stick, and a bone-dry log with a small pit in it— with your arrowhead we can hollow a pit. And bone-dry tinder—maybe from a squirrel nest, or a bird nest in a knothole or decayed hollow trunk. Bone-dry, Professor. I'll get some horsehair to Victoria and hope she can find room enough in her hollow log to plait hair into a bowstring of some sort. With your arrowhead I might be able to cut a long thong from my leggins, but the wet leather won't be strong enough. That arrowhead, Professor—that'll make some moccasins for two of us."

"From what?"

"My leggins."

"That'd leave you too naked in this weather."

"I got this long elkskin shirt and breechclout."

No one remained in the gravel bench where they'd camped. But Elkanah called from within the cottonwood forest, and they turned that way. They'd all removed to the trees, even Cobb and Connaught. The gusting wind cut at them less, and they'd discovered the dry east sides of the massive trees. At one, Elkanah sat with his back to the tree, holding Betsy tightly, warming her as well as he could. And she held Dirk's cradlebasket. The baby fussed, hungry, but was better off than the rest inside his warm cocoon with a hood of leather over it. The cradlebasket itself, in Betsy's arms, gave her some additional protection.

Mary sat in the lee of a tree, stoically making grass bundles, using horsehair to tie the tops of each. She looked numb.

In the dry lee of other trees sat Cobb and Percy Connaught. Cobb sat ashen-faced, in only his wet shirt and pants. Connaught had commandeered all of Mary's grass bundles and had packed them around him. Both trembled convulsively. Their gaze followed Mister Skye and Professor Danzig and the horse, but they said nothing.

"Up with you both now," said Mister Skye gently. "I want you to run in place, wave your arms, make your body work hard. Then we'll stuff these rushes around you."

Cobb laughed sarcastically, between chattering teeth. "Make us die comfortable," he muttered, shivering.

But Percy Connaught obeyed, casting aside all the grass bundles and standing in his muddy underclothes. He flailed clumsily, shivering. In the lee of the cottonwood little rain hit him. In moments he puffed and quit.

"We're done for," he muttered.

"No, mate. The professor here has found an arrowhead that may save us all."

Cobb laughed wildly, but the laugh died away into a shudder and spastic rattle of the throat.

"Mister Cobb," said Mister Skye, "you've lost faith. If you won't save yourself, we will."

Danzig slid off Jawbone to help. Together, he and Mister Skye stuffed the rushes into Cobb's shirt, working them around into an insulating barrier. The rest they stuffed up his pants legs, while Cobb watched inertly, chattering.

"I'd rather die fast than slow," Cobb muttered.

"You'd be better off sitting there with Percy, your back against his chest."

Cobb grinned grayly. "Too intimate for males," he said, convulsing again.

"Professor," said Mister Skye, "perhaps you could sit here with one or the other. I'll take Jawbone and the arrowhead and cut another load."

"I'll go with you," said Danzig. "The rushes in my shirt have warmed me some."

Mister Skye peered at him sharply. They stopped at the tree that sheltered the Morses.

The baby gnawed at a cattail bulb, but fussed.

"If you find some moss," said Mary, "I'll clean him. He's soiled. He's warm, though."

"We'll look," said Mister Skye. Then he addressed the Morses. "Elkanah, Betsy, we'll make it, thanks to the arrowhead that Rudolpho found. It's flint, too, and later we can strike a fire with it. We'll bring back more rushes now, and you'll find them helpful when spread evenly inside your clothing."

Elkanah sighed. "I'm sorry I'm so helpless, Mister Skye. I've become so numb . . . this tree offered a little relief . . . do you really believe that we—can—get out of this? Or are you just buoying us up in hopeless circumstances?"

"It's very bad, mate. Especially without a fire. But there's a chance. When there's a chance, fight for it. Eat on those cattail bulbs. They're nourishing. Full of sand or grit and not pleasant, but they sustain life. All of you, down as many of them as you can. Later we can pound them into an excellent flour.''

Cobb laughed weirdly. ''With what?'' he yelled from his tree. ''Our handy kitchen?''

''I'm coming with you,'' said Elkanah quietly. ''Betsy, will you be warm enough?''

''I'm coming with you, too,'' she said firmly.

''We've only one tiny arrowhead to cut with, mates.''

''I'm coming anyway. I can be looking for things.''

The Morses came. They all stopped at the hollow log and found that Arabella and Victoria were almost comfortable.

The girl nodded mutely, too miserable to talk. But they could see she wasn't shivering. At the other end of the great log, Victoria shivered nakedly.

''I'm damn cold,'' she muttered. ''Dry, anyway.''

''You gave your dress to save my daughter. I've got my wool nightdress under my dress, and I'm going to give it to you now!'' Betsy cried. ''Go ahead, gentlemen. I'll catch up.''

''Goddamn, that'd feel good,'' said Victoria.

As they stumbled ahead Elkanah seemed to gather strength. ''I'll hunt bone while you cut rushes. Give me a rib bone and some sandstone to sand with and I'll make a knife and speed this up.''

''Don't look for skeletons in these cottonwood bottoms. Look on open ground,'' said Mister Skye. ''That's where you'll find sandstone anyway, along the bluffs. Keep moving. Start calling if you go numb. Make your blood work. Better yet, Elkanah, I'll go on Jawbone while you and Rudolpho cut rushes here. I'll return directly. I can cover a lot of ground on a horse, far more than a barefoot man. You keep warm cutting hard. Here, I'll cut some more of Jawbone's tail hair and you can tie the rushes into bundles. We'll take the big load back on Jawbone.''

They watched Mister Skye wheel Jawbone west, through cottonwood forests and brush. Rudolpho cut first, slashing a small handful of rushes with the arrowhead, finding some warmth in the work. Elkanah stuffed the first batch into his shirt, and then began tying them into bundles.

''Let me cut awhile, Rudolpho. I'm cold again. I never

knew what cold was until now. I never even knew I could live, make my body work, feeling as heatless as I do now.''

Danzig handed him the tiny brown arrowhead, and Elkanah began slashing at rushes furiously.

''I'll be back in a bit. I'm going to walk the river flats again. There's got to be some sharp rock I can use to cut with,'' Rudolpho said.

Elkanah stood a moment, looking haggard. ''It's up to us and the Skyes, isn't it, Rudolpho? We've got to try. Use the last bit of our strength if we must. Figure things out. I've never needed to think to save my life, but now I'm trying to think and act to save my life—and Betsy and Arabella's. It's all impossible, I know. But I don't want to die from a lack of trying. Who knows? Some tribe or village might show up. We might find a warm cave. Sometimes these Indians leave ceremonial lodges or shelters. Never give up, Rudolpho. We must never, never give up!''

Danzig smiled. He'd gotten numb standing, and hobbled off toward the riverbank. He kept his back to the driving rain. It seemed warmer somehow than when rain lashed his face and trickled icily down his chest and belly. Behind him he heard Betsy arrive and take over the cutting while Elkanah bundled the rushes.

So many problems, he thought. Shelter and fire first. But food, too. They couldn't put that off. Tools and weapons to make. Bows and arrows, lances, clubs. Clothing . . . he wondered if the rushes could be woven into something much more durable than cattail mats. Surely they'd make carrying baskets. Ancient people and modern all wove baskets from rushes.

He spotted an antler and picked it up. Mister Skye said he wanted one, but the reason for it eluded the geologist. Along the gravelly flats he hunted, his eye alert for something, anything of value. He found the remains of a dead mallard, long since devoured by predators. But the heap contained feathers, and feathers made arrows. He grabbed a handful and stuffed feathers in his pocket. He thought about down, but this duck carcass yielded none. A tough vine tripped him. Vines! he thought. Vines to tie shelters together! He ripped it loose and followed its long snaking stem, finally gathering ten feet of it. He couldn't break it, but with a rock he smashed it off from its roots. Feather, antler, and vine, he thought unhappily. And they were all freezing to death.

A covey of ducks burst from rushes ahead of him, whirring into the air and honking loudly. Meat, he thought ruefully, at last feeling pangs of hunger. The exploding ducks startled something else, and he glimpsed a brown form—deer probably—bounding off. The thought of hot, steaming, tender meat, of hides, filled him with a vast yearning. His eye caught some dun chert among the gravels. Maybe it'd make sparks. He pocketed it. He probed around the gravel with his antler, and then it came to him—he held a knife in his hand.

Excited, he stared at the antler. Not one knife—ten knives! But he needed sandstone in hand-sized smooth chunks to start shaping it. Easy enough. The bluffs to either side of the river were made of it. He hobbled over a carpet of sticks, oblivious to the jabs and slices, and struck through grassy parks, past dense brush, and finally to a sandstone outcrop. Plenty of it, stratified and weathered. Feverishly he began grinding on an antler prong. It'd probably be hollow or spongy in the center, but he could still fashion an excellent knife from one side of it. He set the prong on rock so he could apply pressure, and delighted to see the sandstone in his hand begin to cut into the antler, flattening one side. He turned it over and flattened the other, sanding violently, barely aware of the rain. Gradually he shaped a knife, two flat sides about four inches long, plus a comfortable handle. But he didn't know how to cut the prong loose from the antler. Then it occurred to him to notch it and snap it off.

So intense was his labor that he scarcely realized people called for him. Then Mister Skye rode up on Jawbone and sat, observing the professor's progress.

"That's the most valuable thing so far," said the guide. "We'll cut rushes fast with that. I didn't find any buffer bones, but I found a shelter place. Little overhang, couple hundred yards downstream. Only three, four feet of overhang, but it's dry and we can block off the rest with a wall of brush or thatch. Professor, don't go back to the old place. Just head upstream along this bluff. Do it now. You can sand it in a dry place, get out of the wet.''

"Mister Skye, I'd be more than delighted to get out of the wet,'' he said. He gathered up his antler and sandstone blocks, plus a sharp-edged piece he thought might help snap the prong off, and trudged north. Some of the others had already arrived, carried there on Jawbone. Cobb and Connaught sat under the low overhang in a completely dry place. Rudolpho even noted dust and dead leaves and twigs untouched by rain here. Maybe the sort of debris that'd kindle into a fire.

"I don't see that this rock is any better than the tree," muttered Connaught. "It'll just prolong the agony. I've never been so cold. No heat left in me. I can't imagine why I ever consented to this journey.''

"Here, Percy, come here and work this sandstone over the antler. Keep you warmer," said Rudolpho kindly.

"You really suppose that your little toolmaking exploits will rescue us from exposure and starvation, thousands of miles from civilization,'' Percy said.

But the dry protected hollow had awakened the possibility of survival in Cobb. "Percy," he said sharply, "we're probably within fifty miles of comfortable lodges with warm fires in them. Bridger runs a trading post somewhere southwest of here. Victoria's people, the Crows, claim this basin as their own. We can't be far from a warm Crow village. Mary's people, the Shoshones, often hunt and camp in this Big Horn River basin. I don't know how far we are from Fort Laramie itself—our goal—but I suppose it's not far.''

"Without moccasins," muttered Percy.

Rudolpho said, "Jawbone will carry two of us. Mister Skye says his leggins will make a couple pair. And as we make weapons and fire-starting things, we'll get clothing and warmth. In Europe, many people wear wood-soled clogs. And don't forget sandals. Even an old desiccated buffalo hide might yield sandal soles. Come help me, Jarvis. My arms are so tired with this grinding I can't make them work anymore.''

Jarvis Cobb came at once, a different human being from

the one who sat listlessly in the rain, mocking the gods. "I don't see how we'll make it—unless we're rescued by friendly Indians—but trying is better than not trying," he said. He took over the knife making, bearing down with the sandstone in long smooth sweeps across the prong.

"I'm starving to death," said Percy. "Not that there's any reason to live. I've lost everything. I won't even be leaving my insights behind when I go."

But Rudolpho didn't listen. He'd spotted Mister Skye, Elkanah, and Betsy on Jawbone, all of them carrying bundles of rushes. And struggling barefoot behind them came Mary, with Dirk in his cradlebasket on her back. All gathering here, hauling their few possessions, cattail mats, bits of rock, the clothing on their backs. The rain, if anything, lashed down harder.

The newcomers huddled gratefully in the dry air, all three of them spontaneously hugging each other tightly. Mary set her heavy cradlebasket down. Dirk howled lustily now—he needed food and attention at once. From outside, Mister Skye turned Jawbone around for one last wet trip, to bring Victoria and Arabella from their log. To Rudolpho, this shallow hollow, this dry place, seemed more marvelous than all the palaces of the Hapsburgs and Bourbons in the Europe he left behind.

Chapter 23

Mister Skye had no idea how long it might be until night-fall. The gloomy overcast hid the sun. A lot of time had elapsed since the Bannocks had ridden off in the morning, but perhaps that had been more recent than it seemed. Ordeals did that: time went haywire through trouble. Hun-kering under the shelter of the low overhang, he studied a sky that held its secrets perfectly, neither hinting of the end of this icy rain, nor revealing the hour.

Beside him, the others huddled miserably, trying to draw heat from each other. The overhang might keep fresh rain off them, but it achieved little else. Freezing wind gusted and eddied through it, turning wet cloth and leather to ice. Every scrap of material they'd gathered—rushes, grasses, cattail mat—they'd put to use in and over their clothing, with little effect. They eyed him, waited for him, the gaunt despair in their faces telling him that he alone could save them, that they had run out of ideas. The expectant and defeated looks told him something else, too. None of them wished to venture out into that stinging rain again. Here in the lee of the cliff, when they clung tightly enough to each other, the soaked rags they wore grew slightly warm, or at least didn't suck the last heat out of their bodies. So they cowered there, a bit warmer than out in the weather—but in mortal peril.

Up to him. Their stares said it'd be up to him. He felt as cold as the others, a deadly numbness that seemed to go deep. He shivered violently on occasion, unable to stop the convulsing and shaking of his limbs.

Fire, he thought. They had shelter of sorts, and the only additional thing they could do would be to pile up brush around the overhang to cut wind. Maybe thatch a wall if they had energy enough—and the daylight to do it, which he doubted. He guessed it had reached late afternoon, and an hour of the gloomy light remained before a pitch-black, starless, moonless overcast night descended.

Fire, or some, maybe all, would die this night. He probed around in the debris. Their drenched clothing had wet much of it, but he found a few small dry twigs, some dry leaf, weed seeds, a bit of fluff. One good-sized ancient cottonwood stick, maybe four inches in diameter. Half-wet where someone had sat or dripped on it. Enough to try, he thought.

The baby squalled. Mary had pulled him from the warmth of the cradlebasket and wiped him with wet grasses. The shock of the cold set the tyke to howling and sent pain through Mister Skye's heart. Mary had found a flat rock and a river cobble and began pounding a cattail bulb into an edible mush for the baby. She'd stopped nursing him only a few months ago, and now Mister Skye wished she still might have milk. He watched her slide some of the cattail pulp into the child's mouth. The boy spat it out and bellowed. She tried again and this time the child munched on it, whimpering. He'd be warm again soon, back in the cradlebasket with its seasoned leather outer shell and blanket lining inside.

Fire. He began gathering the dry debris, twigs, fluff, dust and the half-wet stick. Fire. Make a fire with this.

"Victoria," he said, "if your fingers still work, would you make a horsehair bowstring for a fire bow?"

"That hair ain't long enough, Mister Skye."

"I know," he said. "Try it anyway."

Muttering, she pulled herself away from the warmth of the other women and sorted out three small bundles of Jawbone's tail hair, twisted each, and adding new filaments of the twelve- or fifteen-inch hair, began plaiting them into a cord that would run not much more than three feet long, less when she wove the ends into loops for the bow.

The others watched intently, hope and discouragement showing in their gazes.

"Mister Danzig," Mister Skye said. "I need to have a small smooth conical pit chipped out of the dry side of this stick here, maybe half an inch in diameter. A single drop of water will ruin it. I will need a similar little pit dug into a hand-sized piece of wood. That doesn't have to be bone-dry, but it mustn't be wet or spray water."

"I'm so cold that any work will help," Professor Danzig muttered. He dug the wet flint arrow point from his pockets, wiped it on the inside of the cradleboard—the only thing approaching a dry place—and began gouging tiny bits of wood, trying to keep water out of his work.

"I'm going to go out on Jawbone and hunt down a dry stick. Need a bone-dry stick, maybe a foot high, inch in diameter, to spin in that hole. While I'm gone, gents, I'd like you to brave that rain one more time—gather the driest firewood you can find—from the lee side of trees, underside of deadfall. Once it gets dark, it'll be too dark to gather anything beyond firelight—and there's no wood to speak of in here."

Elkanah nodded. "I'll do it," he said, rising wearily. "Will you join me, gentlemen?"

Cobb stood, trembling, and hobbled out.

Connaught said, "I'd not be any good, I'm afraid." He drew grass bundles about him and settled back. "I don't believe in fighting fate or defying destiny," he added.

No one replied.

"I'm trying to reconcile myself to what must come," he muttered.

Elkanah and Jarvis plunged into the sweeping rain.

Mister Skye dragged himself out, felt the terrible icy lash again, and caught Jawbone by the mane. He led the slippery horse to a log and mounted painfully. Then he rode numbly into the cottonwood forest, hunting for the single dry stick he had to have. The rain assaulted him in sheets deep in the forested flat of the river, missing him one moment, deluging him icily the next. He couldn't stand it long, he knew. Perhaps he imagined it, but the light seemed to grow murky and fade. He studied each tree, looking for a knothole containing squirrel debris, scrutinizing each deadfall log that might be hollow or rotten and hold the stick he wanted. At last he found a giant trunk that had lodged against another tree when it fell, so it remained high enough for him to crawl under if he wished.

There in the dull light stood the sticks he wanted, spikes from the old log, projecting straight down, ancient and dry apart from whatever minor windborne spray had touched them. He slid off the horse and hunkered before them, staring. Yes, he could break them off. But then he realized he had no way to carry the precious sticks back to the overhang without soaking them. Bark, perhaps. A piece of hollow log he could put them in? Nothing.

He boarded Jawbone again from a stump, feeling his legs slide over the slick wet hair, and went hunting for a stick carrier in the dimming light. Running out of time. Nothing. He stopped, wondered if there might be something, anything, up at the overhang.

An idea came to him, and he rode back to the others, after sharply peering around to memorize this place in the dying light.

"Need the cradlebasket for a few minutes, Mary," he said. "To keep a stick or two dry."

Her dark glance seemed despairing, he thought, but she wordlessly pulled little Dirk out and clutched him to her cold wet breast. Mister Skye took the cradlebasket gratefully, folded its hood over to keep rain out, and rode Jawbone down into the gray forest again. He felt the slap of yellow cottonwood leaves plastering him with every gust. At the fallen log, he dismounted.

How could he keep his hands dry? He wiped them futilely, first on leggins, then on Jawbone's underbelly. Nothing. He'd have to snap the spikes from the log wet-handed and hope not to touch the ends. As a last measure he rubbed his hands along the underside of the log and then gripped the first stick. It cracked off and he darted it into the cradle-basket. The second snapped harder, but he slid it in also and nestled the dressed leather over his precious cargo. And rode back.

"Keep those sticks bone-dry," he muttered to the others. "We need only one, but keep them both dry. Professor, whittle the ends into points if you can with the antler blade."

Then he turned Jawbone back into the gloom. He still needed bow wood and began searching for a box-elder stalk, maybe an inch or two in diameter. Or anything like it that he could break off. It had grown almost too dark to see. Close to the river, he found chokecherry brush and snapped off the cold wet sapling, having trouble with the clinging bark. He finally mashed off the bark with a rock, hammering viciously until the last of the fibrous material parted. The light had died, and he'd have to make his bow in virtual blackness. He wished he'd done this earlier, but when you're trying to stay alive and keep others alive, time grows peculiar and irrelevant.

He slid off Jawbone at the overhang and plunged under it, bone-cold again, feeing water trickle down his chest and belly, catch in his loincloth, drip from his plastered-down hair. Elkanah and Jarvis had returned with some pathetic, mostly soaked sticks. And they'd managed to pile some brush at the north end of the overhang to slow the gusts a bit. Both of them walked back and forth in the confined space, willing their bodies to move.

"Don't know how we'll see to do this," he muttered.

"I have these," said Danzig, holding up a couple of pieces of wood with small hollows pitted in them, blurred shadows in this light.

"I don't see this hair no more," muttered Victoria. She eyed his crude chunk of chokecherry disdainfully. "That's too fat. Gotta be thinner to make a bow. I'll go get one," she said.

Before he could stop her, she plunged out, a wraith in her white nightdress.

"Don't!" he cried. "Too dark! You'll get lost!"

But she ignored him. Some lingering eerie light gave her

passage. He waited, dripping, desperately cold again, and finally peeled off his sopping skin shirt and wrung water from it. His flesh had become icy. He sat down, easing back into the cold rock wall. Mary slipped down in front of him and pressed her warmer back into his chest. That felt good.

Like a ghost, Victoria reappeared in the blue dark, dripping water. She held a proper wand of wood.

"Goddamn," she muttered. She peeled off the borrowed nightdress and wrung it out carefully, her wizened body all but invisible in the murk anyway. Then she put it on, tugging the resisting wet wool.

"Where's that arrowhead, Danzig? I gotta scrape this into a bow and put nocks on the end," she said.

They could hear her in the dismal darkness. Her teeth chattered. The others huddled silently, night upon them, finding only each other for warmth.

For an endless while, they heard only her steady scraping, her profane muttering, and the soft movement of arms and fingers in the night. Mouse scratching, rat gnawing. It grew colder. Mister Skye could no longer control his shaking. He couldn't see the others, but supposed they might be better off welded together as they were.

Night settled into utter emptiness. They could not see each other, even a few feet away. Vicious winds gusted down the slope from above, chilling them. In pitch black, Victoria sandstoned the little piece of bow wood, tapering and notching ends for the bowstring, muttering in her strange Absaroka tongue. Mary crooned softly, quieting the restless child. Somewhere in that inkiness, Harvard Professor Danzig whittled tiny chips of wood from a dry stick, feeling his way as he chipped a broad point at either end.

Mister Skye stood and paced. He feared his body would quit if he didn't. But he bumped into someone else, two others, also pacing. He didn't inquire who.

"Goddamn!" exclaimed Victoria. "Where's that horse string?"

Silence, and anguish.

"Ah!" she said. She muttered and mumbled. "We make it go now, Mister Skye," she said. "You kneel down here."

Danzig sat there, too, holding things. Victoria handed

him the little bow, first. He felt its tension, felt the taut horsehair string looped and tied at each end. Good, he thought, but so short he'd hardly get up any speed. Danzig found Mister Skye's hand, led it to the wood on the ground, and showed where the tiny pit in it was. Mister Skye assembled it all, the fire stick, with a twist of the horsehair around it, a small hand-held block on top to serve as a bearing, and the bow.

"Now, Mister Danzig. A pinch of that dry stuff off the floor here into the hole, please. And then hold the bottom piece firmly."

"It's done," said Danzig.

He sawed at the bow slowly, feeling and hearing the stick whirl in its sockets, beginning the friction that he hoped would set the tiny bits of debris smoldering. From above, he pressed down gently, taking it easy on the hair bowstring. Blackness multiplied the difficulties. He scarcely knew whether his fire stick stood upright. He sawed at the bow, the stick whirled and squeaked—good, squeaking might mean it's dry, he thought. He couldn't see a damned thing. Gently, gently, he sawed, back and forth, spinning one stick in the socket gouged into another.

Nothing. "Victoria, I'm going to lift the point out of the hole. If your finger is dry, see if there's heat. And add a pinch of tinder. . . ."

"Goddamn, it's warm," she said. "Ain't hot, though."

He set to work again, this time whirling harder and faster, less careful of the bowstring. He sawed madly, feeling the stick spin under his palmed pressure, and finally smelling— he thought—a bit of smoke.

"Close!" he muttered.

"I think I smell smoke!" cried Elkanah.

In the blackness Victoria pinched more of the tinder into the little charred hole, and Mister Skye sawed the bow back and forth. The exercise and tension heated him, at least momentarily, driving back the circling wolves of cold. Smoke again, close, so close.

"Oh, God," cried Betsy, "let it happen, have mercy on us!"

"Oh, please," added Arabella, lifted from her long silence by hope.

"Have mercy on us, Lord!" exclaimed Percy Connaught. "Have mercy on your poor servants!"

"We'll do it, man!" exclaimed Elkanah. "If the Indians did it before flint and steel, we can do it!"

Mister Skye spun the stick, jerking the little bow back and forth viciously. Too short. The bow didn't let him spin the stick for long before he had to go the other direction. He grew tired, but sawed anyway—

—until the horsehair string broke.

"What happened?" cried Jacob Cobb.

Something sagged lower and lower inside of Mister Skye. He felt his muscles weigh down, his body sink, icy air eddy over his bare feet.

"String broke," he muttered.

"Don't give up!" cried Elkanah. "We can make another. Try thong. Can we cut thong with Rudolpho's knife—from leggins?"

"Wet thong's weak, mate. And this bow's too short."

Mister Skye's words sounded like the rattle of a falling guillotine blade.

"It's in the hands of God," breathed Betsy. "If we had moonlight, we could cut a new longer bow and start over. Oh, I'm so cold. . . ."

"Hands of God," murmured Rudolpho, sounding puzzled.

Mister Skye sat in the blackness, seeing nothing of past and future, not even seeing in his mind's eye. Cold and despair snuffed his inner vision, turned this moment into an eternal midnight. Hell, he thought. Hell must simply be a place without light and heat.

"I'll give you my shoestring. Tie two shoestrings," muttered Captain Cobb. "I'll give you my West Point belt."

"We can fix it!" Elkanah exclaimed firmly. "Never give up! Never give up! I'll find something. Who's got something for a string?"

No one answered.

"Some spin the stick by rolling it hard between hands,

mates," Mister Skye said. "Hold the bottom one, Professor. Victoria, pinch in some more tinder."

He tried again. Between his palms he whirled the stick in its socket, harder and harder until crouching exhaustion sprang upon him. He stopped.

"How hot is the hole, Victoria?"

She muttered, didn't reply.

"Anyone else want to try?"

Elkanah tried and wouldn't quit until he fumbled, exhausted, sobbing wildly.

"Hold me," whispered Betsy. "We must be together now."

Mister Skye heard shuffling, and Elkanah's soft sobs, buried upon the breast of his wife.

He peered into the night and saw exactly nothing.

Little Dirk squalled violently, and ratcheted sobs. Mary exclaimed, "What?" The child's sobs muffled.

"Who took the cradlebasket?" she cried.

It took Mister Skye a moment to understand. And when he understood, he still felt too tired and cold to care. His son whimpered and coughed, while Mary soothed.

"Whoever took Dirk's cradlebasket, return it now," he said. "Return it now and I won't be coming for you."

"Oh, God!" Betsy cried. "God have mercy!"

No one stirred.

"I'll be hunting you down," said Mister Skye.

Silence met him. Betsy sobbed. Victoria cursed. Mary soothed the cold infant.

"I'll be hunting right now. And you'll feel my hands," Mister Skye rumbled, in a voice as black as the night.

A miserable thing, he thought. He found someone and patted ruthlessly. And another. And another. His sixth sense told him someone moved silkily, always knowing where the guide was. He jabbed out toward the rain with both hands, touched a bare wet foot, he thought, and met silence again. Nothing.

Not that a cradlebasket would help much . . . he thought. Still, the outer lining and hood would run maybe three feet square. . . . Warm someone a lot.

"Cradle robber!" he roared. "I don't know who you are, but I'll find out!"

From the darkness, Elkanah's voice. "I intend to find out, too. We'll survive this. And someone will return east in shame."

His voice quivered with cold.

"Let's all huddle close now," he added softly.

"No, mates. If you do that, you'll die before this night's over. We'll walk. Every last one of us—get up and walk, all night, right to dawn. We'll walk until we drop, round and round this little place, stooped under here. Up and walk! You—the one with my Dirk's cradlebasket, and his little robe—you won't make it under that. You've got to walk all this long night!"

Chapter 24

The baby whimpered at her breast. She felt its icy limbs and wondered why the little thing wasn't bawling. A placid child, she thought. Her people withstood cold much better than these whites, and the blood of her Shoshones ran in Dirk. She clutched the naked boy, trying to protect him with her hands and with the wet elkskin of her dress. But it seemed hopeless.

She felt the cold and hungry baby's needs as keenly as she felt her own: food, warmth, dryness, relief from the murderous cold that pressed so relentlessly. It had not reached freezing. Winter Man had not come, making Earth white. But he hovered not far away, and could kill wet and unclad people even before water turned to ice. She hugged Dirk tighter, trying somehow to cover the child.

What manner of man would do such a thing? Had these white people no honor? Did they not love children? Her people loved children. Not only her people, but the other Indian people, too. Only rarely did they harm a child. Not even enemy children. Sometimes they captured the little ones of enemies, not to kill or harm them, but to raise them as their own. She knew of enemy Blackfeet children in the village of her people. Arapaho, Cheyenne, Lakotah, too.

But someone among these white people stole from her child, stole selfishly so he might live and the child might die. It seemed so terrible to Mary she couldn't grasp it. Unspeakable, this deed. Were all of Mister Skye's people like that, evil in their spirits, empty, without good medicine? The question brought its own answer in her mind. No, they were not all like that. She thought of each of them here and decided that three would never do such a thing, but the other three might.

The child stirred restlessly in her hands and sobbed softly. Everywhere her hands touched its smooth young flesh, she found numb cold. Its back had grown numb, its legs stiff. Surely that child of her womb and Mister Skye's love, surely it would cease to breathe before Sun came. A terrible bitterness sang through her, and she thought she would find out who did this thing, and kill. Yes, kill. The bad-medicine person who had evil must be driven out, sent to the spirit land, sent where his spirit would wander forever without a home.

Medicine. Her own medicine helper and friend had always been the magpie, bold saucy bird, black and white, daring and smart. Well, Magpie, what would you say to me now? she thought. How would you save my child from the Winter Man?

Dirk sobbed steadily now, choking on his sobs.

"Blanket stealer," muttered Victoria, who trembled next to Mary. "I'm gonna go look," she whispered.

Mary's own coldness consumed her mind when Victoria vanished. How dark! She'd never known a night so black, so black that even the people next to her seemed a long way away, and she seemed all alone. Only the sound of their breath, or a subtle sense of their presence, told her that she wasn't utterly alone with her freezing child under a naked overhang. Just beyond, the subtle whisper of splashing told her the rain still sheeted down.

No one complained about Dirk's soft sobbing. Some shame pervaded them all, the utter evil of the theft of the cradlebasket grinding heavily upon other souls and hearts.

"Let me hold him, Mrs. Skye," said Betsy. "I have skirts that might warm him."

Mary didn't answer.

Mister Skye paced angrily, staying warm, she knew, but also driven by boiling rage.

A clatter. "Here!" hissed Victoria. A moment later Mary felt the old Crow woman touching her, handing her the cradle frame.

"Found the damn thing almost in the rain," she whispered. "Here—feel this!"

Mary felt, and touched wool! The inner liner she'd fashioned from an old Hudson Bay blanket remained inside the basket, a little bag of wool she'd carefully sewn for Dirk. She used it in cold weather. In warm, the outer leather lining sufficed to keep the child comfortable and protect it from rain and sun. That laced-down leather skin had been stolen. No doubt at the crack of dawn, she'd find it on the rock somewhere, carefully abandoned before telltale light came. Wool!

"Thank you, Magpie," she whispered. "We have stolen it back. You have sent Victoria!"

She felt, rather than saw, Mister Skye suddenly crouch before her.

"What?" he muttered.

For an answer, she found his hand and guided it to the cradlebasket and the wool, letting him hold it while she pulled Dirk off her soft breast and slipped the little boy into the dry woolen sack, and felt the child slowly relax in the sudden warmth.

"Goddamn," muttered Victoria.

From afar, Elkanah's sad voice came to them. "I am afraid to ask this, but is the baby—he's stopped crying. . . ."

"Dear God," wept Betsy.

Mister Skye addressed them all, his voice a low thunder in the bitter night.

"Victoria found the cradle," he rumbled. "Outer elkhide's missing. Someone's snatched a robe for himself. But inside, Mary had a wool lining, sewn from a blanket. Dry wool, a bag. She's put my boy in it and he'll weather the night. . . ."

"Thank God!" Betsy cried again, weeping.

Mary heard others cough and sigh.

Mister Skye continued quietly, soft words floating out into the inkiness. "I'm talking now to the one that stole the liner," he said. "All you had to do was ask. We'd have given you that hide liner. We'd simply forgotten about the wool inside. Whoever you are, you stole life from my boy. I'll not forget this. We're all cold, but we'll survive, I think. And one of you'll go back east with a shame in you, a stain you can't erase, a deed you'll never undo."

Cobb laughed sarcastically. "Come on, Skye. I'm so cold right now I know I'm dead before dawn. What time is it, do you suppose? Nine in the evening? Ten? And who's to say tomorrow will be warmer? The sun will rise on corpses."

"Don't give up! Never give up!" exclaimed Elkanah. "Mister Skye's right. Walk. If we sleep, we'll die! Make our muscles work and we'll live! I've walked this whole time, and I'm still living!"

Mary listened for more. Neither Arabella nor Percy Connaught spoke. And neither did Professor Danzig, now that she thought about it. Maybe Professor Danzig was a witch, just as Victoria thought. Bad-medicine man, bringing evil upon them all. She clutched the woolen bundle to her breast, warming the baby within it with her caress, warming herself, too. Beside her she felt Victoria trembling in her wet nightdress. Mary handed the woolen bundle to the older woman, who clutched it to her own chest. She felt Mister Skye gathering them into his arms, sharing what small heat remained in him. And then, when he discovered Victoria's trembling, he pulled off his elkskin shirt and pulled it over her, and Mary heard Victoria weep.

It surprised Elkanah Morse that life remained in him. He didn't see how his body could possibly function, his heart beat, his lungs pump air, when his flesh and bone had lost their warmth. He wondered what his body temperature might be. Whenever he felt the fatal drowsiness seep into him, he bolted up, sometimes hitting his head on the low rock above, and paced a tiny circle furiously, flapping arms as he went. Tiredness had long since consumed him, but he scarcely cared about that. Cold remained the enemy, the stalking killer.

Betsy prayed. He knew that, heard her soft whispers and entreaties. He dragged her up from her seat where she slumped against the rear rock wall, forced her to walk beside him, and all the while she whispered and sobbed and trembled. He'd found Arabella, too, tight beside someone— Cobb probably—and pulled her up and forced her to march, she protesting bitterly all the while. Some of the dampness had left Arabella's borrowed doeskin dress as well as Betsy's linen one; he could feel that with his hands. They'd been under the cliff for hours and body heat slowly dried clothing.

Still it poured. He jabbed a hand out and felt the icy sting. Heard its soft murderous song, too. He sensed Danzig paced also, but not Connaught, who huddled inert somewhere. The shame and rage of the cradleboard affair boiled through him. He could understand the desperation. He felt the same cold, the same frantic need to wrap himself in anything at all. Not Danzig, surely not Danzig, his fine dear friend, and a man of honor. Not Betsy, not Arabella . . . his mind stumbled uneasily upon his daughter. Had she done something so dishonorable? The others, surely— the two he didn't know well, who'd tied on to his plans. He hadn't known Cobb at all; knew Connaught only through business. One of them! He would deal with one of them! The world would know about one of them!

He returned to his pacing, his mind mad with ideas. That's how his mind worked, thinking, trying, planning, studying. No problem he'd ever faced in a long life had ever been so desperate as this. No telling what dawn would bring. Could it only be nine or ten, with a whole night ahead? Surely they'd die. What heat remained? What shelter? He thought of weaving rushes into tight blankets and discarded it. No one could see a thing. In any case, most of the rushes had been consumed, shoved under clothing into thick layers of prickly grasses that did insulate them a bit.

He peered out. Not the slightest sign of a star or moon. What would they do tomorrow? Try a fire again, he supposed. If anyone was yet alive. Make a new bowstring from Jawbone's tail hair. Or Mary's . . . the woman's jet hair hung to her waist when she hadn't braided it.

"Mister Skye?" he whispered. "Let's try the fire bow with Mary's hair. It's longer!"

He waited for a reply. At last the guide responded. "Bow itself's too short, mate. I couldn't get it to spin the stick long enough. Also, hair's slippery. Victoria's loop and knots slid apart. And how will we see to braid it?"

Elkanah heard Cobb laughing sardonically again. "You'll invent something, I'm sure, Elkanah. In Lowell, you'd sit at your warm desk and invent something, sipping tea and eating tarts while you do."

Elkanah didn't reply. Hunger worked on him as it did the others. He'd tried a cattail bulb and found it gritty and bland, smelling of swamp, but he'd managed to get it down, sand and all.

Jawbone. Jawbone! "Mister Skye," he began. "What about Jawbone? Could you get him to lie down here? He's a thousand pounds of warmth. We could all draw warmth from it if the horse would lie still."

"Afraid not, Elkanah. I couldn't get that horse to lie still for that."

"But—a half a ton of warm flesh! Try, Mister Skye!"

Jarvis Cobb said, "Kill him. That heat would last all night. In the morning we'd have meat and a hide for shoes. You've got that belaying pin, Skye, and you can approach him, lead him here, and drop him right here. One horse for nine lives. How about it?"

Mister Skye didn't respond, and when he did at last, the answer surprised Elkanah.

"Ten lives, not nine, Captain Cobb. If you try to touch that horse, he'll kill you, if I don't kill you first."

Mister Skye's tone seemed so terrible that Elkanah couldn't imagine a reply from Cobb, but the captain laughed wildly.

Elkanah said, "That horse is our transportation, our ambulance if one of us becomes ill, Jarvis."

"Too late," muttered Cobb. "Dawn—if there is a dawn—must still be ten hours away, and I'm going right now. Half hour left for me . . ."

The man's desperation pierced the night. Probably true, Elkanah thought. Maybe none of them would live. If only they could have Jawbone . . .

Elkanah himself couldn't get Jawbone off his mind. He could almost feel the warmth of the animal radiating from its wet hair; he found himself conjuring up tasty steaks of horseflesh, cutting crude moccasins from the scarred blue hide of Skye's animal. Using its thong and sinew to make weapons, clothing, stone-head clubs and hatchets, horsehair from tail and mane woven into shirts . . .

He knew his own mind raced. Tiredness caught him again and he slumped beside Betsy, found her numb and inert. "Get up!" he cried, dragging her to her feet. She slumped down, unable to support herself. He lowered her to the cold rock and massaged her limbs, pumping arms and legs, hugging her.

"Mister Skye!" he cried. "Betsy's going."

"I'm coming," muttered the guide. "Keep talking so I can find you."

Together they lifted Betsy and dragged her, but her legs no longer worked and she wasn't responding.

"Elkanah," said the guide. "We'll have to press her between us. Hope you don't, ah . . . Let's ease her down, mate. I'll lie behind, you face her, and we'll press her."

Between them they sandwiched Betsy. Elkanah felt Mister Skye's massive hands reach past Betsy and onto his own back, pressing the three of them together. For a bit, Elkanah felt almost warm. He felt Betsy's heart and lungs work—she lived, sandwiched in a fragile warmth.

Cobb laughed relentlessly. "Should have killed Jawbone, Skye. We'd all make it to daylight with a warm carcass like that. Funny, Skye. You've railed and raged about a missing bit of skin covering for a baby, talking shame and honor and dishonor. But there you are, refusing to save ten human lives by killing a horse."

That accusation had justice in it. A deadly silence sifted through the desperate camp. Jawbone's body would indeed help them to dawn, Elkanah thought quietly. They might also manage to eat some raw hot meat, or hot blood, too. . . .

Mister Skye sighed. At last he said, "When Mrs. Morse is warm enough, I'll fetch Jawbone."

"Goddamn!" cried Victoria.

Mary wept. Elkanah fathomed that killing Jawbone would be akin to killing a brother or a child or a husband.

He felt Betsy's body slowly relax in the cocoon that he and Mister Skye had given her. Perhaps they could make such cocoons, taking turns at being the one in the middle. He lay quietly, his mind more and more on Jawbone, almost feeling the beast's hot warmth. Hair, hide, blood, hooves for glue perhaps, horseshoes to hammer into knives and . . .

"Mister Skye," he whispered. "Is Jawbone shod?"

"Of course, mate. Had him shod at Benton."

Elkanah felt a pulse of wild excitement. "We have fire!" he cried.

Cobb laughed nastily.

"Rudolpho! You found flint?"

"I think so," the geologist muttered. "Maybe some chert, but the arrowhead is definitely flint."

"Where is it?"

"Against the back wall of the overhang, drying out. Couldn't sleep with rock in my wet britches."

Elkanah bolted up crazily. "Mister Skye, get Jawbone fast. Iron! We have iron! Not as good as steel for sparking, but many a horseshoe has struck a spark! Will he hold for it?"

Mister Skye thought. "He stands for shoeing well enough, mate, as long as he knows the shoer. I haven't a halter, but I've got whangs enough on my leggins and shirt sleeves to cobble something."

"Can we get the shoe off?" cried Elkanah.

"Not in pitch black. Those nails, clinched over. I don't see that we have the tools—"

"We can sharpen an antler prong—" Elkanah shouted.

Betsy stirred in his arms. "I'm all right," she whispered. "Go make the fire!"

Mister Skye said, "I don't think we need to take the shoe

off, Elkanah. Victoria can hold him with a halter I'll lash up; I'll hold his foot steady. You and the professor can strike flint and get that tinder under it." He sighed softly. "I don't know that we can ignite the tinder, especially in total darkness. I'd give my arm for my charcloth."

Charred cloth, or charred cotton, heated until little but carbon remained, but not allowed to ignite, made perfect tinder, Elkanah knew. A spark settled on it, glowed into life, and a gentle breath often flared it into flame. But they had none of it.

"Betsy, we'll carry you to Arabella. Never stop hugging her. . . ."

Moments later, Mister Skye stood at the edge of shelter, whistling up Jawbone. They heard a rustling, a soft snort, and then felt the presence of the horse they couldn't see. "Easy," muttered Mister Skye. The very presence of the animal seemed a good thing. Not that they could feel its heat, but they sensed its presence. Mister Skye worked at something, and Elkanah realized the guide pulled whangs from his skin clothing and was tying them into something. In a bit, he heard Jawbone being turned around, the horse's deadly hind legs facing into the shelter, its shod hooves clicking on rock.

"Easy," muttered Mister Skye.

Then the guide's voice, very close. "Professor? Elkanah? Have you your things?"

Elkanah felt around for the tinder while Danzig fetched his rocks.

"Easy," said Mister Skye. "I'm holding his off rear hoof, gents. Hunker down here. Who's doing the honors?"

"I suppose I am," said Professor Danzig. "If I can hold the rock. My hands are numb."

"Easy," said the guide. The horse stirred restlessly. Both Rudolpho and Elkanah reached out, felt the hoof, traced the iron shoe, memorized it. Mister Skye held the foot toe-down, making the shoe vertical.

"The shoe's wet," said Danzig.

Mary materialized from somewhere and handed them a scrap of wool from the cradle—the only dry cloth among them.

"If he kicks, it's as good a way to die as any," Rudolpho joked, "and faster than some. Elkanah, is the tinder down?"

"Piled right below the shoe, Rudolpho."

"Well, let's be about it," the professor said.

He snapped a rock across the hoof. The horse stirred but held, with Mister Skye soothing him.

"That wasn't promising. Felt wrong," said Danzig. "Let's try this one."

Another harsh scrape, and a spray of sparks like fireworks.

"Ah!" cried Elkanah.

"Oh, God!" cried Betsy.

Behind him, Elkanah heard them all babbling.

Danzig struck again, and this time one tiny orange spark caught and glowed in something below.

"More, Rudolpho!" Elkanah cried.

Danzig struck flint again, and a spray of tiny shooting stars dropped through the darkness. Three sparks struck tinder and continued to glow. Elkanah blew gently, cursing the damp air, the humidity.

Then, grudgingly, a bitter blue flame wavered.

Chapter 25

Too late, too late.

Jarvis Cobb stared at the dazzling little flame flickering heatlessly as Mister Skye fed it twigs and sticks. It guttered dangerously in the cold gusts, but grew, crackling and wavering, casting a yellow wash over the dun rock of the overhang. Light out of darkness. Fire out of promises and hopes. They all gazed, bewitched, at this miracle of life snatching at least some of them from the lip of doom. Mister Skye, Professor Danzig, and Elkanah Morse huddled around it, nursing it protectively with their very bodies.

In it lay the possibility of life. Betsy wept. She'd come closest to doom, but others weren't far behind, minutes from the very end.

Light blossomed, glinted yellow off of wet rock just beyond, probed into corners previously black as pitch, struck the planes of flesh on faces, shadowed other planes. Jarvis rejoiced along with the rest—until he realized that they stared at him silently.

Too late, too late. The soft, well-oiled elkskin robe he'd unlaced from the cradlebasket remained tucked up under his armpits, wrapped tightly about his torso, offering steady life-giving warmth.

Too late, he remembered it. He stared at it, this insignia of dishonor, feeling the heat and scorn of their gazes. His mind leaped to find excuses, explanations, mitigating words, but he could think of none. His brain went soft, addled, rattled, and he couldn't string an idea together.

None of them said a thing. What was there to say? He stared wildly about, unable to meet their eyes, and then pitched the robe off with a small strangled laugh. Victoria picked it up and wrapped her small cold frame in it and returned Mister Skye's shirt to him. With the fire and his blanket bag, Dirk wouldn't need the outer lining.

"See? It wasn't needed," Jarvis babbled. "See, she took it."

No one spoke. Mary slipped to the fire with the restless child in her arms and let the rudimentary warmth begin its work.

Jarvis chuckled amiably. "Nothing ventured, nothing gained," he said. "What counts is the life of a man in his prime, fine-honed and educated, and not the life of a little— breed."

No one spoke.

Their obdurate stares told him he had become a pariah, an outlaw here in this community.

He ceased to make light of it. "We do what we have to to survive," he muttered. "You'd do the same if you were dying."

Still no one replied.

"This is nothing. I've done us a favor. The child doesn't even need it—he's got a wool bag. Now we've got moccasin leather from it."

The words drifted out into the strange silence, marked only by the snap of twigs in the tiny wavering fire. Its heat barely reached him where he sat with his back to the wall of rock, and he shivered, not daring to move closer to the life-giving flame.

He trembled, hugged himself. He'd do it again, he told himself. We all do what we must to save ourselves. He had that right—save himself or perish—and he took it. No harm done, either. They'd found the woolen inner lining. . . .

He'd been scarcely aware of that lining when he unlaced the cover in the pitch black. It snugged into the other side of the willow hoops of the cradle frame.

Jarvis Cobb had a sense that his life had changed in a moment, that some great dread crushing force had forever damaged his progress through his days and years. He sensed that he would live with this thing forever, that it might sneak up upon him in his nights, catch up with him as he taught at West Point, follow him about in whispers, ostracism, isolation, pointed fingers, lack of promotion. His wife, if she didn't know of reasons, would wonder why he seemed so isolated, why they never advanced. . . .

Sitting there against the cold rock, he sensed all that, less thought out than intuited in a flash. What rotten luck, having to deal with this, for surely it would follow him. Not a lifetime of valiant service in combat on the frontiers would wipe it away. And yet it had been nothing: a civilized scholarly life for a minor threat to a breed child of the wilderness, half-blooded of a Stone Age people.

He laughed. He'd made a perfectly logical choice; save what was valuable, a lifetime of study, of intelligence, and its applications. Save what was valuable if one had to make hard choices. Save himself, as he had every right—indeed, a firm duty—to do. Still, he thought, it'd go badly, badly. . . . A melancholy settled over him and he tried to turn his thoughts to other things.

A fire didn't mean much anyway. They were all half-naked and shoeless, without food or weapons or shelter, and autumn thundering in—what did it all mean, this shaming?

Mister Skye set aside his damp elkskin shirt and then stood under the low overhang, stripping off his leggins until he wore only his breechclout. Jarvis wondered at this public disrobing.

"Throw a bit of the dry kindling on, Elkanah—give me light. I'm going out for squaw wood. Don't have near enough here, and what we've got is half-wet. While I'm out, pile it close to the fire and start it drying."

"I'll come with you!" cried Percy Connaught. It startled Cobb. Connaught volunteering to do a nasty job in icy rain. But the big ungainly scholar with ghost-white flesh peeled off his undershirt and winced out into the rain, teeth clenched, behind Mister Skye. Cobb caught the glance that Elkanah gave to Rudolpho, the faint smile. A man redeemed, it seemed to say. No one glanced at Cobb. He'd ceased to exist, he thought.

From out in the darkness he heard snaps and the slap of wetness, and then Percy Connaught minced in carrying an armload of sticks snapped from trunks, dry wood but wetted black.

"Mister Skye says we'll need a lot more. We'll need enough for two fires, and enough to be drying and feeding fires at the same time," Connaught said. He slipped tenderfooted back into the gloom, ice water trickling down his cold-pinked body.

Between them, Mister Skye and the Hartford bookbinder brought in ten armloads of broken sticks and set it all to drying around one side of the fire. Connaught looked determined and proud, even when he'd gotten so chilled he could no longer keep his arms and legs from spasming.

"Come sit here, Mister Connaught," said Betsy softly. She made a place for the dripping man close to the fire.

Mister Skye returned almost empty-handed. "That's as far as we can see for wood," he said. "Mostly I'm just feeling trunks for sticks that far. We need much more."

He shook himself like a hairy bear and found a place close to the flames.

Jarvis Cobb found no place at the circle around the fire, but sat with his back to the stone wall. Still, a faint heat reached him, radiation from flame, warm air whirling and eddying through the overhang. He felt colder than he had without the fire, but he knew the whole place would warm gradually.

An outcast, he thought. For doing what anyone would do. Even Arabella, who'd sat beside him through the night, who loved him and shared hardship with him, had deserted him now, gone to sit beside her parents, refusing even to glance his way.

Well, he thought, too bad. A sudden hardness filled him. They had no right to judge. Fools, all of them, or canny rustics like Skye and his squaws. They'd go back east and babble and tell dark stories . . . if they got back at all. Skye and his women and brat might survive out here, living their savage lives, but he doubted they'd say anything, or that the army would take a squaw man seriously anyway. Such drunken louts lived off the scraps from army forts all along the frontier. But Morse might talk, his women might gossip. Connaught might whisper. Danzig might tell a tale or two. If they all got back, of course.

Jarvis Cobb wondered idly whether they'd all make it. Betsy looked haggard; Arabella half-sick. Connaught, soft and scholarly, seemed half-dead in his underdrawers. Oh, they'd try. The squaws knew how to turn rock and wood and bone and hide into useful implements, bows and arrows, knives, snares, hooks, traps, deadfalls. Given time, they'd make shoes and clothing of sorts, lay in wild foods, and hobble their way back to Fort Laramie. Morse had a kind of genius at it—he'd come up with the means to make a fire, something that had eluded even Skye and his savages.

Cobb wondered where he stood in this cozy little society. Would they feed him? Make shoes and clothing for him? Offer fire and shelter? Bid him to come along east? The more he pondered it, the more he doubted it. He'd be there, a presence, but outside of them. Some wall had lowered between them and him. All the sensible argument in the world wouldn't breach that wall, he knew. Well, he thought, if they cared so little about him, for some minor transgression—if it was a transgression—he needn't care about them. In fact, it'd be most inconvenient for them ever to reach the east and whisper their nonsense about him. He had a whole life ahead, glory and honor, and he didn't want it stained by something as absurd as this. Perhaps, if he used his brains, he could contrive to arrive at Laramie alone.

They awoke ravenous. The cloud bank cleared off about the time the smoky sun probed over the tops of the distant Big Horns walling the east. A warm dry day, a day to achieve important things, thought Elkanah. In a curious way, he found himself enjoying the challenge of all this. He had to solve problems—manufacture urgently needed things—or he and his dear ones would perish.

It had been a strange night. With the building heat came

relaxation, and drowsing. Yet no one had slept much. Each wished to guard the wavering fire, feed it, nourish it as one nourished a child at breast. The strange brooding presence of Jarvis Cobb troubled them all. No one knew what to do about him, and each bottled his private thoughts about Cobb within. Not a word had been spoken. In the breaking dawnlight, the captain sat a little distant, walled off from the others.

By common consent, the remaining cattail bulbs had been left to Mary, who washed the grit from them and then mashed them gently, using a river cobble and a flat slab of wet deadfall she had found. It made a poor meal for the infant, but a meal at any rate, and in the end hunger won over his distaste for the whitish pulp.

Their clothes had dried. The fire along with body heat had done that for them. But if the others felt the way Elkanah did, their stomachs howled and the beginnings of faintness from starvation pressed upon them. The last full meal had been two evenings earlier, cooked under the canvas tent fly Elkanah had rigged for Betsy.

Elkanah sat quietly, his mind chewing furiously on the looming problems. He could scarcely even list them, much less arrange them in some order of priority: food, footgear, clothing, firewood, tools, weapons, carrying bags, bedding, means of building a fire more easily, dry tinder for future use. . . .

Mister Skye's women handed the infant to Arabella, who accepted it a bit sourly—the child had soiled its blanket bag—and then walked out into the wet woods and the icy dew-laden grasses. Each found a digging stick, and then the pair of them separated, one working upstream, one down, their gaze steadily upon the autumnal yellow weeds and grass. Root gathering, he supposed. They'd had bread root the squaws dug up several times during the trip. The white meat within the black and repellent skin seemed edible enough. They'd boiled the roots then. He wondered whether they could come up with something to boil them in now— short of fashioning and firing clay pots, a process that intrigued him. He knew nothing about doing that.

Mister Skye, too, had busied himself right from dawn,

roaming widely through the cottonwood bottoms, hauling
sticks and logs in great profusion back to the overhang,
where he carefully set them close to the fire to dry. He
gimped along on bare feet, wincing and wobbling while
he labored. Only his squaws seemed able to go barefoot
without much difficulty.

Footgear. Surely one of the first things, Elkanah thought.
A knife to cut moccasin leather from Mister Skye's leggins.
The flint arrowhead would do it, but slowly. Rudolpho's
antler knife would be too weak and dull too fast. He needed
metal . . . such as Jawbone's shoes. Then an idea came to
him: horseshoe nails. If Mister Skye would permit it, he'd
take a single nail out of each rear hoof—one to beat into a
tiny but effective knife; the other to turn into an awl. Elkanah worked the idea around, growing excited. With a
stone hammer, he'd flatten out one nail into a tiny thin blade,
and bang the nail head into a haft and anchor the haft into
wood, or antler. Then they'd have a real knife—something
to cut leather, gut animals, whittle wood. . . .

And the other nail would make an awl to punch holes,
drill, manufacture. . . . Excited, he wobbled out over gravel
and sticks until he cornered Mister Skye.

"If you'd let me remove a nail from each of Jawbone's
rear hooves, Mister Skye, I'd turn them into valuable
things—a real knife, a good awl. . . ."

The guide paused in his wood gathering and grinned.
"You're the man to do it if it can be done," he said. "I
suppose the shoes would stay on minus a nail. Usually do.
But we're still a long way from Laramie—well nigh four
hundred miles. Maybe a little less. A lot of wear on an
unshod hoof." Then he frowned. "How do you propose to
get the nails out, Elkanah? Those nails are clinched tight
over the hoof."

"Rudolpho's antler spikes . . . and patience."

"You'd better make a mallet first, mate."

"I have that in your belaying pin, Mister Skye."

"What if the nail gets stuck halfway?"

"Pry the whole shoe," replied Elkanah.

"Jawbone's trained to kill people who fool with him,"
Mister Skye muttered. "But I can usually keep him calm

enough for shoeing. It seems like a way to start. Make tools to fashion what we need."

Elkanah felt mounting excitement. "With a little knife, sir, I can whittle wooden soles, clogs. We can attach sandal straps to them and walk, even if there's not enough leather for moccasins."

"Go to it, things-maker. I'll join you soon as I get this load of wood in. If we stay warm, we'll survive the rest."

Elkanah fumbled his way back, his cold wet feet discovering every stick and rock and cactus on the way to the cliffside. Tools and weapons, he thought. Bows and arrows for the hunters. He paused before a chokecherry bush, seeing wands of wood two or three inches in diameter. Bow wood, he thought. Not the best, not dried hard, but useable. Better than the other choices in these bottoms, coarse splintery box elder and cottonwood. He tried to break some off but couldn't. Well, too early to think of bows anyway, he thought. Hunger hung in him maddeningly, souring a bright day that would turn warm and golden by afternoon.

"Daddy, I can't bear this hunger. I'm half-mad with it!" Arabella cried crossly when he returned.

He squatted before her as she rocked little Dirk in her arms. "We're alive, Arabella," he repeated softly. "Before we can get much to eat, we must be able to go out to find game and roots. That means shoes, moccasins, at least sandals. And that means tools to make them."

Tears welled in her eyes. "I'm so hungry. I didn't want to come. I wanted to stay home. I've slept on hard ground. I've gone unwashed for weeks. And now this . . ."

The baby squalled suddenly, and she began crooning, rocking it with unaccustomed arms, half-desperate.

Professor Danzig joined them. "I've been scouting the riverbanks as much as my feet permit," he muttered. "I have more flint. Scared up mallards and mud hens and some Canada geese going south. Things splashed ahead of me— otters, I suppose, or muskrats. And deer. I startled a deer. And fish—I'd even eat fish."

Danzig looked so forlorn and famished that Elkanah laughed. They both laughed sharply, feeling the hollow of their bellies. For a moment Elkanah allowed himself a vision of dripping venison, roasted dark, of tender duck cooked in its own fat, of juicy buffalo hump meat or rib roast half-pink and juicy within and browned hot and fire-bathed on the outside. . . .

"Food is my nemesis," muttered Danzig. "I'd sell my soul—I'd do most anything for a juicy platter of buffalo just now. . . ."

The selling of soul reminded them all of Cobb, and they glanced covertly toward the edge of the overhang, where the captain had isolated himself. He had disappeared somewhere.

We all have Cobb's temptations and weaknesses in us, thought Elkanah. No need to be too hard on the captain. Who among us might not do the same thing, if a bit more desperate? Maybe hunger would drive another to do it, to stealing food rather than warmth. . . .

Ten mouths to feed, he thought. Actually a staggering task without the means. No gardens here or dairies or swine or cattle or orchards—other than what Mister Skye's remarkable women might discover in nature.

"Betsy," he said softly, "if you can manage it without shoes, go with Victoria and Mary next time, and learn, learn everything, and ask questions about every leaf and stem you see."

"Oh, Elkanah, I'll do all I can. But I'm so weak for want of food . . ." she murmured. "And my feet are bleeding."

"Percy," he said amiably. "I'm appointing you our fire tender. Keep it going all day, at least a bit. Bring in wood, and hunt down dry tinder and twigs—rob squirrels!"

Connaught seemed pleased. "Trust me, Elkanah," he replied.

Mister Skye approached the cliffside, leading Jawbone with a whang-leather halter. "You're in luck, Elkanah. Jawbone's near hind shoe's loose. I'm thinking to pull it off. Would a horseshoe and eight nails assist your manufactures?"

"That's wealth for us all!" exclaimed Elkanah.

Jawbone eyed them all viciously from yellow eyes. But he let Mister Skye lift the shod rear hoof. The toe of the shoe had worn almost to a razor edge, which delighted Elkanah—an ax! A metal hammer! A striker to make fires!

An anvil! The guide wiggled the loose shoe, showing them. All the nails remained clinched down, though.

"I think I can bend those," said Professor Danzig. "Give me a minute to snap off some antler spikes and sandstone them."

"Lots of horn under the shoe," rumbled Mister Skye. "He won't go lame soon."

From the corner of his eye, Elkanah saw Cobb stop and listen to Mister Skye. For some reason the captain seemed interested in all this, even from his distance of several yards and several civilizations.

In a half hour, they'd pried the shoe off without damaging Jawbone's hoof. Instantly, Elkanah and Rudolpho set to work hammering tiny blades of iron with patient taps. It'd take much of the day, he thought. Too much for starving people.

"Rudolpho, let's hammer out only one small knife now, one to cut up some of Mister Skye's leggins. I'm thinking to sew up some moccasins so we can hunt food. We've so much to do. Tonight, around the fire, we'll make things—snares, traps, whatever Mister Skye and his women wish us to make."

"You done with Jawbone?" asked Mister Skye.

They nodded. Elkanah noticed the guide had his ancient belaying pin in hand, a formidable club.

"I'm going after meat," he muttered, clumsily throwing himself over Jawbone's back. He sat barefoot and barelegged.

"When Victoria's back, have her cut some moccasins with those fancy nails of yours. From my leggins. I'm going meat hunting."

"With a belaying pin?" asked Elkanah.

"I'm hoping to scare up a buffler calf and jump it from Jawbone's back. Club it down."

The thought of juicy calf steaks set juices flowing inside Elkanah.

"Good luck, Mister Skye!" he cried.

Chapter 26

Jawbone topped the west bluff and stepped out upon a flat arid plain of white clay and sparse bunch grass. The wet clay sucked at his hooves. Mister Skye steered him southwest, the direction the Bannocks had gone in the rain two mornings before. He disliked riding bareback. The ugly horse's spinal ridge sliced into his tailbone, and his bare legs and feet dangled uncomfortably without stirrups. The pad saddle Victoria had made him, carefully stuffed with the hair of a buffalo bull, had vanished along with the rest.

He carried his battered belaying pin with him, ancient relic of his days as a seaman, but once he rode out across the Big Horn basin, he realized sheepishly that even if he brained a buffalo calf, he had no means of getting any of it back to camp. He lacked a knife to butcher it and rope to drag it.

He wanted to get away. Back in camp, people would do what they needed to. Elkanah and Professor Danzig would manufacture amazing tools. His wives would gather food. The Morse women would probably gather rushes, weave mats. Percy Connaught, showing some fortitude after all, would amass wood and tend the fire. Cobb . . . he didn't know what Cobb would do. One reason he had ridden out alone was to think about Cobb. He knew what he wanted to do with Cobb: banish him, tell him he would have to make his way alone, tell Cobb that the services, guiding and food, he provided didn't apply to him. And yet . . . he couldn't bring himself to that. He couldn't abandon the man to his wilderness fate.

The tracks of the Bannocks had washed out, and no telltale scrape of travois or hoofprint marred the rain-slicked basin. But he had reasons. Indians discarded what they didn't understand. Their nomadic life kept them from accumulating worthless things. At the times when government annuities were distributed to the far tribes, the Indians dumped the flour—which they didn't understand—and kept the sacks, which seemed valuable to them. He hoped he might find the detritus of their camp if he could fathom which way the Bannocks wandered.

He zigged and zagged generally southwest, hoping to cut a track. Travois poles cut deep into wet gumbo, and he might spot a trail if he persevered. The weak sun rose as high as it would at the start of October, bringing the temperature up into the fifties, he supposed. Maybe warm days ahead. But not today. His bare legs, bereft of the leggins he'd donated for moccasins, felt the chill. He rode worrying—the problems of clothing and food heavy on him. No worry rested heavier than Victoria's near nakedness. She had only Betsy's thin nightdress, having given her own buckskin dress to the white girl. His leggins might make something for her, but they all needed moccasins. That left the cradlebasket outer cover. . . .

In spite of the fire, they were all close to perishing. He'd experienced several starvin' times in the mountains—any fur trapper had—and he recognized the faintness that came over him now and then, knew it for the slow death that crept along on an empty belly. It and cold could addle people, too, turn them mad, trigger senseless fights. Cobb, for instance. Already an outcast; maybe an outlaw when crazed for food and warmth. Once they got moving, what would they do for shelter? How would they make fire again? What would they do for food?

He angled south, the purple hulks of the Owl Creek Mountains looming along the horizon. The Bannocks probably headed that way on a long circling route home, through the lands of their Shoshone relatives. All of it good buffer country. He cut a travois track at last and peered down from Jawbone to examine it. Southwest. He turned again, picking up the faint dimples of horses passing through mud. No debris, no discards. They'd keep all of Elkanah's efficient camp equipment.

A band of antelope watched him progress and trotted off, sliding beyond a low ridge. Food, he thought. And hide. And every one of the prairie goats fleeter of foot by far than Jawbone. That reminded him to look for horses, too. Nothing would solve their problems better than finding their horse herd. With that in mind, he detoured to peer over ridges, detoured to study grassy gullies. Nothing. He sat on Jawbone yearning for horses, aching for horses and mules. With horses he could take them to safety. They might starve and freeze en route, but he'd get them to the Crows or Shoshones, or even to Fort Laramie.

He topped a gentle sage-covered roll of prairie perhaps ten miles from the Big Horn River and spotted the remains of a camp below. Eagerly he trotted down the slippery gumbo slope. Ashes, a pile of unused wood—and the carcass of a buffer cow, already stripped to the bone by wolves and coyotes as well as magpies, crows, eagles, and all the rest. Flies still swarmed. On the underside of the skeletal remains, lots of hide remained, nibbled around the edges, tooth-torn but mostly intact. An eyeless skull gaped at him, tongueless and hairy. A treasure, he thought. Rawhide sole leather under there. Bone tools, too. The remains weren't foul, kept fresh by near-freezing temperatures. He slid off Jawbone, chased away audacious magpies, and kicked at the rib cage. In a moment he had the remains turned over, the hide up. Except for a few grubby things crawling on it, the hide seemed good enough. Eight or ten square feet of it, he thought. Rawhide soles for nine mortals in peril. Cut out with Elkanah's tiny nail knives. He tugged at it, having trouble working it loose. He found a cannon bone and hammered, finally freeing the soggy thing. He shook the grubs off it, scraped it swiftly with pieces of bone, and then collected some useful bone—ribs for arrowheads and tools, leg bones for war clubs and hammers. He knocked out some teeth and added them—maybe Elkanah would turn them into miraculous things. Satisfied at last, he rolled up his booty and mounted Jawbone again, having a bad time of it, as he always did, without the aid of stirrups. Jawbone peered back at the bundle nervously, his ears flattened.

"Don't like that, eh?" Mister Skye muttered. "You'd better like it. Maybe you'll be the only survivor, Jawbone."

Suddenly filled with emotion, he patted the vicious horse along its black mane, loving the animal that had been boon companion, brother, and warrior, rescuing Mister Skye and his nomadic family countless times. His fingers lingered on the scars. Had ever a horse suffered more wounds? Arrow and lance and war club, bullet crease, too. They'd wanted to kill Jawbone for meat and hide. Kill him. And he might have let them. His eyes watered, and he stroked the horse, his brother.

Mister Skye circled the camp again, followed the trail a mile or so west, finding nothing—neither horses nor abandoned loot—and sadly turned back. His stomach howled at him now, and he fantasized buffler rib steaks, tongue, liver, steaming boudins. He worried about Dirk—the adults could understand hunger and cope with it somehow, but how do you explain starvation, poor doings, to an infant? For that matter, how do you explain Cobb? A man who'd rob infants to stay warm would also rob anyone to eat. Mister Skye puzzled Cobb in his mind as he rode, not knowing what to do.

He headed straight back, hoping to make camp by late afternoon, hoping to scare up game—anything. Even snakes, he thought. But the snakes had vanished for the winter. He knew little about snares and deadfalls, but they'd have to try some, bag rabbits, bag anything. He wondered if he could find beaver on the Big Horn, catch them in their stick-and-mud houses. Nothing like good beaver-tail meat . . . Nothing like any meat.

Changing his mind, he steered due east. He'd strike the
Big Horn and ride north, and maybe he could brain some
game with his belaying pin. River bottoms teemed with animals that might make meat. That and village campsites. A
westerly breeze chased him back, sharp and penetrating and
chill across his naked legs and feet.

By his reckoning, he struck the Big Horn valley about
five miles below his own camp. It coiled green between
silvery-white prairie hills, but the green had dappled into
yellow with the turning of the leaves. Beyond him angled
the Big Horns, blue and snow-tipped from the early storms.
He'd struck the site of a large and recent encampment, a
flat beside the great river, gnawed down by horses, muddy
and dark. Gently Mister Skye steered Jawbone down grassy
slopes and into the camp, his small buried eyes peering
sharply for useful things—food, above all food now. He
passed rings of stone, black ash shimmering with water, a
broken arrow. He slid off Jawbone and picked it up. It had
no arrowhead. Its owner had saved that. He rolled the broken arrow into his salvaged hide. Barefoot now, he trudged
through the place, desperate for whatever had been missed.
He couldn't quite say why, but he felt himself among the
Arapaho.

Two worn-out moccasins of wide Arapaho make, holes
in their soles. He took them gratefully. A purple rag. He
lifted it, tradecloth, once a squaw's long blouse, riddled
with holes, torn and nearly useless—except to him. He shook
it, sending insects scattering, and wrapped it in his hide
roll. An hour of careful searching yielded prizes: several
blunt-headed children's arrows, excellent for shooting game
birds. Two more moccasins. A hide-scraping tool with a
bone blade. A lance point of rusted iron—a great discovery.
A shabby chunk of lodgecover, most of a hide, worn and
weak. Bits of thong and feather. A long piece of sinew in
tiny filaments. A weakened bowstring of twisted sinew,
shredded at one end but maybe usable in a very short bow.

But no food. He circled the camp carefully, looking for
food, nuts and roots forgotten by squaws, jerky, pemmican,
kitchen wastes, fresh bones with marrow . . . nothing. His
stomach growled his disappointment back at him. Dizzily—

he felt the want of food badly—he gathered his prizes into
the roll of wet hide and started north, up the bottoms of the
river. Along the way he scared up a giant jackrabbit, threw
his belaying pin at it, and missed. Irritably, he clambered
off Jawbone to retrieve it. Once, when he was young, he
could throw a belaying pin with deadly accuracy. Long ago.

Victoria and Mary found little food. Nine grown men and
women, plus a child to feed, and little food. It made Victoria cross and unhappy. Her own hunger ate steadily at her
innards, but she ignored it. These whites all seemed to faint
and fall into the beyondland the instant they lacked food.
Her feet hurt. Even though her soles were much tougher
than those of the whites because she had walked barefoot
many of the summer moons of her life, they hurt badly now.
Dense brush, thickets of sticks lined the Big Horn River,
and they'd had to work through the brush barefoot to reach
the cattails. Already they'd pulled up all the cattails they
could find close to their camp. But they had this last small
hard-won pile to take back, rinsed of their grit and the muck
on them in the cold murky water.

Victoria felt continually cold, too, in the wool nightdress
that was her sole clothing ever since she'd given her buckskin dress to Arabella. Sun wasn't warming her the way he
used to. Her old thin body ached, but that didn't matter
either. She felt much warmer now than last night just before
Elkanah Morse and the little man, Danzig, the one she'd
thought was a witch, had made the sparks. She'd felt the
heat going away from her, felt the cold coming into her
center, and she had prepared to sing her song and go over
to the Other Side because the heat had slipped from her.
She didn't tell her man about that, how close she'd come.
He had enough worries. But she'd brought to her mind the
words of her own death song, one she'd thought up when
she had been a girl sitting on a grassy hill and thinking
about serious things the first time, and waited now to sing
soon. She would tell Sun, and the First Maker, to welcome
her, and she'd tell them how proudly she had been the wife
of Mister Skye for most of his days. She'd sing to them of
her love for him, and to prepare a place for him, and Mary,

too, in the beyond land where it never felt cold. But they'd started the fire and she set aside her song for now, for a little while more. Maybe not long. Oh, she felt hungry!

They'd found few roots, but the ones they found came easily from the mud, which was good. Their digging sticks broke at once. No greens at all, for frost had nipped them, except for a handful of wild onions they'd gathered. Berries had dropped, too, long gone, snatched away by birds and rodents, bears and women like herself. They'd found prickly pear, though, and knocked off twenty or thirty of the thick lobes, stringing them with a cord made from the whangs of Mary's skirt. And coming back, they'd found a grove of pines and gathered browning cones that still held the tiny nuts. Victoria set store by pine nuts, and in her mind she saw them all going to little Dirk, giving him strength and life. And at the last they robbed a squirrel, finding a handful of seeds and nuts cached in a hollowed-out place in a decaying cottonwood. Not much, she thought. Not even a whole meal for the nine of them and Dirk.

At least all the whites seemed busy when they got back. Even the strange white goose-man, Connaught, who'd patiently gathered an enormous cache of wood, and in between trips had constructed a rock wall, mortared with mud, along the north side of the overhang to keep the wind out. The women had collected rushes with Danzig's antler knife, and made thick bedding with them. Betsy had woven a rush mat and had started a second. Mats wouldn't help much, Victoria thought crossly. She should be making baskets to carry food and roots when they began the hard journey ahead.

"Goddamn, make baskets," she said sharply. Betsy stared. They all stared at Victoria and Mary, their gaze glued upon the meager roots and cattails and the prickly pear hanging like giant beads from a thong.

"Cactus?" asked Arabella.

"Hell yes," retorted Victoria. For a reply she tossed several on the small fire, letting them hiss and sizzle. The spines turned black and then flared off the green flesh. Victoria dug one of the lobes out of the fire, let it cool, and then munched on it. The warmed juices and pulp would nourish her. They stared, and then tried it themselves. Cactus! Food everywhere!

"It doesn't satisfy at all," Arabella said, devouring the last of a hot lobe.

"Believe I will," muttered Elkanah, rising from his work. Victoria realized that the things-maker and Danzig had been busy doing something. She peered at their tiny factory, astonished. They had finished two tiny knives, their blades made of horseshoe nails patiently hammered flat and sandstoned to an edge. These had been driven through handles made of antler that the whitemen had somehow cut off, so that an inch or so of nail projected. She picked up a little knife.

"Son of a bitch!" she muttered.

Beside it lay an awl, made of a nail jabbing out of an antler handle.

"Mister Skye asked that you make moccasins from his leggins with these," Elkanah said as he roasted a cactus lobe. "He's off hunting."

"Goddamn," she muttered. The men still had five horseshoe nails left, and the shoe itself. She picked up the shoe, ran a finger over the keen edge of its worn toe, and knew how these whitemen had cut off an antler handle for their little knives.

Maybe the things-makers would help after all, she thought. With these things she could make a little bow and some arrows.

Jarvis Cobb appeared, carefully ignoring the others. None of them had any idea how to cope with him, or whether to feed or help him. He simply hovered around. Now, they saw, he'd made some crude weapons. He carried a war club made from a flat river cobble wedged into a split stick, and a lance with a wooden point ground down with sandstone and hardened in fire. He had honed a wooden knife of sorts, too, capable of sawing grasses at least. His gaze focused on the roasting prickly-pear lobes, and some illumination struck him. He struggled off, barefoot, to find his own supply of it.

"We'll have to come to some decisions about him,"

whispered Elkanah. "I hope Mister Skye returns soon so we can talk it over."

Victoria muttered. She would kill Cobb or drive him out. That's what her people would do to a betrayer, a man without honor. Make Cobb a renegade. But these whites seemed soft and forgiving.

She hunkered beside Mary, who cleaned Dirk and packed moss she'd gathered to absorb Dirk's wastes in the cradle blanket. But the blanket had been fouled, and she thought better of it, and took it off to the river to rinse out. The baby would manage in the leather liner for a while.

They ate and looked as hungry as before. "Well, what's for lunch?" asked Professor Danzig, with a light humor no one felt. The pangs of their bellies told them of looming desperation soon, within hours. They'd had little now for almost two days.

Victoria picked up Mister Skye's leggins. She'd made them for him. She hated to cut them up, but maybe she'd have to. At least she'd wait for him to return. Who knows what he might bring? He had ridden out looking, and nothing could be better than looking. That had always been the way of her people. In trouble, start looking. She huddled closer to the fire because the sun had swung around to the far west, casting their little shelter in deep chill shadow. She peered at her thin white thing disdainfully. How could white women wear something so useless? It held no heat and barely covered her nakedness!

"I think my rock wall is holding the heat in here better, making a deep corner of it," Percy said, hunting acclaim.

"Damn! Good wall!" said Victoria. "Maybe you can take it with us when we go."

The white goose-man looked vaguely crestfallen.

The baby fussed, hungry. Mary pounded nuts and cattails into a nourishing pulp, using her river cobble for a pestle, and then began fingering the stuff to Dirk. He spat it out, but accepted the next finger load.

Victoria heard Mister Skye coming, or rather, heard Jawbone snort and mutter his way through river brush. The guide loomed on the horse and tugged his whang-leather rein in the cold blue shadow of the overhang. They stared at him, seeing something in his lap that wasn't food or meat; he stared at them, his knowing eyes finding heaped wood, a rock wall, rush beds and mats, and an array of tiny tools sitting proudly on the dun rock of their refuge. He smiled one of his rare smiles.

"Got a few things, mates, but not food. Couldn't find buffler, and couldn't get anything else."

But as he unrolled the wet hide, he dropped treasure upon them. Part of a lodgecover! Moccasins! A tool for scraping! Blunt children's arrows. A sinew bowstring, broken at one end. A purple something . . .

Victoria pounced on it, held up a woman's thigh-length blouse, rent with holes and half-unraveled.

"Son of a bitch!" she bawled. "That's for me! And maybe enough of that old lodgecover for a skirt . . . and moccasins." She slid it on and tied it at the waist with whang.

As dusk settled, Mister Skye's women resoled the two pairs of moccasins with rawhide, using awls of nail, courtesy of the things-maker. One pair fit Betsy perfectly; the other larger pair fit Professor Danzig. He slipped them on, tied them over his ankles, and waltzed.

With their little iron knives, they cut rawhide soles from the buffalo cow, not bothering to flesh or hair the rawhide. From the old lodgecover they cut uppers, and all of them worked through the evening punching holes for thong and stringing the uppers to the soles. All of them except Captain Cobb, who stared quietly from the darkness of the corner.

Chapter 27

More than anything else, Captain Jarvis Cobb wanted moccasins. Without them, he would be helpless and probably die. With them, and some hide clothing, he could make it to Fort Laramie. It took a long time to starve to death. Give a soldier shoes and water and warmth, and he could struggle a long way.

In his dark corner, the farthest from the fire, he watched the squaws cut soles from rawhide and uppers from the remains of the lodgecover Skye had found. Betsy and Arabella laced them together, with nail awls and some expert help from Skye's women. No one spoke to him, nor did he feel much like speaking to them. A silly thing threatened his life, and he intended to deal with it summarily. If no one but himself returned to civilization, that would be one way. But he bridled at the thought of something that desperate. Moreover, he'd have to take on Skye. The guide sat with a piece of sandstone honing a rusty, pitted iron lance point he'd found, turning it into a large, effective butchering knife—and a swift, brutal means of self-defense. This point, probably of Santa Fe origin, had a hollow iron socket at one end for the lance shaft, but it had split apart and wouldn't hold much. Even without a handle, it made a useful knife, but Morse patiently whittled a wooden grip for Skye's blade, and they'd probably hammer the metal over it and bind the whole thing with the sinew Skye found.

Cobb felt his hunger and scorned it. Surrendering to hunger seemed infantile, the sort of thing no officer would do. Arabella complained constantly of it, and her whining got on his nerves. He wondered what he had seen in her. Just a wilderness solace, he supposed. He knew how to eat now. Ever since he saw them eat the lobes of prickly pear, he knew. Still, the season had advanced to frosts, and the things he might live on had vanished—grasshoppers, snakes, berries. . . . But he'd roamed the hills of western New York as a boy, trapping and hunting and making deadfalls and snares. He needed thong for snares and intended to get it when the rest slept. He could use some bone or wood for triggers, and certainly needed one of those nail knives to cut it. Grudgingly he admired Danzig and Morse for creating them almost out of nothing.

"Try this, Mister Skye," said Morse, handing him a well-whittled knife handle. It slid perfectly into the socket, and the pair of them tapped the split socket tight, using a heel of the horseshoe as a hammer. A fine knife. Skye handed it to Victoria, who laid it on the rawhide and patiently cut a sheath for it. Soon Mister Skye had the weapon sheathed at his waist.

These people were getting closer and closer to success, Cobb thought. And then he knew what he'd do. Hang around until they had manufactured whatever they needed to journey again—no doubt a bow and arrows, moccasins, clothes, lances, awls, and knives. Then he'd steal everything in the night and be far gone by dawn. And just to fool Skye, who still would have Jawbone and that knife—unless Jawbone could be brained to death—he'd strike for Fort Bridger, southwest, rather than Laramie. Reoutfit there on an army draft. He liked that idea. No murder in it, no violence. They'd perish of natural causes, cold, autumnal snow, lack of clothing—he'd try to get their moccasins if he could—and above all, starvation.

All because of their stupid indignation at him for saving his own life, he thought. He huddled in his corner, scorning cold and hunger, toying with his plans, testing them, applying all he had learned of intelligence to the thing he would do. Much of military intelligence consisted not of facts but of educated guesses, surmises. He had to calculate what he could steal, what he would have to leave to them, what his own resources would be, and just what they—Skye and his squaws, actually—would do when they found him gone. A juicy problem. He enjoyed it. All the theory he had mastered put to the test. If he won, he'd recover his life and honor. No one would ever know what happened here, or learn of the unimportant act that threatened his future.

With surprising swiftness they completed moccasins for all except Cobb. Even Percy Connaught helped, awling holes in the rawhide soles and clumsily poking thong through them. Enough rawhide remained to make soles for one more person.

The question of moccasins for Jarvis Cobb hung in the air, and he waited, amused. The rest tied theirs on, walked and exclaimed, their emotions buoyed suddenly by something as important as shoes.

Old Victoria beamed. She'd inherited a pair of the fine Arapaho moccasins Mister Skye discovered, now tightly re-soled and strong. "Son of a bitch!" she exclaimed. "Now I got to make a dress." She began to measure out a vest from the remaining tattered lodgecover. That and the purple blouse and the nightdress poking out below it would suffice for a while.

But Mister Skye intervened. "Mister Cobb," he said gently, "come be fitted for moccasins."

They all paused, absorbing that. Jarvis Cobb relaxed. A major problem had just solved itself. He unfolded himself from his corner and stepped toward the clammy rawhide to be measured.

"It's time to get on with living and put the past behind," said Mister Skye.

It was a message to all. The guide meant to forget the incident and draw Cobb back into their small community.

Muttering, Victoria roughly traced Cobb's feet on the remaining rawhide, using charred sticks from the wickering flame. Silently, Mary cut the uppers from the precious soft lodgecover, leaving Victoria less to clothe herself. No one spoke, and yet the atmosphere eased a little. The whites, at least, had been disturbed that they had moccasins and Captain Cobb didn't.

It angered Victoria; Cobb could see that. It amused him. She had it correct, and the civilized whites didn't.

"Mister Cobb," rumbled the guide. "We'll proceed now without thought of the past. We all become desperate. In the mountains, during starvin' time, I'd have likely eaten my partners as not."

It shocked even Cobb, an admission like that.

"Why, yes," said Morse. "Let's be on with it."

Mister Skye continued. "We're all doing what we can, Captain Cobb. Mister Danzig and Mister Morse have made amazing things and rescued us all by finding a way to strike a fire. My women have found food and have made moccasins. Mrs. Morse and Miss Morse have gathered rushes, made beds for tonight, woven mats. Mister Connaught has gathered firewood, built a rock wall for warmth, and made himself useful. There's much more to do, Mister Cobb. You've made some weapons—a lance and clubs. What would you like to do? Hunt?"

Cobb considered. "As a boy I made snares and deadfalls to catch small game. If I may have one of the nail knives and some thong, perhaps I can do that and feed us meat."

"Very well, then," said Mister Skye. "I'll be off hunting in the morning. Before I leave, I'll cut bow wood—chokecherry probably—for Victoria to begin shaping. I know where there's a buffler skull with horns, and I'll cut a horn for a firecarrier."

"A what?" asked Elkanah, excited.

"Moving villages carry a live coal with them, usually in a hollowed buffler horn. Or used to before they got flint and steel, and sulfur matches. I'll need to have you whittle a wooden plug for the top—tight enough to be airtight. They put the live coal in with slightly moist punk and sealed it. Added punk as they traveled, every two, three hours. Regular firecarrier job, with honors, given to someone reliable.''

"Consider it done!" cried Elkanah.

Cobb took notice. He'd take the horn and fire, and that'd solve another of his problems.

"I'll help fashion it," he said softly.

Victoria glared at him. Mary awled and laced one moccasin, and Victoria the other, jabbing thong with dark thrusts.

"I don't care about fire; I want food!" cried Arabella.

Betsy Morse laid a gentle hand on her daughter's arm. "Fasting is good for the spirit," she said. "It sharpens the mind and makes us grateful for God's gifts."

"But I'm feeling weak and trembly," Arabella replied. "I didn't want to come on this stupid trip. . . ."

Mister Skye said, "With moccasins we can travel far and wide tomorrow. Miles, in fact. You're all starving now, but tomorrow will be fat times."

"As long as the weather holds," added Elkanah. "We're in trouble if it snows."

Victoria handed a completed left moccasin to Cobb roughly. In spite of her anger, she'd done a careful job, and the upper had been bound tight. It had been cut ankle-high, the customary height of all winter moccasins. Cobb slipped it on, delighted, and laced thong. His numb foot began to warm at once. Mary followed with the right one, and then Cobb had shoes. It seemed late but Victoria began at once to fashion a vest out of the remaining lodgecover, shorter now because of Cobb's moccasins but still hip length. Muttering, the old woman sawed and shaped, using Mister Skye's big knife, and soon created a vestlike garment of the last of the lodgecover.

"Damn!" she muttered, after slipping it on. "I'm gonna feel warm again."

Her joy amused Cobb. He eyed the armless tunic, seeing a useful wind-resistant item that would warm his torso. Something he could well use on his journey, he thought. That and the cradle cover that had gotten him into trouble, which he intended to turn into leggins.

* * *

They awoke to a bitter damp day with autumnal slate clouds lowering over them again, blotting out horizons. Worse, they awoke to tormenting hunger and not a scrap of food to be had. Percy Connaught had found he could endure cold, even in his filthy underdrawers and shirt, but hunger made him faint and dizzy. Everything seemed so hard. Even a drink of water could be had only by threading through brush to the river and cupping it up with one's hands. Cleaning himself had become a formidable problem: grass for body wastes and icy water to wash in. The riverbanks here lacked even sand for scrubbing. He completed his morning ablutions grimly, shivering in cold misty air, and hurried back to the fire, grateful to have moccasins.

The lowering clouds with their threat of renewed rain disheartened them all, and he returned to a camp turned sour. Nothing remained of the evening's jubilation at having moccasins. He felt so dizzy from the want of food he thought he might not be able to gather wood much longer. And he needed clothing more than anyone else now that Victoria had fashioned something.

Mister Skye gathered the haggard party together. "Today we'll start our journey," he said. "We have the moccasins we'll need. Winter's coming fast. Staying here is death."

"But—" cried Elkanah, "we haven't anything to eat. You were going to hunt today. Betsy's so weak she can barely walk. And what will we do for shelter?"

"Food's where you find it, Mister Morse. We've exhausted it here. The cattails and cactus are gone."

"But look at the clouds! We'll be caught in another icy drizzle."

"That's a risk we take to escape the larger risk, Mister Morse."

Rudolpho Danzig said, "How far is it to Fort Laramie, Mister Skye?"

"I imagine three hundred fifty miles."

Elkanah groaned. Arabella began to weep.

"How long will these moccasins last?" asked Cobb.

"Maybe a hundred miles—at the outside."

Dirk began to wail, hungry and fretful again.

"If we make ten or eleven miles a day—all we can expect

in our condition, Mister Skye—it'll take a month to walk to Fort Laramie,'' said Elkanah, sounding more discouraged than Percy had ever heard him. ''I don't think we'll make it. Here at least we can shelter ourselves, and make weapons—bow and arrows, and kill game, get hides for coats. . . .''

''Mister Connaught, how far are you going out now to find firewood?'' asked the guide.

''Why—I imagine a quarter of a mile now.''

''Victoria—how long does it take to tan a hide enough to make a coat—assuming we have the hide?''

''Damn long time.''

''And a workable bow and arrows?''

''Damn long time.''

''My son is hungry, Mister Morse. Let's be off.''

''This doesn't make any sense at all,'' said Jarvis Cobb. ''We'll all stumble and fall before this day's over. Starting now, without proper equipment—it's a foolish thing.''

''We don't even have anything made to carry our few things,'' muttered Betsy.

''Roll them up in the rush mats, mates.''

Elkanah stared at the desperate faces around him and apparently came to a decision. ''Mister Skye: up to now I've never questioned your judgment. You're the guide, and we've gladly put our lives and safety in your hands. But we aren't equipped to travel. I'm going to have to overrule you. We'll stay until we are properly equipped.''

''And die doing it.'' Mister Skye peered at them from his small buried eyes. ''We can't walk to Fort Laramie. It's too far. Most of us would die, between exposure and starvation. But we can walk forty or forty-five miles south along this river to a place that's a kind of crossroads where we'll find help. Down at the south end of this basin is a hot springs—biggest mineral springs I've ever seen. It's a favorite place of Mary's people, the Shoshone. Bands come through all the time, take the waters, build shelters—there'll be brush wickiups, maybe a lodge or two for us—and leave messages. The place is a regular Indian mail place, telling who's been where and who's coming. It's a long journey in our condition, but our only chance for help. And once you're there, you can sit through a blizzard in those hot waters and never know it's snowing."

They stared at the guide, haggard and disbelieving. Connaught heard the sound of false hope in Mister Skye's talk. He himself harbored no illusions. In spite of moccasins and fire, they had come close to the end now, and one good storm would finish them.

Elkanah said, "Do you have any tasks for us before we leave?"

The guide considered soberly. "Yes, Mister Morse. We need some thin poles with loops of hide attached to one end. A lot of animals freeze when we walk by. Rabbits, ducks, prairie hens. With a pole, we can lower that loop over their necks, twist and yank, and we've a meal."

He peered around at hunger-pinched faces. "Mister Cobb, food is your business. If you can make snares to set tonight, do it now. Mister Morse, I'll cut some poles—I have the knife to do it—and you and Mister Danzig can manufacture the loops from our remaining bits of hide. Mrs. Morse, perhaps you and your daughter can turn your rush mats into baskets or carriers somehow, and gather our things together. We'll leave in a few minutes."

"What about breakfast?" cried Arabella. "We've got to find something."

"Nothing left here, miss. Maybe we'll find something as we go. If we snare a bird or rabbit with the poles, we'll stop to eat at once."

"Without fire! And look at those clouds!" snapped Jarvis Cobb.

"We have flint and the horseshoe for a striker. Mister Danzig, perhaps you could gather tinder from our shelter, and whittle tiny bits of dry wood, and find a means to carry it dry."

"Quite an order," said Danzig, grinning.

"We're dying," said Arabella. "Why don't you just say it?"

"I've been in worse trouble, Miss Morse. And here I am."

In an hour they were ready. Connaught stared almost lovingly at the little place that had sheltered them, the wall he'd built, the remaining piles of wood, the fire that would soon die.

"Can't we take some coals?" he cried.

"We don't have a way," said the guide. "But we can strike a fire now, long as it's dry."

They all stared at the life-giving blaze, dreading to leave it.

"I don't have the strength," said Betsy.

Mister Skye turned to her. "I'm going to scout ahead on Jawbone now, for a while. And when I return to the party, I'll put one person at a time on Jawbone. You'll each get a rest while I lead him."

"Things would be so different if we had horses," she said.

The guide, back in his leggins now, and moccasined, climbed up on Jawbone. With the sheathed knife at his side and his battered belaying pin, he looked almost formidable again, a man who could bring home meat in any wilderness. But Connaught knew it wasn't so, that Mister Skye himself had weakened along with the rest of them.

Silently they watched him ride upstream, south, and when he vanished into the river brush, so did their hopes. The dour slate clouds cast a doomspell none of them could shake off. Percy's stomach hurt. What had been a dull ache and sullen need had become urgent need now. He'd eat anything; rob an old carcass.

At camp, Morse and Danzig prepared themselves for the long walk, gathering rush mats, slipping their few tools into pockets, rolling up bits of hide to carry. Then, heavy-hearted, they started south along the bottoms, faint with hunger before they even began.

"Elkanah . . ." Betsy said, and then said nothing. "I'm dizzy," she muttered. "I don't know how long this torture will last."

Percy settled himself into a weary shuffle, making his feet step ahead. Forty miles would be impossible. Not long now, he thought. Even if they got an occasional duck, or managed to snare a rabbit, it all added up to nothing. He felt a certain sadness return to him. He'd relived a hundred times the moment when the Bannocks made off with his journals, the outpourings of a lifetime. All gone, just as he would soon be gone, a man without family and soon forgotten. He hadn't expected to become a bachelor, but women found him rather undesirable. He learned that early in his life, when his cold intellect and owlish way of observing the world evoked polite refusals. The owl, he'd privately called himself, growing old totally alone, keeping his bookbinding business functioning comfortably, reading, pondering the state of the world, living out his small lonely owlish life.

The loss of his journals had been a kind of death; and soon he would experience the other kind of death, from exposure and starvation. Well, he thought, it hadn't been a good life, and death held no terror to him because he would lose so little. But one thing remained. He hadn't thought about honor until Cobb did the dishonorable to save himself. And then Percy thought a great deal about honor. A man could die honorably—if not for anyone else's sake, then for his own. Or he could save his skin dishonorably, by any means, and without regard of others, as Cobb had attempted to do. The whole business of the cradle cover had set Percy to thinking, and out of it had come a simple resolution: he would die honorably, and perhaps God—if God existed—would smile.

During the whole journey, he'd disdained camp chores. Those were for menials like Skye and his squaws. His journals, and the careful observations of his good mind, were what counted, not manual labor. But the journals had vanished. Oh, he might recollect some of it, but the truth and immediacy of them could not be recaptured; the detail would blur, the insights would cloud. All gone. And all that remained was a starving man in his underclothing, ill-suited to a frightening wilderness. He could die honorably or not. From the time of Cobb's dishonor, Percy chose honor, gathering camp wood, doing what he could, cheerfully.

From the little blanket bag, Dirk wailed, hungry and sobbing. Percy watched the younger squaw, Mary, stop and slip off her cradlebasket. She pulled out the child to soothe it and clean it with moss. But the little boy choked and sobbed.

Frowning, Mary hugged it, giving all she had, which was love.

"I'll go look, Mrs. Skye," said Percy. "I can find cattails as well as anyone. We're close to the river. And with my moccasins, I can manage."

She smiled. "That would be good. We'll be walking ahead."

"I'd hold him for you, but I'm feverish," said Betsy.

Percy gazed at the woman, realizing how bad Betsy looked, hollow-eyed, gaunt, and pale.

"I'm afraid I took a chill the night we had no fire and it was so cold and wet," she added, smiling apologetically. "I'm sorry. I fear I'll be a burden."

"I wish you hadn't come," said Arabella. "Then I wouldn't have had to come."

That seemed unkind. The young woman might have comforted her mother instead, Percy thought. Still, hunger worked on them all now, making minds cruel. He suddenly realized hunger would twist each one of them into some primal character that lay hidden back in civilization. Percy wished he could record all that in his journals. He wondered what he would become when starvation turned him mad—a beast! What would Cobb become in extremity? And cheerful optimistic Elkanah? And Danzig? And indeed, Mister Skye? When hunger madness came, who would become animal, who would become angelic? Who would kill and rob, and who would give his last bit of something to another?

Oh, for a journal to write it, Percy thought.

"I'll be back shortly," he said, plunging into a cold mist that turned his white flesh to ice. He ventured toward the river, feeling his starving muscles rebel and his heart pound unnaturally. He'd have to walk a considerable distance because Mary had already scoured everywhere nearby for roots and cattails. Honking geese burst into air ahead of him, and his mouth watered. He struggled south through dense cottonwood, willow, and alder forest and grassy parks, working to the riverbank every hundred yards or so. But the Big Horn nurtured no cattails there because the banks rose steeply.

For a mile or so he struggled, feeling his weak body

protest. He entered a small park of yellowed grasses, gloomy under the slate heavens, passed an upright dead cottonwood trunk, half-rotted and hollow. His eye caught the movement of bees, several of them, almost moribund in the cold. In an oval hollow, a bee's nest. Honey. Food for Dirk. He peered in, noting the lethargic movement of the few surviving bees. He found a stick and jabbed it in, and no guardian swarm rushed to the defense of the hive. Heart pounding, he dared himself to poke a hand in, break off comb. Food for Dirk. He plunged his hand in, felt the mass of waxy honeycomb, broke off a large chunk, and then his hand turned into fire, white pain rocketing up his arm. He pulled out a mass of honeycomb, along with a dozen bees buried in his flesh.

Chapter 28

They found Percy Connaught sitting on a log, babbling, holding a large waxy yellow chunk of honeycomb in a hand swollen grotesquely. Tears streaked his puffy reddened face. A scream had drawn them toward the river from their trail under the brown bluffs.

"This is for Dirk," he mumbled, proffering the honeycomb to Mary.

"For Dirk?"

Connaught smiled crookedly. "He's hungry."

"You took the honey like a grizzly bear?"

"I thought they were dead. They die in the fall."

"You are Grizzly Bear Man," she said. "Here."

She thrust the cradlebasket into his lap. "You feed the boy. Food from Grizzly Bear Man."

He peered up at her, his face streaked purple with pain. "But I never—I've never held a child. I've never fed—"

She knelt beside him and slipped Dirk from his nest. He wailed at the insult of cold air, added to his desperate hunger.

"Madam, I don't know what—"

With his good hand he cradled the infant. Mary broke off a piece of the honeycomb still clutched in his swollen red right hand.

"Put in his mouth, let him suck it," she said.

Percy did, forgetting his pain a moment. The baby gummed the waxy sweet stuff, wailed, and then sucked on it in earnest.

"See, Grizzly Bear Man, he likes your gift."

In minutes, the child had eaten a large amount of it, and drifted off to sleep. Percy Connaught stared at this little creature nestled into his gray-grimed underwear, a kind of wonder upon him. Mary slipped the sleeping child back into his cocoon and hoisted the heavy basket over her shoulders.

"There's enough of the comb for us all to have a piece," said Jarvis Cobb.

"No!" cried Percy. "It's all for the baby."

A flash of hatred crossed Cobb's chapped red face. The others stared at him again.

"I don't know how we'll carry that sticky honeycomb," said Elkanah.

"Gimme the little knife," said Victoria. She headed for a poplar tree, and in minutes skinned off a curl of green bark and rolled the remaining honey in it. "There. You carry it," she said to Arabella. "You ain't carrying anything."

Arabella looked annoyed.

Elkanah wished Betsy could have a little of the honey. He'd been helping her the last mile and feeling her weaken with every step. The hot springs seemed infinitely distant, and slipping farther away with each hour.

"Let's go," said Victoria crossly.

Connaught stood—and toppled over.

"Damn—them bees got him," muttered Victoria. "You wait. I'll go find Mister Skye and Jawbone."

A while later she returned with Mister Skye, and they loaded the semicoherent bookbinder on the horse. He'd grown too weak to cling, so they held him upright as they walked, Mister Skye leading the angry flat-eared horse, and Professor Danzig beside, keeping Connaught from sliding off.

Elkanah virtually carried Betsy, step by slow step.

"I'm sorry," she whispered. "I'm sorry."

Arabella trudged along beside, and then slipped into the red bushes. They waited for her. When she reappeared, Elkanah knew—sensed, rather—that some of the honeycomb had vanished. He wrestled with himself about it. Arabella had eaten. Betsy needed it more. But Percy should have shared. They all might have gotten a boost from the sugary comb. The girl covered herself well, never revealing anything.

"How much did you eat, Arabella?" Elkanah asked.

She glared at him defiantly.

Cobb, tottering nearby, heard him, and mocked.

Beside him, Betsy dragged to a crawl. They scarcely made progress at all. He couldn't support her, either. He felt as famished as the rest, and his strength had slid away, until he tottered under her weight. He didn't know how far they'd come—six or seven miles, he supposed—almost nothing compared to what they had to travel.

"I can't go any more," said Betsy. She sagged into him. He put a hand to her brow and found it feverish. "I'm sorry," she murmured.

He clutched her, keeping her from sliding into the grass.

They rested there where the river ran through a broad silvery valley bordered by barren sage-covered hills. The slate clouds lowered all the more, threatening rain but not issuing it. Except for black brush along the banks, this place lay open and windswept. The minute they halted, Elkanah felt the wind slicing through his few clothes and wondered how Percy in his tattered underwear endured.

Mister Skye and Professor Danzig slid Connaught off Jawbone and onto the grass. Connaught looked worse, almost comatose. The swelling had advanced up his right arm, ballooning it monstrously. The man muttered and babbled incoherently. Bee poison, Elkanah thought. Enough stinging and it could kill a man.

As if thinking the same thing, Professor Danzig peered intently at Connaught's swollen hand and wrist. "I count seventeen or eighteen bites," he said. "It's hard to tell."

Mary gratefully slid the cradlebasket off her back and

pulled out the child to clean him with moss. The baby awakened and fussed and sucked at her finger.

"I'll give him more," she said to Arabella.

The girl handed the roll of smooth green bark to Mary defiantly. Mary hefted it, a question in her eyes, and then uncurled the bark. No honeycomb remained. "You have eaten it," she said softly.

"It must have fallen out," Arabella replied haughtily.

Elkanah sighed, heavy of heart. "There's no excuse for lying, Arabella," he said wearily.

"It fell out," she retorted sullenly.

From the nearby grass Percy lifted his head. "If you ate it, then I died for nothing," he muttered, and sank back into a semistupor.

The statement shocked Elkanah twice over. Did Percy think he was dying? Had his own daughter robbed the old scholar of the last shred of meaning in a barren life?

He settled Betsy back in the grasses, noting the goose bumps on her chapped arms, and squatted down beside Percy Connaught, taking his good hand, cold and clammy, into his own. Mister Skye and Rudolpho Danzig hovered close.

"Percy," Elkanah whispered, desperately trying to reach him, "you did a brave thing. No deed is ever lost. For good or ill we leave our mark on the world. Whatever happens, Percy, you've left a noble mark. We'll remember it and try to live up to it, and tell the world about it."

But Connaught seemed lost in some sort of oblivion, and Elkanah doubted that he heard. His breathing came in snuffles.

Cobb smiled crookedly.

"Best we cover him with a rush mat, mate," Mister Skye rumbled. The guide looked as gray and pinched as the rest, Elkanah thought. They spread two of Betsy's mats over the man and weighted them down with sticks, against the probing wind.

"I'd rig a travois but I've got no harness for it. I need a surcingle or a collar or something like that," the guide muttered. "This is a bad place to stop. Wind," he said.

"Betsy could go no further," Elkanah replied.

The baby whimpered, hungry again. Mary thrust the basket toward Mister Skye and slowly toiled down to the river brush. Victoria followed, muttering.

"Betsy's feverish, Mister Skye," said Elkanah.

"Fine decision you made, Skye. We're a few miles from the old camp and all half-dead," said Cobb. "Where's the food and shelter you promised us along the way?"

Mister Skye didn't answer. Ahead perhaps three hundred yards the silver river swung around a bluff projecting from the west. He tried to climb on Jawbone but lacked the strength. Instead, he left them there on the windswept gray slope and walked ahead, growing smaller and smaller in Elkanah's eye until he vanished from sight around the bluff.

Elkanah felt the presence of death again. The wind cut icily through his shirt and pants, starting him shivering. The thought that he had organized this journey, brought his wife and daughter to their doom here, desolated him. Connaught lay dying—that seemed plain enough. From bee poison. From despair. From exposure and starvation. And Betsy . . . he lifted her inert icy hand into his, feeling its clammy cold, its weakness. His gaze turned to Arabella, alive and warm and selfish, his own daughter, no better than Cobb, succumbing at first impulse to dishonor.

What gave some men honor, some dishonor? In extremity, why would some people cheat and steal, think only of themselves, while others would sacrifice, love, encourage, buoy the weak along? Had he failed to bring up Arabella correctly? Spoiled her? Lavished too much luxury on her? Let her become thoughtless of others? It had always been a pitfall of the rich, he thought. He'd failed somehow, and now his daughter shamed him. And yet, Cobb had shown the same traits, too, and Cobb lacked the advantages that he'd given to Arabella. Elkanah stared at Cobb, wondering what lay in the captain's mind. The soldier emanated resentments, mockery, and something else, some cunning and calculation that made him rattlesnake deadly. The man would strike at them again. Elkanah felt sure of that. He huddled closer to Betsy, trying to share his remaining warmth with her, protect her from the bitter wind. A few yards away, Danzig had lowered himself windward of Connaught, trying to keep the comatose man warm.

They'd lost, he knew. Good as dead. Idly, he watched Mister Skye toil back, a burly weary figure crossing a vast empty slope. Without the others, he and his squaws would probably survive, Elkanah thought. But the man remained loyal, doing what he could.

Mister Skye stared briefly at Connaught, noting the bookbinder's inert form, and at the rest. Mary and Victoria toiled up from the river, carrying a few things that looked like roots and cattails. The baby would be fed.

"We've got to get ourselves around the headland there," the guide muttered. "There's shelter in the rock, a good stand of cottonwoods and firewood—and meat, if I can get it. And I think I can."

"Meat? Meat?"

"Lend me a pole with a loop on it. You can get settled out of the wind on the south side of that spur. Victoria will help you get Mr. Connaught up on Jawbone."

Fourteen wild turkeys. They saw him coming and exploded up into the lower limbs of a box elder. They flew easily enough, he thought, but didn't like to fly. If he could slip that loop over the neck of one . . . of all.

Beneath the tree he peered up at the dark birds through yellowing ruined leaves, into a foreboding sky. Some were twenty feet up or so, but a few fools perched low, within reach of his pole. His arms didn't work well now—hunger had robbed him of the adroitness he needed more than anything. But he would climb that tree and wring their necks by hand if necessary.

Mister Skye yearned for a bow. He had the blunt arrows, but lacked even a boy's practice bow. Out of breath, he slid the last distance on moccasined feet until he stood under three of them. They hopped sideways, never letting him come closer than ten feet or so. Meat! He glared at the big nervous birds, mesmerizing them with some violent force of will as he eased the pole toward the nearest. It watched the approaching loop, flapped its wings, but sat. Gently he eased the loop close, and then with a swift lunge he dropped it over the turkey's neck, twisted, and yanked. The big bird fell, flapping and gobbling, to earth. The others leaped to higher branches—except one.

He snapped the caught bird's neck and went for the next one. It seemed warier, dodging the loop. He lunged and missed, but the bird only danced down the limb, clucking at him. He edged the loop close again, hoping the bird wouldn't flap higher and out of reach. He positioned his loop, lunged again, and missed. Angrily, he lanced the thin pole at the turkey, struck it, saw it flap toward the ground, and caught it midair, furiously wrapping his big hams around the flapping feathers. Angrily, trembling, he smashed it dead and walked out of the small forest nested in the ell of the bluff, and dropped the turkeys before them.

Elkanah saw the birds and sobbed. The others gaped and wept, too.

He and Professor Danzig had managed to start a small fire with flint and the horseshoe and tinder, but it'd take a while to become hot enough to cook.

They were too hungry to wait. Victoria and Mary took the turkeys, gutted them with the tiny nail knives, and handed out raw liver and heart and kidney, which were devoured instantly and wildly. Mary saved some liver and gave it steaming and raw to Dirk, who gnawed lustily on it, blood leaking from his small hands.

They would have devoured the rest, tearing off feathers and ripping apart raw meat of breast and thigh and wing, but Mister Skye stopped them.

"There's more birds, mates. You've had a morsel or two. Let's let them cook properly. They'll stay down better. Professor, Mister Morse, Mister Cobb, come along. They're all in a tree and we'll get them all. Bring that lance of yours, Mister Cobb. I hope you can throw it."

They looked unsure, wanting to tear apart more raw meat, but slowly they gathered the other pole with a loop on it and Cobb's long wooden-tipped lance. More food. Enough for days, and it'd keep well in the cold weather.

The turkeys flapped higher into the tree, and one or two fled to a nearby cottonwood. Small, lithe Professor Danzig found he could climb. Mister Skye was too heavy, and the rest too weakened. The turkeys edged away from him, and several more flapped off to the cottonwood. But he looped one and dropped it, and Cobb clobbered another with his lance as it started to fly off. Cobb threw his lance at one several times, missing, driving the bird higher. Then he spotted one roosting low in a neighboring tree, and knocked it to earth with a lucky throw of the lance. In an hour of trembling labor and endless near misses, they'd knocked down four more birds. By then they'd reached utter exhaustion, and gave up. Six turkeys!

In camp, Mary and Victoria had roughly plucked the birds and had them spitted over the fire, which burnt off the remaining pinheads and feathers, and whirled a wild voluptuous aroma of cooking meat into the eddying cold air.

The exhausted men grabbed a half-cooked bird and ripped half-raw flesh from it, wolfing it down with trembling hands, too tired to care what or how they ate. Only when they'd devoured one of the turkeys did any of them remember the comatose Connaught, who lay inertly near the fire, bee-poisoned and cold.

Guiltily Mister Skye cut some juicy breast meat from the second bird and carried it to Connaught, hunkering over him.

He shook the man, who seemed cold to his touch.

"Mister Connaught," he said. "Meat! Meat!"

But Percy Connaught didn't respond.

Mister Skye shook him. "Grizzly Bear Man. Meat! Meat!"

Only then did he realize that Percy Connaught had died.

He peered up. They'd all drawn around him, frightened. "He's gone," Mister Skye muttered. "The bees and the cold did him. Gave his life for my Dirk."

Mister Skye sat quietly, scarcely aware of the sobbing of the women, peering into the puffed face of a man who no one knew, least of all himself. Percy's opinions, yes. His conceits, yes. But the Percy Connaught who lay behind the life of the mind had been a stranger. A stranger who, in the end, had revealed some strength of character, some courage, some manhood. Whatever his failings, Connaught had been a man.

He stood wearily. "Here was a man," he said softly.

They stood about Connaught, letting the reality of death soak into them. Percy's spirit had fled somewhere, forever gone. Death subdued and chilled them all. Connaught's face had twisted in death into an agony of pain.

"I think he was lonely," Betsy whispered. "He had no one."

Arabella said, "I don't know why you forget so fast. He never did a lick of work or helped out. He complained all the time. I didn't like him."

Uncharitable, Mister Skye thought. That girl would never be charitable. He bit off a withering response, but Elkanah didn't.

"Arabella, Percy Connaught proved to be someone . . . larger than that. Pay your respects!"

They had no way to bury him and could scarcely find enough loose rock to keep the wolves and coyotes off, but they mounded what they could over the puffy body, leaving his filthy underwear but taking his moccasins. They had no strength, and tottered through the job poorly. But in the end, Connaught lay beside the cottonwoods, in a gentle amphitheater opening on the river, protected from the cold wind that had sapped life from him as much as anything else. They labored in eerie silence. Mister Skye knew they were all contrasting Connaught with Cobb, selfishness with generosity, caring for others in extremity, or caring only for self. Courage to do the dangerous, reaching into a hive, all for a hungry infant. In the end, Mister Skye put a finale to it by reciting the Lord's Prayer. He didn't know what Percy believed, if anything, or what anyone else believed. But it seemed fitting.

"I will have a memorial made, and a service back east," said Elkanah.

In the dusk of that gloomy day, they ate another whole turkey, slower this time, gathering life from its sweet dark meat and juices. They made themselves as comfortable as they could in the deep silence, gathering rushes and firewood. They built a second fire so that both reflected from the protecting mudstone that became their refuge that night. Filled at last, they would sleep.

Mister Skye looked over his small exhausted band. Betsy—his deepest worry—looked a bit better with food in her, but still hollow-eyed. Sleep might help. Arabella seemed young and vital and too self-engrossed to surrender her courage. Elkanah lay back wearily. He had an innate courage. Professor Danzig seemed indestructible, quietly doing what needed doing—he'd gathered the firewood this evening—and making life work somehow. All along the route he'd stripped off buds and seedpods, munching on them, finding bits of nourishment. Now, against the cliff, he emptied his pockets of flint, set the precious horseshoe beside the flint, and arranged his nail knife, antler knife, and awl. Cobb, enigmatic and still vital, made his bed a little off, perhaps still feeling the sting of his shame, Mister Skye thought.

Victoria and Mary had made a place for them near the fire, piling brush on the far side for a windbreak. It would be a good night, even though Percy Connaught's death lay heavily on them and would fill their private thoughts through the long cold dark. He went out as he always did, wrapped his paws about Jawbone, and whispered a few things to the animal who had become a part of himself, and then slipped back to the fire. He set his big rough knife beside him, instantly available, and settled into sleep. He knew they'd all sleep that night, filled to bursting with good turkey meat, with plenty more in the morning.

That was the last he remembered. When he awoke before dawn, with gray light slitting the eastern horizon above the silver river, he knew something had gone wrong. He felt for his knife—missing. He sat up, wary. He counted heads and recounted. Cobb gone. In the gray light he stood up and studied the camp. Cobb gone, and every tool they'd made, every flint, the horseshoe, Connaught's moccasins, and every turkey. They were back to nothing.

He could not bear to tell the others, or even awaken the camp. The news, he thought, would kill them.

Chapter 29

Something sagged inside of Elkanah Morse. Mister Skye watched the man die before his eyes, the gleam of hope and determination fade from Morse's haggard, weathered features.

"All the tools gone," muttered Elkanah. "He took everything—the knives, awls, flint, and horseshoe. He took the spare moccasins and the cradle cover again . . . even the blunt arrows you'd found . . . It's the end, you know. We can't live without tools."

"You're alive, Mister Morse."

"Never should have come. Should have turned back when the season got late. I've killed me, my dear Betsy . . . Arabella . . . Rudolpho. . . ."

"All of you are alive, Mister Morse."

Some terrible pain flashed into his face. He looked awful, a man surrendering to death and guilt; his jaw stubbled with a week's growth of beard, dirty and ragged.

"I have killed us with my foolish quest," he muttered.

"Get wood, Mister Morse. If the fire dies, we'll be in worse trouble than we are."

"What for? Why prolong it?" Elkanah muttered.

Beside him, Betsy sat round-shouldered, gaunt, and dejected. Arabella burned with bitterness, her accusing eyes first on her father, then on Mister Skye. "Well, do something!" she snapped. "I should have guessed about Jarvis. He takes what he wants."

Professor Danzig seemed almost as subdued as the rest, but somehow not broken. "I have a full belly from last night," he said. "I think I'll hunt for cattail bulbs along the river."

"I'll go, too," said Victoria. "Damn, white people give up without trying."

The baby bawled, and Mary dug through turkey bones, finding tiny shreds of meat for the child. Wearily, she trudged into the cottonwoods for some squaw wood as long as none of the whites bothered with the fire. The day had dawned clear and frosty, and without fire they'd perish all the sooner.

"I'll see what I can see," said Mister Skye, hunting down Jawbone. He thought Cobb had probably pitched most of the tools into the river, kept what he needed, and hauled three heavy turkeys with him. Finding moccasin prints would be tough—much harder than tracking horses. All his hunches about Cobb had been true. The man meant to save himself and save his reputation by letting the others die in a wilderness. Mister Skye barely understood a man like that. What would he see in the looking glass when he scraped his brown whiskers off each day?

Mister Skye had mastered the most important lesson of the mountains long ago, and that was to keep on trying. To give up, to sit down and die, would result in exactly that. By tonight they'd be dead unless . . .

He had to make a rein of whangs from his elkskin shirt. He could ride Jawbone with knee pressure alone, but he never felt comfortable with it, and sometimes Jawbone took perverse notions. So he knotted his rein together, and around Jawbone's jaw, and rode off. He spotted nothing on the west bank of the river. He found nothing in a great arc around the camp. So he forded at a likely-looking place with riffles, and the water rose belly-deep but no more.

Jawbone shook and sprayed on the other side, almost tossing off Mister Skye. He found no prints there, either. Cobb had made his escape expertly, no doubt with some cunning, the cunning Mister Skye had observed in the man from the first.

Wearily, the guide rode south along the east bank, doubting that Captain Cobb would turn north, even for the sake of cunning. The bottoms lay barren and frost-covered in the dawn light, and virtually devoid of brush or forest. He had only the belaying pin, which Cobb had mockingly tossed a hundred yards off from camp. Cobb would have a knife, the wooden lance, and his stone-and-wood war clubs. Still, Mister Skye had Jawbone. One word to the horse, and Cobb would be flattened.

Laramie or where else? Fort Bridger? Platte River Bridge, off to the south on the Oregon Trail? Mister Skye had been heading toward the Platte River himself, knowing that it would be a great artery, even this late in the year. But Cobb had stayed on the west bank—he felt sure of it. He wouldn't risk a freezing swim across. He'd stay dry, haul himself and his tools and turkeys south or southwest. . . .

Jawbone's ears came up and he froze, a signal as familiar to Mister Skye as shaking hands. It meant horses, and horses usually meant people, friends or enemies. Sometimes Jawbone stayed quiet; sometimes he whinnied or screeched his welcome. This time Jawbone screeched, and Mister Skye didn't mind. Some black heads bobbed up from a grassy crease in the eastern bluffs. He steered directly that way. Four, no five. Odd-looking dark horses, edging away from Mister Skye but not running. No owners in sight. Unusual. Indians rarely lost horses from their herds, and when they did, those animals quickly found new homes in other bands.

The five dark animals turned and stared. They weren't horses; they were big black mules. The guide reined up Jawbone, trembling. Some warriors scorned slow mules. Mules were no warrior's dream of speed and glory, of warhorse or buffalo runner. Some warriors would turn mules loose after a successful raid, or give them to squaws for beasts of burden. But to Mister Skye, those five dark longeared mules, nervously watching him, meant salvation. He talked at them quietly. They likely knew English, he thought. He talked at them and eased Jawbone forward gently just as the sun cracked over the eastern mountains, sending amber shafts that lit the mules like torches. Each mule had a U.S. brand. Army mules! Captain Cobb had come perhaps one mile and one river away from United States Army mules. But that was a piece of intelligence he'd missed, thought Mister Skye wryly.

They turned out to be docile, humbled by long familiarity with profane army muleteers, men who knew how to apply the carrot and the stick, and do it with a briny tongue. He rode among them, talking, cajoling, loving, rejoicing.

"Ah, you bloody buggers. Come to save us, have you? This is how the United States Army operates? Send the bloody mules but spare the men? Captain Cobb should know it. Bloody colonials never did learn how to make an army. All right, you bloody buggers, I'm pressing you into service. You've joined Barnaby's Army!"

He howled. He howled at the sun, at the blue-stained sky, at the frost. He howled at the wolves and coyotes. He terrorized a magpie. He howled at Cobb, wherever he'd gone. He bellowed like a buffler bull and laughed thunderously across the frosted sagebrush. Jawbone twisted his head back to see this display, and snapped at Mister Skye with vicious yellow teeth.

"Ah, you bloody horse! Think I'm mad, do you? Well, I am, mate. Now, bloody horse, get these four-footed clodhoppers lined out. Get them moving. The bloody blue army of this here republic has arrived."

With a lunatic hoot, he booted Jawbone. The horse leaped under him, snarled, clacked his teeth, circled mules like some lobo wolf, and set them to trotting, then loping, then galloping and farting and dropping green pies, and shrieking madly, on down to the silvery Big Horn. They never paused, but plunged in, tall fat ears rotated behind them, listening to demons and devils. Jawbone splashed after them, snorting and snarling, screeching to wake up the dead and send Indian spirits into flight. Jawbone bit rumps and shouldered laggards. Mister Skye howled like a hundred wolves, cackled and hooted, roared and bawled.

"Give up, will you, Elkanah Morse. Ye goddamn lily-livered easterners. Give up, will you? Quit on me, you bloody idjit! Whine and die will you, you miserable excuses for manhood! You damn fools!"

He saw them huddled, dejected, around a thin column of blue smoke. He saw them rise. He saw Victoria and Mary start to dance and hug each other. He saw the others stare, not yet grasping, stare as if the world had sucked them into its belly and no blue sky would they ever see again.

He drove the dripping mules straight into camp. They whirled fearfully, penned by an ell in the bluffs. The Morses stood staring, not really comprehending. Only Professor Danzig really understood.

"I believe the army has come to our rescue, Mister Skye," he said quietly. "They sent these by express, of course."

"Git on board, you idjits!" Mister Skye roared.

"What good will these do?" asked Elkanah quietly. "We have nothing. No tools. Nothing to make meat. Nothing to strike a fire . . ."

"Railroad tickets to Lowell, Mister Morse. What more do you need—? If we push on right now, and if you can stand long riding, we'll get to the hot springs sometime tonight. The springs are on the river, so we can't get lost. You've got full bellies, mates. Ate like hogs last night. If we can't find help at the hot springs, we'll ride down to the Oregon Trail southeast of there. Can you sit an ugly mule for a week? If you can sit a week, you can live to old age."

"I suppose we can try," muttered Elkanah.

Victoria yelled. "Get your goddamn ass on them mules!"

Elkanah looked at her, aghast.

Professor Danzig gaped, and then howled with laughter.

They paused long enough to fashion some reins from Mister Skye's remaining whangs. They weren't adequate but they would do. And then they trotted south, while Mister Skye roared bawdy ditties at the blue sky and Betsy held her fingers to her ears.

From the grassy knoll where they paused, the whole village shimmered before them, silvery and moon-splashed and alive. From scores of lodges amber light radiated translucently, and the soft perfumed smoke of piney lodgefires drifted lazily east. Beyond lay a massive black hulk of forested mountains, and Betsy caught glimpses of moon-silvered heights far away. The glowing lodges seemed to illumine the grassy alleys between them like porch lights welcoming Christmas carolers, Betsy thought, staring at her salvation. And beyond, shimmering white, rolled silvery water, steaming in the cold night. The hot springs.

She'd passed the endless day in pain and desperation, sawed in two by the bony ridge of the mule beneath her, no supporting stirrups for her aching legs, and constantly chilled by an icy breeze slicing out of the north. That mad guide wouldn't stop, except for a nooning, and spent hours bawling out awful sailors' ditties that numbed her soul. They lacked one mount, so Mary and Victoria rode together on the largest mule while Mister Skye carried Dirk in the cradlebasket. They'd nooned beside a whole estuary of cattails, a small swamp of them, and the squaws had swiftly gathered armloads, peeled off the long blades, and stored the slim brown and white bulbs in their bloused clothing.

They'd all munched on the tasteless slimy things, and no one had gone hungry all day. Still, they'd done over forty miles this day—a cavalry march, Mister Skye had pronounced it—across endless sage-covered hills, fording five or six small creeks, never stopping. She thought her legs would break off, her spine would snap. She slumped, clutching black mane, and rode through the chill clear day, blind to everything except her pain and the numbing cold within her.

Elkanah rode grimly beside her through the day, absorbed in his own recriminations and doubts, unable to comfort her as he had always done. She'd never seen her husband in such a state, his buoyancy gone, natural optimism sucked out of him by crushing fate. Arabella, younger and defiant about death, sat grimly on her mule, skirts hiked high, daring her parents to rebuke her. Betsy didn't. Her own dear daughter had shown the world a streak of selfishness. But what did it matter? Betsy thought she might have devoured the honeycomb, too, had it been entrusted to her. How could one blame a desperate girl for that?

Mister Skye had ridden behind them, looking sharply for Cobb, while Jawbone harried and frenzied the mules into constant trotting that jarred her body into acute pain. She'd never known such ache and cold. Her feverishness had gone with the turkey meat, but this cold brutal day had been the worst ordeal of her life, and the melancholy of her family had only deepened it.

Once Mister Skye had pulled alongside Elkanah. "Be hearty, mate. You'll have the best hot soak tonight in your life. And if no village is at the springs, one soon will be. It's the Snake spa. It's where they have fun."

"You're feeding us illusions to keep our morale up, Mister Skye. Without tools and weapons, without shelter and—"

"Things!" roared Mister Skye. "You think only of things! Be thinking of friends! Mary's people! Victoria's people! When you go back to makin' things in Lowell, think about people and friends, family and clan and band. Stop makin' things in your bloody head and start makin' friends!"

"You don't need to shout so," Betsy had said wearily.

"Even friends, and Mary's people, couldn't exist without tools and weapons, Mister Skye," said Elkanah softly.

"Invent a mule, mate. A little bit of jackass, a little bit of horse, and a lot of Elkanah," the guide retorted, and rode off.

Behind her, Betsy had heard something awful, something unthinkable and unforgivable. Professor Danzig had laughed!

Now they sat on the wind-whipped knoll and waited, for whatever mysterious reasons Mister Skye may have had. Jawbone shrieked, and the screech of that awful horse rattled her ears, invaded her head like a violation of her womanhood. She loathed Mister Skye's horse. Ahead, Mary slid off her mule and cried, jabbering wildly, clapping her hands like a small girl, dancing about the frosty sagebrush. From the luminous village, dogs harped the wind now, and dark forms of horsemen trotted toward them.

Then Mary danced and cried in her strange tongue, and men on horses laughed and talked, their eyes nonetheless observing the rest of the haggard party in the silvery light.

"Her own bloody people," bawled Mister Skye. "Mary's band. Her father and mother, her brothers and her sister. They're all down there. We'll bloody well have a party!"

"I'd never have believed . . ." muttered Elkanah.

Betsy didn't want a party. She didn't want to cope. Her body was a cold-numbed mass of pain. She desperately wanted just a small corner of a warm lodge where she could curl up and feel safe and loved.

Others on horseback rode out, and soon a procession of Snake warriors escorted them into the village, while before them the town crier gleefully announced these unexpected and welcome visitors, and kin. At the edge of the village Mary screamed, slid off the mule, and ran toward a short broad man whose hair had been drawn into a single braid. She hugged him, dancing in his embrace, jabbering in their strange tongue.

"That's her brother, mates. His name is"—he stared nervously at Betsy and Arabella—"name is . . . Strong Stallion. Yes, Strong Horse."

Behind her, Betsy heard Professor Danzig wheezing with laughter again.

They rode the last distance, through the curious, laughing, shouting throng, and stopped at last before a glowing lodge. Betsy clung mutely to the mule, too exhausted to care what happened. Someone lifted her off. She needed to relieve herself, but there seemed no place to go. Someone lifted Arabella off, too, and helped Elkanah and Rudolpho down. Her legs gave under her, but warm hands and arms kept her from collapsing.

"Thank you," she muttered.

A lot of Shoshones did a lot of talking, and all Betsy knew was that their story, their ordeal, was becoming known among the villagers. She sat mutely in a warm lodge, patted and fondled by beaming Shoshone women with seamed brown faces—Mary's mother and other relatives, Betsy gathered. At last, through her weariness, she smiled back at them, and a sense of gratitude at this surprising salvation purled through her spirit like fresh springwater.

Mary seemed to be everywhere, radiant, beaming and laughing, chattering and hugging, smiling. Victoria clucked and muttered, not knowing much of the Snake tongue but welcome here as Mister Skye's elder squaw, welcomed because her man had always been a great ally of these people.

They fed Betsy a bowl of something warm, and it tasted strange.

"Goddamn! Good antelope," said Victoria.

Smiling women plucked at Betsy, beckoned her to go outside. She didn't want to, except to relieve herself. Maybe that was what they had in mind. . . .

"Dammit, git up and go with them women," Victoria muttered. "They gonna give us a hot bath."

"I just want to sleep," Betsy said. "I'm—so tired. . . ."

But the Snake women dragged her almost forcibly into the icy moon-washed night air, dragged her toward a place of white rock stairs that glinted with water. They took her to a shrubbed place first for her needs, and then led her to the springs. The mineral smell drifted to her nose. She didn't want this. She didn't want a chill bath in the middle of a cold night. She didn't want to disrobe before these strangers. But they tugged her onward, laughing, fondling her gently. She wanted Elkanah. She wanted to curl up and sleep for a week.

They paused at last before a large pool that had been dammed at its lower end with rock. She stared into its depths and saw the moon wobbling up at her. The Shoshone women laughed, beckoned.

"Goddamn!" exclaimed Victoria. Betsy scarcely realized Victoria had come. Arabella, too, crossly, some resentment flaming in her.

Victoria didn't wait an instant. She yanked off the leather vest, the riddled purple blouse they'd salvaged, and the grimed nightdress that had once been Betsy's, and slid her slim old body into water.

"Ohhah!" she snorted. "Son of a bitch!"

Betsy peered about. How could she go naked in open air, and a whole Indian village a hundred yards off? But laughing women were peeling off her tattered green dress, until she shivered whitely in moonlight. She put a tentative toe in—hot! She tried a foot and ankle and calf. Delicious! With some gladdening of soul, she slid into the pool, finding a solid smooth rocky bottom, slid deeper into a kind of paradise, feeling hot water, almost as hot as she could stand, flow about her, warming and massaging her aching body, drawing pain out of her like some magic laudanum, lifting her spirits, making things right.

Around her women smiled shyly.

Betsy eyed them dreamily and then she laughed.

Chapter 30

A triumph of intelligence, thought Captain Jarvis Cobb, West Point. He'd made it his business to know everything, and by knowing everything, he'd escape the deadly trap.

He knew about when in the night frost formed, and intended to escape camp before leaving tracks in it. He knew where Danzig emptied his pockets of flints, nail knife, antler knife, and the rest. He knew where Morse would place his knives and the precious horseshoe flint striker and emergency ax. He knew where Skye put his big lance knife. He knew where Skye's squaws would lie, and how to get the knife. He knew how to fool Jawbone. He knew they'd all fall into a deep sleep after that terrifying day.

But that was only a part of good intelligence. He had surmised, from long observation, what Skye would do at dawn, upon discovering that Cobb had left with literally everything. He surmised the weaknesses in his own plan and questioned himself ruthlessly and unsentimentally about what might happen and what he could do about it.

The weakness would be Jawbone. He'd kill that horse if he could; hamstring the animal if possible; poison it, blind it, whatever it took. But in fact, that murderous horse would kill him and instantly arouse the camp. And yet, Jawbone remained the only weakness. It gave Skye mobility, a chance to seek help, hunt down Cobb, ferry them all to some safe place. But Captain Cobb knew his own limits and sensed that the better option would be to elude them all.

He struck out early, after gathering weapons and moccasins and the turkeys with perfect ease. The turkeys—which would keep for days in the frosty air—he carried on thongs he'd devised. The horseshoe hung from a thong on his belt. He strapped on Skye's big sheathed knife, kept a nail knife, flint and awl, dumped everything else, except Connaught's moccasins, into the Big Horn River. He'd done it all by starlight, too, shadowy and silent. Jawbone scarcely perked up his ears.

He struck due west out of the Big Horn River valley. He knew that you stayed well away from traveled routes when you wished to elude all eyes. A mile west of the river, he turned ninety degrees, and headed south, roughly paralleling the river, and guided by the North Star in the clear night.

In the morning, Mister Skye would mount Jawbone and go search, especially the west bank. Morse would despair. The things-maker, as the Indians called him, wouldn't fathom survival without tools and weapons. Danzig would be stronger. The white women would want to stay in camp. Skye would return after finding nothing, and they'd begin making new tools halfheartedly. Some turkeys would still be roosting in that patch of woods, so they'd make a new pole with a loop, for food. Danzig would hunt flint so they could strike fire from Jawbone's horseshoe again. Some of them would keep their fire going desperately because losing it would be fatal until they got flint. They'd struggle halfheartedly in that protected camp, and then trudge south along the river again after a few days of preparation, but they'd be demoralized and their progress slow. Or maybe they'd roll over and die there, dead of exposure and discouragement. He didn't wish death upon them, but neither did the thought of their death torment him. Life would always be dilemmas, ambiguities, circumstances . . . and the survival of the best.

Captain Cobb paced himself. He'd had a bad day along with the rest, and needed to husband his strength. He wished he could have nabbed Victoria's windproof leather vest. But he couldn't. Even so, he felt content. No plan ever devised had lacked pitfalls. Generals who waited too long usually were crushed by opponents who seized opportunities, stayed mobile, created new chances by flow and advance. Every textbook said it; every lesson they taught at the Point said it. So he paced through the icy night, ignoring the cold, pausing every fifteen or twenty minutes to rest and conserve himself. South to those hot springs for a healing bath and maybe opportunity—his mind danced with the possibility of stealing a horse there from a passing band, and he weighed the ways and means of doing that as he walked, reviewing everything he knew about how Indians guarded their herds. But even if he found no one at the hot springs, he'd follow trails south to the California-Oregon Trail, and go on home, retiring home from the field, as they liked to say in the army, with honor. . . .

At dawn he found a small gully and hunkered down in it, out of the wind. He built a tiny fire with ease, a palm's breadth across, and with it cooked turkey breast he sliced from a bird. Then he settled down for a three- or four-hour rest. He planned to do the same at dusk. And thus dozing as the morning sun probed down into his little gulch, he missed the passage of several horsemen—or mule riders to be more precise—a mile and a half east, over open prairie.

En route again under a pale autumnal sun, he found himself wrestling with his conscience. He regretted leaving Arabella to such a doom. They'd come together only the one time, in the Crow lodge, and once Arabella discovered lust, her appetite grew boundlessly, beyond Cobb's means to satisfy her. Well, he thought, she has had her great moment in life, and will die reasonably fulfilled. Still . . . he wished she might survive. He wished they all might survive. But he could not permit it. They'd die peacefully of illness and exposure and starvation, and no one would know his part in it. All because of a preposterous code that turned a simple act of self-protection against a freezing death into a crime, a blot on his honor. He deserved life! He deserved success! How could such a small stupid thing hang like the sword of Damocles over him?

He sighed. That had been nothing. A desperate small act that came to no bad end. But what he'd done last night was another matter altogether. It could be construed as murder. Angrily, he shook that thought out of his head. Nature would do the killing; he hadn't. He'd be free to pick up his career at West Point, unblemished, but he felt no joy in it. The thing would always stare him in the face. He'd have to be careful. What if he talked in his dreams and Susannah pieced it together? What if, in dying, Skye and the rest managed to leave behind a message, an accusation? The thought curdled him. Well, after all, what would they have? Charcoal, easily washed away by fall rains and winter snows. Tattle-tale carbon. He wished he'd buried their fire under earth before he slipped away. Too late to worry about that: the odds against messages were astronomical anyway. They'd think only of surviving, making tools, getting food and shelter. Intelligence, the knowledge of how the enemy would act, the educated surmise . . . He felt comforted.

His long walk proceeded like clockwork, and all went as expected except that his moccasins wore out much too fast, and he squeezed into Connaught's pair, worried that he'd be shoeless soon, a long way from the California Trail. Surely there'd be discards around the Snake encampments at the hot springs. . . . He rested and cooked turkey twice a day, and proceeded by easy stages south, under clear skies, the weather cooperating in his plans and lifting his spirits.

He fought demons the second day and recognized them as phantasms of guilt. As always, he put them front-center in his mind so he could examine them, understand them, banish them. Had he contributed to the death of others? Well then, agree to it. Yes, indeed. But how might he proceed through life staggering under a burden like that? Why, judge them. From a mental throne, he did exactly that, weighing each of them. Skye and the squaws, nothing, barbarians. No loss. Morse, some enterprising genius and inventiveness, but devoid of a soldier's virtue and courage, and in the end a fool to come out here. No great loss. Danzig, a dry-as-dust professor, who had no business out here. Actually, though, the best mind of them. Some loss there, he had to admit it. Betsy, an amiable amateur artist. Harebrained. No loss. Arabella, spoiled by wealth and empty-headed . . . He remembered her passion, and sighed. No loss. No great calamity. Why let it eat at him the way it did? He'd get past it, he knew. As soon as he returned to the Point, all this would vanish. . . .

At dusk of the next day, he topped a rise, saw a flat layer of blue smoke, tiny cones of lodges, and to the south, rising purple mountains. A village! The hot springs! Horses! Swiftly he settled flat in the dry dun grass to observe, to reconnoiter. He needed, simply, one good horse. He had plenty of thong for a rein. One horse.

A time to put intelligence to work! The herd, shifting dark dots, grazed in the Big Horn valley north of the village and rather close to him. Good. He wouldn't even get close to the village. He'd steal a horse and ford the river and strike east and south, and get down to the trail in a few days of hard riding. He closed his eyes, concentrating on what he'd learned of tribal practice. They'd have boys herding by day, warriors of their police society at night. Favorite horses would be tethered or picketed close to lodges in the village. The night guard would look for commotion among the animals, look for horses with ears pricked all in one direction. Usually two guards. He'd either have to elude them or kill them. He chose to elude. He wanted to slip a horse out of the herd undiscovered, perhaps undiscovered for weeks. Not easy. He wouldn't know which horses would be broke . . . unless he hunkered here in the little gulch long enough to see what the youths rode and trained by day. But that would take endless time, cold harsh exposed time. Evening now, and not until the next evening and the following night could he strike. No, he'd strike tonight, select a big docile animal, and hope he had blackness for a blanket. He thought a moment about the moon, observing it. It lay low now and quarter full. Probably set around ten or eleven. He frowned, trying to remember whether it had been rising or setting

early evenings. A lapse in intelligence. It irked him, this
carelessness.

Still, he'd try. He felt numbly cold here with the wind
whipping relentlessly over his back and the ground half-
frozen under him. Dark lowered swiftly, and he thought to
get his horse at once. Good tactics. They all supposed horse
thieves would strike very late, near dawn. He'd fool them.
He observed the night riders now—one circling, the other
sitting blanketed near a cottonwood, his horse close. Cobb
itched for that blanket, but decided not to risk it.

At last he rose, driving numbness from his limbs, and
slid down toward the herd, from the wind side unfortu-
nately. He couldn't get downwind, not with the river to the
east and the village to the south. He stole gently into the
herd, seeing them shift uneasily from him, like waves from
a bow. A horse snorted, and he froze for minutes. Then he
eased ahead, and they dodged as he went. One didn't move,
though, a big one and fearless, of a color he couldn't de-
termine in the blackness. Familiar with man. Heart stabbing
his chest, he slipped closer. This would be it! He unrolled
his thong, slid a hand along the big horse's mane and neck,
and started to knot the thong around the horse's jawbone.
That's when something struck him from behind, and he felt
himself falling and then felt nothing.

"This is the one," said Strong Horse. "See, even the
horseshoe."

"He's the one," agreed Mister Skye as Mary's brother
eased the semiconscious Cobb through the lodgedoor.

Strong Horse laid Cobb flat, while two other warriors
entered as well, seating themselves, and waiting for their
captive to come to.

"We made it easy for him," said Strong Horse cheerfully. "He saw only Elk Antlers in his blanket under the
cottonwood, and Whistling Deer on his pony, riding the
herd. He never saw the rest of us, not even when we were
very close!" He laughed easily, staring at the foolish white
captain slowly coming back into his head. "It was exactly
as you said. He came to steal a horse!"

Mister Skye translated all this, with Mary's help, to the

Morses and Danzig. Mary's parents, Rutting Elk and Stealing Jay, had turned over their large, luxurious lodge to the Skye party, and had moved in with relatives. Now, in the glow of the tiny lodgefire, they all looked rested after their ordeal, luxuriously dressed in soft skin clothing, quilled and beaded. Professor Danzig looked startlingly Indian in buckskins in spite of his beard, slim and dark and sharp-nosed. Betsy, washed and rested, radiated something vibrant in her doeskin skirt and red tradecloth blouse. His own women, Victoria and Mary, lounged on the thick curly-haired brown buffer robes in happiness and peace.

But now Captain Jarvis Cobb lay before them, intruding upon their idyll. His eyes flicked open and glanced about the lodge, focusing at last on Mister Skye. He groaned, and felt the knot on the back of his head.

Then he shifted his brown eyes away and wouldn't look at them again. Nor did he speak.

"Well, Mister Cobb, it didn't work, did it?" asked Mister Skye.

The man said nothing.

"I'll satisfy your curiosity. The army came to the rescue," the guide rumbled.

Cobb's eyes flicked around, looking for soldiers, wanting soldiers.

"What would you like to do, Cobb? Go back to West Point?"

The man closed his eyes, feeling the antagonism of the Morses on him. He'd left them to die, and they knew it and understood why.

"We should take him back whether he wants to go back or not," snapped Arabella. "And I'm going to tell the world about him."

Mary translated softly for her brother and their guests.

"I haven't made up my mind," Cobb muttered. "This all happened too fast."

"I think we should forgive and forget," said Betsy, always the generous person.

"Never!" cried Arabella. "He takes what he will and he should die!"

The girl's tone was so vehement that the senior Morses stared at her.

Mister Skye had an inkling of meaning in it.

"Mary's people don't mind the horse stealing. That's Indian sport, Mister Cobb. You're not their prisoner, nor ours. Quite free to go if you wish."

"I am?" exclaimed Cobb, astonished.

"Strong Horse, Mary's brother, has even volunteered to give you an old pony."

Cobb considered that. "Will I have my—the . . . weapons?"

"Exactly what you came with," said Mister Skye. "Perhaps the California goldfields, Mister Cobb?"

For a long time Cobb remained silent. "What if I choose to go east?"

"We would escort you to Fort Laramie. These good people have agreed to take us there, even though Laramie is deep in the lands of their enemies, Sioux and Cheyenne, who tried to jump them at the peace conference last year. If you come with us, we'll naturally take your weapons from you. But you'll be free to tell whatever story you wish to the commanding officer there—Captain St. James, I believe he is now."

"Susannah," Cobb muttered, and fell silent.

They waited patiently, comfortable in the warm luxury of the robes, and filled with buffalo tongue and sausages of boudins and two days of feasting.

"I'll head west," Cobb said. "I can't escape the ruin you plan for me with your exaggerated stories. I'll be a deserter technically, but the west is large and empty."

"No one's planning your ruin, Mister Cobb."

"I am!" snapped Arabella. "Ruin for ruin!"

Some sudden awareness blossomed in Betsy's eyes, though Elkanah missed it all.

"All right, then," rumbled Mister Skye. "You'll go west. One thing, though. If you sneak east tonight, these people will kill you. They'll escort you to a trail over the Owl Creek Mountains. Take it and be on your way southwest."

Mary translated, and Strong Horse and the other warriors

escorted Captain Cobb into the cold night. He did not look back or say good-bye.

Mister Skye and his people sat thoughtfully in their luxurious robes. Tomorrow they'd begin the trek to Laramie, graciously outfitted and protected by Mary's people. In a week or ten days, the Morses and Danzig would be ensconced in the old fur post the army bought, and would go east with the next army supply unit.

"He might have lived down dishonor easily enough, if he'd wanted to," mused Elkanah. "No one blames a desperate man much for trying to keep himself alive. It might never have come to light anyway. I've never been inclined to tattle about desperate moments and desperate mistakes. I don't suppose the rest of us would have said anything either. The fear was in his head. . . . But the second episode—stealing all we had so we'd die of exposure and starvation and keep his secret by dying—that's something I would talk about, and intend to talk about."

"It can't be ignored," agreed Mister Skye.

"We owe your people much, Mary," said Elkanah.

"My people are always helpful to those in need," Mary replied proudly.

"I want to paint them!" said Betsy. "I'm making images of them in my mind. I think I'll be able to! How could I forget these dear people? I've been remembering each of my paintings and those I painted, and I think I'll be able to do them again, maybe even better. If I have a few things—these beautiful clothes—I'll make them all come to life."

"My mother and my sisters are pleased to give them to you," Mary said. "We are pleased that you'll paint them, and will think of us when you paint them."

"We'll be wintering here, you know," the guide said. "We'll outfit at Laramie—I've a bit in my account with the sutler there, enough for a rifle and a few things—and then we'll ride here. Or walk . . ." he added, remembering he had no ponies other than Jawbone.

Mister Skye worried about that, actually. He'd lost everything, every bit of gear. His account would cover only the barest necessities. But maybe he could trade the army mules. . . .

He slid out onto the frosted night, sensing that Cobb had vanished forever from his life, sensing the calculating captain trotting his ancient pony west, escaping from dishonor that had once lain largely in his head rather than in reality.

Barring surprises, they'd make it to Laramie in utter comfort. He peered around this lodge with its warm cowhide skins, parfleches of jerky and pemmican, white backfat—perfect for stews—hanging from lodgepoles, thick robes, medicine pouch hanging in place of honor, and all the rest. It'd be a good winter with Mary's people—a time of hunting for buffler, trapping for skins to trade, eating fat, making love, hugging his women, telling tales, tanning hides and sewing a new lodge, training colts, giving parties, attending ceremonies, all beneath the eastern shoulders of the Wind River Mountains where this band wintered each year, in a paradisiacal valley. Mary's people, like Victoria's, loved him and made him a part of themselves, and he made them all a part of himself, feeling more Shoshone and Crow than he felt whiteman or Briton or Yank. When spring came and the grass freshened, they'd go back to Laramie and do some guiding and trade some furs to the sutler, and wait for the summer trade.

Chapter 31

Captain Walden St. James liked to shout. "What are you talking about!" he sputtered. "Cobb? Head west? Preposterous! He was a year ahead of me at the Point. I know him well enough to know something stinks here! Desert? Head west? I'll hold you all in irons until I get answers!"

The young Fort Laramie commanding officer had whirled like a tornado into the sutler's store where Mister Skye and his party had only moments before arrived in the company of a band of Shoshone warriors.

"I have instructions from the western command—Leavenworth—to send him along as soon as he arrived. Months late now! Cobb and some civilians. What've you done with the man? You're talking about a United States Army officer and West Point instructor and foremost authority on intelligence!"

St. James struck Mister Skye as someone unduly excited, so he said nothing.

"Well, out with it!" he cried, whirling on Elkanah. "Who are you? Where's Cobb?"

"I'm a New England businessman, Morse by name, and

these are my daughter Arabella, wife Betsy, and Professor Danzig of Harvard College.''

"Well I want the truth about Captain Cobb or I'll detain you until I get it!" bawled the beet-faced captain.

"I don't believe you have authority to detain civilians, sir," said Elkanah. "And in any case, Mister Skye's story is correct. Captain Cobb chose of his own free will to depart and head west, perhaps to the California goldfields."

"I have the authority to do what I damned well please, including detaining who I please. And your story is full of lies. And the squaw man's story is full of lies. Skye is notorious, and a bigamist."

"It's Mister Skye, mate."

"I don't care if it's Honorable Lord Skye. Your story is bull and you'd better give me reasons or I'll have you all for murder and insurrection." He jabbed a finger at Arabella. "You, miss! You tell me what happened to Captain Cobb or I'll put your father in irons."

"Captain Cobb did a dishonorable thing, and chose to escape whatever fate awaited him," said Arabella angrily.

"Dishonorable thing! Cobb hasn't got a dishonorable bone in his body! Finest man to come out of the Point in a decade."

Arabella blazed. "Dishonorable! He took me—took me into his bed. Had his way with me! Ignored his poor wife and children and had his way, and then fled, knowing what would come!"

Elkanah gasped.

"Arabella!" cried Betsy.

"It's true!" she snapped.

St. James sputtered, then turned crafty. "How come this young lady claims to know things the rest of you don't know? It stinks, all of it."

"I have nothing more to say!" Arabella said, and flounced off.

St. James stared around him. "Get these savages out of here!"

Old Colonel Bulluck drew himself up. "I'm sorry, suh, they are my guests and customers, and your writ, suh, doesn't run here."

"Like you to meet my brother-in-law, St. James. This is Strong Horse. Meet Lieutenant St. James."

"It's Captain, squaw man!" snarled the commanding officer.

Mister Skye considered something, and plunged ahead on the proposition that could end up just one way.

"We recovered five army mules some three hundred miles from here in Big Horn basin, Captain. I thought I'd trade them back for a couple of your older mounts for my women."

"Trade them? Trade them, Skye? They're army property. I could have you arrested for horse theft. In fact I will. Guard!"

Elkanah Morse intervened. "If you arrest everyone who returns army property, young man, you'll get no property back. I fear I must say a word in certain places about you. You are a most rash young man, and I fear for your career. . . ."

Elkanah's quiet powerful tone conveyed something to the young commander. St. James glared at them all, grew cautious, and muttered, "I'll get to the bottom of this. Guard, confiscate those mules outside."

He stormed off, and Mister Skye sighed.

"I hadn't expected unpleasantness, mates. I fear your long journey with the quartermaster command won't be very happy."

"We're glad to be alive, Mister Skye. We wouldn't be, but for you and these good tribesmen of yours. I've been thinking. You've been wiped out, lost everything on our account. If Colonel Bulluck here could arrange credit, we—Betsy, Arabella, and I—we'd like to buy you horses and make sure you're properly outfitted—and make sure these Shoshone colleagues of yours get their reward. That's the least we can do, Mister Skye. . . ."

"And a way of giving you our love, all of you our love," cried Betsy.

"We've gained everything," continued Elkanah. "I lost a few goods but gained knowledge and—I hope—wisdom. Betsy lost something dear to her, but gained something profound. She just told me that when she does new watercolors, they'll express something—something inside of them—larger than her earlier paintings.'' He slid an arm about Arabella. ''And my daughter's learned, too, bitter lessons, and will return to Lowell a better person.''

''I daresay I lost some and gained a lot more,'' said Professor Danzig. ''I have books to write, maps to spin. And memories, my dear friends, memories. I never dreamed that my geology and anthropology would someday save my life!''

''Goddamn!'' bawled Victoria, hugging Betsy, then Arabella, and then the rest.

Two hours later, Victoria and Mary had good ponies, clothes, blankets, and kitchenware. Mister Skye had a new Sharps .60-caliber rifle and all the necessaries, along with boots, a fine bowie, flint and steel, and a raft of other things. Their escort of Shoshones found themselves the owners of thick new blankets, knives, powder and galena, and red ribbons for their ladies. And buried in Mister Skye's new kit lay a jug of amber stuff to warm him on cold nights.

''What do I owe, Mister Bullock? And will you carry me to the next season?''

Colonel Bullock stared at his old friend. ''Mister Skye. Elkanah Morse asked me to tell you the accounts are even.''

Mister Skye roared, found Elkanah, and hugged.

''Is this what the mountain men do?'' gasped Elkanah, taken aback.

''It's what Mister Skye does, mate.''

They made their good-byes with the Morses and Professor Danzig, and the more Mister Skye tried to see them, the more blurred they became.